Ossa

OSSA

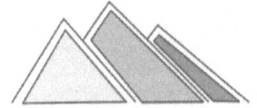

Vincent P. O'Hara

espiral press
631 E J St
Chula Vista, CA 91910
619-980-6170

ISBN 978-0615966991

Western Ossa

0   100   200
Ossian miles

MOUNTAIN

Hilev

Rahap

KINGDOMS

R Jen

Green Ossa

Rajappa R

Kyen

Lesser Tarhad

The Middle Hills

Joshin

SUMA

Brown Ossa

Anneglen

R Shem

Joshin Rd

Long Wall

TUMI

XUMI

Great Tarhad

TARHAD

R Laso

Moaz

Long Lake

Rivercamp

Klaxxis

Southfening

Ria

Zoha

Xaxi Mts.

Xexi Mts.

Last
L.

Riverport

GILDI

R Xo

Riverrun

EMPIRE

Gildesh

Sidoc

Upper
Dyrads

Pendaflax

Inner Sea

Havne

Saroka

Two Harbors

Dell

Yebol

Inner Run

Vanis

North Pointing

OuterSea

Eastern
Ossa

Istel

ISTELIAN CONFEDERACY

N
W   E
S

0   100   200

Ossian miles

O'Hara
2014

1

A GRIEVOUS SMALL WOUND

Ossa is a land of plains and autumnal winds; of encircling mountains and wide rivers: the Ossa, Green and Brown, the Shem and Laso, which drain the great lakes of the interior, and the Narva of Taelin. In most quarters the summers are dry and the earth yields reluctantly to tillage.

A dark-complected child dreamt each night of Ossa. Her dreams mingled harmony and nightmare, realization and frustration, past and future. They were mighty dreams, more than her waking mind could envision. She had seen but a tiny corner of Ossa. She was greatly unhappy and didn't know it.

Two men who had no idea they had been that night in a small girl's nightmare stood on Sidoc's seawall, buffeted by Squallblow, the gusty wind of autumn. It swooped in from the sea, warning of winter and worse winds to come. They stood apart from their attendants, holding private conversation and watching the newly acquired galleasses and galleys of Bar-Lev paraded raggedly in the blustery offing.

"Every day," the man in green and gold said, "they taunt us so. I have tired to my full measure." He turned and looked behind at the press of ships riding idly in the walled harbor.

The second man followed his gaze; shrugged his shoulders.

"Lord, these shows are intended to confuse our reason. Winter comes. Be thankful Bar-Lev isn't using the fleet to victual his host. We'll be hungry, but it will be far worse for them, I'd say."

The Prince of Sidoc grunted. "And next spring? He has the shipyards of Tarhad at his beck. Now our numbers on the sea are not so unequal. This choice won't exist forever."

"Perhaps. His rule is hardly popular and his back is to a devastated land."

"Fie on that. I hired you because you were known as the best captain in Ossa, Talo of Taelien. Well, I don't wait on other people. I want a success of my own and I want it now."

"Action is no guarantee of success."

"Fie, fie and fie. I'm no milkling. You say rash. I say bold. Bold action has brought me my position, not cravenly sitting." The Prince looked once more at the passing fleet. "See those broken formations? Fishmeal for my captains. But enough, I know my mind. There will be a council at the fourth hour."

Talo bowed to the Prince's departing back. He rejoined his attendants and walked the walls in a bitter mood. Compromise and diplomacy were, in Talo's estimation, his true talents. But he had failed here. Patience was running thin in Sidoc. Talo could feel it in himself as clearly as he could see it in the Prince. But his impatience was of a different kind. Maybe he was growing weary of compromising his own will. If so, his days as a hired captain were clearly numbered.

The council went as expected. The prince feared his city's mood. His citizens were unschooled in emergency and unaccustomed to privation. Misunderstanding the noise of discontent, the Prince proclaimed his plan for victory. Action, he said, would dispel the black mood of the city brought on by short rations and random death. It might even disperse the forces that ringed Sidoc so tightly by land and sea. That would be best of all. It was the Prince's first siege. Talo counted it as his twelfth.

After the Prince's plan was acclaimed, he unleashed a surprise.

"Master Talo, you and your men have been of assistance to me and mine during these dark days, but its clear our aims are no longer in harmony. I have spoken privately with my counselors and we agree that the time has come to terminate your contract and settle our account. I will not oblige you to participate in a venture you are so set against. You are free to take your ships and go. Does that make you happy?"

"No, Lord, it does not."

The Prince stroked his chin. "I didn't think it would. I never said you were without honor."

"Your plan will strip the city dangerously short of men. If you are willing, I'll remain and look to your walls. Upon the conclusion of this venture, you may dispense with my services if that is your wish."

The Prince nodded. "Fair enough. All right, Master Talo, we'll do it that way. Now, a toast to victory."

The next day at first light, the horns of the city sang out. The engineers released gears and the barrier chain at Harbor Gate sank out of sight. The fleet, preceded by the Prince's double banked galley, filed between the towers of the gate. Talo stood in the left tower with Pen, his mate. It was a brave sight and all the population of the city gathered on the walls to witness. (Talo would have kept the walls clear, but the Prince required an audience.) He could hear the blaring of trumpets as the Levites rushed to prepare their response.

In the morning the sea breeze round Sidoc's island was strong. The Prince was able to pass his entire fleet out of the harbor and set his formation before the Levite fleet could threaten. As the wind died slowly away, the Levite fleet struggled to gain sea room and the Prince maneuvered to counter. As noon approached, the forward divisions of both fleets finally clashed.

As Talo watched, he began to hope in spite of himself. Bar-Lev did not have the ships he had estimated, nor the Prince's nautical savvy. The afternoon waned and the melee grew general. Ships rammed and grappled one another till a continuous field of vessels were chained together. The waters round Sidoc grew dark with wreckage and bobbing heads. The tide slowly carried the battle away from the city's walls, toward shore. A dark line of soldiers was visible along the beach.

A cheer went up from the city when the Prince's pennant appeared on the Levite flagship. Talo wonder what words to use to confess his error when another cry sounded from the tower lookout. "Sail ho." For a second Talo thought it was the Istelians responding finally to the frantic messages the Prince had sent months before. But as the sails rose in the offing, they revealed themselves to be of all hues and that meant Levite. Talo realized the Prince had been tricked. He ordered the chain raised and a fast boat sent to warn the Prince of his danger. Then Talo rushed from his vantage to form his men into ready companies.

Talo's men were steady, as always, but the Prince has left the dregs of his own people and rumors were flying among them. Talo worked mightily to counter panic, but he couldn't be everywhere. Even more disturbing, his orders were not being obeyed. Men scurried helter skelter, thinking of their families, or just themselves. Finally Talo ordered his crew to draw weapons. Obedience improved, but already bobbing hulls dotted the harbor. Small boats were setting out through the harbor gate as if there was somewhere to flee. And at sea the battle continued. The Prince had seen his danger and struggling to disengage, but few vessels had succeeded. Instead of returning to swell the defense, these craft sailed forward to engage the Levite reinforcements. Talo shook his head and wondered if the Prince was still hoping for victory. After that, he was too busy to think much of the Prince.

The *Daughter of Shee* was anchored beside one of the two lesser entrances to the harbor, protected by an iron grill like a land gate. As the biggest ship left in the harbor, it was attracting the lesser craft of people trying to flee. Talo sent a detachment to reinforce the guard on board. He didn't intend to lose his own ship to boarders, Sidocian or otherwise. Then he looked to the Prince's walls.

The greater part of the Levite fleet joined the sea battle, but individual ships peeled off and veered toward the walls. Talo dispatched a few more of his precious men to the towers to take charge and kept the rest, barely a hundred souls, as a brigade to counter threats wherever they developed.

There was little missile fire to keep the Levite ships away from the walls; only the natural defense of reef and shoal. Rocks were not enough to prevent the landing of small parties equipped with scaling ladders. Soon Talo was leading his men at a jog (incongruously thinking he was too old and overweight for such exercise) from one spot to another, casting ladders down and slaughtering pockets of Levites who had gained the top. One threat was dispatched only to have two more flare in other locations. Talo had lost all track of time and outside events. His legs and arms were heavy and his lungs burnt. He was covered with sweat, but he was keeping the walls clear for the Prince.

As Talo fought, the initial surge of panic subsided. The townspeople steadied and began to assist. This was godsent because ever more Levite ships were directing their attention to the city. Talo saw old men, young boys and even women fighting. A ship with yellow sails floundered on the shoals and people cheered. Talo heard and began to think, regardless how the sea battle goes, the city might hold out. This inspired the strength, old and overweight as he was, to lead his men at a jog to the next intrusion.

Ossa

This one proved the most dangerous of all. Two galleys had located a sink where deep water came right to the wall. The crews swarmed up directly from the decks. They held the walkway, protecting their ships from rocks that would stove hulls and make short work of their attack. Talo pushed through men running in the opposite direction, ordering them to turn and follow. Then, he was at it again, standing aside and letting Pen lead the charge. (Talo had never been much of a swordsman, even in his prime.) Talo's mercenaries slowly cut their way forward. They were as tired as their leader, while the Levites were fresh and on the wall in greater numbers than ever before. Moreover, the Levites had gained the objective they had been staring at in frustration for months and this made them fight all the harder. Still, Talo's men advanced. Talo glanced up and saw that already twilight was growing. The sky was glowing unnaturally, lit from below by the burning ships in the bay. Talo paused and said, to himself: `Ah, and where is the Prince? If we hold another hour, we've succeeded, though he has failed. He has lost his city, thought it stands still.'

Then, a pain. Talo found himself on his knees with no recollection of falling. In his side he saw an arrow. Someone was kneeling beside him saying: "Master, you're wounded." Talo couldn't focus his eyes to see who had said such a ridiculous thing. In uncounted actions, battles, skirmishes never had he been wounded. Another part of his mind said relax, it's painful, but hardly fatal. A third part had lost control and was plunging into despair. He wondered if the end had come, but immediately came a comforting whisper, tiny and clear. He was not meant to die in the defense of Sidoc. That thought, without logical source, prevented him from blacking out as a fourth part of him wished.

"Master," that voice again, "what shall we do?"

"The ship," Talo gasped, "take me to my Daughter."

Someone broke the arrow shaft, others lifted their captain. His crew retreated along the wall to the spot opposite the *Daughter of Shee*'s anchorage. The Levites rallied and followed. The sight sowed panic among the Sidocians as nothing before had. They fled toward the city or called boats in the harbor to pick them up; or just jumped into the water, preferring the mercy of nature to that of sword or axe.

Talo lost consciousness as he was carried but regained it when he was set in a small boat to be rowed to the Daughter. He felt the change in motion and thought water better than land by far. Pen was beside him. When he saw Talo awake, he began speaking:

5

"Master Talo, I've sent two men to open the gate beside the ship. I think if we up anchor now, we can find a passage out. To go down fighting in the bay will be better than this."

Talo nodded. He couldn't think clearly.

The *Daughter of Shee* slipped through the gate and into the bay. It was now fully dark. The Levite fleet was clustered along the walls, emptying their crews to join in the rout. Already fires were springing upon the city itself.

The Daughter sailed away unheeded.

2

CHILD OF DELL

An event such as the fall of Sidoc has unexpected repercussions. The night the city died was, for Getlof of Dell, a night of nightmare. When she awoke, she knew something bad had happened, but she didn't know what or where and that made it worse. . . .

Or was it at hand?

She leaped from her pallet, looked wildly about and saw only Geto, her grandfather. This calmed her. The spectral land of vision had receded safely to the other side of consciousness.

Geto stared at her steadily; mornings were his lucid time.

"I know, you had a bad one, child. Twice you screamed and woke me." Midnight disturbances of this sort had been occurring more frequently. Secretly, Geto feared her. "Well, you're all right now. Stop staring,." Soon, she would be an adult and responsible for herself. That time was coming none too soon.

Getlof stretched, feeling shivery: some unnamed excitement was fingering the strings of her heart. "Will you be wanting me at hand?" she asked, exchanging her night shift for the day one.

"Eh? Today? No, just fix me something to eat and I'll be happy if you stay away till dark."

She nodded. Geto was a smith; but he had no helpers and rarely worked anymore. Getlof herself hated the bellows, the heat and the monotony. She was glad to obey.

"All right, Grandfather." She uncovered last night's coals and dropped a handful of grain into a pot. "Maybe I'll walk the rims today.

Geto shook his head without looking up. The girl was strange. "As you wish. Just leave me alone. I slept poorly last night and I reckon it was your fault."

Getlof saw nothing strange in hiking to the rim tops. From above, Dell was an emerald, banded by gullied ridges, brown and gray. A deep bowl in the dusty plain, it was the only source of water within a three-day walk, or so the elders said. Water was important; it was forbidden to tease or insult the Water Spirits and that was about as far as religion went thereabouts. The spirits made Dell a favored spot in an inhospitable land, but it took the constant labor of the inhabitants to keep it so. Geto's neglect of his smithery was extremely anomalistic. He spent his days drinking swill, yet purchased this very swill in coin. People remembered how, a decade and a half before, he had mysteriously acquired an infant girl, some two years after the death of his wife. Why and how were subjects for speculation, but plainly he hadn't neglected his own advantage.

Just as plainly, Getlof wasn't a natural child of Dell. Her bones and frame were too small; her skin too dark and her features too even and refined. Her thoughts and actions were foreign as well. But even foreignness becomes familiar, when viewed from infancy to the end of adolescence. Getlof had few friends, but for that her personality was to blame. She was sensitive to insult and often provoked disputation without cause. Extreme in her actions, she often carried these disputations too far, even when she had cause. Unpredictable, she could end a feud with an expected kindness and just as easily with an effective revenge. She was subject to extremes: episodes of energy and restlessness or depression and sloth. She was rarely uncertain about anything (expect herself), but her judgment had gained respect despite her youth. Within these traits, like berries behind thorns, was a charm that compelled people to repeatedly forgive and oblige her.

While general opinion held that Geto was doing her little good by letting her run wild; that the inconsistencies in her character could be moderated though the exercise of discipline, Mama Riza, wife of the headman, was the only adult in Dell who had ever tried to discipline Getlof. More than once.

By the time Geto was fed and settled into his day, the sun was already above the Rims and bearing down upon the valley with typical intensity. This early heat, with its promise of worse to come, had a way of vanquishing energy. Getlof didn't walk far before she discarded the idea of climbing the rims. Afterimages of her dreams jangled in her mind. She began to feel jagged and helpless, and somewhat reckless.

To reorient herself, Getlof tried to think ordinary thoughts; that is, about Delea.

Delea had just turned adult. This was the major threshold in the life of a Dellite. Ever since, her behavior toward her younger friends and acquaintances had been calculated to impress them with her new superiority. That was obnoxious, but even worse, Delea had spied on Getlof swimming in the upper spring six days before and bore the tale to Riza. A beating, light but humiliating resulted. Knowing she had been in the wrong and that it would be better to forget it, Getlof began to wonder how she would get even.

In no hurry (she had the whole day in front of her, and after that the next, and the next) Getlof followed the west stream. The springs, situated at the north end of the valley, welled up from the mountain in six pools terraced one above the other. Water tumbled to ground level and branched into two channels. These meandered through Dell and reunited in the lower pools (wherein no spirits dwelt and bathing was allowed) and there disappeared back into the ground. Groves and fields alternated along the streams; each family cultivating its own plot. Watching the children and women bent in the unentertaining business of weeding made Getlof thankful such was not her lot.

She left the field behind. The path ran on a dike separating the stream from a stretch of cattail and rush. Then a voice hissed her name. Getlof stopped.

"I heard. In trouble again?"

The voice belonged to Elp, two years younger than Getlof. She was his idol, but rather a bother to her. But, at least he never said a thing was wrong, especially when it was. Elp poked his head above the rushes, looked up the trail and down, and said:

"I might be. Father's in a terrible bad mood. He beat Earp for nothing and I didn't stick to see if I was next."

Getlof smiled, this being completely normal, and would have kept walking but he said:

"Wait, don't you want to hear why? It's big news."

Getlof shrugged her shoulders: "All right, but come out. I'm not going to crawl through the muck to talk to you."

Elp fell in beside Getlof, apparently unconscious of the mud, which did indeed cover him. "Last night a new collector from Razedaze's came in. That's why my father's in a mood. He owes money, the collector says, and he can't pay. And he's not the only one."

9

This did interest Getlof, though she didn't let Elp see.

"After what happened to the last one, Old Sam, there could be trouble, don't you think?"

Getlof nodded. Geto was still sober enough to talk to. She considered returning to tell him.

"Did he come alone, Elp?"

"He did. Spent the night with the Opahs, they say."

This time Getlof's face showed her surprise. Elp grinned.

"You still mad about that whipping last week? It was nothing to Pa's."

Getlof stopped. They had come to the fork in the stream. From there the trail climbed to the springs. Getlof was suddenly aware of the faint, but deep music of water in motion. A wayward breeze eddied through the top of the plane trees and set their leaves to shivering. Getlof changed her mind again.

"I'm going up. Want to come, Elp?"

Elp's grin got bigger. "Today should be safe. People are too worried to worry bout us."

But Getlof already had started and Elp had to run to catch up.

The ascent to the first two springs was easy, but it was steep after that. The water cascaded beside them, down a series of short falls. Mist wetted them through. They passed the fourth spring and the tumult of falling water faded. The top was only a hundred paces off, mostly straight up. Then Getlof heard a noise. Laughter, followed by a splash and then more laughter. She froze and Elp did the same. With absolute certainty, she knew who it was. That knowledge came from out of nowhere, a gentle whisper on a liquid breeze. Getlof circled to a spot above the spring. From there she finally looked down and was rewarded with the sight of the tail end of a female form disappearing into the water; a blur of pink that surfaced and became Delea, indeed. A man lay on a rock watching her. In a whisper Getlof asked Elp if that was the collector, although there was no one else it could have been. Elp let out a low whistle and nodded. The man glanced up. Getlof punched Elp. Delea, seeing her companion's attention wander, splashed water into his face. He slip into the pool and chased her.

"Sorry, do you think he heard?"

Getlof shook her head. Of course, she was an adult and free to do what she choose, but in the highest spring and with a collector?

"Listen. I want you to sneak down and steal their clothes. He probably has his horse around here. I'll find it. Hurry while they're busy."

10

Getlof found the horse by the third spring, the one known as Asha, which was about as high as a large animal could be taken. A secondary search revealed the collector's saddle and bag. The hardest part was wrestling them onto the horse. The fear of discovery made her clumsy but she finally managed to get the saddle on.

Elp was waiting in the grove.

"What took you so long? I was going to come back and look for you."

"Be quiet. Did you get their clothes?"

He nodded and held up a tight bundle. "His boots were too big so I hid them."

"All right. Did they see you?"

He shook his head.

"Then help me get this saddle on right and let's get out of here."

After they were off the slope, Getlof slowed the horse to a walk and directed it toward the closest field, which happened to belong to the Rizas, who were also in debt to Razedaze. The women straightened and watched the walking horse approach.

"Getlof, child, where did you get that fine nag?"

Her heart was pounding, but Getlof swallowed her nervousness and said: "I borrowed it from the new collector. Anybody who wants to see something interesting should climb to the fifth spring."

"What would that be, Getlof?"

She turned. It was old man Riza, a spade over his shoulder. From the height of the horse, Getlof felt suddenly fearless. She smiled and kicked the animal into a trot.

By the time they had visited several fields, the news was ahead of them. Delea and the new collector polluting the springs! By the standards of Dell the scandal was deliciously unprecedented. The Riza women, assisted by various other families, ended by driving the discovered lovers into the hills behind the springs.

Delea snuck back after dark. She was filthy; feet and body lacerated, pride shredded even worse. The Opahs, let her in, foolishness sufficiently punished. The collector, however, had forfeited his meager claim to hospitality. Delea watched her family drive him away with stones. She sobbed quietly in a corner the entire night.

The next morning, a member of the Rhis discovered a man sleeping in a storage shed out in the fields. They chased him away. The collector quickly became known as the wild man and every time he surfaced, people greeted him with rocks. He kept to the fringes, stealing and becoming, in a surprisingly short time, another feature of everyday life.

Getlof gave the horse to old man Riza who turned it into a community plow animal (a change the horse didn't care for). That lasted a week before it disappeared one night. The wild man vanished at the same time.

People were grateful Getlof had postponed the inevitable reckoning with Razedaze, but that gratitude had a cost. Recalling Delea, mothers instructed their children—once again—to avoid her; people began to remember she was different. Her nightmares increased in frequency and poor Geto seldom got a decent night's sleep.

3

A NEW COMMISSION

Five quarters of the moon had passed since Sidoc's destruction; the season of storm was waxing full. The Daughter of Shee had stayed near Sidoc's island long enough to teach Bar-Lev to protect his shipping and to raise the hunt. Now she reached south, well off the rocky coast. Her captain stood alone on the elevated afterdeck, buffeted by wind and icy spray. Occasionally the watch glanced aft and was reassured by Talo's stance and by what it portended. In Talo the Taelien's restless mind another plan was evolving; some scheme to bring them profit at no great cost.

Talo felt the cold of the driving spume, but not as the mental goad his crew imagined. He was exploring the rare, titillating sensation of failure. Normally Talo considered introspection a useless vice that sapped the powers of decision, but in this case he justified his inner thoughts as a quest for peace of mind, unattainable until he understood and explained to himself that wound received on Sidoc's wall.

The pain had left almost as soon as Talo arrived on the Daughter's deck and he was walking that same evening. Such a recovery was as embarrassing as it was ambiguous; it opened his debility to doubt. Talo, at least, would have disbelieved had it happened to anyone else. It was his natural assumption that doubtful interpretations were occurring to everyone who had knowledge of his wound, especially his crew. Talo mourned for his easy manner of command, which seemed as lost as his powers of concentration. He was so accustomed to ideas shouting and competing for his attention, his present condition seemed stark and permanent indeed.

Self-knowledge is typically another name for self-delusion; Talo's knowledge of Ossa's south-east coasts, however, was certain. All day the clouds continued to lower as the gale gradually increased. Before the Daughter risked too great a danger, Talo neglected his introspections long enough to turn her toward a nearby haven. This was Yebol, a fishing port in the disadvantaged mainland district of Istel: a dozen dozen earthen dwellings and a few wood and stone structures scattered on the sandy margin between bay and a precipitous, deeply eroded ridge. A broad wash terminated the village on the south. Fishing coracles were beached inside its dried mouth.

Knowing Yebol's citizens would find unsettling the appearance of a strange warship late on a stormy day, Talo decided he'd best reassure the headman that evening and so, with Pen, he put to shore in the longboat rowed by several of his crew.

They landed near the coracles. Talo noticed first the flavorful scent of cooking fish. In the twilight -- the time of balanced opposites -- he felt a vague sensation that all impressions and appearances were subtly inappropriate. Pen inspected the men sullenly watching their landing, sniffed the air and remarked:

"A populous village and more prosperous than just a fish camp. I catch a hint of piratcy in this place. I'm rather mazed to see no fort or strong place."

Talo shrugged his shoulders. Instead of commenting on how he would defend Yebol, or confirming Pen's guess he said: "Ask directions."

Pen did, but he might have been talking to statues. The fishermen merely stared at them harder. Talo shrugged his shoulders again.

"I am in no mood to deal with sand peasants. We'll find it."

Pen tried to object. The longboat's crew stood at hand fingering weapons and ready for the obvious order to enforce better manners, but Talo had turned away and was already climbing the bank so Pen ordered the crew to wait with a whispered admonishment: "You heard the master, make polite, then."

The light was blue and violet and ebbing, but the wind had ripped huge gaps in the clouds, delaying the advent of total dark. The two men threaded their way through random lanes with Pen slightly preceding Talo. The town was strangely still. Then a man came limping into view on a path intersecting their own. Pen's glance had already swept past him when his mind said: `here is someone deserving another look.'

The man had a maimed foot and was dressed in the rags of a beggar. His skin was a shade rarely encountered, almost green, although it may have been the light that made it seem so. Stranger still was his presence. His limp seemed a stride and his stoop the posture of a prince. He was like no beggar Pen had ever seen. The stranger reached the path they followed slightly before them and stopped. He found Pen's eye and in a low voice said:

"Greetings, good mate. I have a poem for the master."

This reassured Pen, being a typical beggar's line. Talo looked up and studied the man for a long moment. His lassitude seemed to be surging. It was a struggle to inquire: "What is this poem?"

The stranger's skin now seemed to be yellow in hue. He smiled.

"That was not goodly put, good sir. Such shortness implies a slur. Perhaps you're distracted, so I won't be protracted. The poem is as follow. It goes:

"'Tis but a rumor I hear;

A wound unexpected, and fear.

A man carried in haste

From his duty and place;

I doubt he'll find peace to be near."

The beggar-poet bowed as Talo frowned and nodded slightly.

"That, my presumptuous friend, I'm sure you'll hear in due time." He turned, then turned back and tossed a silver Istel which the stranger caught, turning the motion into a mocking salute.

"You'll remember my name. It is Yetit."

As Yetit limped off Pen stood flabbergasted.

"Master. Why do you reward insolence with silver?"

Talo stared directly into Pen's eyes for a moment. "You are my oldest companion . . ." Then he bit off whatever was next and turned oppostite to the begger's course. Swirls of wind sent dust driving against Pen's face followed by the first drops of rain. The mate scratched his head and, looking up, realized it was dark. "Well," catching up to his master, "let's try that place yonder. With two stories it'll either be what we're looking for or at least an inn."

Pen's guess was a good one. A servant called a small man who turned out to be the headman himself. Talo gave his name, one well known within a hundred leagues of the southern coasts, and especially in a place such as Yebol, and the man bowed very low. He hurried them inside to his table where the evening meal was set. Four guests were present and while extra places were made, Talo make a few diffident remarks saying they were anchored only for the duration of the heavy weather. Then, to reinforce their peaceful intentions, he had Pen present the headman two napkins fashioned from fire-washed linen, fabric which, when cleaned in fire, came out brilliant and pure—a commodity in great supply aboard the *Daughter* after a recent capture.

The headman, however, thought this a marvelous rare gift and passed the fabric round for all to see. All the same, as the meal progressed, he couldn't refrain from covertly glancing Talo's way. A discerning man with a politician's fine-tuned sense for moods, the incongruity between the mild, stocky man before him and the high deeds he had heard of Talo the Taelien bothered him. In truth, the beggar-poet had plunged Talo into another introspective funk. Pen recognized this and it irritated him to have his master accorded less than his due of respect. In the face of Talo's mood, however, there was little he could do.

One of the guests watched Talo more closely than even Pen or the headman. This was Razedaze the Tarhadian, richest man in Yebol. He also thought the man didn't match the stories, though he didn't doubt Talo's identity--the gifts established that. He just assumed the stories were mostly fancy. Razedaze was prone to exaggeration so he thought everyone else was too. Moreover, this interpretation suited his plan, for if Talo was a man of high deeds, he would scorn the deed which had occurred to Razedaze.

After the wine gave out, as the guests were taking their leave, Razedaze bespoke Talo privately.

"Master, honor me tomorrow by paying a visit to my poor establishment. I would discuss that which could be to our mutual advantage."

Talo looked the unctuous little man over and shrugged his shoulders thinking if he were to accept commissions from people like this, he had fallen far indeed.

Pen returned to the Daughter, but Talo passed the night at the headman's. By morning he had forgotten Razedaze's invitation. If Pen had known this, he would have been really worried because usually Talo forgot nothing. Razedaze, however, with only his impressions of the night before to go on, took the precaution of sending a boy with an ornately lettered invitation to remind Talo.

When Talo received this missive his first impulse was to send the boy back with a verbal refusal; but he looked again at the fine paper, the gold ink, and the faultless calligraphy and decided he had, after all, nothing better to do.

Razedaze received Talo with courtesy, blended with just the faintest flavoring of contempt. Talo caught this as he stepped under the lintel and it was like water dumped upon a dreaming man. Talo was amused--for the first time, it seemed, in weeks. He even found himself starting to encourage Razedaze's fanciful impressions; the slightly slack jaw and mazed expression was a familiar mask, if from a much earlier time.

They had refreshments in an inner chamber. Razedaze described himself as a merchant, but Talo had noticed the bulk of his stock, cluttering several storerooms like brassy rouge and powder on an ancient dowager's face, was goods left as security on loans. Then a door opened and a reflection captured Talo's eye. Razedaze disposed of the interruption as Talo went to inspect this thing. He saw a casket, picked it up and Razedaze flew to his shoulder.

"Ah, master, it is plain you have an eye. That which you hold is ancient indeed. The workmanship is primitive, perhaps, but of abounding interest, and, of course, the materials are all genuine. The stones are malachite and jade marrow, I believe, and the silver is pure. And, if you press here, so, you see the lid opens and that the contents are of an interest equal to the exterior."

`No,' Talo thought, `of interest greater by far.' A thin sheet of beaten, purple gold rested on a bed of brocade silk, the color of clouds at sunrise. Characters of inlaid green decorated the sheet of metal forming a script Talo couldn't decipher. It was signed, however, with an intelligible hierogram: : the symbol by which the Pau, an ancient and mysterious people from the north, indicated the name of Josh. Talo had heard tales about the Pau, even as a child in Taelin, and about Josh who was supposed to speak to them with the words of their god. The fact that Josh had been killed some fifteen years before and most of the Pau exterminated from Ossa made this relic an interesting find indeed. Talo became aware that his heart was pounding and this amused him. To Razedaze he said:

"How came you by this casket?"

Razedaze struggled mightily not to smile. "That I had of an old man who lives away in the back country. He was in need of money and I was able to oblige. The words I wish to speak to you are not unrelated to this event."

"Then speak. I'm ready to listen."

Razedaze led Talo back to his inner chamber and brought out a far finer wine than served the night before, the dark brew of Loren. He proceeded to lay forth his proposition.

There was a village, hardly noteworthy, by the name of Dell. In a time of hardship three years past its people had borrowed heavily from him. Sympathetic to their plight, he had made the terms reasonable. They, however, had repaid his reasonableness with acts of cruel violence. Of the two men sent to collect the interest due ("with no mention, mind you, of the principal") the

17

first suffered what had been described as a fatal accident, while the second returned beaten and robbed.

"So, master Talo, you understand the problem. I could, of course, request troops from the Islands, but expensive gifts would be required and the troops would like to be ungentle with the folk of Dell, as is their habit."

"And you think I would be less ungentle, not to mention cheaper?"

Razedaze waved a hand vaguely in the air. "The truth is that I have a great desire to finish this business. I know you could do that quickest, being here with trained men of war. As for the other, well, acts of excessive cruelty are not associated with your name, although in the circumstances, a few such acts could hardly be considered unjust."

Talo sat back and smiled at Razedaze's bent flattery. Ordinarily he would have ignored the man who offered what was, after all, the work of a tax farmer. Razedaze, however, possessed something he had suddenly come to want very much and this decided Talo's mind. After a pause long enough to cause some discomfort, he said:

"I believe I shall look into it. I will journey to this place myself, and by myself . . ."

Razedaze opened his mouth in protest, but Talo stilled his words with an upraised hand.

"Oh, with a guide, of course. I will promise you nothing and this is in consideration of your profit, for I do not work cheaply. To start, I shall require the casket of malachite and jade marrow for my trouble. If I undertake your collection, we will discuss further considerations. If I find my men are necessary, the cost will be very high."

Razedaze nodded. Perhaps, just perhaps, he had made a mistake. But the casket, for all its fine materials, would be no great loss. An Istelian lord had scorned it not two quarters past, being, he said, of a style too primitive to excite interest.

"Very well, I accept your conditions."

Talo smiled serenely. "Oh, I'll also need to know the name of the old man from whom you acquired the casket."

4

TALO GAINS A RING

It was harsh country Talo traveled. Harsh light, reflected from stone fields attacked his eyes--accustomed though they were to sea glare. Harsh, spiky shrubs clung to rock fissures. Harsh and bitter odors irritated his nose. His usual ability to make the best of any situation was not encouraged by the sharp spine of his Tarpan mare that was slowly bifurcating his body. Talo's only comfort was the casket he carried and the speculations it brought to mind.

In his entire life Talo had seen only one Pau, in Gildesh, before the Times of Trouble. They were said to be the flotsam of an earlier age, the original people of Ossa and holders of strange and primitive beliefs. These beliefs centered round a nebulous figure named Josh, or The Josh; Talo wasn't certain which was correct. Talo had certaintly encountered his share of strange beliefs. He had watched the cult of the Disembodied King come into its own. This cult had begun in Moaz when the Magnas ordered the devotion and offerings of his people be directed from the traditional gods unto himself, taking the titles and attributes of those gods as well. With the Magnas of Moaz a god, the emperor of the Gildi had little choice but to become one as well. More lately, every liege-lord up and down the coast was affecting similar pretensions.

Even though Talo knew this was nonsense, he endorsed the trend. The idea of offering sacrifice and prayer to a man possessing real power of life and death seemed more consistent with reality than the worship of some entity whose existence was based upon the tales of crones and beggar-poets.

According to the tales, the apotheosis of Magnas Raos had caused the Pau great harm. They would not desert their old gods so Raos embarked upon a slaughter that ended only when there were no Pau left alive within a month's march of his kingdom. This genocide convinced religious conservatives throughout Moaz that his worship was appropriate.

Talo was a young man in those days. He first came into Ossa from his natal land of Tael when Raos mounted his famous campaign into the Middle Hills against the many leveled city of Joshin. Along the coast Moaz and Josh were just names, but Talo could recall the approval Raos' deeds received. Joshin had been razed and the line of Josh extinguished; the Pau of Joshin had been killed or driven north to their mountain retreats and since that time, rare was the man who had encountered a Pau in Ossa.

Talo was certain the casket figured in these old tales. He expected to find some manner of refugee; at the very least, an interesting tale. To envision the most his discovery might bring required the full exercise of his imagination. It was a relief to find something to think about other than his grievous small wound.

In mid afternoon, Talo and his guide reached the rims and looked out over the valley and village of Dell. It was similar to countless valleys back of Yebol, except that instead of supporting a few yellow-green trees along the line of a seasonal watercourse, the prospect was verdure, almost painfully so.

"Dell," the guide muttered laconically. "They know me for Razedaze's man so I'll not go down."

So Talo traversed the steep trail down the face of the rims alone. He noticed that Dell, like Yebol, had no fortifications. Buildings were scattered throughout the valley, no area appearing to have a density higher than any other. At the foot of the rims the trail bisected a copse and then crossed a small stream over a wooden bridge. Beyond the stream people labored in a field, but to Talo they paid no heed. Talo thought this strange. He led his Tarpan down a path amid the field, but people rotated, keeping their backs to him. This made the snub more amusing than strange. Talo stopped and, in the voice used for giving orders in high winds, tempered by the tone used for getting information from shy children, he shouted:

"Ho, good people and greetings. Who will guide me to the abode of the goodman Geto?"

They turned at that, giving the curious stares Talo had expected from the first. He put on his broadest smile and waited. Finally, an adolescent boy, with much backglancing, approached.

"I can take you there, but why do you want to see Geto?" If you be a collector, he has no debt."

"I imagine he doesn't," Talo laughed. He gave the boy a copper Istel. The boy's eyes widened as he clutched it; he looked up at Talo, who nodded, then said:

"It's this way, master sir."

They followed the stream, walking in the shade of the tall plane trees. Then the boy stopped. Talo saw a girl running toward them.

"Getlof," the boy said with evident relief, "this man wants to see Geto."

The girl stopped and returned Talo's stare frankly. The Dellites were darkly complected their lips thick and nostrils wide. The girl was darker still, however. Her hair was black and fine, and her features delicate and thin. As he stared, Talo grew ware of other subtleties. Her age was difficult to gage; at first look he thought her a child, but quickly realized she was a young woman and that he had been misled by her small size.

Talo released his breath with a hiss. She was Pau. The impulse which had led to his accepting Razedaze's commission was proving inspired and he still hadn't seen Geto.

"All right, Geto won't like it, but he never likes anything so that doesn't matter. My name is Getlof and Geto is my grandfather. What's your name?"

Her voice had Talo's heart beating rapidly and he wasn't sure why. "Talo the Taelien at your service."

She nodded as if she had expected no other answer.

She led Talo to a dwelling distinguished only by its shabbiness. Geto sat outside leaning against a wall and smoking a long pipe from which rose the bitter, unmistakable scent of weed. Talo saw at once that although Getlof had called him grandfather, it was an honorific, not a natural title.

"This man is Talo the Taelien," Getlof said as Geto rose unsteadily to his feet. "He wants to see you."

Geto blinked rapidly, looking first to the right, then to the left of Talo. He said: "Which mistake brings you . . . sir?"

The casket sat in Talo's purse, but he was suddenly shy about bringing it out in front of the girl. Playing a sudden hunch, Talo said:

"No mistake, as I think you know. Business I would discuss and possibly your profit."

Talo was gratified to see a kind of shrewdness filter into Geto's expression."

"Business, do you hear child. Well go then and leave us be. Business is no concern of yours."

21

Talo expected the girl to protest, but she didn't. The look she gave Talo as she left, however, seemed to contain a warning. Talo turned away amused with his imagination.

Geto led Talo inside and offered him swill. Talo declined, but that didn't prevent his host from partaking. Talo took the casket out and carefully unwrapped it. He hoped to salvage something from his disappointment.

"In Yebol I was led to believe you once possessed this casket. . . "

Geto shook his head and cut off the rest of Talo's question with unintelligible muttering. Talo shifted into a more reassuring manner and poured Geto another glass. After several more, Geto began to relax. He finally admitted he did have one other item related to the casket.

This item proved to be a ring fashioned from purple gold like the plate inside the casket. It was plain, without gems, but etched in green the hierogram of Josh. Talo felt vaguely ill at ease, but he ascribed this to Geto's nervousness and having to watch the man drink cup after cup of the horrible, cheap swill. The ring obviously went with the casket and, as with the casket, Talo was possessed with the desire to have it. He looked up and said:

"How much."

Geto shook his head violently. "No, can't sell. Belongs to the child."

"Didn't the casket belong to the child as well?"

"A container only. I needed money. For her. The ring they said to guard as I guarded her. That I can't sell."

"They? Tell me this story," pouring another drink.

Geto's telling was uneven and hard to follow, but the sense of it was that sixteen years ago he had been an important man. He had a good wife, a strong son and a thriving trade as a smith. Then, his world fell apart. His wife died unexpectedly. His son left to improve his lot in Istel and had not been heard from since. Talo sensed some old guilt, but into this he didn't inquire. Not long after these events, a strange party of strange people passed by night through Dell. Geto lived, at that time, in a house on the north slope, separate from other people. They came to his house, a party of about fifteen, men and women both and with them there was an infant. They were smaller and darker than any people Geto had ever seen; handsomer, but frightening. Geto said they told him they were on a journey. The infant had been born on the way, but now that she was weaned, they had to leave her behind. They didn't tell Geto why. They said he was the one they would leave her with. Geto said he wasn't the one, but after

22

they delivered to him a generous sum, an enormous sum, for her upbringing and his trouble, he agreed he was, after all, the one.

Geto lost his trade as he slowly grew used to the possession of specie. He admitted the money finally ran out and so he had been forced to sell the casket. He had been told that it, along with the ring, belonged to the child and were to be given to her when she came of age, but he had decided that the casket was just a container and the ring was all that really that really mattered. He ended on a note of pride.

"That was long ago, but here you see the ring. Old Geto is a better guardian than people might think."

Talo poured him another drink and agreed he was amazingly faithful. Geto nodded as he drained the cup. Talo poured another, wishing he had thought to bring some of that Loren wine. Geto drained the refill; within ten minutes his head was cradled in his arms. As Talo watched, he began to snore.

Talo took his purse and put a stack of gold Istels beside Geto's head. He picked the ring up from the shelf where Geto had carelessly set it and departed.

Sunset was coloring the sky when Talo regained the rim top. The guide was surprised by his prompt return, but not by his insistence they leave at once. The moon rose early that night; its creamy light illuminated their passage through a landscape that was like a portal to the imagination. This suited Talo, for he had many things to consider.

First, there was the casket, then there was the ring and finally there was the girl. They shared a common source, but the connection eluded Talo. The girl was plainly of gentle birth and she had plainly been fostered in Dell. But why? And why Dell, halfway across Ossa from Joshin and farther still from the mountains of the Pau? Talo rode with the casket at hand, running his fingers over the raised script on the sheet of purple gold. It provided an answer, no doubt, but few people in Ossa could read that script.

When the moon set the guide said: "We're close, but no farther tonight. I can't pick my way in the dark." Talo didn't argue. He wrapped himself in his cloak and fell asleep at once.

It was very cold when Talo suddenly awoke, without his usual period of disorientation. The eastern quarter of the sky was filling with gray light, but to the south he saw a rose-colored glow. He stood and poked the guide with a toe. The guide looked and said: "Yebol."

Dawn passed, as if to mock their attempts at speed, and swallowed the glow from the sky. The scent of salt, and ash was coming to them when the guide stopped and pointed out a man descending the ridge before them.

"Over the rise is Yebol."

Talo nodded. "And there is a man to spare us from riding pell-mell into town without news." Talo turned his Tarpan in that direction. The guide followed for a short way, then he suddenly reined in and turned.

"I've come with you far enough." He spurred his horse as Talo watched bemused. When Talo turned back toward Yebol, he saw the stranger from whom he expected news was suddenly much closer. Then he recognized who it was: Yetit. That made the guide's actions a lot easier to understand. Talo recalled Yetit's regard for courtesy and thinking it wise to get the first word in, called out:

"Good day to you, poet-beggar, maim leg on the empty fields. What profit may I bring you?"

Yetit laughed. It was a silvery-clear sound, but unpleasant none-the-less. "You, master Talo, fear to hear another poem." Yetit's face became, for a moment, unclear, as if expressions were flowing so swiftly over its surface it had no set form. It was a very unsettling thing to watch.

"However, your first words were a greeting and your next words expressed concern for my condition. Thus, I will say what I will say in prose and I will ask for no profit. This day all profit belongs to you, though the profit I speak of will not seem as such."

"Say on, prince of the poets," Talo said, thinking the guide was no fool.

"I say this: you are pursued from the north by one who neither hates nor fears you--especially now that his long arm has struck your Daughter down. Her blacken timbers lay in Yebol roads. Yebol town was defended, by your men above all others, but you'll find no love there today. But you already suspect. Not this do you fear to hear from me."

This was all true. Talo bowed his head: "Speak my deeper fear."

Yetit laughed. "Brave man. You embrace the nexus as a lover; I observe with delight. Unsettled times attract me, it is true. You may not see me, but I shall be near until the end of your days"

The wind was cold on Talo's forehead; he licked his lips and tasted the salt of his perspiration.

"Yes, master Talo, prose is so obscure. At the mid-point we shall walk; there the nexus has power. Again and once again. Good day, master Talo." Yetit circled around Talo's mare and limped north at great speed without a backward glance.

Over the ridge Talo found the beginnings of the wash and followed it down to the harbor. The Daughter of Shee had been burned to the waterline. The town itself looked hardly touched; several building along the waterfront were charred, but that was all. A crowd stood on the beach opposite the Daughter and in the roads a cloud of small boats clustered round the wreak. Talo could see people diving--his crew, presumably, for the Daughter contained much treasure. Then a figure detached itself from the crowd and ran toward him. It was Taxis, under master behind Pen and Turns. He shouted:

"Master Talo, good it is you've returned so quickly."

"That I see. Where are Pen and Turns?"

"Dead. They had but one ship, but we were taken unawares with the crew scattered about town. Turns was on the Daughter. Pen gathered us and drove their landing party back. He fell here on the beach."

Talo shook his head. "And how many besides them?"

"Many. You see us here. Under four score and half wounded."

Talo nodded, suddenly very weary. In his mind's eye he saw the headman berating him for bringing war into his narrow land. Two under masters, his oldest companions and his Daughter torn from him. He had expected the latter, but not the first. Unnoticed his hand slipped down to his purse. It found the casket and rested there. Then Talo's head cleared. The beggar's words stood clear in his mind. Maybe the hand on the tiller of his plans was not his own, but the course was there and he would follow. Talo regarding Taxis, the young man chewing his lip, eyes fixed on the sand.

"Well, the Daughter was unnecessary for the journey I have in mind; and alas, so is the crew."

"Master?" Taxis said, looking up and not understanding.

"Three men, no more because we can't attract attention such as this. I leave the selection to you. Choose two whole men, they who acquitted themselves most bravely last night. I shall ride to Razedaze's and inform him I decline his commission. He will find compensation in the salvage from the Daughter--enough to pay off any debts owed by the village up-country."

"Yes, master Talo," Taxis stammered. "But, may I ask, where are you proposing to ride?"

"To Moaz, Taxis, Moaz. There is some script I would know the meaning of and only there, I suspect, may I get my answer."

As he rode into town Talo could see Taxis liked this plan not at all, but there was no help for that.

5

THE MIDDLE CITY

The direct route from Yebol to Moaz led over the Innersea, through Gildesh and up the Riverrun. This way was unavailable to Talo because of his activities a decade before in the Times of Trouble. He choose instead the circuitous eastern route for himself and his three companions, Bren and Finig, rough but capable members of the crew, and Taxis, his only surviving under master.

"Go north from Yebol (by-passing Dell) to the Innersea north and east of Saroka; cross the steppes to the Xaxi--the further east you bear the lower you'll find the passes--and pick up the broad Ossa by following the northern foothills to the west." Distilled to their bare sense, such were the directions Talo obtained in Yebol. It was a long journey (spring came while they traversed the Xaxi foothills) but it was completed without incident.

The great central plain of Ossa -- which washed against the north side of the Xexi-Xaxi ranges like a sea -- presented its most congenial aspect in the spring; a vista of fertility crowding every horizon. Bunch grass, sage, sorrel and wild flowers competed in hectic growth before the descent of the summer-autumn drought. The air was balmy and so was the rain: balanced perfectly between excessive cold and heat. The great Ossa spread over its vast flood plain like a roiled mirror, surfeited, but not satisfied. They rode along the eastern bank all the way to Rivercamp before finding a ferry.

Rivercamp was an outpost of the Magnus of Moaz. Talo had prepared a bribe for the frontier warders, but in the event it proved a needless precaution. Speaking Southcoast, the master warder asked their business.

"We ride to Moaz-town," Talo answered. "I carry a gift for the Magnus."

The warder studied them, particularly Bren and Finig, and finally said: "You come from the east, yet little like Levites do you look to me."

Talo perceived his misconception immediately, aided by the rumors of traffic between Bar-Lev and the Magnus. He said: "His lands are wide and growing wider. His people are the people of Ossa."

The warder shrugged his shoulders, as if used to tolerating barbarian delusions. "If you say." Then: "All right, I suppose you know the way to Moaz as well as I. Pass by."

They rode from Rivercamp across the neck of land that separates the Shem from the Ossa, coming to the Long Lake of Moaz above Ria town. This was a pleasant district. The road ran between orchards and through a succession of well-ordered villages. Food was cheap and plentiful.

They reached Moaz in the middle of the next morning. From a distance they saw a collection of towers thrusting above the milky airs of the lake. The city lay hidden behind tall walls of gray stone. The road now ran through stone fields toward a massive gate.

The guard at the gate stopped them and asked if they were outlanders, to which Talo replied yes, adding they had been sent by Bar-Lev. In a way this was true; by burning the Daughter of Shee, he had propelled Talo on his journey. But while the guard accepted this assertion, Talo's hope, that they would gain entry into the city as easily as they had into the realm, proved false. The guard instructed them to bide in the temple beyond the gate while he sent for someone to conduct them to the citadel.

If a city was to have a waiting room, the temple was a suitable place. It was a massive edifice with broad steps climbing to four arched doorways each the width of five men. Talo and Taxis entered, leaving Bren and Finig with their dice cups on the steps outside. It was like stepping into night. Talo reached out until he felt the coolness of a wall and waited for his eyes to adjust, but even then, there was little to see; just two statues against the far wall. Taxis wandered by himself, his footsteps lost in the vast interior spaces. Talo walked toward the statues and walked and watched them grow as the entries shrank behind him. Two huge, stone men sat hands upon knees and stared out above their supplicants of whom Talo was presently the only one. On the left Talo recognized Raos, bane of Josh. He was carved with a long, hooded nose, thin lips and narrow forehead. The statue on the left Talo assumed must be Caos, present Magnus. His features were balanced, benign and pleasing. The juxtaposition of real and ideal was slightly jarring. Talo looked for a priest, having in mind some questions, but the temple was empty.

"Master, we are called." Taxis spoke from near the doors, but his voice carried easily across the vast space, lingering in the dark, high corners. Talo glanced at the statues a final time and realized this edifice was, in fact, not a temple at all.

Emerging, Talo was momentarily halted by the need to let his eyes adjust, once again, to the light. He almost didn't notice that a voice was addressing him. He shaded his eyes and waved his other hand in the direction of the voice.

"Sorry. Do you speak Southcoast?"

"Of course." Talo saw a tall, thin man with the fair skin and hair more commonly encountered on the eastern coasts. He was clad in a full length coral gown; a garment which the trousered Talo considered peculiar. A wispy beard hung on the man's face like lines trailing from a dismasted ship.

"But I was informed you came from Klaxxis. How is it you don't speak the language spoken there?"

Talo nodded, squinting to take in the two men standing behind the gowned man. Their arms were crossed over uniform coral colored tunics.

"You were misinformed, no doubt," Talo said carefully. "I said I came from Bar-Lev; never did I say Bar-Lev sent me."

The other nodded, as if Talo had said a wise and profound thing. "Well, I am not sorry to find my expectations confounded and a civilized man before me. The Tarhadian tongues are harsh and I find it difficult to express myself completely in them. Southcoast I prefer even to Moazian."

The gowned man looked past Talo. "I see there are three in your party. My name is Baken-Lie. Come with me, please, all of you. I shall guide you to the citadel where you may explain the business which brings you to Moaz." With a swirl of drapery he led them into the alleyways of Moaz. It was slow going. People pushed by and around them, bearing on their backs, some of them, amazingly large burdens. Most of the buildings were low and surrounded by walls, like fortresses within the fortress city.

By the time they neared the citadel, Talo was feeling hot and buffeted. Around the walls was cleared space a hundred paces wide. Emerging into the open gave a sense of relief, like the feeling after successfully conning a channel full of uncharted shoals. It also gave a clear view of the citadel. Talo gazed up at walls constructed of coral stone, height augmented by the hill they enclosed. The gates were shut, but a stream of people wound up to a small portal on the side. Above the walls, Talo's eyes encountered an architecture gone wild. Towers shots up from every imaginable foundation; galleries stretched forth and back like stone spider webs. Irregularly shaped windows stared down; random walls, seemingly unattached peeked in and out of the confusion. On the coast, people built for function. The citadel of Moaz was quite unlike anything Talo had ever encountered before.

Bren and Finig were dropped off in a barrack close to the gate and seemed content enough. Baken-Lie led Talo and Taxis up into the citadel. There was much movement of people within the lower precincts, but Baken-Lie greeted no one and no one greeted him. The stream of conversation he had maintained passing through the city likewise died out and they made their way in silence. They walked down long corridors with closed doors, past open gardens and fountains.

Finally Baken-Lie stopped before a door, seemingly identical to the many they had passed. He pulled out a large ring of keys and opened it.

"You can clean yourselves of the dust of your journey here." Baken-Lie turned.

"A moment. Will I see Caos today?"

Baken-Lie turned back and smiled. "Are you in such a hurry then? My good sir, you must realize you are not whom I expected; nor have you seen fit to introduce yourself and your business to me, although I have provided sufficient opportunities. To be honest, I have no idea of what to do with you." He paused. "But perhaps my departure is unnecessary. Muk seems to have located the lower captain without trouble."

Talo heard the measured footfalls and looked up the corridor to where it terminated in a staircase going up. Baken-Lie had folded his arms and was still smiling, but faintly. Then, with a clatter, a group of men appeared on the staircase. A short man with a heavy face and belly was in the lead. Directly behind him was one of the men who had come with them through the city. Behind the familiar man was a file of six soldiers.

The heavyset officer stopped before Baken-Lie and nodded. His gaze deliberately seemed to avoid Talo.

"Why are you in the corridor, then?"

Baken-Lie shrugged his shoulders. "You came so quickly. We just arrived ourselves. I was about to look for you, in fact."

"Humph. Isn't that why you have servants? Your man knew where to look."

Baken-Lie opened the door. "Muk is an excellent man."

The chamber on the other side of the door was not what Talo expected. There were two rooms. The one they entered was hung with intricate, geometric tapestries on all the walls and furnished with couches. In the other room was a large pool, filled with water from which steam was raising. It had a skylight and a profusion of potted shrubs and trees set around the pool.

"After all, Captain," Baken-Lie went on, "these men are weary and I though it would be a politeness to permit them to clean." Baken-Lie added extra emphasis to his words with a wrinkled nose.

"Politeness is a luxury you can allow yourself, but not me, good Fanbearer." Then the captain finally swung around and faced Talo. His men were waiting outside, but Muk, Baken-Lie's servant had followed them in.

"So, I am told you have come from Bar-Lev, but that Bar-Lev did not send you."

"In a manner of speaking," Talo replied. He was having trouble deciding how best to deal with the direction events seemed to be taking. They were very suspicious folk in Moaz. The captain, however, didn't wait for Talo to shape events. He turned abruptly to Taxis.

"What is your master's name?"

Taxis hesitated just slightly. "He is Talo the Taelien."

Silence followed this revelation. Talo was slightly annoyed. He hadn't thought to discuss this possibility with Taxis, but old Pen would have known enough to lie. Then the captain looked at Talo.

"Talo the Taelien."

"That is I, at your service."

The captain looked at Baken-Lie. "Talo the Taelien. It is a name that tugs the memory."

Baken-Lie laughed. "As well it should." He bowed to Talo. "Sir, it is an exceeding honor to make your acquaintance. I presume you are the man who most lately defended Sidoc against our ally, the indomitable Bar-Lev."

Talo returned the bow. "I can hardly claim credit for the work you quote."

Baken-Lie turned to the captain. "I suppose he falls into your jurisdiction, but still, the puzzle remains. How did Bar-Lev send you? And what business can you have with the Magnus? I ask now before the captain takes you and asks these questions in his own way."

"Gentlemen, I have no secrets. My business with the Magnus concerns this:" said as he pulled the casket from his purse. Baken-Lie did no more than glance at it; then, with raised eyebrows he addressed the captain.

"Nothing is simple anymore. Talo the Taelien, it does no harm to tell what you already know. We do not trust you, but what you bring merits special consideration. Captain, I say we withhold judgment and bring this to the attention of the Magnus. You are familiar with his feelings on matters that pertain to the Pau."

The captain nodded. "I am, I am. But I have recalled this man now and I think he is dangerous. . . "

Baken-Lie interrupted. "Yes, I will not obtrude into the functioning of your duty, but do know I shall make a report and delete none of the particulars."

The captain stared at him in silence. "Right." Then to Talo: "I'll leave a guard on the door. Remain here and take advantage of the pool. I assume Coastals care how they smell."

Baken-Lie added. "I will take this casket, with your permission, of course. Also, my man Muk will abide in the next chamber. If you need anything, go first to him."

After everyone had departed Talo went into the poolroom. Taxis said: "Master, our well-being seems on the balance. Did we do wrong to come here?"

"I don't know, Taxis, but look here: when you twist this valve, hot water enters the pool. Come and see."

6

ALL CUSTOMS DIFFER

Talo made the pool water as hot as he could stand and took a thoroughly enjoyable bath. Taxis was more reserved. He could understand where the water came from, but not how it was heated. He regarded the whole arrangement with distrust.

"What if they let boiling water in and we roast?"

Finally he eased himself in, submerged and jumped out, all in one motion. Talo laughed.

"You've no idea what you're missing."

When he was finally clean, Talo sat naked in a patch of afternoon sun coming from the skylight. Taxis ran in circles around the pool to dry himself. Talo was going to wash his trousers and tunic next (much campaigning had made him practical) when the door opened and slaves entered carrying folded robes and gowns. Talo eyed these garments reluctantly (a look Taxis assumed was suspicion) but resigned himself to wearing them.

After they were dressed more slaves entered, this time bringing food. Neither Talo nor Taxis had any reservations about eating the spicy inland food laid before them. Talo frustrated the slave's attempts to serve them and hustled them out of the chamber.

A half-hour later Talo felt fat, fit and happy. He examined Taxis reclining on a couch and said: "You don't look the same man who rode so dry and dusty into Moaz this morning."

"I don't feel like that man either. I feel better, but worse, if you know what I mean."

"You'd feel better yet if you had given the bath a chance. As for feeling worse," he shrugged his shoulders, "every new situation or commission is uncertain. You must be confident. Start doubting yourself and everyone will doubt you."

The door opened before Taxis could reply. It was Baken-Lie.

He walked into the center of the chamber, rubbing his hands. "Ah, I see you gentlemen now look like gentlemen. The food was acceptable, I trust?"

"Acceptable and very welcome," Talo said.

Baken-Lie stroked his sparse beard and nodded. "That is good. Now, master Talo, I must inform you have upset my whole routine for today and probably for many days to come. I have been pushing your business forward and little else."

Talo stood and bowed, drawing back the folds of his robe as if he'd been wearing drapery his entire life. "I thank you, gracious Baken-Lie, Fanbearer."

Baken-Lie laughed and waved a hand in the air. "Oh, I am sure you know I have my own reasons. But we may speak of those later. Now, the first thing I did was to write a report. Then I delivered the casket you brought to those men whose business it is to know of such things, the scholars of Pauic. They were very excited; a comfort to me and an indication I am making no mistake with you, as maybe, the lower captain is. Now I am returned on their errand. They have an exceeding desire to question you, Master Talo."

"I'm ready. Indeed, next to an audience with Caos, all respect to him, my greatest desire is to ask a few questions of those gentlemen myself."

Baken-Lie smiled. "Well, be not surprised if that desire is frustrated. You will see soon enough what I mean."

"And Taxis? Does he come with?"

"Not for now. I will instruct Muk to come in and entertain him with conversation."

The Pauic scholars proved to be two ancient men, dry and crisp. They looked up with unfriendly expressions when Talo and Baken-Lie entered their dusty chamber. The casket was sitting on a table before them. Talo glanced at it and thought it looked quite out of place. In that same instant, he was aware of the cool touch of the ring secreted against his body. Having a secret served to increase his natural confidence.

The scholars greeted Baken-Lie, then they called in a slave to translate and the questioning began. They were concerned where and from whom Talo had obtained the casket. Talo had entered the interview with enthusiasm and might have responded with most of the truth if the questions hadn't been put to him so offensively. ("You are a barbarian; what made you think this was important?") As it was, his temper stepped in and the clarity of his answers suffered. There were long periods as he waited for the translator to understand another interminable question, having repeated his monosyllabic reply. During one of those periods, his thoughts got lost somewhere else.

Danger sat on the other side of the table from him. Why was he courting danger? It wasn't hope for reward. A prince did pay for good news or important intelligence, but Talo wasn't sure he had either. Nor did he care. Much gold had passed through his hands, but it had never weighted him down. Curiosity was a trait, however, akin to greed, and one which held Talo particularly in thrall. It was a physical sensation, his desire to know what the tablet said--a cavity in his chest begging to be filled. But there was something more. Plain curiosity would never have sustained him through the long journey to Moaz. It was intuition, he thought: intuition so strong it could go by the name of certain knowledge. Intuition apparently guided by luck and strange encounters (thinking of Yetit, the twice-met beggar of Yebol).

Talo figured he had his motivations trapped, skinned and on the rack drying. Dimly he was aware that there were other animals of his mind--red eyes staring unblinkingly from beyond the light of the fire--ignoble and misshaped beasts, but he choose not to consider them. The scar on his side, left from the arrow in Sidoc itched and Talo ignored that too.

The translators toneless voice intruded on Talo's meditations. If he remained uncooperative, torture was next. Talo could feel Baken-Lie's eyes seeking him out, and he wondered (on Baken-Lie's behalf as much as on his own) why he was doing this to himself.

Then Talo was graced with another insight. He realized, suddenly, they were afraid of him--that they were afraid of everything foreign. Why else affect an ignorance of Southcoast (people who knew old Pauic, the most difficult of languages must know Southcoast, the easiest). Talo didn't answer. He stood.

"This has gone far enough. What is the message written on the tablet?"

The first scholar looked up before the question could be translated. His lips quivered, as if about to give reply, but he looked back down. Talo continued.

"What manner of men have I encountered. In peace I came, offering more than I ask and in return I am threatened. I have asked a question. I will have an answer. Now!"

Talo laced his voice with both the custom of authority and the expectation of obedience. Perhaps because these people were accustomed to responding to such tones, the results were gratifying. In unison the two men rose to their feet and blinked. The translator dutifully began rendering the question, but was silenced with a gesture.

"Most noble sir," in unaccented Southcoast, "we regret if cause for offense has been given. However, we must study the tablet and prepare a report. It is written in old Pauic, a subtle and blasphemous tongue. Moreover, its sense in wrapped in riddle. If we knew where you obtained it and from whom, it is possible these riddles would make better sense. Moreover, there are certain phases which we must check against our books before we can be certain of their meaning."

"I see, Talo said. "In that case, I will not keep you from your researches." He rotated on his heel and walked loudly from the chamber. The guards at the door made no attempt to detain him. Baken-Lie hurrying to catch up, tugged at the sleeve of Talo's new gown. Talo turned and because the mood was full upon him, said:

"Ah, the good, the venerable Baken-Lie. I trust you do not intend to conduct me back to the holding chamber I was put in this morning. Its location in the palace is low and is neither a suitable nor honorable place for me to remain."

Baken-Lie stared at Talo. His mouth twitched, as if uncertain which way to turn, up or down. Finally, he smiled.

"Perhaps not. I acknowledge its location is not in harmony with your reputation."

Talo, still probing for Baken-Lie's anger threshold, lifted his hand in a magnanimous gesture. "Mistakes happen. I take them not to heart. You may oblige me by expediting my request for an audience with his most gracious Magnus. When can this be done?"

"At his pleasure," Baken Lie said; then in a tone more confidential, "but I will begin working on it. Now, if we can collect Muk and your man, Taxis, we shall see about a more suitable chamber."

Talo followed Baken-Lie down the corridor thinking he was a man well schooled in the way of patience.

7

INTERVIEWS

After they'd settled into their new quarters, Talo related his interview with the Pauic Scholars to Taxis. It was late by the time he finished. The day had been long and filled with interesting events. They were both tired, but Talo wasn't quite ready to let Taxis go to sleep. As before, Baken-Lie had left Muk in an adjoining room to be available if they needed service. Talo was curious about the man and questioned Taxis about the time he'd spent with him. Taxis yawned and said Muk was indeed a close man who never smiled; none-the-less, he had faithfully fulfilled Baken-Lie's order to entertain. "He's a Shonian by birth and told me some stories about the lakes. Also a good one about a mix-up two years back at the big sacrifice to Caos when they dedicated that statue we saw today."

"That one I want to hear," Talo said, "but tomorrow." At that moment the object of their conversation, Muk, opened the door. He announced the Captain of the Lower Guard.

The Lower Captain entered their chamber. Although the Captain was clearly no friend of theirs, Talo found he rather liked him. The Captain was similar in height and build to Talo; but best of all, whereas Talo did have some hair on the top of his head, the Captain had none. The Captain crossed his arms and looked around. Talo was aware of more men in the corridor.

"I have lately been informed your quarters were changed. This move was made without my knowledge or approval. I am responsible for security in these precincts of the palace. This chamber fails to fulfill the requirements. Gather your possessions and accompany me."

"To a more secure chamber well within your gaze," Talo said. "No thank you, Captain. I must decline your invitation."

The captain looked at Talo, disbelief flitting across his face like a gull dipping in a rain smeared sky. "That was no invitation, it was an order."

Talo crossed his arms and placidly smiled.

The Captain abruptly began to pace the length of the chamber. Talo noticed he glanced at Muk who was standing by the door, observing everything. Finally, the Captain whirled to face Talo (`this one practices his gestures,' Talo thought approvingly).

"All right. But don't be so confident you won't eventually find yourself in my hands." After the Lower Captain was gone, Muk surprised Talo with an unsolicited observation.

"He takes his charge seriously." Muk related a story of the Lower Captain before this one and the fate that befell him after a would-be assassin penetrated the citadel. Talo asked what had happened to the assassin, but that question Muk couldn't answer.

The second day in Moaz was uneventful. Baken-Lie stopped by in the morning and advised them to refrain from exploring; in fact to remain in chamber. After that they saw no one, with the exception of Muk. Talo didn't take well to the waiting. Some spirit within him, always present but particularly strong at the moment, demanded action. Fortunately, on the morning of the third day Baken-Lie returned with welcome news. The Magnus Caos had consented to an audience in the Hall of the Chair that very day. Talo left immediately to be instructed in the procedure necessary to properly approach the Presence. Protocol didn't allow for Taxis' attendance, dooming him to another day of sitting.

Talo had no difficulty picking up the etiquette for the occasion; it was much the same throughout Ossa. After the masters of ritual passed him, Baken-Lie returned. They journeyed to the very highest portion of the palace to the Hall of the Chair. Talo was winded when they arrived and it rather distressed him to hear his name announced immediately. However, approaching the chair of Caos in the prescribed manner gave ample opportunity to catch his breath.

According to the procedure, Talo was supposed to keep his eyes on the ground; however, he found this impossible. For one thing, the hall was an amazing sight. The walls were of a coral-colored stone; the ceiling, vaulted high overhead, was garnished with mosaics mostly invisible in the floating smoke. The lamps were shaded with a translucent coral material which imparted to the light a murky, reddish quality. The hall was crowded with guards and courtiers, but of them Talo could form only the dimmest of impressions. Caos himself seemed to float in his elevated chair. Finally, Talo arrived at the base of the chair.

He stopped, performed the oblation and waited. He waited until it was Caos' pleasure to notice him and this took time. But finally:

"Master Talo the Taelin; the famous captain who acknowledges no lord. Come and approach our presence."

Talo slowly mounted the steps of the dais. He looked up and for the first time beheld Caos' face. This sight surprised him. He recognized Caos from somewhere, and then remembered the statue. This was cause for further surprise: the stone depiction was true to the living man. No, if anything, it was more impressive to see such beauty on a living face, even conceding the majestic proportions possible with stone.

When Talo was but a few steps below the chair he stopped again. Caos looked him full in the face and smiled. Talo got the impression he was confidentially ridiculing the surrounding pomp. His smile was without affectation and for the briefest of moments, Talo wondered if he was the victim of some elaborate joke. Then Caos spoke again. He spoke in a public voice to the whole hall.

"Who does not know this man? Who does not know of the Troubled Times in Gildi?" . . . a pause. . . "Who does not know he put to flight their armies, yea, even the celebrated guard of their emperor? Who does not know of his heroic defenses of Vaanis and of Kell and most lately of Sidoc where only the massed hoards of our ally, Bar-Lev, could rout him out and that at the expense of an entire campaigning season? Who does not know this man?" Caos paused again. "Then join me all in welcoming this man to our service and in honoring him."

Talo had to stand for the ovation that followed Caos' order. When it was finished and all was quiet again, Caos said:

"We are entirely pleased, Talo the Taelin." Then he sat back and his face appeared to blank out. It was a moment before Talo realized he'd been dismissed. Nothing had been said and nothing had been done. He couldn't believe it. He even dared to say:

"Gracious Magnus . . ." but he stopped because Caos gave no sign of acknowledgment. His face was curtained. Talo stood for a moment while a surge of irritation passed, then he made the departing oblation and retired down the length of the hall. People were whispering, but Talo didn't pause. Baken-Lie was waiting near the entrance to the hall. He was quite pleased.

"The Magnus has chosen to honor you," he said, "things are going very well. I imagine the Lower Captain's happy he listened to me."

"Do you think so," Talo said. "I'm happy for the captain, but I think this was a waste of my time."

"Not so loudly, please. And not so foolish. These things proceed at their own pace. You will understand. And do you think it is just anyone who is proclaimed in this hall? I'll tell you now, what happened today has happened only twice before and once was with Bar-Lev. I would dearly love to have my time wasted so."

"I didn't know Bar-Lev had been in Moaz. . . "

Baken-Lie was motioning for silence. A small boy, dressed in the finery of a page, was standing beside them.

"Greeting most gracious fan-bearer of the second degree. I relay the commands of Gavin, Captain of the Upper Guard. He bides me say unto you that your presence is desired in his chambers." This message erased the smile from Baken-Lie's face. Talo said: "Gavin . . . ? Is that the name of the. . . ?"

"No indeed," Baken-Lie muttered, "here in the higher precincts another man commands the guard. That is Gavin."

The boy spoke up again. "Gracious fan-bearer. My master's request permits no delay."

"Of course not," Baken-Lie said. "I have no intention of causing you trouble with your master, my boy. I am coming." Then to Talo: "There is no telling what this is about. Be not concerned about your audience today; it will not be your last talk with the Magnus, that is certain. Now I must run."

Whispering anxieties haunted Talo's journey back down to his chamber. He was relieved to find Taxis waiting when he returned, anxious to hear how the audience had gone.

"Well, I'm told there's reason to be confident. I received honor today equal to that accorded Bar-Lev himself. I just wonder why I don't feel as confident as I did yesterday."

"Master, I feel worse than that. You gladden me, but you frighten me as well. This place I do not care for. . . .Bar-Lev? When did he find time to come all this way?"

Talo laughed. That was the way he was: if someone's thought paralleled his own, he was likely to swing one hundred eighty degrees in his feelings.

"If I had to stay in this room all day as you did, I'd be just as depressed. But be of good cheer. I wish I'd known of Bar-Lev's visit when it could've done me some good. But maybe next year people will be saying the same of us. And if this doesn't work, we'll just collect Finig and Bren and be gone."

"If we can."

They spent the remainder of the day in their chamber, growing progressively more bored and disenchanted with Moaz. Talo wanted to talk with Baken-Lie, but not even Muk was present to answer their questions. They made ready for bed quite early because there was nothing else to do. But just when Talo had trimmed the lamps, there came a knocking at their door. It was another page-boy, maybe the same one who brought the summons to Baken-Lie that morning. Caos required the presence of both of them, at once.

They had to hurry to keep pace with the boy who acted as their guide. He led them up countless corridors, past innumerable turnings, broad stairways and narrow concealed steps. They were both hopelessly lost early in the journey. Somewhere along the route two guards fell into step behind Taxis. The boy didn't seem to notice, but Talo and Taxis did. They refrained from comment, however. Dungeons were traditionally placed in the lower, not the higher portions of a residence. Finally they stopped at an ordinary looking door at the top of a long and winding stairway. The boy knocked twice.

They he turned and bowed:

"Wait here."

Talo nodded. He was puffing too hard to answer. He glanced back and noted the guards had disappeared. Then the door opened. An old man peered vaguely in Talo's direction. Talo didn't recognize him. Then the old man's glance appeared to come into focus. "Oh, there you are. But who is he?"

"Taxis, my second mate. I was instructed he was to come with."

"Well, I don't know about that. You come in, but let him wait by the door."

Talo shrugged an apology to Taxis and entered the room. It was plain, almost austere. Caos was sitting on a divan at the further end. The only other furnishings were a desk, two chairs and a smoking lamp. There were no windows. Caos looked up and smiled.

"Good, you're here. I trust the trip was not too tiring. I like the stairs. They keep me fit."

Talo bowed and was about to answer, but Caos turned away, talking again.

"As a rule I don't receive in my chamber. It's plain and out of the way, but what it lacks in comfort, it compensates with intimacy, wouldn't you agree?"

Talo started to do just that, but the old man began coughing violently. Caos' face--his perfect features startlingly beautiful--assumed a look of grave concern.

"Uncle, a glass of water?"

The old man shook his head. "No, hack, hack. Just bile." He pulled out a yellowed linen and spat into it. After inspecting the product, he returned it to an inside pocket.

"I don't think you've had the pleasure of meeting my uncle, his most gracious peer of the realm, the Lord Raden."

Talo bowed again. He still hadn't spoken a word.

"He doesn't completely approve of you. You're an outlander and according to the Lord Raden's way of thinking, outlanders are barbarians."

The Lord Raden grunted and turned away.

"But that is neither here nor there. We have summoned you for a reason. It is our constant regret we are unable to afford the time to pursue our pleasures and cultivate friendships with such men as yourself. Yet, our obligations we accept with . . "

Caos paused. Expression came flooding into his eyes. "We are never safe. We recall with grim distaste and longing for vengeance the fate of our divine father. We ourselves are blessed with divinity . . . His eyes bore into Talo's. Talo was sweating and his neck itched, but he didn't scratch it. "Some seek to oppose us with violence. From these we withhold all mercy and return to them the harsh violence they have espoused. That treachery most foul and sorrowful comes from within. From our servants in this palace who have been seduced by evil we withhold all pity." Caos sat up and pointed at Talo. "However, you have come to us guided, we have no doubt, by our ancestors, bringing disquieting evidence the evil our blessed father did his utmost to eradicate has once again arisen in this world. Both within and without the conflict of our age is at this moment rushing to confront us. But it shall not confound us. Even now we ready ourselves; even now, more than ever, we feel our need for trustworthy and able servants. We have it in our mind you are such a man. We have honored you highly because your instincts have directed you toward the right. We are prepared to go even further, but not without a test."

Caos blinked rapidly. Lord Raden had been noisily shuffling parchments during this speech. Noticing the silence, he looked up and said: "He speaks like that when the spirit is strong within." Then he returned to the documents, his interjection hanging in the air.

Questions were welling up in Talo's mind. He thought it was something other than the `spirit' that made Caos talk so and whatever that something was, it disconcerted him. But of these thoughts his reply gave no indication. He stood and said:

"My lord, I am a man in the habit of knowing his mind. Any tests you devise shall be welcome. I can state confidently I shall be able to fulfill them to your satisfaction."

Caos stroked his chin. "I see. Well, confidence is good. I shall waste no more time and explain my commission at once." He stood and walked over to the desk where Raden was sitting. "Uncle, where did you put that box?"

"Don't shout. I have it here."

"Ah, yes." Talo watched Caos gingerly pick up his casket and bring it over. Again he was aware of the ring hanging against his skin, of it's cool, detached touch. "This, Talo the Taelin, is the casket you so rightly brought to our attention, is it not?"

"It is the same, my lord," Talo said, rather amazed they were finally coming around to a topic that interested him.

"Yes, I find it highly commendable you have come to us seeking explanations. A man, if truly a man he is, must understand the nature of evil."

"Of evil, my lord?"

"Of evil indeed. Listen and I shall explain. First, know that the Gildi, for whom you have no love, have for many years maintained forts on our southern territories, obstructing our rivers and holding our city of Zoha. This is most obnoxious to me as it was to my father of divine memory. Until this time, however, my temporal strength has not been sufficient to correct the situation. Now, we have powerful allies who await our word. You know of Bar-Lev and you know his power." (`And I know he can't be trusted,' Talo thought) "All is favorable. All is ready. But now you have brought a matter of grave concern to my attention and that is the casket." Caos picked up a scroll of linen paper. "This is a summary of your interview with the scholars of Pauic. I read you have forgotten where you acquired the casket."

"Forgive me lord; such was only what I told them."

"Yes. Of course, knowing you were in Sidoc until recently helps. I presume it was found somewhere in that vicinity."

"No," Talo said, forcing the word out. "I found it south of Sidoc. In a village called Dell. Eastern mainland province of Istel. It belonged, at one time, to a child I believe Pauic born."

Caos had stood and was pacing back and forth down the length of the apartment. Lord Raden, who had dozed off, awoke with a start. He mumbled and then saw Talo. "Oh, its you. I wanted to say . . . "

"Silence!" Caos commanded. He turned to Talo, expression going in a blink from stern to eager and bright. "This is fantastic. I won't ask why you lied to my officers; often they obstruct my business rather than further it. But the child as well. This is fantastic. You have devised your own test. With the threat of another Pauic rising, another Josh, I felt my hands were tied. But now. . . ." He paused and looked at Talo who couldn't help but be fascinated by the man's liquid face. "But you still don't know what's at stake. You don't know the traditions pertaining to the casket and the translation of the tablet that was inside."

"No, Lord. I admit I've tried, but. . ."

Caos smiled; it was such a horrible expression Talo fell silent. "Through the agency of your good friend, Baken-Lie. No, don't be concerned by the way I spoke that name. I'm well aware you're innocent of his designs. He is in custody and will harm no further." Talo opened his mouth. This was completely unexpected. "Don't ask. I won't mention his name again. No indeed. Instead, we wish you to listen to this:" He picked up the tablet and read:

> North to South the rivers flow\
>
> Springs unquenchable\
>
> South to North you shall go\
>
> Paths unmentionable\
>
> Little one\
>
> As you shall do it shall be done\
>
> It shall be done as you shall do\
>
> Blessings permeate you, little one\
>
> Blessings through and through\\

Ossa

And it is signed with the hierogram of Josh. What do you make of it?"

"It sounds like your scholars played with the meaning to make their translation fit the original rhythm scheme."

"Caos laughed. "A critic. Well, perhaps they did, but the meaning is still clear enough. Listen and I shall explain. The Pau claim primacy because they are eldest in Ossa. That claim, that they are eldest, I don't dispute. Their age, however, makes them not foremost; it makes them an abomination in the eyes of the younger races. It makes them tradition bound, decadent and stinking of death. They follow a god who is no god at all. Even they admit he is unknowable and call him Paulac, the unmanifest one. I ask you, how can a god be unmanifest. It's ridiculous. How could I be a god to my people if I secluded myself from them? "Josh was the prophet of this ungod. That is, only to him would their god show himself. The line of Josh was very old; a lingering vestige in this world of an earlier age. My sacred father--who shares the void with no Paulac, I know, he's told me--ended this line. You must know that."

"Yes, I do, but what I fail to understand is how there could be a Pauic child so far south. How could the child be related to Josh, as the tablet seems to imply."

"My dear Taelin, please understand: the child you saw is Josh, or at least, he could be. Know that the first Josh, many hundreds of years ago, was, according to their tales, born on the island of NorthPointing. Are you familiar with it?"

"I've landed there. It isn't a favored place."

"Not surprising. When the line of a prophet dies out, as happened in our time, then it is the custom for the sacred families, their nobility, to pilgrim to the birthplace of the founder of the old line. How unfortunate this birthplace was in a land beyond my control. The object is to establish a new line. Any children born during this pilgrimage are left behind with appropriate tokens. They think Paulac will then choose his new voice from these children and help the one to return to the Pauic lands. If one does, they have a new Josh; if not, after a space of two decades--what they call a long year--the process is repeated."

"How strange," Talo muttered. "But that means the child I found could be just one of many."

"Undoubtly. Of course, the odds against any of them finding their way north are great, particularly now for I haven't been idle. My agents are scouring the lands between the Hill kingdoms and NorthPointing for signs such as you have brought. It is such a wide land, however, they have been without success,

45

except in one instance. So, now you understand. We must make arrangements, of course, but Talo the Taelin, well beloved of Caos, your test is this: be prepared to ride on the day following this. The task I lay upon you is to bring this Pauic child to me. Alive and undamaged I want him and in a state of innocence. Since the last one it has occurred to me that a Josh might be a handy thing to have around after I have completed my war with the Gildi. Do you understand?"

"Completely, Lord."

"Good, good, good. I say uncle, the luck has returned to us."

Lord Raden muttered something about being commanded to silence.

"I would like to have the child by the beginning of summer, but east of the Innersea . . . that is a long way away. Still, I trust you to complete this test as quickly as possible. I can begin my campaigns with a calm mind knowing you are on your way. And now, for details. You are acquainted with Baken-Lie's ex-servant, Muk, I believe."

"Yes, my lord. I am," Talo said with a sinking heart.

"He shall be your companion. Fewest travel fastest, I say."

"Very good, my lord. But what of the people I came with?"

"What of them? Your two servants are fighting men. Of fighting men I've constant need. I'm sure you don't begrudge me them."

"No, my lord."

"And the other one, Taxis, I believe his name is, shall reside here as our guest until your safe and successful return."

"I understand, my lord."

"Good, I thought you would. But now it is late. One thing more and you can go and get some rest." Caos took a metal disk from a pocket inside his gown. "This is a sign I want you to carry. It will give you authority over my servants and serve also to remind where your allegiance lays."

Talo accepted the disk. It was heavy, stamped with Caos' profile on one side and an inscription on the obverse. Caos held out his hand. On his ring finger was a heavy, jeweled signet ring which Talo kissed. "I shall not see you before your return. Let it be soon."

As Talo was going to the door, Raden suddenly said: "He is a good man, nephew. I feel you can trust him."

Caos laughed. "Hear that. It is a rare thing indeed for a man to win the Lord Raden's trust."

A page was waiting to guide Talo back down. Of Taxis there was no sign. Although he had been expecting this, it still angered Tal.o.

8

MUK GETS HIS MISSION

In a different part of the upper citadel, secluded and difficult of access, Muk underwent an interview of his own.

Gavin, the captain of the upper palace guard was a close man; his face a secret to all but a few. This was a function of his job, but even more of his personality. He abhorred gossip more than treason; even prisoners who broke under his interrogation earned his contempt.

It was extraordinary that he decided to conduct the interview with Muk personally; but his preparations had reached the point where mistakes were unacceptable and he was the only person he trusted to avoid mistakes.

Muk was shown to a chill, windowless chamber, furnished with a table and two chairs. He was kept waiting several hours before the captain entered. Gavin noticed at once that Muk had been standing the whole time. This made a favorable impression. He took a chair behind the table and said: "Sit down." Muk did so, showing no signs of weariness. Another point.

"All right, you are Muk, formerly Ruba Talbekh ni Shon, nine years in the possession of the Magnus and in my employ in the capacity of informer. As Ruba you had a wife named Kista. Two hands shorter than yourself, green eyes and a blemish, a scar from a sledding accident, I believe, below the left ear. This is right?"

Muk's face gave nothing away. "Yes, captain."

Gavin nodded, watching closely without seeming to do so.

"What would you do to have her and your freedom restored to you?"

The color drained from Muk's still impassive face. "Kista? She is dead." He had begun to tremble slightly. Gavin noted this and said:

"To you she is, but she need not be. I have spoken with her and what I say is true. It remains to be seen if you remember her as she remembers you, Ruba Talbekh ni Shon."

Muk abruptly stood. "Anything, lord. If this is true I will do anything, betray anyone, go anywhere." He put his hands to his face and the trembling stopped. Gavin was pleased. He had begun to wonder if Muk were too cool a character for his purposes, but he would be perfect: a man of deep reserve and suppressed emotion. Someone who could remember.

"Good. There is an assignment for you. If you carry it out satisfactorily, you may expect the reward mentioned. But there must be no reservations. Are you prepared, then, to hear this?"

"I am captain."

Gavin nodded. Not by picking the wrong man had he come to the threshold.

"You have been ordered to accompany the Taelin, Talo, on a special mission for the Magnus. You have received instructions?"

Muk nodded.

"Disregard them. The Pau, if he truly exists, must not arrive in Moaz. He must not be suffered to remain alive. This you will see to. The arrangements for the restoration of your wife will be explained. Is there anything you need to say?"

"Nothing, captain." Muk's control was perfect again, except for the spots of color in his cheeks.

Gavin remained in the questioning chamber, thinking. The Pau was a small matter, but dangerous to ignore. He would be the type of tool Caos knew how to use, and effectively. But Gavin was satisfied with the arrangements devised for the Pau. Lord Raden was what worried him. Gavin could feel him slipping away. Worse, he suspected if Raden were pushed much further he might even expose himself to Caos; he might confess and let Caos do what he would. The only solution was to cut Raden loose, assassination being too risky for the present. Gavin would miss the information, but he could afford the loss. The tide of affairs was set and no one could stop its motion. He had but to sit back and exercise only ordinary caution, letting his person become but a memory and his doings a rumor in the city, and, someday, in the lands beyond. All things would come to him of their own accord.

49

9

A CHILD COMES OF AGE

In Dell, the sixteenth birthday marked the threshold between child and adult. It was a day eagerly anticipated by most children, but as Getlof's sixteenth birthday drew slowly near, her anticipation came to dominate her thoughts almost unbearably; as if the day signified something much more. This engendered an amorphous terror that was especially strong at night. Her childhood had taught her that it was normal for expectations to be disappointed and she tried to apply this knowledge like a balm to make the days pass; but there were moments when her heart would suddenly begin to race. She was ill with anxiety.

Finally, the day arrived.

It began with a moment of panic. She woke, not remembering who, or where she was, from a dream so strange its afterimage left a forgotten web of wonder. Then she saw Geto.

"When will I have peace?" he grumbled when he saw her eyes open. If he remembered what day it was, he gave no sign.

This hurt Getlof so that she lay almost stunned. Yet, there was a trace of satisfaction as well for having correctly foreseen what would happen. Geto continued talking whispering, early-morning complaints. Just like any other day. It made no sense. Nothing did.

That was the difference.

Nothing made any sense at all and it had taken her so long to see. She jumped up abruptly and ran from the house, leaving Geto blinking in astonishment.

The back of her head was buzzing. She bore each moment expecting the next to be unbearable. She ran, feet making small, frightened thuds as they hit the giving ground. She ran, following the twisting stream up to the springs. The ground was rocky there and the fields far below. She had to be alone.

Finally she stopped. Panting, heart pushing against ribs. She was at the third spring: Asha, densely overgrown, quiet, deep and away from eyes. Slowly she caught her breath.

The pool bubbled with emerging water, but the margins were still. Getlof stepped out on a rock and squatted, gazing at her reflection: large, unhappy eyes, thin nose, ears sticking out through stringy black hair, skinny neck. Then, of a sudden, a bird trilled from across the spring. Getlof glanced up at the sound. When she looked back, someone else was there. It was too abrupt not to believe. Someone else. A young, old woman with green hair and white skin and eyes like sunlight through water. All of it weird, but correct.

The woman smiled, as if from a distance and then she spoke. Getlof couldn't say how she heard, but she did. The woman said:

"I saw you and I came."

"You are Asha?" Few people indeed had ever claimed to have seen a water spirit.

"Who else. And you are Getlof Josh. That is known."

"I am Getlof. Josh I don't know." The panic was gone and the disappointment and wrongfulness suddenly not so important. Water bubbled up unceasingly and the wind was liquid.

"You are Josh. Would I have come otherwise?" said in a way that disallowed question. And it made sense. Josh, whatever it meant, must inform the difference she felt.

"What should I do?"

A sound of laughter, high and thin. "You don't know?" Getlof stared, her gaze becoming as fixed as the other's. Then she realized she did know. Green hair and skin of white, nothing was strange in its element. More was real than she had ever believed.

"You're right. I know." She finally said and saying it she was taken with the desire to act.

"But wait, a boon," Asha said, just as Getlof thought of leaving.

Getlof hesitated. Yesterday that request would have been unthinkable. Today she could deal with it. She said:

"What boon, Asha?"

Asha's expression was incalculable, yet, Getlof felt the spirit had lost something she would rather have kept.

"Just this: today is your first day and in that is great power; a power that will linger to good effect. The people who honor and live by me are my life; our fates are shared. I feel a disharmony rippling toward us that I have no wish to experience. Spend this day here in the Vale of Emerging Waters. Turn it from us. I feel you can. That is my boon."

Getlof stared, not answering. They seemed to speak more with eyes than lips. Getlof drank in Asha's eyes and got the feeling that somewhere she had gained an advantage and if she didn't go forward, she would lose it. She might drown.

"I will do as you ask."

"Asha of the jade pool thanks Getlof Josh. You will be as foretold, but different: something more and something less." Then there was nothing at all in the water, neither Asha nor Getlof's own reflection. Quiet and still.

Getlof stood and saw that the sun was over the rim; it was midmorning. She never thought to wonder where the hours had gone. She started down from the spring, taking little notice of where she was going.

Getlof didn't know she was in the Riza family fields until she heard a voice call her name. She turned and saw that the voice belonged to Mother Riza. She had dropped her hoe and was coming with outstretched arms. "Getlof, only now I was thinking of you. This is your big day. Come and let me kiss you."

Getlof smiled and surrendered herself to Mother Riza's embrace. Although they had often clashed when Mother Riza had tried to exert a mother's authority over the motherless child, Getlof liked and respected the old woman.

"What is this. You're still in your night dress, you strange thing." A flicker of worry: "Nothing happened, did it? Why aren't you getting ready for your party. I hope you aren't letting Geto handle things."

"He forgot."

"So, that's it, stingy lout! This morning I thought about coming by. I should've. But don't worry my dear. I'll straighten him out. I feel I should and I will. You'd just let it go and that wouldn't be right at all."

Having made her decision, Mother Riza called two daughters over and together they walked Getlof back to the house. Several people along the way called greetings to her.

Geto was not there when they arrived. That was unusual to the point of strangeness. After Getlof changed, Mother Riza said:

"We'll stay here and begin preparing the food. I really can't think where he's gone off to, but don't worry about it. You must go and invite anyone you wish and don't worry about anything. If Geto won't provide, the Rizas will."

Getlof hadn't forgotten her promise to Asha. It suddenly came to her how she could best fulfill it.

"Are you listening? Be off with you, child."

"I heard, but it isn't right the Rizas provide. I'm going to ask everyone, and . . . Geto can afford it. Wait."

Getlof ran inside and over to Geto's pallet. Beneath there was a patch of dirt darker than the floor. It was a moment's work to uncover the box she knew was there. From it she took two of the gold Istels Talo had left there three months before.

Back outside she held them up, bright and glittering. "See, Geto provides."

Mother Riza took them and looked at Getlof strangely. Finally, she said: "Everyone. That is an idea and a good one. Bless you, Getlof, there's been some bad blood in this valley of late and maybe a grand old party is just what we need. But I must get started. Everyone. I'll have to send for help. This will take the rest of my daughters and their daughters too." Then she laughed. "It's a grand idea."

The first person Getlof saw when she left the house was appropriately enough, Elp. He came running up and said: "Getlof, I've been looking everywhere for you." This was his standard greeting and the familiarity of it made her laugh (not without a bit of sadness and regret). She gave the standard reply:

"Why aren't you in the fields. You know your father will beat you when he finds you ran off."

"But I didn't. I mean, he told me I could. So I could find you, I mean. Happy birthday. Who are we going to invite. Will you still be my friend?"

"I'll always be your friend, Elp."

He was worried; Getlof could sense it, but the concern seemed greater than the question implied.

"To answer your first question--if you still remember it--I'm going to invite everyone. Will you help?"

Elp's eyes went wide. Getlof found herself thinking Elp could open his eyes wider than anyone she had ever known. She wished there were some way she could freeze the moment so she would never lose it.

"Everyone? Even Delea?"

"Delea first of all. Come on if you're coming."

They started at the Opah's fields and from there worked their way from west to east. Everywhere they went it was as if they were expected, and, as the news got ahead of them, they were. By midafternoon they were finished and no one had declined. They returned to the house to see how the preparations were progressing. Mother Riza beamed when she saw Getlof, hugging and kissing her again. Elp she cuffed lightly on the ear. The house had been cleaned as never before and converted into a big kitchen. The younger Rizas were cutting vegetables. Four pigs and several dozen chickens had recently been slaughtered. Getlof asked if Geto had ever returned.

"It was the strangest thing. He finally did and do you know, he was out looking for you. I sent him off to our house so he wouldn't get underfoot here.

"Elp, run outside for a second. I must speak a word to Getlof."

"Getlof won't mind if I hear."

"Elp," Getlof said, "I think you'd better."

Elp shrugged his shoulders and left. Mother Riza shook her head. "Getlof, you are the only one who can do anything with that boy. His poor mother."

"Did you want to talk about Elp?"

"Oh no. Not about Elp at all. I wanted to talk about you, my dear. You've been on my mind all day and I've been thinking that the treatment you've received has not always been as good as it should've been."

Getlof turned away at that. "Oh, Mother, how can you say that. What child is happy with the treatment they receive. Besides, I'm a child no longer."

"Well, bless you for thinking that. You are definitely not a child, no indeed and I never doubted it. You are an adult now and now I think there are some things you should be told."

Getlof looked up quickly and saw Mother Riza was struggling with embarrassment. She shook her head. "I think you should wait and give Geto a chance."

"Geto!" she said with contempt, but didn't expound because at that moment Elp came flying into the house pursued by one of the Riza boys. Mother Riza threw her hands into the air. "All right, Getlof, but if he doesn't, come and see me tomorrow and we'll have our talk then."

With twilight the time for the party finally arrived. It was an occasion such as few could remember; even Geto, who for once in his life, followed the majority and surrendered to the good feelings that prevailed. He drank swill and became merry, not moody. He gathered a circle of children about him and regaled them with ghost stories and tales of the old days--high novelty for most of them who hadn't dreamt he was capable of serving up such good entertainment. Geto's good mood last as long as there were people, but the people finally had to go. The new day was already well along and it was no holiday. Getlof and Geto together said goodnight to the departing and even that became ritualized. The people of Dell walked in a procession past the new adult, like an old form long forgotten. Mother Riza was one of the last. She was drunk. She hugged and kissed Getlof. Then she turned to Geto, one arm still around Getlof.

"See, this has been party such as I can't remember. Geto, isn't she a fine adult?" Another kiss. "Yes, my dear, come to me tomorrow, but not too early, and I'll tell you what you should know. This niggard will never do it." Then she grabbed Geto and kissed him as well.

"What did she mean?" Geto tried to ask, but more people were coming by so the question had to wait.

Finally they were alone, standing before their house, facing the grove which was always empty, but seemed strange now for being that way. Geto asked again: "What did Lady Riza mean?"

Getlof was surprised he remembered. She took his arm and led him toward the house. "She wanted to tell me. . ." Then she stopped, surprised again, this time by the expression on his face. If she didn't know him so well, she would have thought he was going to cry. The house was only a few steps away. Quiet and still. A gentle night wind and a soft chill. In the distance a heavy beating of wings: a large owl emerged from the grove, gliding.

"I know what she was going to say."

Getlof looked at him without answering. Geto's stoop was so bad they were the same height. He whispered:

"I've done everything wrong, but I can do this right. I'm afraid not to."

"Then tell me," Getlof said.

Geto nodded unhappily and began. "I've sold everything and there's nothing of yours left. I'm sorry because this day they were to be yours." The words came faster, ancient inhibitions falling away like the gathering momentum of a landslide. "I almost kept the ring. I was going to, but I couldn't even do that." Still Getlof didn't speak. This was more, much more than she expected, and yet, something in her had been waiting for this very thing.

"They left you with me when you were just a baby, hardly weaned, with tokens for when the time came. And they left me with money so you wouldn't have to be brought up in want. There was a lady--maybe she was your mother--I remember she was very tender on that point. A casket they gave me too, with writing on a tablet inside and a ring. They were yours. My only obligation, save raising you, was to hand them over to you when you came of age. That's all." He looked at her almost slyly, as if she was about to give him something he wanted very much. Getlof saw this and felt badly for him.

"Come inside; I'm not mad at you," she said, discovering she could no longer call him grandfather. "Tell me of these people. Who were they? Why was I given to you?"

"I used to wonder, but now I don't think there was a reason." He stumbled going over the low step into their house. "They were Pau, old ones from the far north. Haven't you ever looked at your reflection? I never said nothing, but you must know you're different." He looked down and his voice dropped.

"I didn't want a child, but they came at dusk. I lived by myself. Mylof was my wife, and we had a house further up toward the north rim, but she had died the year before. I was alone and they came at dusk, maybe a dozen of them. Fine lords and ladies. Rich folk. I've never seen finer. They came from the north. The north. They said take our child, hold her for us. I said thank you, no. There're better folk for that below. But they said I was the one and they gave me gold and I saw they were right. I was the one. And they gave me a casket and a ring. I kept them many years, but the gold couldn't last forever. I remember the lady and how she didn't want you brought up in want. She was very tender on that point. I sold the casket in Yebol to Razedaze when I was getting poor and couldn't provide for you. I didn't think it would matter." He stopped and put cradled his head on the table. Getlof stood watching until she saw he was asleep.

Her decision had been made that morning beside the spring of Asha. Geto's story affirmed it. Dell was not her home and its people were not her people. She looked at Geto again. Anger was impossible. His task had been hard, and knowing him as well as she did, she knew he had performed it better than might have been expected. She shook her head and began at once with her preparations. She took half the gold Istels and left one in the stables of their nearer neighbors, taking their mare in return. She cropped her hair with a knife, knowing it was not safe for a girl to travel alone. She took a short bow and a long knife and a pack stuffed full of the left over food.

Ossa

Dawn was near when she began the ascent of the north rim. The mare was excited by the prospect of exercise that didn't involve a plow. People were beginning to stir, but no one marked her departure. She was sorry she couldn't say goodbye to Elp, but he would have wanted to come. Mother Riza also deserved a word, but she was older and smart besides. She would figure it out for herself.

10

A MATTER OF TIMING

Talo's return to Dell was no repeat of his earlier journey; the pace was sharply accelerated, the season was swinging into its full heat and the company was not as good. Talo had hoped Muk would be more forthcoming away from Moaz, but the opposite proved to be the case. Muk practiced economy in all things: speech, action, gesture and expression. On his face a scowl was as foreign as a smile.

Being naturally gregarious, the lack of fellowship disappointed Talo, but in time he adjusted to Muk's company; it was much the same as being alone. Muk only came forward with an opinion when questions of speed arose. Talo had always preferred a bucking deck in the wildest of weather to the spine of a horse. All the practice in horsemanship he had gained since making port in Yebol--three months and half a lifetime past--had served only to reincarnate, in fire, muscles Talo had gleefully eulogized years before. Talo bore with Muk's driving not because it conformed to their commission, but because he considered it beneath his dignity to argue. Knowing their progress was only half as fast as Muk wished also helped.

They reached Rivercamp on the afternoon of the second day. The captain of the frontier warders recognized Talo.

"Found a new friend and leaving already," he said. "Well, another two days east you should find a new camp of Xumi. Word is the whole tribe's on the move."

On the far bank of the Ossa they struck south and slightly east, angling away from the river. It was a land of few inhabitants, but those they saw repeated the rumors of Xumi. Talo didn't doubt the veracity of these tales, but they gained the heights of the Xaxi without seeing a single nomad.

On the Xaxi's southern slopes it was already high summer. The sea of bright wildflowers Talo remembered from his journey up had been baked into extinction. The streams were dry and the distances between potable water were great. Muk suffered far worse than Talo; what sailor doesn't know thirst. Once he even complained and that was music to Talo's ears.

However, the day that found them on the rims north of Dell came quickly enough. The sight of greenery and open water was enough to mellow even Muk. It was late morning on just the other side of the midyear equinox.

They zigzagged down the steep trail marking their approach with pillars of dust. The valley floor was quiet and still. Talo rightfully thought this strange. He considered that something untoward might have occurred and the new muscles in his stomach contracted.

"I don't know what, but something's wrong. Be thinking of caution."

Muk must have felt it too because he said: "There is smoke yonder."

They turned toward the smoke, following the trail into a grove. As they were about to emerge, an old man suddenly stepped into their path, startling Muk's horse. He was burly with sun-blackened skin and a gray, squared beard. He waited for Muk to control his mount and said:

"Greetings, outlanders. I am Riza, the headman. I ask your business here in our valley." He spoke an outmoded form of Southcoast, using archaic pronouns. Talo smiled and leaned forward in his saddle.

"Greetings, headman. We have come from the north having business of some urgency with Geto of Dell." Talo observed some of the tightness ease from Riza's body at this information, and felt encouraged to indulge his own curiosity.

"Pardon if I inquire into business which isn't my own, but you have the aspect of a man who expects enemies. Surely this isn't usual?"

Riza looked at Talo shrewdly; then he coughed and waved his arms over his head. Suddenly there were people everywhere. A few men with bows dropped down from the trees behind them, but most appeared in the field behind Riza. Muk seemed startled, but Talo had already noted the nervous rustlings in the trees. Riza said:

"Forgive me if we appear rude. No, this is not usual for us. If your business with Geto permits, I should like to make amends with my hospitality and with an explanation for this reception."

"I would be honored," Talo said. "Certainty Master Geto will be here in an hour's time and we are hot and thirsty from our ride." Talo ignored Muk's sharp glance. He didn't get a chance to complain until they were alone at Riza's house, stripped to the waist and sluicing the dust from their bodies at his trough.

"I like this not at all. By now we could've had the child and been on our return road."

Talo rubbed water on his forearms and didn't answer.

"Even a days delay makes a difference." The urgency in Muk's voice was beyond the usual. There was a quality to it as if the world was to end tomorrow. Talo, careful to keep his thoughts off his face, grabbed a cloth and dried his body.

"Our instructions are to keep the child innocent. That takes time and patience. Kidnapping will be our last resort." Then he went inside, cutting short Muk's reply.

They were seated on stools and given a dark, beer like beverage to drink. Riza sipped his drink.

"In the time of the great drought, three years ago it was, many people here were forced to borrow money from the house of Razedaze in Yebol. . ."

"The pawnbroker," Talo interrupted, "yes, I know him."

Riza looked up with fresh suspicion; then, seeming to think better of his thoughts, he smiled and continued.

"Then you will understand. We are not rich here, but we are honest. We have been paying, but not at the rate he thinks fit. Periodically he sends collectors to take what he says is interest due him. This is very hard on my people. The collector before last had an accident here and died of it. Then the last one was discovered grossly transgressing against our custom. He was driven out for that reason. Then, three months past three hired men came. Rough, unpleasant men. They murdered Slipdec. Naturally we had to protect our own. Now we learn from a friend in Yebol, that Razedaze has appealed to the Islands. A force of soldiers has gathered in Yebol. Not only do they want interest, but they say we owe taxes for nine years. I don't know how this will end."

Talo nodded. He wondered if the 'rough, unpleasant men' had formally been of his crew. Then he looked up and said: "You have scouts in the hills, I presume?"

"No, we will be warned when they descend the rims."

Talo looked at him incredulously. "Perhaps I failed to understand you. Are you prepared to pay Razedaze and the taxes as well?"

"I would like it, but we can't. It would destroy us."

"So I gathered. If you don't intend to pay, then you'll need more warning than the sight of them on the rims above your homes. Send scouts out now on your fastest horses. Are there many men skilled with the bow?"

"Ah, most people here are acquainted with its use."

"I said skilled. We'll need only ten men or so; any more would be too hard to hide." Talo was beginning to plan, talking more to himself than to Riza. "I wouldn't send more than a troop to deal with a place like this. Say twenty to thirty riders, with transport, if they intend to return with taxes. We'll ambush them, of course. With luck, one volley and it will be over. No one will fight if they don't think they have a chance."

"A moment," Riza said, holding up his hand and shaking his head. "Are you suggesting we should fight soldiers?"

"Of course. Soldiers exist to be fought. Why did you put armed men into the trees when we rode in?"

Riza began to examine his seamed and callused hands. "That was different. There were only two of you. When the Islanders come, we shall take to the hills and hope they don't block the springs."

Talo stood and looked down at Riza. "Are you telling me you're going to wait until you see mounted troopers descending from the hills and then try to run for . . . the hills? Does that seem very wise to you, headman?"

He shook his head. "When you say it like that, no, it doesn't. But I am inexperienced at this sort of thing; it's hard to know what to do."

"Then listen to me. I have much experience and I know exactly what to do. Send out the scouts now. Then assemble all the men who are willing and able to fight. I still have my business with Geto to discharge, but after that you can take me around the valley and we will look at the possible ambush sites."

Riza stood. "Good sir, I thank you for your interest and I shall do as you say, but tell me one thing. Why? You know we cannot pay."

Talo grinned. "Headman, I'm no bystander. Besides, I have both a particular interest in seeing no one comes to harm here and a debt I would gladly repay. Now, let's not waste time."

Talo walked from the headman's house with Muk stalking beside him. Turning over the best ways to deal with a troop of Istel light horse, Talo had quite forgotten Muk, until his thoughts were interrupted with:

"What did you mean, promising to that old man things we can't deliver?"

"What's that," Talo asked absently.

"I mean this," Muk said in a voice that actually carried some emotion, "we are here for a purpose and all depends on speed. It's no good if we return with the child and are too late."

Talo stopped and faced Muk, his eyes focused and hard: "Too late for what?"

Muk looked down and didn't reply. Talo noted that he was trembling and trying hard not to let it show. "Who gave you your instructions, Muk? Caos gave me mine. And yes, he was interested in speed, but he was interested in other things more. How will innocence be maintained if we resort to kidnapping? It takes time and trust. And now we have a wonderful opportunity to gain all the trust we'll need. By the way, Muk, what is your best weapon?"

"I am a palace slave, not a fighting man."

"Come, certainty a man of your accomplishments must be skilled in one of the killing arts."

"I say again, never have I held a weapon."

"Pity, well, here we are, Geto's house."

The house looked abandoned, but Geto was inside sleeping, his head cradled in his arms. The place reeked of swill. Muk wrinkled his nose and stood by the door while Talo shook Geto awake. Finally, he lifted his head and gazed about with veiled eyes.

"Who are you?"

"Talo the Taelin. You know me. I've come to speak with your granddaughter."

Geto barely completed one shake of his head before dropping back into his arms on the table. Talo grabbed and pulled him up again.

"Your granddaughter, Getlof."

Geto wiped his nose. "She found out two days past, at the party. She's gone."

Muk interrupted. "What of the Pau?"

"That's her, Muk; I've been asking."

"You never said the Pau was female."

Talo shrugged his shoulders. Muk crossed from the door to the table in one long step. He came face to face with Talo and locked gazes. Talo didn't look away. He saw in Muk's eyes a fire and an emptiness which frightened him. Muk turned to Geto, lifting him off his seat with one arm and shook him.

"Where is she?"

Geto gurgled.

"Drop him. He'll never answer if you choke him to death."

Muk stood back, breathing deeply and trembling again. Talo crossed his arms and gazed at him for a moment. He was watching a brand new Muk and liking him even less than the old Muk. He said: "Wait outside. I'll ask again."

Muk shook his head. "I'll stay and listen."

"You don't trust me. I would hate if our trip proved to be a waste here at the end because of your idiot behavior. He's frightened and I'll get no sense from him until you're gone. Wait outside."

Muk hesitated a moment more, but he went.

Talo knew the medicine for Geto. He set a silver Istel on the table and asked again what had happened. Two more doses got all there was to be had. The same story as told to Getlof; basically the same story told Talo the day he had acquired the ring. It made more sense this time, but as regards Getlof, it only told him that she was in the same state he had been just prior to setting off for Moaz -- less his experience, resources and talents.

Geto had dropped immediately back to sleep. Talo stood for a moment looking down at him and then he passed his eyes quickly around the house: crude, dirty and depressing. He tried to put himself in the place of a sixteen year old girl raised in this environment and given the garbled information Geto had available. What would he do. She had run away. That indicated guts. But where? He'd go north, certainty, but had she?

Talo emerged from the dark house, shading his eyes. Muk was waiting. "Well? I heard him speaking. Where are we off to?"

In that moment Talo finally realized Muk was much more than the companion he was supposed to be and the informer Talo had assumed he was. He realized, in fact, the time had come to get rid of Muk altogether.

"Did you hear me? Where off?"

Talo paused before he answered. Muk did indeed have a very authoritarian manner for a palace slave. He said: "She has gone south. To Yebol on the coast where, apparently, she has relations."

"That is certain?"

"As certain as anything."

"Then we must hurry. She has a two day start on us."

"If by that you mean we should leave immediately, I must remind you, I have pledged my aid here."

63

"Unpledge it."

At that moment a boy came running up. "Master," he cried, breathless and excited, "they have been sighted."

"Already?" Talo said.

"Now we must hurry," Muk said.

Talo shook his head, secretly smiling. "Go then, Muk. I won't stop you. This business won't take long one way or the other. If we are successful I will ride as soon as I can and meet with you in Yebol."

Muk agreed to this at once, secretly smiling.

Talo found Riza in the center of a milling group of men. "What news?" he shouted as he dismounted.

"You were right. The men I sent out sighted the dust of many riders directly as they reached the rim tops. We have two hours, maybe."

Talo and Riza went to the south rim. The trail passed through a thick grove not far from its base. A canal bordered the grove on its northern side and a wooden bridge crossed the canal to the field on the other side. There they decided to stage the ambush. Riza wanted to send the women and children up to the springs, but Talo dissuaded him.

"They won't be safe no matter where you send them. It's important to present an air of normalcy. Put some women in the field. We want them to be confident."

Talo collected about twenty men and a few women who struck him as particularly truculent and armed them with spears. These were to serve as pikes. Talo put Riza in charge of that group and hid them in the field beyond the bridge.

"Your part is the most important. When the lead rider is on the bridge, stand and block his way with your spears. This will cause them to bunch up. The important thing is not to panic. A man will commit suicide, but a horse won't. If you keep your sticks up and don't break, the horses will stay back long enough for our purposes."

Ten men more were placed in the trees. Talo gave them strict orders to let the riders pass without giving themselves away, and only to beginning firing when they were bunched at the bridge.

"Your part is the most important," he told them. "One dropped arrow or one sneeze before its time and all is lost. And when you do begin to fire, make every arrow tell. The more that fall in the first volley the easier this will be."

Talo himself took command of the third force. He found eight men who claimed acquaintance with the short sword and mounted them on an assortment of horses gleamed from throughout the valley. Positioned up-stream from the bridge, he told them:

"Our part is the most important. We charge their flank when the confusion is at its height and the rout will be complete."

As a final precaution, Talo taught his eight cavalrymen the Levite war cry.

"Scream it at the top of your lungs when your charge. Believe me, it will make them pause."

The preparations were barely completed (certainly not to Talo's satisfaction) when the Istelian light lancers crested the rim. The Dellites were confident and in high spirits. Talo waited with his heart in his mouth, fearing some untimely noise would give them away. If he had been able to put them through several practice runs, then he would have been confident. As it was, he could only wait.

When the Islanders were halfway down, Talo moved to a position where he could observe them. He counted twenty-six riders in single file. He had been in agony, fearing there would be more. As they neared, he saw they were indeed Istel light lancers, second-line troops that specialized in operations like gathering back taxes. It was likely the younger ones had never seen real combat.

The troopers entered the grove. There was a moment of suspense as everyone waited for the shout that would mean they'd been discovered. Then, the lead rider was through the trees, reins jingling. He continued onto the bridge. The women in the field beyond looked up. Suddenly, a line of pikes emerged from the ground, barring passage. The lead rider reined in. The whole troop was now out of the grove. Just as Talo hoped, they began to bunch up.

One rider, an officer judging from the gold trim on his livery, rode onto the bridge and shouted:

"What nonsense is this? We're government troops Drop your weapons . . ."

Then he slumped forward with an arrow in his back. Talo exhaled. There were shouts and screams. Several men were down. Talo waited. His riders were fidgeting, very ready, but it was not yet the moment. A group tried to charge the bridge, but Riza held the pikes firm. Horses reared and one fell off the bridge. Arrows were coming from both directions. Then Talo saw they were going to break toward him. He screamed the Levite cry (never imagining those words would come from his lips) and spurred his horse. There were other cries and, Talo thought, at least some were following. Then he was among the Islanders, hacking at a lance aimed for his chest. Talo's business was war, but he was no warrior. From behind, he had the peripheral impression of a horse rearing, its rider about to throw his lance as if it were a spear. Then the horse stumbled and the toss went awry. A pikeman stood behind. Talo looked around for fresh enemies, but there were none. It was over. A dozen troopers remained. They were holding their hands high, calling for mercy, faces mirroring looks of dumb astonishment. The Dellites were cheering.

Talo left Riza to deal with the problem of the prisoners. After congratulating him and saying that if hadn't been a village headman, he would have made an excellent under-officer of infantry, Talo asked for and received two extra horses.

Within an hour he was wearily climbing the North rim in pursuit of Getlof.

11

A CHANCE ENCOUNTER?

The horizon shimmered; the sun hung relentlessly close in the heavy sky. Getlof had little notion of distance; her longest journey had been to Yebol, but already she knew she had come farther than that and was still nowhere. But this didn't discourage. She knew she was different, but there were others like her in the north, far away. She intended to find them. Distance didn't matter; she couldn't conceive it anyway. Time was cheap; she had nothing else to do with her life.

Getlof had chopped her fine, black hair as close to her skull as she could manage with her knife. She was flat chested and slim; her features were attractive, beautiful to some eyes, but it was the beauty of youth and unspecified gender. She thought she looked like a boy and was pleased with her disguise. She was eager for an opportunity to test it.

Getlof didn't know when such an opportunity would come. The land north of Dell was arid and mostly uninhabited. She had heard that shepherds sometimes appeared from the north, but the pasturage was poor and even a small herd of sheep would have to range far to live. What surprised her were the birds. In the air, starlings, crows, vultures and even gulls. On the ground, grouse, quail and brush-runners. They sang to her and kept her company, recalling Asha whose appearance she associated with bird song. It was lonely, but with such company she bore it, riding slowly, sitting out the heat of the day, the sun rising on her left and setting to her right.

After five days of plodding progress, Getlof's confidence was evaporating. She felt worn and anxious to arrive somewhere. Her mare (she had named it Sweetheart) was especially unhappy. It was a plow animal, unaccustomed to continued exertion. Sometimes it would just stop and refuse to move. Other times it played lame. By the second day, Getlof was on to its tricks. After five days, she had become an expert at coaxing every possible effort from her reluctant companion.

Late in the afternoon of her fifth day out from Dell, Getlof arrived at the foot of the high ridge she had seen since that morning. Like all the ridges she had crossed, this one was rocky and steep, deeply indented by dried gullies and sparsely covered with shrub and cactus. It ran east west and the sun was already behind its crest. Getlof shivered in the shade and decided to ascend before stopping for the night. Her food was getting low and her water even lower. Sweetheart protested vigorously. Getlof dismounted and led it by its reins, saying: "Come along, maybe there'll be water on the other side."

Even out of the sun, the climb was hot and sweaty but not as bad as Getlof expected. It was still light when she reached the top and saw that the land, finally, was beginning to change. Below her, to the north, there were swatches of green and beyond that, far, far away, an uncertainty in the haze--a lightness that was, perhaps, the sea. Then a thrush, an afternoon singer, broke into song. Getlof felt like doing the same. She remounted and jingled the reins.

"A final effort, Sweetheart, and I'll let you have the rest of the water in the bag."

The light was failing fast, but Getlof could still see she had entered a land of small steads. After awhile, she even found herself following the suggestion of a trail. Columns of smoke rose below her from evening fires and she considered making for the nearest one. She knew in Dell a stranger would be received, but she reminded herself she was not in Dell. She camped the night in the empty elevations above the farmsteads.

The next day Getlof was in the saddle at first light. She had slept without dreaming and was ready for anything. The haze of the afternoon before had cleared and the view was expansive. She could definitely see the ocean; there were orchards along the shore and numerous dwellings between. It amazed her that one side of the ridge could be so dry and the other so fertile; that after so many days of the same, the change could be so abrupt and absolute.

Getlof had heard of Saroka city -- it was her first destination, but strain her eyes as she might, she couldn't see it. This puzzled her slightly. She decided she would have to ask the way.

The opportunity to do so came quickly. Getlof followed the trail down along a dried stream between two shoulders of the ridge. The sea dropped from sight. She turned a corner and there was a small house. In the dirt out front lay a dog. Catching sight of Sweetheart, it sprang up, barking, but wisely keeping its distance. A man came out. He was smoking a pipe from which rose the unmistakable scent of weed. He returned Getlof's greeting with a nod, emitting a quick series of puffs. The dog left off barking and padded over to stand beside its master. Getlof had a sudden fear, wondering if the whole world was full of Getos.

"Good sir, can you tell me in which direction I ride to come to Saroka town?"

The man laughed. Removing the pipe he said: "There's a question. Its plain, my lad, you're an outlander, although what you're doing coming from up there," he pointed, "I don't know."

Getlof smiled. It seemed the nicest way to avoid answering the question that the man had paused to hear. Finally, he continued.

"Saroka town, we call it The City, is north and a little east. Just follow the coast north; its maybe a five-hour ride to one well mounted like you. Plenty of time to come inside and tell me your tale and still make the gates before they close for the night."

For a moment, Getlof was tempted; he did seem friendly enough, but finally she refused on the strength of her first impression. He shrugged his shoulders, but did get her to accept a ladle of water for herself and a bucket for Sweetheart before she continued.

An hour down the road (for such it had become) Getlof encountered a long, two-storied building--larger than any in Dell, although Yebol had some to rival it. Several horses were tied in front. Sweetheart, thirsty again, smelling water broke into a voluntary gait. Above the door hung a board painted with the likeness of a swan. Getlof supposed it was a public house and again experienced the desire for company. Again, she suppressed the impulse. People looked at her curiously as Sweetheart drank from the trough. Their greetings were friendly, through their accents were strange. When Sweetheart was finished, she took the branch that angled north and continued on her way before she could change her mind.

It was late afternoon when she topped another in the undulating series of humpback ridges that fell from the high divide to the sea and saw Saroka.

The sight was unexpected and impressive. Tall walls studded with towers, massive gates, spires and beyond, more towers raising even higher than the wall. Getlof sat on Sweetheart and stared. Her imagination had not prepared her for such a sight. She dismounted and stared some more.

Talo made it from Dell to Saroka faster than if Muk had been along to hurry him--only three days after the ambush of the Islanders and a day ahead of Getlof. He first went to the gates and questioned the guards, but they could tell him nothing. He had trouble believing he was ahead of Getlof, but spent the rest of the day riding back and forth along the Saroka road. By late afternoon he found himself uncertain and discouraged. A thousand things could have happened to her. He finally stopped along the road, on a ridge with a vantage of the main gate, to rest beneath a tree before entering the city for the night. And there he was when Getlof rode up and dismounted. She couldn't see Talo, but he saw her, and disguised or no, there was no mistaking Getlof.

To a man seriously doubting his luck, it was so sweet he felt for a moment dizzy. Indeed, a tingling, rushing sensation passed from his forehead to his feet. Talo took a breath and another, shook his head and then crept up behind her:

"Big, isn't it, especially at first sight."

Getlof jumped at the sound of his voice and before he had completed the sentence, she had Sweetheart between them. Talo grinned, overwhelming her with his good feelings and tried again:

"Sorry, didn't intend to startle you. . ."

Getlof saw a short, somewhat shout man with a bald patch on the crown of his head. He looked familiar, not dangerous. Almost without thought, she decided he would be the first acquaintance in her new life.

"That's all right," trying to make her voice deeper than it really was. He did look like someone she should know. "Why do you think I've never seen the City before?"

Talo laughed. "The City. This is very good. And so is the disguise."

Then she remembered.

"You came to Dell. Several months back you came to see Geto and took something away from him."

Talo nodded. "I did. And I left something as well."

"Gold. I know. But what you took belonged to me. It was a ring, wasn't it."

The ring was hanging in a pouch around Talo's neck. He felt it suddenly a point of fire. Then he thought, `why not? Why have I kept it so long if not for this?' He pulled the pouch from around his neck and emptied the ring into his hand.

"Here. Consider me just another guardian. The ring now goes to you, several days late, perhaps, but who's to say when you really were born anyway."

Getlof fought back her surprise. She slowly reached out her hand, even more slowly opened her palm and took the ring. It was cool. She slipped it on. It fit perfectly. For a moment she was lost in its beauty for she had never possessed such a thing in her life. Then she remembered Talo and looked up to see him as if for the first time. He was watching her with a smile. She felt a warm wind brushing against her face and was suddenly aware of a buzzing, a mixture of many noises, floating faintly from off the city. She inhaled and then exhaled, feeling her breath like an ocean tide. Talo was still smiling. No time had passed at all. She remembered his name, then, and wondered who he was, and why she felt such a great inclination to trust him. She took the ring off.

"Here, take the pouch. Keep it in that and wear it around your neck. Safer that way."

"Thank you, Talo."

Talo blurted: "You remember my name!" and then momentarily scolded himself; she had done a better job keeping her surprise than he just had.

"You told it to me once. But why are you here. Why did you take the ring. Were you looking for me?"

Talo rubbed his cheek and thought, `here comes the hard part.' He began with the easier questions first.

"I'm here because I was looking for you. In fact, I was in Dell only three days ago looking for you and learned you had left. Didn't know where, but this seemed the logical place to start looking. . . ."

He proceeded to tell her about Riza and the Islanders and the ambush and his talk with Geto, but said nothing about Moaz or Muk. Getlof heard his story with amazement, and thought about Asha and the disharmony she had predicted. He had diverted it, not her, but it had been because of her. This decided her mind about Talo -- as Talo hoped it would, but not for the reason he supposed.

Getlof was silent when Talo finally finished. She looked up and noticed the sun was setting. The man back on the ridge had said it was a five-hour ride, but Getlof had taken more like nine. She said:

"They close the gates at night. If we want to enter the city, don't you think we'd better get started?"

Talo gave her a calculating look and when to fetch his horses. Later, when they were halfway down the ridge to the city he said:

"Getlof, you seem to have accepted my company. You realize, I'm sure, that I never really told you why I was waiting for you or why I took the ring."

Getlof looked over and smiled faintly. "I presumed you wanted to give it to me yourself because you want to come north with me. I'm not sure why, but you seem to know a lot about my . . . my situation. I wasn't sure at first, but the idea of a companion is nice--I think I'll have a hard time doing it all on my own."

"Especially mounted as you are," Talo laughed. "We'll have to do something about that first thing." Talo was vastly pleased. Everything had gone far better than he had allowed himself to hope. And he was pleased with Getlof. Intelligence always attracted him. It was hard to picture how things would finally work out, but for the moment, everything was perfect.

They made the gate just before complete dark and plunged into the city of Saroka. It lay within the dominions of the Emperor of the Gildi--the greatest city on the eastern shore of the Innersea. Indeed, with the wasting of Sidoc, it was the first city in the eastern third of Ossa between the Brown Ossa and the Tarhad. It was a city larger by far than Getlof had ever imagined could exist. She was amazed at the way the streets were paved with stone and at the height of the building; riding between them was like being in a canyon. And there were people everywhere, strange and familiar, crowding and pushing, in bright clothes and rags and in some cases, almost nothing. Sweetheart didn't care for the commotion at all and she wasn't shy about letting Getlof know it.

"Careful," Talo said. "If we get separated I'll be a long time finding you again."

Getlof nodded and held her reins all the tighter, thanking the chance that had saved her from facing all this alone. She had never imagined.

Talo knew a good inn close by the waterfront. The moon had risen by the time they maneuvered and pushed their way through to the docks. Getlof could see the spiring masts of the ships dimly in the dark. Then Talo turned suddenly into a courtyard. A boy came running up and grabbed the bridles of their horses.

Talo flipped him a copper. "Two rooms. Stable the horses. We'll eat in the commons."

Getlof amazed Talo by the quantity of food she put away. He thought sadly that if he ate like she did, he would soon be too huge to mount a horse. Afterwards, they discussed the route. Talo told her that from Saroka the only practical way north was over the Innersea. The economics of it were such that it would be better to sell their mounts in Saroka and buy new ones in Gildesh where horseflesh was cheaper. He expected some objection to this plan, already respecting Getlof's independence of mind and assuming young girls always became attached to whatever horse they were on. Getlof surprised him for a third time by agreeing.

That night, for the first time in her life, Getlof slept in a bed raised off the ground.

The next day they purchased a new outfit for Getlof. Talo thought her male disguise a good idea, but the effect was entirely too rustic and too slapdash.

"People in the Imperial lands scorn anyone not richer--at least in appearance--than themselves." Accordingly, Getlof was fitted in a soft woolen cloak of green, leather breeches and an embroidered linen shirt. The quality was high and so were the prices, but Talo paid for everything. "Save your money. If I need it, I won't be shy about using it, but for now, I'm well stocked with the stuff."

Getlof was pleased with her new attire; it was finer than any she would ever have selected, but the sense of wearing it was plain. Less plain, at first, was the trip they took to the street of armorers. He picked out for her an inscribed short sword in a scabbard decorated with semi-precious stones and insisted she wear it.

"But what am I supposed to do with it? I'll never use it."

"I hope not. I intent to keep us well away from swordplay. You have to wear it because you are now a young and noble gentleman and believe me, such people don't set foot outside without the proper accessories, of which this is foremost.

Getlof gave in at that. The scabbard was very handsome and after she got used to having it rub against her thigh, she came to think it was not such a bad thing after all.

From the street of armorers, they went to the street of barbers. By the day's end, Getlof was, to all appearances, a different person. Talo was quite pleased with his handiwork.

"I dare say if we took you back to old Geto, he'd be bowing and scraping and asking the young lord's wishes, never guessing who the young lord is. I mean, you even move right."

They were back at the inn. Getlof was turning and studying her new appearance in the polished surface of a piece of steel.

"I like it," she finally said. "I look good."

"You do indeed. And what's more, you look like you should."

Getlof nodded and gave a little hop. Talo smiled. An echo of her excitement was affecting him. He tried to warn himself; he couldn't afford to grow fond of her, but the warning somehow didn't grab. Talo coughed, mostly to hide the beating of his heart from himself.

"There is one thing I should warn you about."

"Oh?" Getlof said turning, "what's that?"

"The ring. Don't show it around, especially as we go north. Not everyone will react in a favorable way."

Getlof looked at Talo shrewdly and for a moment he was certain she was going to ask why. But she finally smiled and nodded and went back to the study of her reflection.

They sailed the next day.

12

A SMALL DECEPTION UNCOVERED

Muk had things to do; he couldn't expose himself to danger. He reached the rim top comfortably before the Istelian troopers; watched them descend, then circled round to their trail. Muk followed it, not pausing even to see what came of Talo's defense of the valley. He didn't care.

Without Talo to slow him down Muk rode swiftly, reaching Yebol by twilight. That night and the next day he searched for Getlof. Yebol wasn't a large town and Muk was prepared to go to every house if he had to. However, his demeanor and errand were so unusual, that by the middle of the day he had a pack of children following him calling: "Getlof of Dell, Oh Getlof, come out, come out wherever you are." Muk tried to drive them away, but that just attracted more attention. By the end of the day, the accumulated weight of all the refusals, blank stares and shrugged shoulders convinced him no one in Yebol even knew who she was.

Muk left Yebol riding slowly north, considering the meaning of this. It was possible Talo had been wrong, but it seemed more likely the girl Pau had met the Istelian troopers on their way in. If so, they had probably done his work for him. However, things were still too ambiguous. He needed proof that would satisfy Gavin. Gavin was not an easy man to satisfy.

Muk was cautious about entering Dell the second time. He scouted from the rims, expecting to see a scene of waste and destruction, but all appeared normal. He could even see tiny figures working the fields. As he descended, nothing dispelled the appearance of normalcy; he concluded (almost against his will) that it was real.

Muk rode along the stream path beside the fields. People stood to watch as he passed. Then, to his surprise, someone waved and greeted him by name. To Muk, ever the stranger, recognition seemed an affront. He returned the salute awkwardly and hurried on his way. When he came to the house which, as he remembered, belonged to the Headman, Riza, he stopped and dismounted. An old, fat lady came out. She smiled and said:

"I remember you: Muk, companion of Talo. Greetings, I am Doolan, the headwoman."

Muk nodded curtly. "Greetings. I seek Talo. Is he here?"

Something in his tone erased her smile. She crossed her arms and appeared to look at him anew. "Someone must have missed a message if you're looking for Talo and think to find him here. He rode out the same day as the battle; three days past, that was."

Muk frowned and wondered why he had not seen him. "To Yebol, you mean?"

She shook her head. "Talo rode north; in a hurry, before we could even thank him properly for what he did. A strange man, but a good one."

Muk had grown aware of his bad habit of trembling in times of stress. He was trying to stop it now. "North?"

"North. He was mighty closed about his business, but between you and me, I suspect he was trying to catch up with a runaway of ours. Getlof. Do you know the name?"

Muk managed to nod.

"Yes. She left two days before you gentlemen arrived. Thought she was sneaking out, but Mother Riza knew what was on her mind. I was too late to say goodbye, curse me for being a bed slug, but I did see her up on the rims. Poor Getlof. But if I knew he found her, I wouldn't worry. He's a good man."

Muk couldn't force himself to agree with that.

"Are you well? Come inside and I'll get you something to drink."

Muk turned without answering and sprang on his horse.

"Goodness," Mother Riza called, "its enough to just say no."

Muk turned in his saddle and said: "I must catch him." He felt ashamed afterward that he had made even such a slight concession to courtesy.

When he was away from Dell, on the dry uplands facing north, Muk regretted he had not paused long enough to acquire a fresh horse. He found it easier to fault himself than to think about what had apparently transpired. He had been deceived, roundly deceived, maliciously and with purpose. Talo had deceived him. A flaw in his perceptions had blinded him to the fact that Talo was even capable of such a deed. His experience as a slave in Moaz had taught that a man in Talo's position wouldn't condescend to put one over a man in his position. Moreover, he harbored an unarticulated belief that all secrets belonged to him. It was as if Talo had stole something precious to him: the only real possession that was all his own. As Muk pursued, he told himself he was doing it for Kista and the chance they still had. However, had Kista been with him at that moment, she would have been burned in the fire of his determination and he would never have noticed.

Muk picked up Talo's trail on the north rim and followed it three days from waste to sown, where he finally lost it for good. By then, it didn't matter. Muk was reasonably certain Talo had been headed for Saroka. Three days of travel under sun and moon had taken its toll, especially following the hard riding that had come before. There were moments when he thought of sacrificing all he stood to gain, of turning his horse around and riding to a place he would never hear of Gavin, Caos, Talo or even Kista again. If he had not been extraordinary lucky in Saroka, he might have succumbed to such temptation. He rode through the gate of Saroka a worn man. One of the guards commented on the condition of his horse, which was truly deplorable.

"You've come a ways, friend. If you want to go farther, you'd best see Scarper, purveyor of horses. His prices are the best in the city. Say Lutho of the South Gate sent you."

For some reason, this attempt to earn a commission brought Muk's frustration back to the boil. Not admitting that his horses' condition was his own fault, he was angry, thinking he could never hope to catch Talo mounted as he was. He asked the guard where Scarper was to be found.

Scarper had no prejudice against people who mistreated their horses. They were a major source of trade. He greeted Muk fairly and when he learned Muk wished to acquire a beast less blown, he inspected the old one to determine its value. He checked its teeth and legs; he ran his hands over its flank and stopped and looked at Muk.

"Interesting trappings. If you wish to part with them, I'll throw in a new set and knock down the price for a better horse by a fair margin as well."

It made no difference to Muk how he was saddled. He agreed and Scarper's face lit up, as if he had expected some hard bargaining.

"Well, good. You're a reasonable man. I see the Lake Serpent here on the horn. Highly unusual to see riders from Moaz and I suppose it will become more unusual still what with the way things are going. You might be interested to know that just yesterday I acquired a horse from a gentleman which might have been the brother of this one. Had the same saddle too. Its good luck for me to get a matched set; they'll be worth a lot more once I clean them up. And if there is a war, may all the gods forbid, then they'll be worth even more." Then Scarper looked up and saw Muk's expression. He took a step back.

"Say, is something wrong? Don't think I'm deceiving you. I stated my interest plain. Say, if you're mad, I'll even let you reopen the bargaining."

Muk shook his head. "Describe this man."

"What man? Oh, the one with the other saddle? Well, I don't know--short, heavy set, not much hair. Actually, I bought four horses from him. Two were Island animals, they breed slightly smaller in Istel and one a country nag; a strange mix of horseflesh. He had a young friend also."

A warm rush of blood flooded Muk's head. He steadied himself and asked: "Did he buy replacements?"

"Oh no. I recall him saying they were off to the north. Going to Gildesh and who would buy a horse here and ship it when they're cheaper up there? He must be a friend of yours?"

"You have done me a service. What price will you give me? I will make a present of the saddle."

Scarpers' face became calculating. "Ah, I see. I talked myself out of a sale. Well, well. How much? It had more value in trade. Let's see."

Muk took a step forward and held out a trembling hand. "Enough! Give me the price of it now."

Scarper retreated another step.
"Oh, it's like that." He looked nervously about and then reached into his pocket and came out with three silver Gildis. It was twice what he had intended to pay, but he was suddenly very anxious to see the last of Muk.

Starlight found Muk on the water of the Innersea, in a small craft hired at great cost. Its skipper had a reputation for speed.

13

HARBOR DETOUR

Waterwalker was a tall vessel of the type that plied the Inner and Outer Seas. Getlof thought it very large until they entered the frightening expanse of lonely water stretching beyond the harbor mouth. Then it seemed ridiculously small. Talo laughed at her worries, but the voyage proved worse than anything her imagination had dreaded. Seasickness struck her the minute they hit the swells of the open water and she knew nothing but misery until they reached the roads of Gildesh next day. When the pitching and rolling subsided, Getlof felt it like a freezing man would feel the first patch of sunlight against his back. She gathered herself, cleaning up as best she could and came wanly on deck. Getlof leaned against the deckhouse and tried to focus her eyes. She was amazed to be alive. She looked for Talo and finally saw him on the poop deck aft, inspecting the offing.

"So," turning at her approach and smiling broadly, face glowing from wind and air, "you can walk. That's good; we'll be docking soon."

Getlof grabbed a stay as the Waterwalker stumbled (as it seemed to her) down a swell.

Talo laughed. "Be thankful we had a smooth crossing. Here, come stand beside me. I have a few things to say before we dock.

"See those ships?" He pointed toward a fleet--both galleys and tall ships--riding in the roads some distance away. "That's the Gildi fleet, armed for war. I had a conversation with the master of this vessel. There's interesting news."

Getlof nodded. The breeze was freshening; gulls soared and dipped in the upper currents. The water sparkled and the distant view of Gildesh promised sights more amazing still.

". . . and after he defeated and killed the emperor, he crossed the delta of the Tarhad, not satisfied with the eastlands. . . ."

"What? I'm sorry. Who killed who?"

Talo had been staring at the Gildi fleet. He glanced at Getlof, surprised. "Weren't you listening?"

Getlof shook her head, bringing her gaze inboard, away from the dipping horizon. "I thought I was going to get sick again, but it passed."

"It doesn't matter. We're on the windward side. I was saying that two years ago nomads from east of the Tarhad killed the emperor of Tarhad. A man named Bar-Lev led them. In those days he was just a chieftain, but since then he's brought the tribes east and west of the Tarhad under his sway, and now he's calling himself Grand Overlord of Ossa. He's an amazing man and talented; the way he drew out the Prince of Sidoc proves that and it was just one of his lesser victories. His greatest talent, however, is for destruction. Nomads have their own way of looking at things. Fields and villages take up a lot of good grazing land, you know."

Up and down the Waterwalker proceeded. Getlof clung more tightly to the stay and tried to concentrate.

"How does this affect us?"

"Right now it doesn't. But the master says Bar-Lev's fleet has been raiding south. The Istelians have had to defend NorthPointing. . . "

Getlof glanced over. "NorthPointing. I know that name; its the big island south and east of Yebol!"

"Very good. From you tone I assume you didn't know Yebol was raided even before that. My ship was burned there."

"Your ship? No, I never heard. You had a ship, Talo, and it was burned in Yebol?"

"That's right."

"I was wondering . . . But it makes sense." Then she shuddered. "I can't imagine being a sailor."

"This is your first time. It grows on a person. But I'm not done yet. Have you ever heard of Moaz?"

Getlof shook her head.

"A city north of Gildesh. The captain tells me its ruler, Caos, has been making demonstrations along his border with the Gildi. That affects us most directly, but it's something we'll have to deal with when we get there. The gist of what I want you to know is that Gildesh is a city preparing for war. Such cities are niggardly in extending the hand of hospitality to foreigners. We're touching here only for customs and to pay a transit tax, but, it'll be best to stay out of sight. And if anyone asks, you travel with Boyce of Taelin, not Talo. All right?"

There was a long delay in getting a pilot and by the time Waterwalker had been towed to a berth along the Gildesh waterfront, it was afternoon.

Talo and Getlof remained below, each in their separate cabin while customs men boarded and made an inventory of the cargo. Then they collected the transit tax. Getlof had the money ready (one silver Istel) when they came around to her. The customs man, tall, uniformed and armed, stood in her doorway and stared while she handed the coin over.

"Is that all?" when he didn't go away.

"No, young lord, I must ask some questions. What is your destination?"

"My destination?" caught slightly off guard. "The Riverrun."

He lifted his eyebrows. "The Riverrun?" and appeared to stare at her harder. "The Riverrun. There are problems with that. You had best come with me."

"Where?"

He laughed. "Just on deck. You'll have to speak with my superior."

Something seemed wrong. The ship was going to the Riverrun and that was no secret. Getlof could see no way to decline, then she reasoned that surely Talo would be on deck as well because their destination was the same, so she went with the customs man.

They emerged and in the glaring afternoon light, Getlof shaded her eyes while the customs man called out:

"Lord Sardin. I have found someone who will interest you."

A heavyset, older man, dressed in bright orange leggings and jeweled armor waddled toward them. His face shone, as if just oiled. He made Getlof uneasy and she hoped that whatever the problem, it would be cleared up quickly.

He stopped in front of Getlof and stared at her with little red eyes. She didn't know what needed to be said, so she remained silent. Finally the man called Sardin said:

"What is your name?"

"Getlof."

"Just Getlof? No city, no land, no father, no family? Your appearance is very uncommon. Perhaps your city is so distant we have never heard of it?" Turning to the first man, "was he more communicative with you?"

"Yes, my lord. His destination he gives as the Riverrun."

Sardin smiled. "The Riverrun! Indeed!" He turned back to Getlof. "My young and pretty lord, this is a time of approaching war. Along the Riverrun goes our military highway to the north. Are you a spy? Are you an easterling? A Tarhadian? A Levite? Come, tell me."

Getlof shook her head. "No, lord Sardin, I am none of those things."

"No? But still you decline to state just what you are." He smiled and rubbed his hands. "Suburg, return to your duties. I will remember your alertness in bringing this delectable problem to my attention."

The customs man bowed and thanked Sardin.

"Now, Getlof, you had best gather your belongings. There will be a delay in your journey. I intend to satisfy myself as to just exactly who you are."

"Wait, you are taking me off this ship?"

"So I just said. If you don't want to leave with just what you're wearing, you'd better hurry."

This was too sudden for Getlof. "But, I'm not alone. I must tell my friend."

"You have a friend?" Sardin said, frowning. "What is his name?"

"Boyce of Taelin."

"A Taelin? Another foreigner deserves another look. Suburg, are you still around? Oh, go and fetch this Boyce of Taelin. Perhaps he equals the young gentleman in looks?"

Suburg grinned and shook his head. "No, he's an older man, fat and balding."

Sardin shuddered. "Oh dear, bring him up anyway."

Getlof felt a wave of relief when she saw Talo's bald crown emerge from the hatchway. He was blinking also. Then she heard Sardin gasp. He put his hand on the hilt of his sword and shouted: "Suburg, take that man!" Two other customs men appeared and a file of soldiers from the dock clattered up the plank. It was very fast. Getlof's eyes never left Talo. For the briefest of moments his face showed some reaction, but it was gone before she could read it. He stood passively as armed and unfriendly men ringed about him. Sardin sheathed his sword and sauntered up in a self-satisfied fashion.

"Boyce of Taelin. The Taelin, that's what recalled you to me. Older, aren't we all, but it's master Talo if it's anyone."

"Who are you?" Talo asked in a neutral voice.

"You don't recognized me? I'm disappointed. I'm Sardin. Sardin formerly of the emperor's guard. The Fourteenth, Osprey. Surely you remember Pendaflax. I do. I was your prisoner."

Suddenly Talo smiled, "Of course. You brought a good ransom; I recollect you Sardin, it's just that there's a lot more of you now."

"Yes, it was awhile ago. Time has been cruel to me, but sometimes it does come up with little surprises. Master Talo the Taelin, you are under arrest and your young friend as well, I suppose. I remember you as a man of honor, and that you treated me fair back when our positions were reversed. Do I have your pledge you will respect your spoken bond and make no attempt to escape."

"Well, that is decent of you. Yes, you have my word, Master Sardin."

"All right; you, you and you, come with me. The rest return to your stations. Suburg, have the master of this ship send their things down to the Basilica."

Getlof was forgotten. She could've slipped away and no one would have noticed, except she had nowhere to go. So she trailed along, following in the pathway Talo, Sardin and the three guards, cleared through the Gildi crowds. Gildesh was a city that stood in relation to Saroka as Saroka did to Yebol, but Getlof had no eyes for sightseeing. She was confused. It appeared Talo had been arrested. She was going to be arrested, but she wasn't now. Talo didn't seem worried, but she was. She had thought Talo was a sea captain, but listening to the talk between Talo and Sardin--which was familiar and friendly--she learned that Pendaflax, the contest in which Sardin had been captured, was a land battle, and that Talo had been in command of an army. She had to blend amaze with her worry and renewed speculation about just who Talo was. In the midst of her thoughts and worries she never noted any of the famous sights of the first city of Ossa.

Getlof almost missed it when the conversation turned finally to her.

"I am much taken by your young friend. Tell me, when did you get the taste? I can't recall you were that way before."

Talo shook his head. "It is not that way."

"No?" Sardin turned and subjected Getlof to a distastefully speculative glance. Getlof looked down. Sardin rubbed his hands and said:

"You, master Talo, can say goodbye to all this, but I'll try to see that Getlof has a choice." Talo and Getlof made eye contact then, while Sardin commenced to plan how he would engineer this choice. She perceived now that Talo, behind his buff heartiness, was indeed very worried. He seemed to study her and she saw he was trying to ask a question with his eyes. She nodded slightly, not sure exactly what she was saying yes to.

Talo cleared his throat. "Of course, Sardin, there is one thing you have missed and that surprises me."

Sardin gestured expansively. "Don't be. I was never one to claim infallibility. But whatever it is, must be to your advantage or you'd not bring it up. Therefore, I'm not sure I want to hear."

Talo smiled. "You want to hear, gracious master of the customs, and if there comes a time when I need a favor from you, I want you to remember the favor I am granting you now."

"Oh, if it's like that then speak; speak by all means. The time when you need favors from me has certainly arrived."

"It is this. Getlof, whose appearance pleases you, so is a Pau of noble birth and important station. He travels not with me, I travel with him."

"And that's all? I mean, you think to bribe my favor with that information?" He looked at Getlof again. "Of course, it has been years since I saw any Pau in Gildesh, but now you mention it, I do see where he might be one. Not that it makes any difference to me." Sardin stopped speaking and appeared to be considering something. "Then again, I see your point. Yes, thanks for the warning. I will make sure he is taken to those people who can best verify your claim. And if it is true, then I will consider it a favor done. If not, I will consider it just the opposite. Here we are now. No more time for chitchat."

They had come to a massive mountain of a building that loomed over the square they had just passed like the rims over Dell (such was the comparison that occurred to Getlof). They climbed a long flight of wide steps. Two sentries stood at the top beside the enormous open doors. They saluted Sardin but otherwise showed no signs of life.

"The Basilica of Mowry the Just," Sardin said to Getlof.

The interior of the Basilica was more overwhelming than the outside. It was a high cavern dimly lit by shafts of light coming through windows cut in the walls far above. Twin rows of columns marched the length of the interior. Craning her head back, Getlof could see that near the ceiling, the columns branched like trees, apparently supporting the roof. A gallery ran one third of the way up between the floor and the ceiling. Curtain hung from the galleries, screening the remainder of the ground floor from view. Tight knots of people were scattered the length of the Basilica and from them disputatious voices rose up in a steady buzz. Getlof heard Talo remark that some things never changed.

Sardin turned to his left, passing through an opening in the encircling curtain. They followed, entering the small room on the other side. A wooden counter divided the room in half; two men sat behind it. One was young, diligently at work copying a manuscript; the other was older, diligently at work doing nothing. The curtain was surprisingly effective in deadening the noise from the hall. Both men stood when Sardin entered, saluting him. Sardin returned the salute and then eyed them, as if considering whom to address. He selected the younger one who was quite handsome. By this time they had noticed Getlof and were both gaping at her.

"Golab, I have someone here who might interest you."

The one called Golab nodded. "I see, Lord Sardin."

"Ah, then he is indeed a Pau?"

Golab looked up, surprised and pained. "Indeed, Lord Sardin."

"Golab, I can say nothing right with you, can I. Well, my prisoner claims he is of noble birth and important station. I wish you to verify or disprove this. And show him around as well; there is no harm if you take him up to the second level, but do remain in summons. Understand?"

"Perfectly, Lord Sardin."

"Perfectly, of course. Getlof, I am handing you to Golab and Miram. They advise the emperor on all questions considering the Pau. You have come to save them from uselessness."

"Golab bowed and Miram nodded.

"All right, and now, master Talo, you and I have business with the prefect Tael."

Talo and Getlof exchanged glances once more before Talo was taken away. In his look she read encouragement. Looking at Golab, who was pleasant to look upon, she felt she had improved her situation over Sardin.

When Sardin and Talo were gone, Golab and Miram held a whispered conversation. Getlof could see Miram shaking his head; then Golab shrugged his shoulders and stood. He beckoned to Getlof and led her though a door out the back in the opposite direction Talo went in. They ascended a twisting stone stairway to the second level. Two soldiers fell into step behind them and followed silently.

They entered a small, empty room on the second level and there Golab turned and spoke to Getlof for the first time.

"I regret this is necessary, but I must search you for concealed weapons. Please strip."

At first Getlof thought she had misunderstood because Golab did speak with a strange accent. But as he watched her with his arms crossed, she realized she had heard right. She said:

"That isn't necessary. Here are my weapons," and handed him the jeweled sword and Geto's old knife.

Golab smiled.

"I believe you, but it's still necessary, so, with your cooperation, we can get this done and go on to something more pleasant."

"No," Getlof said, regretting she had so readily handed over her weapons.

"Please, if you won't I must order the guards to do it."

Getlof shook her head and the two soldiers stepped forward. She was desperate, then she felt a pain against her chest; perhaps from the violence of her pounding heart, perhaps from the sudden weight of her ring. "Wait! I have one other thing concealed I would show you!"

Golab frowned, but nodded. The two soldiers stepped back. "You told me you had no other weapons. . ."

"Not a weapon. This!" And she pulled out the pouch from inside her shirt and spilled the ring onto her palm. It was cool and heavy. Golab stepped forward and looked; then, to Getlof's amazement, he fell to one knee and blushed.

"What's the matter? Please stand up."

"My apologies," he muttered, still on the floor. "I understand my orders not as well as I thought. Return your ring to its place. I am not the man to put you through the indignity of a search."

Getlof was beginning to understand that in her ring she possessed a thing of great effect. Golab finally stood and even though she was not sure why, she was happy if it kept her from being exposed as a girl.

For the next several hours Golab guided Getlof through the upper level of the Basilica, showing her the statues and tapestries and beautiful mosaics and chatting idly about life in Gildesh, but never speaking of her or what would come. The two soldiers had been dismissed; his own conduct was so deferential, Getlof found it embarrassing.

A bell had periodically run throughout the time Getlof had been with Golab. It rang again, twice then three times more. Golab said: "That is the summons, follow me."

They walked a surprisingly long time, going to a room so deep in the second level Getlof became quite lost. Unlike the other room she had been shown, this one was richly furnished. She especially thought the thick, green carpet most extraordinary, never having seen a floor covered in such a fashion. A large table occupied the center of the room and behind it sat a small man with gray hairs and eyes dressed in a white robe trimmed with green. Talo and Sardin sat before the table. Two guards stood outside, beside the door.

Golab proceeded Getlof into the room. He saluted and said:

"Prefect, Undersecretary Golab delivering the Pau Josh, known as Getlof."

The man behind the table, the prefect, inclined his head. "Ah, thank you Undersecretary. What did you say?"

Without expression, Golab repeated himself. Getlof was turning the word Josh over in her mind. It seemed no less correct than when Asha had used it.

The prefect lifted an eyebrow and glanced at Sardin.

"Prefect, he bears the Ring of Kinship."

"The Ring of Kinship? I fail to understand."

Golab glanced at Sardin and then back to the prefect. The serious facade of his expression was beginning to leak confusion.

"The ring of Josh."

"The last Josh died many years ago," the Prefect finally said. "Explain this, Undersecretary, for plainly you deliver news."

"The Pau bears the ring of Josh. It proclaims a direct kinship with Josh and if there is no one of that name, it proclaims a claim to that title."

"Indeed," the prefect said slowly. "Indeed." Then he stood and looked at Getlof. Getlof returned his gaze steadily. She said:

"My name is Getlof, Josh. I give you greetings, Prefect." Getlof Josh, she liked the sound of it. It added to her name and seemed right.

The Prefect stared some more, then he returned to his seat.

"Welcome to Gildesh, Getlof Josh. I am Prefect of Justice to His August Majesty, The Manifest One Ducitos XI, Tael at your service. I trust you have not been inconvenienced or bear any complaint against your hospitality."

Getlof shook her head slowly. She was aware of Talo to her side. He seemed nervous and surprised.

"Thank you Perfect. The Undersecretary's hospitality has been of satisfaction."

"Good, you will not be offended if I ask to see this ring?"

Getlof sensed a test in this and was not certain how to pass it. "No, prefect," she said slowly, "I am not offended." She stepped forward, bringing the ring out, but was suddenly reluctant to hand it over. She held it up on its chain. The Prefect, Tael had to lean forward over his desk. He looked at it for a moment and then sat back.

"It looks pretty much like any other ring to me." He glanced at Golab.

"There is no doubt, Perfect." Golab said.

"Ah, yes. Well, then the question is this: how does a son of Josh travel from the south into Gildesh? There will soon be war and your companion, Josh, is of questionable worth."

Getlof stepped back, secreting the ring again. She considered how best to respond; finally, for lack of a better idea, she said what she thought:

"I think, Prefect, my companion's worth is best known to myself."

Tael shifted in his seat. "Indeed? Is it possible, perhaps, we are suffering from a mutual lack of understanding?"

"I can be of assistance, sir," Golab said.

"Yes, that is your function. Please assist my understanding."

Golab proceeded with a short dissertation on the Josh. He told them the legend of the first Josh, about the island of NorthPointing and the pilgrimage; about the fostering among foreigners and the tokens and how the first of these fostered children to return was blessed. He, or she, for a female Josh was not unheard of, was the new Josh and his children succeeded him.

This was all new to Getlof and she listened with growing amazement. She hardly noted when Golab finished, lost in herself. She still didn't know what it meant, but she felt that every instinct she had followed since Asha had named her Josh has been right and this increased her self-confidence tremendously.

"Interesting, but incredible. I never realized." Tael said.

"It is necessary," Golab said. "There is no other way to find out who has the blessing. But do not think it is a common occurrence. The books only record one other instance when a Josh died without issue."

"I see. Well, that explains why the Josh travels from the south, but it still doesn't explain the companion he has selected."

"Prefect, is that an invitation for me to speak?" Talo asked. "Like Golab, you may find I can be of assistance in furthering your understanding of this matter."

"I never doubted it. Please proceed."

"I find your ready acceptance of the Josh surprising. Getlof seems like he could be no one else, but he has been in possession of the Ring of Kinship for only a few days. I never explained its significance (not that I was certain I knew myself) and I am sure that Golab's lecture on the succession was the first he heard of it. . ."

"A moment. If this is a deception, why do you expose it now?"

"No deception. Let me explain in my own time, Prefect. You are aware the Prince of Sidoc hired me to assist in the defenses of his city?"

"Yes, it did not displease us either."

Talo smiled. "I left Sidoc suddenly with but one ship under unhappy circumstances. I remained in the area raiding Levite shipping and would be there still, perhaps, but for the fact that my crew lost its enthusiasm for the work, and maybe I did as well. We sailed south to rest and came to the port of Yebol."

"A moment. That name is not familiar to me."

"Yebol. It is north and slightly west of NorthPointing on the eastern mainland providence of Istel."

"Small wonder then. Proceed."

"In Yebol I discovered an artifact pertaining to the Josh. This came from a village inland named Dell. I went there to learn more and found the Josh, although this was before I knew who the Josh was. When I returned to Yebol, I discovered the Levites had followed me south. They slipped into Yebol during my absence and burned my ship. By that time I had the ring, still not knowing what it was. It drew my curiosity and I traveled though lower Ossa seeking to learn. One conversation with Golab would have saved me much time, but I managed. When I hurried back to Dell, Getlof had already departed on the very errand I had come to suggest. Fortunately, I found him again outside your city of Saroka. I returned the ring and from there we came directly to Gildesh where the ever efficient Sardin spotted him and then me. And that is that."

"Very strange. I'm sure your tale has been abbreviated heavily, but the rest can wait until others have been brought into this problem. In the meanwhile, I find myself believing. It would take something like this to bring you within our grasp, Master Talo. Yes, I think this requires the strongest action. Talo, you are released from direct custody. Sardin will find you suitable quarters and assign you an honor guard. Undersecretary, you will put yourself in the Josh's service. I must seek an audience with Ducitos and see if I can interest him in this." Tael stood. He bowed to Getlof. "Josh." To the others, he inclined his head and said: "Gentlemen." They returned his salutation and left the room.

Muk reacted to Gildesh like a blind man to the dark: it had no independent existence outside of what it harbored. He never thought to compare it with Moaz, perhaps because there were no comparisons to be made. Gildesh was the first city of Ossa and that was fact. The monumental architecture was designed to inspire awe. Muk never saw it. He pushed his way through the narrow, always crowded streets as if he had a grudge against each and every person. He roamed like a wraith day and night peering into faces because he didn't know what else to do. He went into the parts of the city where the stranger is harmed more often than not, but was avoided and came to no hurt. The price he planned to extract from Talo became higher and higher.

14

FIRST ENCOUNTER WITH A KING

Getlof left the Basilica of Mowry the Just following her interview with the Prefect of Justice. She thought she'd seen the most massively grand building in the world. This was before she and Talo arrived at the Palace of Ducitos, also called the Place of Ajum.

Getlof found so many sights in the polyglot city to distract her eyes that she paid little attention to where they were going. She passed through the palace gate and looked up to see a structure that was to the Basilica what a man is to a child. Known as the city within the city, the jewel on the ring, the fire within the jewel, the palace occupied the site of the first Gildi city: the ancient Gildesh of forgotten legend, scoured by the fresh wind of the first days, pressed by the ghosts of forgotten generations. Ajum was dominated by three structures that, from a distance, appeared to be cubes stacked one atop the other: massive, but subtle in their very enormity. Weight was balanced by arched causeways sprouting from the three levels of the building, some at incredible heights. There were unexpected courtyards and long gardened walkways, densely shaded and loud with bird song that left her quite disoriented.

There was one human encounter in this passage that seemed unimportant at the time, but which grew in Getlof's mind to exceed in her memories her first impressions of Ajum. This happened at no great distance within the gate; Getlof was twisting and straining her neck attempting to find a context for the mountain of worked stone. Suddenly a lame man, a beggar of uncertain race stepped into their path.

"A poem for the lady, a poem for the master,

"who hasten on business I help to go faster."

"Go on then, how'd you get in here. I'll help you go faster!" spoke one of their guards, thrusting his pike around to knock the old man down. Somehow,

Getlof couldn't quite see how, the beggar sidestepped the blow and tripped the guard.

Watching this, Getlof suddenly found herself looking into green eyes of drowning depth and a cocked smile. She felt a pounding excitement in her chest. Then, a party coming through the gate behind them pushed their way around. The lame man whispered one word: "you." and vanished. She glanced over for Talo's reaction and saw a pallor over his features that was gone as quickly as he was aware of her gaze.

"Crazy man, I'll give the word and they'll run him out. Lady indeed. Just plain crazy," the guard muttered as he recovered his pike.

Getlof's trip ended high in the second level in a suite that faced the sea breeze from the south. She spent the next three days there, mostly in the company of Golab.

Getlof was satisfied with this arrangement; too much would have left her dazed, but talking with Golab on her balcony high above the city, she was able to regain her disrupted perspective. It helped that she didn't know all the reasons the Gildi were treating her so well and that around her machinations were beginning to grind.

Talo saw very little of Getlof during this period. Somewhere it is said that old enemies make the best friends, especially those who are eventually overcome. All the aging generals, in their prime during the Times of Trouble, were eager to fete Talo and reminisce about the old days. Talo was thrust into the circles of society and his name became the talk of the town. He wondered occasionally what Caos would think when word came to him and at those times remembered the young man he had left in Moaz as surety for his return. Taxis would be delivered, one way or the other, Talo promised himself and only by that promise did he achieve relief from himself.

Golab was an imperial slave, raised by the state. He had spent his adolescence within Gildesh being trained under Miram in knowledge of the Pau--to the extent such knowledge was available. He had never seen a live Pau, but one of his secret fantasies pictured him playing tutor to the young Josh. He was reluctant to acknowledge that this fancy had, apparently, come to pass. Getlof pressed him to teach and there was so much he knew that she didn't, they never knew where to start. At the start of every day Golab expected he'd be thrust back into the windy corridors of the Basilica.

Getlof was caught by the excitement of knowledge, but she felt other attractions of a less didactic nature; Golab was young and Getlof had had no companions of her age since Dell. He was also very handsome and though Getlof knew nothing could come of that--he thinking she was male--he was still nice to look at.

One morning, less than a week after her entry into Ajum, Getlof was summoned and delivered into the keeping of two unbearably self-important eunuchs. They set her to the task of learning the ritual of the Gildi court. The emperor, Ducitos XI, had most graciously consented to see her and, moreover, to address himself to her problem.

That evening Talo came by to see Getlof for the first time in days. He related stories of the parties he had been to and said he had made important contacts. Her presence in the city was a loosely kept secret, and, respecting it loosely, he had been doing everything possible to advance her position. None of this seemed of much importance to Getlof. She preferred his stories about Ducitos.

"He's still a boy just out of his minority and considered simple by most. Don't repeat that. What we have to consider are the people who will decide your ultimate fate. Actually, this is a good time for us. The old regent is only four months dead and no one has been able to gather in all the lines of power he held."

"So, Ducitos is older than me? Younger? What?"

The next morning, the fifth since Getlof's arrival in Gildesh was the time assigned for the audience.

There were several hours of impressive, boring ceremony preceding the event. By the time Getlof was finally approaching the throne in the Hall of the Sky, pacing slowly past the glittering rows of brightly armored guards, splendidly gaudy courtiers, smoking torches and drifting clouds of incense, she could only think how silly it was.

Getlof arrived at the base of the throne. She knew Ducitos was approximately her age, but hearing and seeing--especially given the setting--was like imagining the swooping hawk from the spotted egg. When she finally arrived in plain view, she was surprised and stopped, staring up at him. Ducitos stared back and suddenly Getlof had a vision of what it was like to always be under the scrutiny and domination of old men. In the sympathy of her sudden understanding, she neglected to follow the details of the ritual as she had been instructed. She climbed the steps of the throne because it was just too far away down at the bottom. Ducitos frowned and then looked anxiously at a gowned man standing beside him. Behind her, Getlof could hear a disturbed rustling in the hall. The old man cleared his throat. Getlof could hear footsteps somewhere behind her. Three steps from the top, practically eye to eye with Ducitos she stopped and smiled.

"Greetings, Ducitos. I am Getlof Josh.

"You're so young," he finally replied. "When they told me I expected an old man with a white beard.

The gowned man finally came to life.

"This is outrageous. You come too close and neglected the oblation."

"Who is he?" Getlof asked Ducitos.

"Lord Xem, my privy counselor."

Getlof turned to him and gave a courtly bow. "Lord Xem, know you not we are of a rank?" Golab had told her this. "It is proper we speak as equals. We could hardly see one another if I stayed down there."

"He's right, Xem," Ducitos' voice was fast and excited. "I want to talk to Josh up here."

"You have spoken, Lord," Xem waved back the guards and shot Getlof an icy look.

Ducitos stared at Getlof for a moment longer, then: "I'm forgetting what I'm suppose to say. Ah, first, greetings. I was suppose to say that first, before you greeted me, but I suppose it doesn't matter. And then, after that, I can't remember. This is all mixed up."

Lord Xem spoke from the side: "We are aware of your plight."

"Enough." Ducitos drew himself up straighter and cleared his throat. Getlof noticed his feet didn't touch the ground. "We are aware of your plight and in the graciousness of our favor we have decided to uphold you honor here in our city until such time you can return to your state in the Mountain Kingdoms of the far north. That's all. And now you're supposed to thank me."

"I do thank you, Ducitos," Getlof said slowly, "but what gave you the idea I was in trouble?"

"Aren't you? They told me you were."

"Of course not. I mean, I like your city; I've found it a wonderful place, but I can't stay here. I have no choice. You can understand that."

"I can, I can. Every time I think I have a choice, Xem or someone else explains how I don't really and there is only one thing I can do."

"My Lord. . ." Xem began.

Ducitos absently waved his hand. "If you don't stay, what will you do, Josh?"

"I shall do as I've been doing. I shall travel up the Riverrun through Moaz, over the Middle Hills, through the Nomad lands of the north, until I am in Hilev over the Jep." (Golab had introduced her to maps.)

"All that way? And by yourself?"

"No, master Talo shall accompany me."

"They told me about him. Is he not an outlaw?"

Getlof laughed and after a moment, Ducitos joined her, as if he had said something funny. The laughter spread throughout the hall.

"I think he is, perhaps, slightly dishonest, Ducitos; but, it sounds like a long road for a completely honest man." Then she looked at him slyly, an idea having just occurred.

"If you wish to be generous, you can grant me a favor."

"Really, what is that?"

"For the past several days I've been in the care of your servant, Golab. His knowledge of the Pau is deep. I request he be given leave to accompany me and Talo."

"Is that all? I can do it easily. Is he here?"

"I don't know," Getlof said, looking around. There were too many faces down in the hall to try to pick one out.

"Well, that's no problem. Xem, send out the call and have this Golab come hither."

"You have spoken, Lord."

Golab was in the hall. He came forward according to ritual.

"There," Ducitos said, "that's how you were supposed to do it. But I'm glad you didn't; it takes so long and I've seen it a thousand times."

Finally Golab prostrated himself before the throne. Getlof noticed that Ducitos' tone hardened when he told Golab to rise.

"It has come to our attention that Getlof, Josh of the Pau, considers you a worthy man, fit to accompany him on his journey to the north. Holding his opinion dear we now release you from our service and hand you over to Josh to be his slave in all matters." He made a gesture of dismissal.

Anxiously watching Golab's expression, Getlof satisfied herself that this command was also his wish.

"Well, that's that, but are you certain I can't do anything more?"

"Thank you, Ducitos, you've already done a lot."

"One man is nothing. Wait, I have an idea. Through the Riverrun and all the way to Zoha you'll be in my dominions. I can at least provide you with an escort. Yes, that's what I'll do."

This struck Getlof as unnecessary and excessive. She was about to say so, but something in Ducitos' eyes made her stop. She had an insight that it was foolish to gainsay a person, particularly a king, in a generous mood.

"Thank you, Ducitos, your generosity is famous."

He nodded. "I know. Now where is Angus?" Then he shouted, dispensing with the proper forms. "Angus, I know you're here. Come forward."

A tall, gray man dressed in battle armor detached himself from the crowd and approached Ducitos, giving an abbreviated version of the oblation. "Lord?"

"Angus, I am putting you and a company of my guard at the Josh's service. I want that recorded and the orders drawn up. Right away so I can put my seal on it."

"My Lord. . ."

"Oh, Angus, you're not going to argue with me, I hope. My mind is quite made up. Go do it quickly." Angus bowed. As he walked away, Ducitos whispered: "I have to do things like this or they'll find a way to get around me. But don't worry, once my seal is on the order, its as good as done." Getlof nodded. She was suddenly anxious for the audience to end.

"You know, Josh, you're really a most stimulating person. I've just had another idea. Why shouldn't I accompany you, at least as far as the borders of my realm."

"Lord," Xem said, bursting forward. "My Lord, that is quite impossible. Respects, Josh, but I think His Most Divine Presence is growing tired."

"I am not tired. I will end this audience when I please."

"May I speak a word to this," Getlof said.

"Yes, if Xem will permit it."

"I would be delighted to travel in your company, Ducitos. You could do me no greater honor. Thus, you will realize this is hard for me to mention."

"What is?" a look of wariness coming over his face.

"Just this: we each have our own place. You are fortunate that you are in yours. I am unfortunate in that I am far from mine. I could never repay your generosity by taking you away from your proper and predestined place. That would be a grave wrong."

"But I want to go with you, even all the way to Hilev. I would like that best of all."

"Indeed, so would I. But consider: you will be with me in the persons of your servants, Angus and Golab. Thus, you can be here in your place and be with me as well. And, of course, I will write you, such letters as people of our rank exchange. It will seem there is no distance between us at all."

Ducitos suddenly jumped up and embraced Getlof. She was so startled, she almost stepped back over the lip of the throne. Only with the aid of the emperor's arms did she keep her balance.

"You are right. Now I do wish you really were in trouble so I could keep you here to talk with me every day. Except then," he suddenly became grave, "you wouldn't be in your proper place."

"No," matching his graveness, "but this way everything will be as it should."

"Right!" Then, with his arm still around Getlof, he turned toward the hall. "Listen, I Ducitos XI, Emperor of the Gildi, do proclaim Getlof Josh to be my brother. Any who harm or hinder him do the same to me with the attendant consequences." In a more private voice: "Xem, draw up a document and I'll put my seal to it."

"You have spoken, Lord." Xem's tone was lighter; he realized Getlof had saved him some hard talking.

That ended the audience. Getlof retired from the Hall of the Sky looking neither to the right nor to the left, but feeling, none-the-less, the eyes of the world on her.

Outside a group was gathered to offer congratulations. Then she heard Talo call her name and broke away. They embraced and Talo whispered into her ear: "You were magnificent."

"Did I do all right?" feeling inadequate now it was over.

"All right? All right? Be serious. You heard what they intended. It might have been fine enough, at least for a time, but you would have been the Josh of the Gildi, not of the Pau and I don't think you'd have been happy."

Getlof shook her head.

97

"And old Angus is going to come along. Its almost too funny to be true; almost worth the trouble its certain to cause. Getlof, you were magnificent. I just don't know how you did it."

That very day Getlof and Talo began preparing for the journey. It was like the market day in Saroka but on a much grander scale. Ducitos sent rich gifts: a new wardrobe of the finest textures, gem encrusted weapons; useless for fighting but splendid for pawning, according to Talo, and a beautiful stallion. Talo received armor custom made; gear that finally fit him right and a new horse as well. Golab was the most excited; he went in terror of some last minute problem that would deny him his place in Getlof's train, but nothing like that happened. In less than a week they were ready to go. With Getlof, Talo and Golab, there was the sixth company of the first column of the Emperor's own guard; ninety-six men and officers, the very best fighting men in Ossa, Talo said. There was also a baggage train manned by teamsters from the city. Getlof considered it quite the grand procession.

On the night when all the preparations had finally been completed, on the eve of their departure, Talo took Getlof aside for a private talk. It was becoming hard to see her alone.

"Well," he began, closing the door to his chamber and sitting on the bed, "we certainty are going to leave Gildesh in more style than we entered."

"Is that all you wanted to tell me?" Getlof laughed. "Golab could've heard that."

"No, that's not all. I'm glad to see you in good spirits, but I've been thinking. There'll be a cost behind all this Gildi generosity and I need to satisfy myself that you see it."

Getlof was dressed in the new clothes Ducitos had given her. They seemed to heighten her foreignness, at the same time giving her an aspect of nobility and splendor. She was so comely it was almost uncanny and for a moment, Talo wondered if she would have enjoyed such success had she been ugly or even plain. He didn't think so; she looked her part to the hilt.

"First, there's the escort. Of course, at the time there was no way to refuse Ducitos' offer, but realize that as well as escorting you, they'll be guarding you. If we contemplate any action that might not be considered in the best interest of the Gildi, you can be sure Angus will have his say. And there won't be much you or I can do. And consider this: by traveling with a troop of imperial soldiers, you automatically associate yourself with the government they serve and gain the enmity of all who oppose that government. That includes just about everyone between here and Hilev. Finally, even if everything does go fine, think of the obligation you'll be under."

"I'm already under that obligation. I don't see what can be done. Besides, Talo, I heard they're coming with us only as far as Zoha."

"We'll see. But you must also know that not everyone holds you as dear as Ducitos. I've heard whispering to the effect that you're some kind of wizard or other to have gained such a hold over him. That's the chief reason you haven't seen him since the first audience."

Getlof nodded. "I figured it was something like that."

"Good, I want you to think about why things are; I especially want you to remember that Angus will have his orders and not all of them, I suspect, will come from Ducitos."

"Consider me warned." Getlof smiled. "I can't help but remember something you told me. What should be, will be."

Talo looked at her strangely and shook his head. "I never said that; I couldn't have because I don't happen to believe it. If experience has taught me anything, it is that what should be seldom is. If fact, with your permission, I'll sleep in you antechamber tonight. There is no sense in taking chances."

15

SWEET SHONIAN

Muk sat on the street edge, head in arms, dozing in and out of sleep. He had been four days in Gildesh, destroying himself in his search. His money was gone and failure, the unthinkable, was at hand; and with it, self pity unimaginable. He was always one step behind; even in Shon, nine years ago, one step behind death, one step behind escape, and so enslaved. Muk had banished Shon from his thoughts; it was a sign of his dissolute state he was thinking of it now. Kista, young and beautiful, marred only by the scar behind her ear.

Ah! Muk remembered that day. The bitter winter, the icy winds rushing down the canyons of the Roganspire. The two children flinging themselves down snowy slopes on pieces of cured hide. Kista thrown off, screaming with laughter and then with hurt. The rock buried in fresh snow. Ruba standing, fixated; red blood on white snow. In his arms he carried her, stumbling through drifts, all feeling lost, holding on by force of will alone. And Kista laughing, at last, saying she was all right now and could walk. Even though his arms were numb, he hadn't wanted to put her down. . .

Suddenly Muk's head jerked up. A voice speaking Shonian. A dream he thought, and heard it again. Two men, walking away were conversing in Shonian.

Muk blinked and convinced himself it was real. He stood and trembled as his sleeping foot buckled under him, and followed.

They were rich men, or at least attired to give that impression. Muk closed until he was right behind them and could easily hear what they said. Sweet Shonian. None of the jangling discordancies of Southcoast. How long had it been?

" . . . be that as it may, my friend, I can think of no place safer than Gildesh. Oh, if you're desperate I imagine the eastern route through Fain and Sitnoe will stay open, but winter will find you by the shores of the Fakanahafaf. Surely you find this prospect better than that."

"You know I do, but all profit aside, I think this will be war and a big one. Its only intuition, you understand, but that's what I think. I'd feel better sitting it out in Shon. What satisfaction could I get in Gildesh not knowing if my family is safe?"

"There is that point. . . Oh, excuse me."

The one on the right looked around past Muk.

"These Gildi are the rudest people!"

Laughter. "At least in the south they are. But you were saying?"

"I was saying? Ah, yes. You are acquainted with the rumors coming out of the palace?"

"I imagine you're referring to the Pau. Somewhat hard to believe."

"I know, after all these years another Josh appears. Somehow I find it comforting, but even more amazing; I mean, after the wasting of Joshin and the way this world has grown worse ever since. If it is true . . ."

"Oh, I'm sure it's a long way from being true and that is the problem."

"No, listen to this. I heard the boy, Ducitos, received him and he charmed him so he had Ducitos proclaiming him brother, over the wishes of his advisor, Xem and that crew. Isn't that something? And there's more. I heard Ducitos undertook to assist him, even to the point of lending a company of guard commanded by no less than old Angus himself. You know the prophecy of Nivila, if it was a girl, I almost might be willing to believe in that."

Muk could restrain himself no longer. He reached forward and put his hand on the shoulder of the man on the left. He looked around, said: "Excuse me," and turned back. Muk said, in Shonian, "Greetings and blessings, brother. May I have a word?" When speaking Shonian even a man like Muk could only be polite. It was that kind of language.
Both of the men stopped and turned to regard Muk.

"Greetings and blessings, brother. A word you may surely have."

Muk stood still, suddenly unable to hear or see. Dizziness rampaged up and down his body. The man's words had transported him.

("Sir, I would have word with you about your daughter."

A pleased smile. "Come in, Ruba. A word you may surely have.")

Hands on his arms, steadying. "Brother, you are ill. Are you eating?"

"Cruel and unhappy city, it permits its own children to starve. What chance has the stranger?"

"Come, come with us."

. . . He brushed you off as he would a fly. He deceived you as if you were a child. And like a child you were deceived. Unhappy, unhappy, unhappy. He will know the day . . .

Two days Muk spent in the house of Ostler ni Shon, merchant stranded in Gildesh with a full consignment of goods for the north. Such were the perils of trade. He slept until he woke, was fed and slept again. On the morning of the third day, he awoke burning for the pursuit and not certain how he had come to be where he was. All he recalled was that kind chance had given him another opportunity. Unless, unless he had fallen one step behind again. His first words to Ostler, that day, was a question about the Pau.

Ostler laughed and asked if that news was even being spread in the land of dreams. Then he gave reassurance. The Pau was still in Gildesh, but was riding on the next for the north. There might be a procession and if he liked, they could go and watch.

Muk relaxed back onto his bed. He was not too late after all, amazing as it seemed. He had their trail firm and plain and would not lose it again. Ostler continued talking, as if the Josh were a topic of only passing interest.

"I have thought that meeting you could be a lucky chance. I have determined to return to Shon this year and will take the eastern route. I need men, and Shonians whom I can trust above all others. Have you sword-craft or other weapon skills?"

Muk shook his head. "No killing skills." Then he did something unthinkable; he revealed to Ostler details of his biography.

"I am a slave. I am on my master's commission. I cannot go with you."

Ostler frowned. "A slave. That is not a fit condition for a child of Shon. More than ever I say come. You will attain both your freedom and your home. Is there anything more?"

Muk thought this was not even a beginning, but didn't say so.

"Ah, I see that your face has lost the habit of gentleness. You harden it for to refuse me again. So be it, friend. I will not press for that is rude. But have pity on my habit of kindness and let me do you some favor."

"The favor has been given," Muk mumbled.

"Ah, no it has not. Tell me, you're on your master's commission. What thing can I give you to help further this commission?"

Muk looked up and saw there was no refusal. Sweet Shon. There were no people like the Shonians. He pressed these thoughts back down.

"If you must than I need a horse." He hesitated, "and a dagger as well."

Ostler frowned more deeply than before. "So be it, a horse and a dagger you shall have and rations as well. But friend, a word of warning: soften your heart."

Muk nodded and thought for the sake of this man he had already softened it far too much.

The next morning Muk was at the gate when the procession issued forth from the Place of Ajum. He waited only until he saw Talo riding near the front; then he rode, pell mell, to the northern exits of the city. The Riverrun was a straight road with no junctions. Talo could follow him for a change.

He rode all day and into the night, not noticing the beauty of the gorge, although it was his first time and it ranked as one of the wonders of Ossa. He rode until he approached the northern end, all the time considering the ways one man could penetrate such a strong escort. Then, under the fading starlight, he was waylaid. Dark forms emerged from the roadside and commanded him to halt. They spoke Southcoast, but their accents were Moazian. Muk gave them peace in that language before any of the drawn bows could be released. He had his own sign of authority given to him by Gavin. It was only slightly inferior to the one given Talo by Caos. He used it to take command of the party of raiders. He was one man no longer.

16

THE RIVERRUN

The Ossa hurtled in colors of green and foaming white through its gorge in the Xexi Mountains. The Riverrun road followed on a ledge carved from the canyon wall. The column rode in double file along this road--slippery in the fine mist that overhung the gorge--with the wains following behind. Progress was slow; they made only one march in the morning and camped by midafternoon. Ducitos' guardsmen were chosen for their size and discipline. They rode in a silence broken only by the drumming of hoofs on stone. Getlof rode near the end of the column, just in front of the wagons. Usually Golab was beside her.

Getlof had studied the maps and it seemed to her that Hilev was really not that far away; in traveling to Zoha she had already come one third of her way. On one occasion she tried to discuss the subject of their future route with Talo, but he was difficult to draw out on that subject.

"It all depends where the Xumi happen to be grazing their herds. That is assuming there is peace along the Ossa and we have no reason to think there will be." He glanced back at the column strung out behind them. "Our escort might look impressive, but even if they followed us onto the plains, I wouldn't care to match them against a couple thousand Xumi warriors."

Angus was riding near by and he overheard this last remark.

"You fear the nomads," he said in his slow, heavy voice, "but the nomads fear us more. They are bandits and will avoid fighting a company such as this, each man trained in the skills and devices of Yetit. And if they were so unwise, they'd regret it. Each of my men, Josh, is worth twenty Xumi. With us you have nothing to fear."

Getlof thanked him for his assurances. She didn't know what to make of Angus; since the march had begun, she had seen little of him. Usually Angus rode at the head of the column, with Talo beside him. She thought they seemed very friendly considering Talo's warnings made the night before their departure, but this observation didn't cause worry. Most of her attention during this period was absorbed by her talks with Golab.

They covered a whole range of subjects, but always they returned to the Pau. He told her of their history; how in the past of the epics and heroes, they occupied the whole of Ossa. Then the nomads invaded from the east and the Sea Peoples from the west.

"The Moazians are descended from nomads. My ancestors were Sea Peoples. The Tarhadians themselves were once nomads as well. I suppose in time, a hundred years or a thousand, all the nomads in Ossa will be settled, unless in the farther east there are new wanderers waiting to trouble our land."

"I've heard so much about the nomads I'm rather anxious to see some. Do you suppose we will?"

"I hope not; certainty not if we can help it."

Getlof nodded. She thought it strange that there could exist a people hostile to everyone. Something in her just couldn't believe it.

"Then tell me about Josh."

Golab tried very hard to look exasperated. "Again? What is there I haven't told you?"

"Each time it's a little different."

Golab shrugged his shoulders. It obviously wasn't that Getlof was stupid; she was like a child with a favorite, well worn tale. "All right. The first Josh appeared sometime after the Pau had been driven from the coasts and middle plains. How he came to be born in NorthPointing is a mystery, at least in Gildesh, but they might know that tale in Hilev. It's said that the Pau, divided into many tribes and clans, were at odds with one another and prey to all. Josh brought them unity. He dreamed of a new god and spoke the words of that god, Pauic, to his people. Under his guidance, the Pau became one people and were not killed from this land. That was long ago and long have they survived. Raos' sack of Joshin was their greatest disaster since the time of the first Josh; they were hunted from the Middle Hills and Moaz and it seems their present need must be greater even than in the days of the first Josh."

Getlof nodded and gazed out over the river. The water was dark, but flecked with foam. The mountains reared abruptly from the far bank. It was early afternoon, but they rode in shadow. Getlof had heard they would spend only two more nights in this canyon. Its chill was beginning to affect her. It seemed ages since they had passed travelers from the north.

"Pauic means the unmanifest. I've said that often enough; I've said all this often enough. I can't imagine what could possibly be new." Golab paused, but Getlof said nothing so he went on. "Think of Josh as being the man in the middle. He listens to the god, words the people cannot hear and speaks those words to his people. . . ."

This part always reminded Getlof of Asha. She had never shared that story with anyone, but was on the point of doing so now, when suddenly she shivered and looked away. She heard Golab asking what was wrong. From somewhere a cleft of light penetrated the mountains. The river was suddenly golden. Full golden and searing.

"Getlof?"

She looked back. The light was gone. "I'm sorry, it was just a chill."

Golab looked worried and stared past her trying to see what had drawn her attention, but there was nothing.

They pushed on that afternoon past the time they were accustomed to stop and came to a small town. A stream fell from the mountains at that point and the town was built up along the cut it had eroded. Angus said they would spend the night there, under a roof. He had not been in the field for years and sleeping on the ground was even more uncomfortable than he remembered.

Angus hired an entire floor of the inn that faced the road on the lowest terrace of the town. This was for Getlof, Talo, Golab, himself and the four officers. The rank and file quartered in houses further up the town. There was some grumbling because ninety-two men are many for a small town to host, but to an officer of the guard no one dared grumble loudly.

Getlof had fallen into a quiet and withdrawn state after her talk with Getlof. The light on the river lingered like burns on her retinas and perception had shifted. Events seemed to be rushing forward with such certainty, there was no leisure to examine the wisdom of what she was doing; or what was being done to her. She wondered how she could be the person in the middle as Golab described it. How did one listen to a god, supposing even He chose to speak? And if He did, how did one make others listen?

106

Downstairs in the commons people were drinking. Getlof could hear the commotion. Talo had tried to get her to come, but she had no sociability in her that night. Solitude, her closest childhood companion, had become a rare experience since meeting Talo. It was a calm night--clear and cold. Getlof decided she would take a walk down to the river. Maybe if she listened very hard. Without thinking why, she strapped on the sword Talo had purchased for her in Saroka. Compared to the one Ducitos had presented her with, it seemed very plain.

She descended the stairs and skirted the smoky commons. One man by the door, a stranger, made a drunken grab at her as she passed, but she evaded him easily and made it outside without otherwise being detected.

It was cold; colder than it had seemed when they camped in the open. There were few lights in the town, but she could hear the sounds of more merrymaking further up the hill. A holiday seemed to have been declared among the soldiers and that struck Getlof as unusual if for no other reason than because the discipline in camp had been so strict.

Suddenly, from the edge of her eye, she noticed a shadow shifting position; a man trying to remain hidden. Getlof edged into the shadows next to a hedge. She moved along the shrubbery quickly, but quietly, hoping the man hadn't seen her as she had seen him.

Getlof didn't scout her surroundings until she had climbed to the terrace above the inn, beside an alley that led even further up. Looking down, she couldn't make out who or what had startled her. The inn was bright, illuminating the area around it. To the right of the door she saw a guardsman standing watch on the road. There was another one on the left. The thought they weren't all busy getting drunk was reassuring, not knowing why there was any reason to worry.

No, something was wrong. She didn't know what, but she could feel it. She stood for a second, watching the guardsmen and wondered if she should go back and fetch Talo.

Then it happened.

Almost simultaneously both men fell and strangers carrying bows began crawling up unto the road from the ditch on the other side. Some had torches. They began to spread out and Getlof realized they planned to fire the inn.

This happened in an instance. Getlof knew there was no time to go back and warn them. Without thinking, she cupped her hands to her mouth and screamed "FIRE!" The intruders stopped and to a man appeared to stare at her. Getlof turned and raced up the alley toward a lighted house where she hopped to find help.

Behind her there was shouting. A red glow took hold on the sky.

Men were already spilling out of the house when she arrived. To her relief she recognized a good many of them as guardsmen.

"Quickly, she cried, her voice breaking, "we're under attack."

"Why, it's the young lord," one of them said. "What is this?"

"Raiders! They've fired the inn!"

The man appeared to be a sub-officer. He muttered a curse. "Quickly, Sepan and Doy, go rouse the Eagle and Hawk and have them follow as they can. The damn Falcon was supposed to be on guard. Come on men, you were looking for a fight tonight and here it is."

They cheered and commenced running down the alley. Getlof trotted beside the tall sub-officer whose name, she suddenly remembered (she knew not from where) was Narhad. "We can't just rush out into the square, there's too many of them."

He looked down at her, grim smile creasing his face. "We, my young lord? It's you I trow they're after. You'll remain behind."

Then they were in sight of the square. The inn was in flames past saving, it seemed. Men were deployed around it, caught in the flickering crimson glow like nightmare images, picking off those who tried to flee. There looked to be over a hundred of them. Suddenly, the man beside Getlof fell with an arrow in his chest. Narhad spared Getlof a glance of no uncertain meaning. Then he cried the Gildi: "**Ah Kal la Kal!**" and sprang forward, the others right behind. Getlof hesitated, then she followed.

There was a detachment covering the alley to intercept them, but Narhad and his men broke through easily, killing all who stood against them. Getlof ran in a zigzag with her head down. It was hard to tell what was happening. Then suddenly she found herself face to face with an archer, not knowing how he had come to be there. He cursed, threw down his bow and began to pull a long knife from its sheath. Getlof found she was holding her sword. With both hand, she brought it around and down onto his shoulder. He cried and sank to the ground. Getlof stood over him and cried also.

More voices from her left: "**Ah Kal la Kal!**" and other guardsmen came sweeping up the road from that direction. She was almost to the inn now. The heat was intense. She looked around--the shouting was fading away--and saw to her surprise it was all over. Everywhere the intruders were fleeing. People emerging from the inn and town's people from off the hill were joining in the fight and giving chase. She had forgotten about them. It had been no more than ten minutes since her scream.

Then Golab was beside her. "Getlof, thank goodness. We heard you. We thought . . ."

She nodded and leaned against him. He put his arm around her shoulder and led her from the fire. Narhad came up, his face shining with sweat and his eyes far away. He appeared to wrench his attention back from wherever it had been and fixed Getlof in his gaze. "Next time I will assign someone to see you follow orders."

They ended sleeping in the open after all; those who slept. Angus was putting the prisoners to the question and that kept Getlof awake. The next day, at first light, he drew his men up.

"Their leader was stupid," he said, pacing up and down the line. "If he had waited another two or three hours we would have been roasted as we slept. As it was, they did better than they should have. I accept the fault. The danger was greater than I look for and the reach of the Magnus longer than I thought." He turned to Renix, the officer of the Falcon who had been in charge of security. Renix stood stiffly. Sixteen of the guardsmen had died as well as a number of the townsfolk.

"Still, I am at a lost to understand how more than two hundred foemen managed to surprise us. Renix, explain that to me."

Few of the enemy had escaped. Their ambush collapsed when the four sub-companies converged from three directions. The fourth, the Peregrine, which Getlof roused, had been first, but the others were not far behind. Confronted with the crises, they acted independently and with consummate skill, disposing of a force three times their own size in ten minutes despite the fact they had been surprised, dispersed and drunk at the time of the attack.

"Sir," Renix said, "there is nothing to say. The guards I posted were inadequate. I await your judgment."

"I see," Angus said. "Well, a subordinate is no better than his superior. You are reduced to the ranks, but you will remain in the guard."

Renix clearly expected worse. "My lord, you are generous. Your confidence will be rewarded."

"I hope so. Narhad, step forward. You were quick; maybe Josh is to thank for that, but at any rate, you now have the Falcon."

Narhad nodded and almost smiled. A field promotion was a promotion none-the-less.

They moved out that afternoon having disposed of the prisoners. In private conference Angus told Talo and Getlof of the spy from Gildesh who had ordered the attack. It had been determined his name was Muk but nothing more was known. Talo heard this with a sinking heart, but his private knowledge he kept to himself.

"This is war, you know," Angus said to Getlof as they moved out. "And sooner than anyone expected. The road beyond Zoha will be closed to us. There is no shame if you admit to this and return to Gildesh."

Getlof looked at him and wondered if Talo's fears were to be realized.

"I recognize your wisdom, sir, and am comforted by your presence, but regardless of where duty leads Ducitos' guard, I must go on."

Angus regarded her with serious eyes of dark gray. "You have spoken." He spurred his horse. As Getlof watched him take his position at the head of the column, she remembered how Xem had used that form of reply with Ducitos.

17

DIVERGENT DIRECTIONS

By the afternoon of the next day the canyon walls were lower and farther apart; the current of the Ossa seemed slower and there was a new, dry quality to the air. Scouts worked the road both ahead and behind the main column. There had been no further incidents, but they hurried on, feeling vulnerable in the confined canyon. The distant view of two rock towers that reared on either side of the river was an encouragement as these marked the terminus of the Riverrun. They reached this gap shortly before sunset. The river spread out in the flat expanse of the Last Lake and the view swept on past even that. It was a land huge and empty.

They camped that night with the most careful security, but nothing disturbed the illusion of peace. Getlof rose early, before light, suffering from restlessness. Wandering in the darkened, sleeping camp, she happened upon Angus doing the same. For a moment they looked at each other, then Angus nodded and fell in beside her.

"Well, my lord Josh, this day we should discover whether the route north is blocked."

Getlof nodded and without thinking why said: "I have a feeling it will be."

"Indeed? I have heard you are one whose premonitions should be heeded. Was your warning of two nights past based upon premonition?"

Getlof looked up into his face and changed the subject. "Tell me, Angus, what do you think?"

He returned her gaze for a time before answering. "This won't be easy as you made it sound, speaking up there with Ducitos. You see that, it's plain. Maybe you saw it then." He paused and looked away. "I must know your desire."

"The same as always."

"Even so." She thought he smiled, but in the light it was hard to say. They began walking again.

"I am accustomed to thinking of a situation according to the instructions I have received. You don't know my instruction in this situation, but I think you should." He looked at her closely, once again. "I am to escort you to Zoha. There I am to use my judgment. If the way is not safe, I am to escort you back to Gildesh."

"And if the way is safe?"

And then Angus did smile. "My judgment is to be this: the way is not safe."

There was something anomalous about being taken into the confidence of this close man that alarmed Getlof. "Why do you tell me this? Was to be, you say; and you say you always follow instructions."

"And you scold me for that." Around them the sounds of the camp waking. Angus' tone was harsh. "I tell you for this reason: recall when Ducitos placed his arm around you and called you brother. He said those who harmed or hindered you acted as if they harmed him? I'm sure you remember, but maybe you thought they were empty words? To me they are words of full import. My family has served his family for more generations than I can remember. Obedience is the same whatever the vessel of the order. I have not forgotten although some have." He stopped and Getlof said:

"I understand."

"Yes, I think you do; you have great understanding for one of your years. Heated words. I have spoken them often in the present reign and I expect I shall continue to do so, but you understand also, I shall do with you as Ducitos intended and not as those who order in his name."

Getlof nodded and Angus touched his finger to his forehead, excusing himself. Getlof watched as he walked away, feeling a new warmth for the man.

They reached the Gildi fort near the southern end of the Last Lake before midday. The gates were open; then sentries were surprised to see soldiers from the south. They rode inside right into the center of the local market. One soldier upset an old woman's cart of melons. Her curses resonated as they gathered in the compound.

Hours passed before the fort's commander was located in a nearby village. He was the son of an acquaintance of Angus', a young noble in his first command. This didn't save him from being relieved of his command and replaced by the officer of the Eagle.

Getlof didn't hear of this until later. Angus wanted her out of sight so she had to sit in the hot and narrow confines of the commander's quarters. The day passed drearily by with nothing to occupy her except the sounds of the guardsmen driving the market outside the walls. They took a surprisingly long time and the clamor of lamentations made it sound as if Angus had ordered a slaughter.

It was under these circumstances Getlof found herself doubting Angus once again, recalling Talo's warning and the slaughter of the prisoners after the battle of the inn. But more disturbing, perhaps, were Golab's words on the function of the Josh. Now they were in danger, those words assumed a new immediacy and meaning they'd never had in Gildesh. She strained to make herself receptive, yearning for some clear sign to tell her what she should do. But, in the end, the decision she reached was her own. She decided she had to strike off as soon as possible with Talo and Golab only. How she would do that, however, she didn't know.

After a long time Talo came in. He looked around the room and said:

"What, you're alone. No Golab?"

Getlof was at the point where she would have welcomed anyone, but Talo was the person she wanted to see most of all.

"No, Golab is neglecting me now, just like you've been neglecting me all week."

An unusual expression passed over Talo's face, the meaning of which she could not read.

"Have I been neglecting you? Let's say there has been more competition for both of our attentions. In Saroka we had each other to ourselves."

"Maybe," she said slowly, "it would be better if it were that way again."

"I'm surprised to hear you say so. And pleased. It makes it easier for me to say I was thinking along similar lines. I've been thinking this escort business puts you in more danger than it protects you from. Angus has been more agreeable than I expected, but still, he is Angus, if you know what I mean."

"Does Caos know I exist?" she suddenly asked.

113

Talo looked startled. "Yes, but don't think all this is just for you. He has long had designs on the territory north of the Riverrun. Its just bad luck he's trying to realize his ambitions at the very time you're passing through."

"But if I fell into his hands it would all be over."

Talo looked away and Getlof suddenly knew he was hiding something.

"Yes, if you fell into his hands it would all be over."

Then, a knock at the door and Golab stuck his head in. Talo appeared embarrassed by the interruption and left soon after. Getlof was sorry. She was sure he'd wanted to say more.

The morning of the next day was spent in loading the horses into boats. Angus had commandeered the transport, feeling it was safer to travel thus, rather than risk the ride along the shores of the Last Lake. Getlof expected Talo to tease her about her pledge never to travel again by boat, but he didn't.

The wind blew fresh from off the mountains all afternoon, saving the oarsmen much hard work. Getlof was sick again, but this time she was not alone. Most of the guardsmen were landfolk like her and suffered as well. Several hours past sunset, the little fleet finally came to the harbor of Zoha. They were able to pass freely in and Angus took this as a good sign, but events proved the omen false. Zoha was a frenzy of activity. People of the outlying districts were pouring into the city. Under torchlight workcrews hurried to complete, and in some cases to begin, last minute repairs to the fortifications. Groups of men-at-arms wandered through the dock sections and crowded into the taverns shouting and fighting. There was little sign of discipline.

Getlof formed only a vague idea of the town's mood, and that was from what the others said. She was weak and woozy from the trip. She didn't protest when Angus dropped her off at the harbor master's station with a guard. He then formed up the remainder of his command and marched them up to the citadel of Zoha.

It was dark when Getlof awoke. The first thing she noticed was that her stomach felt fine. Then she heard a faint shouting, thought from where it came she couldn't tell. She sat up and looked about. She was in a bed and remembered being put there and told to sleep. She had done that and it was good. Then she noticed a form sitting in a chair near the door.

"Don't worry. It's Narhad."

"Oh. What's the noise? What's happening?"

"I'd like to know. The shouting has been going on for some time."

"Where are Talo and Golab?"

"Golab is asleep in the other room. Talo I don't know. He went with Angus. We haven't heard from them since they left, but don't worry, this is a strong house and it's well guarded; rioters will find easier picking elsewhere."

"I wasn't thinking about that. Are they rioting?"

"To my ear that's how it sounds."

"Why?"

He shook his head. "I would say Ducitos needs to look to the loyalty of his chief servants here in the north."

"Then it's not an attack?"

"Not yet. That is the garrison you're hearing. Listen."

Getlof listened. The noise was a low rumble, which suddenly crystallized into meaning. It assumed a voice fraught with urgency. Her head cleared and certainty flooded in. It was time; the time was now. She even imagined it was those words being chanted outside.

This feeling took hold of her so completely that at first she didn't hear the knocking at the door. When she did, it was like waking from a dream.

Narhad stood, almost scraping his head on the ceiling, and opened the door. A young woman stepped through. She smiled at Getlof.

"I'm sorry we had to bed you in your clothes. The man named Talo insisted. Are you feeling better now?"

"Thank you, I'm fine. But who are you?" Then she stopped, aware she was being rude. The woman didn't seem to notice.

"I'm Dedre, the daughter of the Harbor Master. This is my father's house." Dedre looked at her in a curious fashion.

"I thank you for this hospitality, Dedre." Getlof didn't know what else to say. It was difficult to be suddenly snatched from sweeping elation to the ordinary.

"Is there anything I can do?"

Getlof hesitated. "Is there a water closet?"

"Of course, right back here."

Getlof was glad for the chance to be alone. There was something in the appearance of Dedre that touched off a welter of ambivalent feelings. And outside they were still chanting. She needed to sort it all out, but surprisingly the only thing she could think of was Dedre's white dress. It had been very pretty.

Just when Getlof was thinking they might be missing her, she heard more voices, including Talo's.

The bed chamber was crowded: Talo was there with Golab; Narhad and several other guardsmen, among whom she recognized Renix; Dedre was sitting in a corner listening, and servants hurried about with trays of food. When she entered all talk stopped.

"Well, Talo, is there news?"

He smiled, although she noticed it was a smile lacking most of his usual candor. "I see you're yourself again. Never seen a person more prone to motion sickness. Are you fit to travel?"

"Yes, and yes again."

He raised an eyebrow. "I've been telling the news from the citadel. Count Elran was the commander here. It seems he had some sort of arrangement with Caos. He was also Ducitos' uncle. You might remember that, Getlof and take it as a lesson on how far you can trust people."

"Where's Angus?"

"He's busy with Elran's guard, but that was almost over when I left. Still, it's apparent someone will have to take command here, and who else but Angus?"

"Is Caos close?"

"That no one knows, but he can't be far off. My advice, which I came to give, is for you to get out of this mousetrap city before dawn." He hesitated. "Do you remember what we said before?"

From his corner Golab said: "If you are talking of setting off on your own, don't forget me." Getlof nodded. It was difficult to say where her ideas were coming from, but coming they were, with force and clarity.

"Yes, first south again and then straight west. We can skirt Moaz and then head north. It's out of the way and should be unexpected to our enemies. Dedre, can I ask you another favor?"

"Of course," looking grateful to be remembered.

"Good, if this Magnus of Moaz is truly on the watch for me, he'll be expecting a male, not a lady. If you'll lend, or give, I should say, a dress or two, I can become a lady very easily."

She glanced shyly at Talo but he looked abstracted and inattentive.

Then Narhad spoke in his deep voice that was impossible to ignore. "What says Angus to this? He must be consulted."

Talo looked up at this. "He should be, but is there time? At the moment he's deeply occupied. And you know as well as I his mission was only to escort Getlof as far as Zoha which is where we now are."

"That is truth, but still he should be consulted."

"Narhad," Getlof said, "listen to me. Yesterday I spoke with Angus on this very matter. He recalled to me the time Ducitos placed his arm around me and called me brother. He told me also I was a person whose premonitions should be heeded. Heed me now. I have a feeling we are almost out of time. It is this night or never. You are the senior officer here. I put it to you."

Narhad looked down. He sat solidly with both hands on his knees, betraying none of his thoughts with gesture. Getlof looked at him and saw him as if for the first time. She suddenly knew she needed him, perhaps more than anyone else.

"There are the wishes of Ducitos to be considered and they do override all other considerations." Then he looked up and met Getlof's eyes. "If your wish is firm than I say this: take three companions more. I am here and Renix and Doy who knows the land you speak of. Angus would not have you set out into the wilderness without strong swords to shield you."

"Good," Getlof said briskly, "you are accepted. See to your gear and also to getting a boat. I'll go with the Lady Dedre. We leave as soon as we can."

Getlof rose and was at the door when Talo said: "Is this not too hasty? By morning we can speak with Angus." She stopped and looked back, frowning.

"I have spoken, Narhad has spoken, Talo. I would have you come."

She left before he could reply.

When Getlof reappeared in one of Dedre's gowns, everyone gasped. Narhad was the first to speak. "Aye, that's good. Your hair is too short, but if I didn't know you a man, I would never guess."

"Thank you," Getlof said, well pleased. She decided it would be a long time before she would ever again put men's clothing on to deceive.

117

"We are ready, Lord Josh," Renix said. "There is a boat waiting and it still lacks two hours to dawn."

"Good, but from here address me as Lady." She smiled. "It's more realistic."

18

THEOLOGY AROUND THE CAMPFIRE

Dawn unfurled from beyond the limitless horizon. Sunlight touched the plain and wrapped welcome fingers of warmth around the six riders hurrying along the uncertain trails of the undulating chaparral. Brambled ravines, deep and dry, bisected their path. The mellifluously bitter scent of crushed and tramped scrubs surrounded them; mingled with dust and flying insects. The smell saturated their senses with awareness of change.

Getlof was glad to be in motion and gladder still to have her number of companions reduced: she wanted to know them and not be merely an object they were conveying. The morning sky was perfectly blue; she was constantly calling upon Talo, or Golab, or Narhad, or anyone or no one to look at this or at that. Everything appealed.

Getlof's mood was infectious. Before the morning was over it was hard to believe they had fled in uncertainty that very night from a city in riot; even the guardsmen were chattering like friends on an excursion. Only Talo, who rode at the rear, remained silent and wrapped in himself.

Getlof learned that Narhad was reticent, but capable of unexpected and greatly amusing ironies. Sudden mood swings that came and went like the sun on a cloud-dappled day marked Renix. Getlof wondered if it had to do with his demotion after the battle of the Inn. Doy, the youngest of the three, had a ready laugh, but obviously wasn't used to the kind of company chance had given him. Golab would have been perfectly happy except that he was having trouble with his horse. He was learning the hard way that sitting atop a walking horse on a paved highway was to riding at speed along the uneven terrain like stepping over a stone was to climbing the face of a cliff. It puzzled Getlof that every misstep embarrassed him.

That night she lay to sleep under a blaze of starlight. Hilev seemed very close indeed.

Their second day on the plain was much like the first. By the third day spirits were beginning to flag under the huge sameness of the land. That was the day they crossed a narrow track that wandered in a vaguely north-south direction. Doy identified it as the High Road from Moaz to the Xexi foothills. The land had no other landmarks to gauge their progress.

Talo's continued to behave strangely. He had, apparently, abdicated the leadership role Getlof naturally expected him to assume. Each day he rode at the rear, in their dust, without complaint. His enormous fund of entertaining small talk had vanished. Narhad was the other natural leader, but he was always careful to defer to Getlof. At first she found it strange to have such a tall and grim looking man look to her for decisions and even more strange when they were carried out, but she got used to it more quickly than she would have thought possible.

Once on the second day and again on the third Getlof tried to find out what was bothering Talo, but he could deflect questions far better than she could pursue them. She finally decided he was hiding something that distressed him strongly, but she reasoned that as a woman masquerading as a man masquerading as a woman, she had little right to pry too closely into the secrets of others. Talo was still Talo and she was confident he would come around when she needed him.

On the night of the fourth day they camped in a gully below a low hill. Silk tassel and honey sage grew tall around them. Getlof had told herself not to worry about Talo, but his funk had lasted too long: she was having trouble thinking about anything else. She sat, hugging her knees, watching Doy light the fire. He had a talent for woodcraft, the only one beside Talo capable of building a smokeless fire. Golab squatted beside him trying to learn the trick of it. Narhad was cleaning a rabbit. Renix was collecting wood. Talo was in a clearing above the gully feeding the horses. He'd been at it a long time. Except for an intermittent whispered conversation between Doy and Golab, everyone worked in silence. Getlof knew the others were beginning to wonder about Talo and it was doing the group no good; depression was the most infectious of emotions. Doy struck his flint. Renix cracked a branch with his foot. Getlof suddenly stood and said:

"I'm going to see what's taking Talo."

She scrambled up the bank, into the high shrubbery. A whinny led her to the clearing where Talo had the horses hobbled. She saw him before he saw her.

He was sitting on a rock, staring at the ground. Then something happened to Getlof's vision. Talo grew vague and ill-defined. She shook her head and blinked, but her vision didn't clear. The motion caught Talo's eye. He looked up and said: "Getlof?"

The question in his voice made her wonder if he saw her as she saw him. The point of heat on her chest had to be the ring. She hadn't thought of it for almost two weeks. It was a sign, but of what. A dwarf oak grew close by and she put her hand against its trunk. The bark seemed to flow against her touch. That frightened her. She withdrew her hand and took a step forward.

Again Talo said: "Getlof?"

She took another step forward and shook her head. At that Talo smiled wanly. "Not Getlof?" Then, unexpectedly, he began crying. No wails or cries did Talo make. The water just ran freely down from his eyes over the broad paths of his cheeks. He shook his head.

"All right, this can't go on. I can't make myself leave you and I don't want to, but I don't know what else to do."

Getlof made no reply, although she was considering several. This was Talo's secret.

"I must be getting old to find myself in such a situation. I must be."

Getlof made up her mind. It could be only one thing. "You are caught between two promises. You are divided between two loyalties."

The tears were already gone. Talo looked up and a slow smile spread across his face. "Getlof, did I ever underestimate you? I shall confess."

"No," Getlof shook her head. She was surprised to have her guess confirmed so easily. This encouraged further guesses. "I trust you, Talo. That first day I made a decision to trust you and I have trusted you and I will trust you to the end. If Caos holds your pledge, I still trust you and I don't need any explanations or confessions."

Talo's smile remained, but Getlof perceived it was now hiding some other emotion. He shook his head.

"You make it sound so easy. Trust is a frightening thing. Strange things have been happening to me, Getlof." He rubbed his hands across his face, as if trying to wipe away more than the stains of his tears. "I can't just set it aside. I suspected you knew I was in Moaz; there was no help for it. But, you see, I had to leave there a young man; a person not unlike yourself in that he trusted me also. I don't know what it is; such things never bothered me in the past, but they do now. He trusted me and you trust me, I hold both in my hand, but whatever I do, it will be either his death or yours. I can't stand it."

Getlof nodded. It explained so much, but left little for her to say in reply. The best would be that they could go to Moaz and deliver this young man -- she wondered what he was like and felt a slight distress that some one else had proceeded her in what she had come to think of as her unique relationship with Talo -- but before any reply was possible there was a crashing noise behind them.

Narhad emerged from the silk tassel. He stopped when he saw them, eyes darting from face to face. Narhad saw a smile on Talo's face, but it appeared sudden and grim; about Getlof there was an aura of oddity. Something had happened, but he thought better of asking what.

"The stew is ready and the others will be just as glad if you two don't come to claim your share."

Talo stood and rubbed his eyes again. "Well, well, well, we shall come then. This stomach requires too much maintenance to skip even a single meal."

Narhad nodded. Definitely odd.

Darkness enveloped the little company as they sat around the fire dipping stew from Doy's cooking pot. Afterwards Doy built the fire back up. Renix cracked more branches under his foot. One rolled rather than broke and he had to do a wild dance to save himself from falling. He kicked it and cursed it soundly.

To Getlof his anger seemed both real and excessive, but he turned and grinned:

"Blasted piece of termite-eaten mother-rotted wood."

That was offered in a friendly tone and again she was amazed by the way Renix could turn his anger on and off.

"Indeed?" Narhad said. "You really should take some care in your language, at least in the hearing of Josh."

Renix scowled. He and Narhad locked eyes. Then Renix grinned again. "I'm a free follower of Yetit and such language is consecrated to him. Besides, Getlof has heard worse from me and you've said naught before."

"Narhad's right," Golab began, but Getlof cut him off.

"I don't care. They're just words and not worth an argument."

Narhad's face clouded and Getlof saw he wasn't going to leave it. To change the subject she said:

"I've heard of Yetit. Is vulgar language really consecrated to him?"

Renix, Doy and Talo broke up at that. Even Narhad and Golab smiled.

"It is indeed," Renix said, punctuating his affirmative with a loud crack as he successfully split the offending branch. "Yetit likes a man who's blunt. There, Doy, will that do it?"

"It should."

"Good, you see," wiping his hands and sitting with the rest, "he is an honored god in Gildesh, especially among the military. We acknowledge that the Divine Emperor is greater, of course, but Yetit understands our special needs. When a man is off his head drunk, full of spite and fight and talking to burn the ears of a stevedore, he is protected by Yetit. Yetit protects me constantly."

Getlof smiled. When he was in a good mood, Renix was easy to like. "He sounds like a suitable god for you. Narhad, Doy, do you follow him as well?"

Doy nodded and Narhad said: "Aye, but don't think he is just what Renix says. Every god has multiple aspects."

"What does that mean?"

"Well, the masters have to make a living same as anyone and not everyone is suited to be an adept. This is everywhere true. In the case of Yetit, it is like Renix says, but he doesn't mention that Yetit is also the patron of discipline and concentration. Hard is the road and many are the sacrifices one must make to come to his inner mysteries."

"And Narhad would be an adept, but he can't speak of that to us," Renix said. "Gods require worship and he values my worship just as much as Narhad's for all his discipline and concentration."

Narhad laughed. "I don't deny it, Renix."

"And you, Talo? You're of the military classes. Do you follow Yetit as well?"

"No," he said slowly. "We have other gods in Tain, but, if I may say this without offending anyone, I have seen much, but I've never seen anything in Ossa that would incline me to believe in anyone's gods."

Golab seemed shocked. "No gods at all?"

Talo smiled. It was his careless, mischievous, slightly evil smile that told Getlof things were okay. "Well, if you insist on pushing me into a corner, I'll say I think the cults of the disembodied emperors'--to which you all give empty homage--make more sense to me than any other. At least, you know they exist; but I still think they're only men, not gods."

"That's hardly what I expected, Talo the Taelin, especially after what I've heard about the Troubled Times."

"Why, Golab? Because I fought for the alliance of all the gods against the disembodied emperor? That was business. I never said I thought they were right."

"Golab shook his head. "You're a strange man."

"You haven't told us about your gods, Golab," Getlof said. "What do you believe?"

"That's not hard to answer. First and foremost I believe in the paramount god of the Gildi: His Disembodied Majesty, Ducitos XI. The other gods, the ones I know and the ones I've never heard of, exist no doubt. Obviously I know most of Pauic whom I've studied and I believe in Him, but for the daily ordering of our lives, we must acknowledge that power and rule reside in the vessel of a lord. To deny the authority of that vessel is clearly heresy."

There was a moment of silence following Golab's statement. Then, surprisingly, Doy said: "May I ask the same question of you, Getlof? I mean, as long as we're taking about that kind of thing. The men were saying things after that night the inn burned and well, I was just wondering."

Getlof shook her head, suddenly reticent. "I was as surprised as anyone." She recalled how strange she had felt that evening, but she didn't think that had anything to do with it, so she didn't want the others to think so either.

"Well, then" Renix said, "tell us about your gods."

Carefully Getlof replied: "Talo has said he has never seen anything in Ossa to make him believe. I won't presume to say I've seen more because I haven't. Perhaps what I'm trying to say is that I think perception has much to do with it. The same thing can be different for different people. Renix, you and Narhad make Yetit sound like two completely different gods with the same name. Or, our journey on the lake, take that as an example. Talo enjoyed the roll of the deck, but me it made sick. Pleasure and pain; belief and disbelief, you see what I'm saying? They seem to arise from the same thing."

Narhad smiled. "All true, although it surprises to hear one so young saying such words. I am impressed also with the way you avoid the original question."

"Did I? No, I answered. I believe in them all, Narhad. All of them or nothing. Talo and I are the same, except where he says nothing, I say all."

"Does that include, then, the disembodied emperors?" Talo asked.

Getlof glanced over at him and smiled. "If I may say this without offending anyone. . . . But, no, Talo. You are wicked. You know I wanted to avoid that question."

"Have no fear of offending, Josh," Narhad said with formality. No one will insist on the divinity of Ducitos."

"All right. The gods are gods and men are men. Maybe some aspects are shared, but the essences are quite different. Ducitos is a man."

"A boy," Narhad corrected.

Golab looked shocked and thoughtful.

Later that night Golab drew Getlof aside and resumed the conversation privately.

"I notice that most of us are acting out the the beliefs professed tonight. Renix and Doy are shaking the dice cup, doubtlessly in honor of Yetit. Narhad is off doing his exercises. Talo is sleeping and you and I are still talking."

Golab stressed Talo's name and this caused Getlof to ask: "What about Talo, are you trying to say something about him?"

"No, I wasn't, but if you bring it up, I can. He's a strange man playing a strange role in this journey of yours. Repeatedly he makes the point that he'll go anywhere, do anything, if its business. Right, wrong, and his own feelings all stand aside for business." Golab took a breath. "All right, so what's the business that concerns him in this? If not you than nothing. And what is his business? Mercenary soldiering and organizing. I don't see the connection."

Getlof nodded and watched Golab not watching her. "I know. I think sometimes he talks so people won't know him well. Maybe he's a little too fond of the stories about him. All I can say is I trust him."

Golab appeard to examine the sky. "In Gildesh I rarely went out at night. I never realized how many stars there are, and how bright. They're there every night."

Getlof laughed. "Except when it's cloudy. Are you changing the subject?"

Golab gesticulated in the dark. "Well, actually I wanted to talk about you, not Talo."

"Indeed?" Getlof said. She sensed his discomfort and for some reason it made her playful.

"Yes, it's about this disguise of yours. We're almost pass Moaz, there's no one here to see you; do you think it's still necessary?"

"Why? Don't you like it?"

He shook his head. Another gesture lost in the dark. "No, I don't. I get uncomfortable always looking at you dressed as a woman. People are going to forget you aren't one. Besides, it doesn't seem right to pretend to something you aren't."

Getlof yawned. She was suddenly very tired. "I still say it's just a question of perception, Golab." Then she giggled, very much as a young girl would, thereby increasing his discomfort. "I'm going to sleep now. You can stay up all night if you want."

During the next day the landscape finally began to change. The horizon opened before them as if the world had suddenly tilted in the direction they were heading, hurrying them along. The gullies began to contain running water; scrub and chaparral were yielding to trees. At first they passed yellow-green stands of pine standing stranded on the plain, but Doy told about Fakanahafaf and the Hafaf: the Great Lake and dense forest surrounding it on almost every shore. If they veered but a little toward their left they would enter that land of trees neverending and would quickly long for the open plain. Talo had changed too. He was riding in the front again and was more like the man Getlof remembered, but there were times when she wondered if it wasn't an act. She hoped he would volunteer what Narhad had kept him from saying the night before. She also wondered if there wasn't some way they could rescue the young man he had spoken of.

That evening Talo pronounced the greatest danger to be past. Unless he was in error, or his map, or both, the next day should bring them to the margins of the Fens of Laso, the swamp surrounding the lake of the same name. These marked the eastern border of Moaz. Once past, there would be nothing to worry about. Except Nomads.

The next day proved Talo and the map both to be right. Late that morning they climbed a low range of eroded, piny hills. When they came to the crest they could see the valley of the Laso on the farther side.

Talo broke the silence. "And to think, we came all this way without seeing a soul."

Renix stood in his stirrups. "You speak too soon." He pointed to the left. Further down the ridgeline a solitary mounted man was observing them.

Getlof shaded her eyes. He's dressed in yellow and his lance has a red pennant."

"You can see so far?" Talo said. "Well, doubtlessly a scout and probably Moazian. Nomads wouldn't dress their lances up with flags, or wear yellow, for that matter, but I could be wrong. Whoever he serves, he must have seen us ascending this ridge."

The scout turned and galloped away toward the Laso. They watched the dust of his going hang in the air.

"And now," Renix said, "do we return the way we came or is it south?"

"I don't doubt more are coming," Talo said, "and I don't care for the idea of a chase back across the plains. Our horses are worn from poor grazing and I, for one, am not a horseman capable of such hard riding. South is the Hafaf. I know of no trails through that wood."

"There are trails," Doy said, "but I fear the people who use them. They are rude and barbaric and practice strange magic on strangers. I don't want to ride into the Hafaf."

Renix snorted. "You call yourself a guardsman."

Narhad remained silent with his eyes turned inward. Concentration and discipline, Getlof thought. She said: "Why not go on? We must be ahead of any news from Zoha so they've no reason to consider us unfriendly, but if we ran they wouldn't have to be told."

"Sure," Renix said, "and what happens when they look at us? A Pau and a bunch of Gildi?"

"That wouldn't necessarily make a difference," Golab said. "It's been a generation since any Pau were seen in Moaz and as for us, do the Gildi look that much different than Moazians? Doy speaks it and so do I. There are a few signs we would have to divest ourselves of, but," he shrugged his shoulders, "it could be done."

127

Talo rubbed his chin and listened to the arguments. He had not forgotten the sign of authority Caos had given him. Talo was reluctant to use it, knowing its very possession would alarm his Gildi companions, but it still gave them more choices than the others were aware of. It made him support Golab's suggestion rather than what he otherwise would have considered to be the better idea of hazarding the Hafaf.

"I say we go down boldly and confront them, as Getlof and Golab suggest. That seems the better choice."

"Do you," Narhad said, his voice edged. "I guess you have reason beyond those given."

'Here goes,' Talo thought. He took the medallion from his pocket and held it up, Caos' golden image reflecting in the sun.

"Yes, I see it. Is it what I think it is?"

"I don't know what you think, but that is an image of Caos and I was in Moaz and he did give it to me. He said, as I recall, that it would give me authority over his servants. I wouldn't have brought it out, except for this. With it, however, going forward is clearly a better option than the Hafaf."

Narhad's face was a mask. "A sign of authority from Caos, which means you had a commission. What is was--or is--I can guess. Does Getlof know?"

Getlof had been watching with growing fear. Given her opportunity, she quickly intervened.

"I know, Narhad and you remember how and when. There is no time to fight it out. Talo, are you saying that with that big coin you can order and they'll obey?"

"I haven't put it to the test, but, yes, I think so."

"The test!" Narhad said. "The test is here and now. One question, Talo the Taelien: Do you, or did you ever, intend betrayal?"

Talo looked at Narhad and slowly smiled. He suddenly felt better than any time since the dock in Gildesh. He needed danger and life had been far too uneventful since then. Maybe that had been the problem. "Does my answer matter, Narhad? I say no, but you believe what you will."

High and shrill: "I believe Talo. Who gainsays my trust?" Getlof regained control of herself as soon as the words were gone and looked around slowly at each of them. She expected arguments, but, amazingly, none came.

"Josh has decided," Narhad said at last. "We will do it then as Talo suggests."

19

THE WELL-WATCHED FENS

The guardsmen stripped themselves of their Gildi insignia and started down the ridge. Before long, they spied dust clouds that marked approaching riders. At the same time, the riders spotted them; two flanking detachments split off to prevent retreat. As the strangers neared, it could be seen they were dressed in leather armor cured to yellow brown. Lances and helmets bore the device of a lake serpent in coral. That signified Moaz. The Moazians halted when they reached hailing distance.

"Ho outlanders, ride forward with the authority that gives you leave to pass from the domains of Moaz."

Talo rode forward. "Leave we have, soldiers of the Magnus." He paused briefly then plunged into the story they had agreed upon. "Know that I am Olat, a freeholder from the eastern marches of the Xexi. With my children and surviving liegemen, I flee across the dusty plain, harried by the foe that burned me out of my stead for the love I bear your lord."

The Moazian said: "Words I hear. Have you a sign to verify them?"

"I have." Talo held forth the medallion so that it reflected the light, sending a bright flash into the Moazian's face. He squinted and rode forward for a better look. In the next instance he was off his horse and bowing low to Talo. "Lord Olat, forgive my rudeness and presumption. Your sign is indeed known to us."

Talo leaned back benevolently in his saddle. "I expected it would be. Know, good soldier, that we ride east to Sitnoe on the Great Lake's shore, wherein flows the River Ti from the Roganspire down. There resides my brother. Do you bar our passage?"

"Lord, I may not." He was standing beside his horse, holding its reins. The other soldiers were still mounted, but they had halted at about three dozen paces distance. The spokesman looked back at his fellows and then up again at Talo. "However, please know that my captain, the esteemed Sunol has been informed of your coming and he has sent me with orders to bring you before him. I must do so and trust your journey will not suffer from a slight delay."

Talo nodded. He had expected something of the sort. "I look forward with pleasure to meeting your captain, the esteemed Sunol. Lead and we shall follow."

Talo dropped back to ride beside Getlof. "They were impressed. This should go all right." Narhad overheard.

"I hope so. These men strike me as true soldiers under discipline. I doubt we could safely take them."

"Don't even think of it," Talo said.

Narhad glanced over, eyes veiled. "I think of what I must."

They descended into the valley of the Laso. It seemed to Getlof that the air grew warmer and closer. The sharp smells of the upper plain were being replaced by their opposites: fetid and unpleasant. `Another change,' she thought and wondered if it would be marked by a threshold like it seemed all the others had been.

The post was a wooden stockade set on a hillock. The path leading up wound through the beginning of the marsh. Intensely green vegetable matter coated the still ponds of water that lay on every side. Tall plants that looked like grass, except they were much larger, grew out of the ponds. They were tipped with thick cylindrical brown growths. Doy saw Getlof staring and said: "Cattails. Haven't you ever seen them?" Getlof shook her head. "Ah," Doy reached out and broke one off. "See," they pull apart. You can make a flour out of this if hunger presses."

When they entered the stockade Getlof was interested to see it was different than the Gildi fort on the Last Lake, her only comparison. It was smaller and perhaps because there was less to maintain, it was much cleaner. She couldn't imagine its commander being absent, or a market in its center square.

They dismounted and men came to take care of their horses. The Moazian who was acting as spokesman clapped his hands and ordered one of the servants to see they were refreshed and accorded every honor. By the way he said it, Getlof could tell he meant it. Then he turned to Talo and said that the esteemed Sunol waited. Talo waved goodbye to the others with a grin that said not to worry. Narhad watched him with crossed arms. His only consolation was that they had been allowed to retain their weapons. He would stay close to Getlof and if treachery occurred (it was truly out of his hands) he would guarantee a contested outcome. He had a fleeting moment of gladness that Talo had not seen him fight and thus didn't know what his discipline and concentration made him capable of.

Talo's first moment of doubt came when he saw Sunol. This man stood stiffly in a sparsely furnished office. His face was without a trace of plasticity, molded in a permanent expression of doubt. His eyes were green and contained all the expression he made his face do without. Talo, an excellent judge of character judged this man to be as hard as they came.

Briefly he asked for Talo's story and listened to the tale of Olat and his brother in Sitnoe without comment. Then Talo showed him the medallion and was gratified to see a spasm of expression flicker over Sunol's face.

"Ah ha, the greater sign of authority. Truly, Olat, you must be a man high in Caos' confidence. That explains why you so boldly rode in with such an unlikely story, however, it makes the behavior and hesitation of your party even more perplexing."

"How is that?" Talo said with a confidence he hoped masked the sickening feeling that was creeping into the pit of his stomach.

"I've had you under observation for some time; obviously for longer than you realized. One of my men returned with these." He produced three red plumes that had lately been affixed to the tops of Narhad's, Renix's and Doy's helmets.

"The sign of authority protects you from whatever I may think, but in these times of trouble, I expect your place is not with your brother. It is with your lord. I will arrange transportation with a suitable escort to see you arrive safely in Moaz. There you can explain your actions and plans to one better able than I to judge." He nodded his head abruptly. "That is all."

When Talo entered the room where the others were resting he was greeted by a variety of expressions. He stood there for a moment and watched them become uniformly sober. He said:

"I'm sorry, Getlof, but it looks like you're in for another boat ride." He then told what had happened. Narhad groaned when he heard about the plumes. Silence followed until Getlof said:

"It looks like Moaz after all." For some reason, the words sounded right to her. It wasn't a thing she could explain to herself so she didn't try to explain it to the others. All she knew was that she wasn't frightened like she should be. "One thing: I want to be sure about is that we all trust one another."

Narhad looked up. "Are you asking me about Talo? You've made the decision, Getlof. I'm a soldier. I'll follow."

Talo shrugged his shoulders. "You overwhelm me, Narhad."

Sunol entertained them that night and afterwards Narhad apologized to Talo; seeing Sunol made the miscarriage of their plan easier to understand.

The boats were ready on the morning of the next day. As they were loading up they had a surprise. One of the boatmen kept staring at Doy; after a time he came forward and asked him if he was Doy of Nikelden. Doy, with considerable surprise, replied that he was. The boatman gave a cry and embraced him. It made sense after he identified himself as Darno of Nikelden. They were cousins, separated since the day, ten years before, when slavers had descended upon their village.

The fact that one of their party was known made a big difference to the Moazians. But their sudden friendliness didn't affect the size of the escort Sunol assigned. Shortly after the reunion, they were on the lake. Getlof was preoccupied and even forgot she was suppose to be seasick until Talo hailed her from the other boat and asked how she was feeling. Even then it didn't hit her.

20

A YOUNG MAN AT LOOSE ENDS

The hostages were accorded limited freedom during the march south and east from Moaz. Taxis' comrades consisted for the most part of Moazians--sons and a few daughters of the free lords of the city--and mostly children; people whose loyalty the Magnus doubted. Of foreigners there were few: a scattered ambassador from Shon, Fanakalahph and a nomad or two. Taxis wasn't surprised. It was apparent why the independent states shunned relations with Moaz.

His last sight of Talo had been a month ago, at the door of the high tower room when that fusty old man had denied him entrance. Taxis hadn't liked that, but then, it hadn't surprised him either. He had always been a junior man: to have stood by Talo's side for the past few months had been for him an honor rare and a pleasure great. Talo was his ideal of the perfect man; the man who knows success and treats it like an adoring little sister: always at hand, teasingly and lovingly.

The guards had marched him away and below to an office in the same tower. In a little, windowless room furnished with only a table and two chairs he had waited, it seemed for several hours. The chairs were hard and the room was cold. When finally the door behind him opened, he jumped up, but the man who entered was not Talo; he was tall, and gaunt, dressed in a brown robe with raised hood. The man walked past Taxis and sat in the chair on the other side of the table.

"Sit. Your name is Taxis, originally of Istel, I understand, but with no loyalty other than to your captain, Talo the Taelien. I am correct."

"You are correct, and have the advantage over me regards names."

"I do indeed. I have every advantage over you and the more quickly you realize this, the longer you may expect to survive."

Taxis felt his face flush, but wisely refrained from comment.

"Just so. You are here for two reasons: first to give information and second to learn a lesson. So, let us discuss your master. Why is he in Moaz?"

"Sir, I believe he has said it plain to the fanbearer, the man who has been our guide in this city."

"You believe. I see. I assume, then, that your master does not share with you his total confidence."

"I think he does. Talo is a great man, sir and sometimes, maybe I don't know all his thoughts, but he has always been honest with me. Never have I seen him come out behind in a situation. I trust him and that is good enough for me."

"That is the proper attitude in an underling. Even after the loss of his ship and crew, all men who trusted, I assume, your feelings are no different."

"That was not good, sir, I admit. But that story isn't closed. My master always said nobody is an enemy unless good money paid makes him so. But, I think--he hasn't really said, understand--that for the first time he has taken on an enemy of his own choosing."

"And that enemy would be?"

"Sir, its no secret. That enemy is Bar-Lev."

"Is that not a conflict--Bar-Lev is the friend of our Magnus. Would not the enemy of one be the enemy of the other."

"Maybe, maybe not. I don't know. I don't know the friends of the Magnus or the relations he has. How could I? Bar-Lev is an enemy to me; of that there is no doubt. But coming here was necessary for some plan of Talo's that has to do with the Pau. I'm not sure how it relates to Bar-Lev. Perhaps he hopes to find allies."

"Perhaps he does. Strong allies and strong enemies make a strong man. The talents of your master have gone without question, but that is only reputation."

Taxis didn't feel he could say much to that and so remained silent. He had his own questions, but it was so much easier to trust Talo than to doubt him. He wasn't to be shaken just by a series of questions, no matter how hard.

"Very good. We shall proceed to the lesson. After that my questions may strike you in a different light. Come with me."

Taxis was led back to the spiral stairway and down for several hundred paces. The hooded man seemed to disdain the need for guards. They entered a dark, spacious chamber lit only by a brazier on the further wall. Taxis involuntarily put his hand over his nose, it smelt that bad within. It smelt of fear, of excrement, of burnt flesh. Taxis gripped himself. He was in a question chamber of a different kind than the one he had just departed. Then, as his eyes adjusted, he saw a chained man hanging from the ceiling. The hooded man stood back with folded arms. Two other men stood on each side of the hanging man.

"Approach him. Tell me who he is."

Taxis' first fear, that he was looking at Talo, was almost immediately put to rest by the fact that this man's torso was long and lanky. His face was hard to make out in the flickering, reddish light. Then he saw the wispy, blond chin beard--one of the only features still intact. It was Baken-Lie. Taxis whispered his name.

"Just so. A man trusted of the Magnus who didn't repay his trust. Give the foreigner a knife."

Taxis felt the cool hilt of a long knife placed in his hand. He gripped it from instinct.

"A man you considered your friend, I believe. Well, now you have the opportunity to return his friendship. Can you do it?"

There was no doubt what the hooded man meant. Baken-Lie was still alive, his breath audible as a choked, bubbly sound. Taxis fought the need to faint. He staggered one step forward. Then the ability came in a rush: here was a wounded comrade on the field of battle. A comrade wounded unto death. He drew the knife across the remnants of the torturtered man's throat before he was ware of what he was doing. After that, he remembered little else.

Taxis never learned exactly who the hooded man was, but neither did he make a serious attempt to find out. He returned to the custody of Daken, the lower captain and spent his time in a loosely guarded chamber--one with cold water only, and that from a bucket--waiting Talo's return. He was advised this wait would be considerable. Talo had been sent forth from Moaz on a special commission, back to the southern coast to fetch some person important to the Magnus. Taxis had no trouble guessing that was the Pau. In the meantime they assigned him a female servant, one several years his elder and not shy about men. She couldn't speak Southcoast so Taxis rapidly developed a proficiency in Moazian. He rationalized it would make him more useful to Talo.

Daken himself brought Taxis the news that he would be accompanying the Magnus in his march south, to open the war against the Gildi. The news came at a good time because the servant was starting to think herself the master and

Taxis was becoming very bored. He had served with the free companies seven years since he was fifteen and never since had he sat around doing nothing for such a long time.

"You grin as if you welcome the news."

"I do. Getting so I can hardly stand it here any longer."

"Well, I see your point. Wouldn't mind some action myself before I get too old for it. But three captains will be staying to keep the city secure and I'll be one."

"Liego told me about a riot or something the other day in the old city."

"Hardly a riot. Your master didn't school you very well in caution. Let me give some advice: take care in what you hear and take greater care who you repeat it to."

Marching in the midst of the Magnus' army, Taxis couldn't help but form impressions. He observed three major elements: One fifth archers, solid looking troops well equipped and disciplined. A third light horse, men of nomad extraction or vassals from subject tribes; troops Taxis had always held in low regard. Infantry, armed with sword, spear and sling formed nearly half. Some companies looked good, others seemed little more than rabble. The entire army counted perhaps twelve thousand men. Taxis was no general, although he had his ambitions, but never would he have thrown such a force against the Gildi. Of course, Bar-Lev was the extra factor. Such an ally made all the difference.

There was also the growing question of Talo. When everyone is neglecting and ignoring a person, his outlook bends sensitive. For the first time in his seven years with Talo, Taxis had begun to wonder. The questions asked by the mysterious man in the upper tower returned to nag his mind. Had Talo deserted the crew; had he deserted Taxis? What was his game, really, and did it involve anyone else? Only Talo could answer and Talo didn't come. Taxis began to wonder if that was his answer.

The army arrived before Zoha and with pick and spade, with bravo and sweating labor (from which Taxis thankfully found himself exempt) commenced its investiture of the city's landward side. The siege seemed it would be a short affair, if the mood of the army could accurately measure such things. The first assault was launched on just the second day, enthusiasm being deemed, apparently, preferable to preparation. On the third day, following a bloody repulse, Taxis was, at long last, summoned into the presence of Caos. This unexpected call enabled him to witness a significant moment.

The campaign audience hall of Caos consisted of a large tent supported by two columns of tapered poles--stripped pine trees of some maturity. Members of Caos' personal guard surrounded it. Taxis had some short dealings with this group and couldn't say they had impressed him, despite their burnished cuirasses inlaid with the lake serpent and their gold tipped spears. There was a current underflowing their collective demeanor that struck Taxis as dangerous, and not in any fighting sense. At the far end of the cavernous tent a conference was underway; Caos and his captains were gathered around a long table. A guard conducted Taxis to this table. He cleared his throat and said:

"Great lord, the man you summoned, Taxis of Istel, undercaptain of the Taelien."

Taxis stiffen his posture to better withstand to the scrutiny of the great ones of Moaz. The coldest gaze of all belonged to a man who could be no one other than Caos. He was younger than Taxis had expected, easily the most handsome man present, but with beauty marred by a feral shine in his eyes. Had Taxis encountered such a gaze in the streets at night, he would have gone to his sword without a word. His stomach clenched and sweat began to trickle down his face.

"Rowenna, you may question him."

A man standing close to the left of Caos bowed. Taxis wrenched his gaze away from Caos, suddenly realizing his stare had been both rude and dangerous. The man called upon to interrogate presented a contrast. He was dark of skin and eye; clearly a man from Tarhad and just as clearly a man of gentle birth. He projected an air of sympathy and understanding that was a welcome to see.

"The Taelien concerns us now. The manifest lord of Moaz has intelligence that even now your master resides in Zoha and does direct the defense of that town. What say you to this?"

"Taxis swallowed. He had an intuition that his answer would be the most important words ever he had spoken in his short life.

"Lords, your Manifest Holiness, I cannot answer if he is or if he isn't. I can only say that Zoha is a city of the Gildi and my master has no dealings with those people. Their memory is long and heavy is their ill will against him. Even I, an undercaptain who did not fight in their Troubled Times, would be forfeit of my life in that land simply because of my associations with master Talo. Even to reach the shining city of the holy lord of Moaz we did travel months out of the direct route rather than risk the unlikely chance of risking Gildesh and being recognized."

137

"Need has its way of enforcing forgiveness."

"It does and well do I know it. I know little of the Gildi, but never did I hear they were a folk to admit to need."

Suddenly Rowenna laughed. "Well, my Manifest Lord, he does make a point. The Lord of the Uncounted Herds does not ignore veracities and as his mouth, I must recognize the arguments of your hostage. They strike me as greater truth than reports of Gildi guards being led to battle by the Taelien. As for the other one," he shrugged his shoulders, "He of the uncounted herds does not see how that merits concern."

Caos did not glance at Rowenna. His gaze remained on Taxis. "It is a concern of the lands of the west and of the north of Ossa of which Moaz is the center; your master's failure to think of the Pau does not surprise."

A quiet descend then. Rowenna didn't appear to Taxis to be the type to face down a king in his own hall, even a makeshift hall, but apparently that was what he was witnessing.

"However that may be, the Taelien is a concern. I will tell you now of my great lord's desire. That this man be given to me for He would question him directly."

Caos' features flowed and he became suddenly magnanimous and gracious, as if he had no ability to be any other way. "Certainly, I give him to you. Let your master question in whatever matter he deems fit, remembering that I will require his return at the end of that time, but tell him this: when I sit in the citadel of Zoha, then will we assess the summer's work and determine what things shall be our concern."

Rowenna bowed, not speaking a word. He turned and strode from the tent, catching Taxis' eye in a private glance as he passed. It seemed to Taxis he smiled. Then Taxis discovered he had two dark Tarhadians, at his side. They assisted him in following Rowenna out of the tent.

There were more men waiting with horses close by the tent. Everyone mounted and Taxis perceived he was in the midst of a sizable escort, several dozens of light horse with a core of Tarhadian gentility. They proceeded slowly from the precincts of the Moazian camp and once in the open Rowenna called out:

"Let the Istelian ride by me."

Taxis was brought forth from the center of the escort. Rowenna greeted him fairly; his face appeared open and full of mirth.

"So, from the hands of the mad Magnus to the evil one of countless herds. I imagine this is a little more than you expected when you followed your master north. Well, you are young and you seem to know when to keep your mouth shut and when to open it. And, even better, how to speak with some effect. You've seen more lands than most and more events and more of the famous people of our time at closer quarters than a man of your age and station can expect. Have you ever considered you're lucky? These are times such as seldom come; the whole world is changing and you are in the center. I wonder what you are going to do with all these advantages?"

At first Taxis thought he was being ridiculed. He heard Rowenna out, staring straight ahead toward the line of the river, then glanced over and saw himself reflected in thoughtful brown eyes. The man was serious.

"I, I have never considered it in the way you say it. It has never seemed I have had say over this or over that to make or take any advantages from my circumstances."

"There is where you must change your thinking. Just now I saw you maneuver with fair and considered words and as a result you are with me and no longer with Caos. There is an advantage. Believe me, it is a great advantage as you shall see before the next day is past."

The west bank of the Ossa was held in force by Levites. Taxis recognized members of several tribes: Xumi, Sumi, and others. A long bridge of boats had been constructed, anchored at points in the wide, steady flow of the Ossa by trees driven into the bed at what cost in labor Taxis couldn't guess. Temporary camps were scattered along the eastern bank. It appeared to Taxis that Bar-Lev would shortly be making a major move across the Ossa.

They rode four hours before and arrived at the main camp in the early evening amid the fragrant haze of cooking fires. There had been movement all along the road from the river to the main camp and Taxis had long since given up trying to estimate the men Bar-Lev had under arms.

"I must report directly. You'd better come as well. My master has heard of you and I suspect he'll have some questions. He doesn't like his news second hand."

They rode at a walk another half-hour to reach the center of the camp and the tent of Bar-Lev. Unlike the field abode of Caos, it was a simple structure seeming little larger than the thousands surrounding it. There was no evidence of direct security, none of the formality or pomposity of Caos' headquarters. Their escort had dropped away and Taxis was alone with Rowenna. Rowenna jumped from his horse and caught the eye of an old man sitting on a three legged stool outside the yellow tent. The old man nodded. Rowenna ducked under the flap and Taxis followed.

The tent was larger than it seemed. There was another, black tent pitched inside the yellow one. They entered this. A man was sitting against the far side, a scribe sat on the floor before him. Two boat shaped, Tarhadian oil lamps illuminated the space with a steady light. The sitting man held up his hand. The scribe stood, bowed and exited out the back.

"Prince Rowenna. You wait till the very last moment. How fare the western barbarians?"

"There is no fresh news from the west, Great Lord. It goes as expected. However, I paused to pluck for you one final fruit from the tree of their innocence lest it be trampled and bruised in the violence of your outstretched hand."

"Indeed. And I may assume the man standing behind you is the fruit of which you speak?"

"Great Lord, you know me well. He is no other."

This banter confused Taxis. There could be no doubt that the man he was seeing was the infamous Bar-Lev, the great one of the uncounted herds. Certain notions had developed in his mind about this man during the months in Sidoc and after. Those notions had nothing to do with the man reclining like a leopard before him. Bar-Lev was a powerful man with a large head set on a bull neck. His arms were like the thighs of a horse, his chest like the kettle drums of Tarhad. There was amusement in his features, in the curl of his thick lips, the flash of his black eyes. His forehead was broad and unfurrowed; his hair was braided and clean. An aura surrounded the man: an aura of power and force. It beat against Taxis like the heat of the desert sun and without thinking he found himself on his knees.

"Great Lord."

"Stand and tell me who you are and what you can do for me."

"Great Lord, I am Taxis of Istel, third undercaptain of Talo the Taelien. I have come with my master to these lands on an errand of his devise and have been detained by the Magnus of Moaz whilst he fetches one whom the Magnus has great desire to hold. I have heard that he has been waylaid or that he has betrayed this commission, I am not sure which, and I am alone in this world.

You are the third great man I have been before this year. I can answer questions for you certainly, in accordance with my knowledge, but the rest depends upon the task to which I am set."

Bar-Lev laughed. "Your speech is becoming practiced. Rarely have the servants of my enemies displayed such fluency when they are first brought to me." He stood and held out a pair of massive hands, thick and callused. "I keep no headsman nor torturers; these are the tools of my displeasure and I do not set others to tasks I can do better myself. Your neck would be like a rotten branch before my grasp. What do you say?"

"Ever has it been, but I am alive before you. I . . . I serve my master, but I am uncertain of his thoughts and think maybe I have been deserted. He holds you no love, you burned his daughter and killed his friends. But I, I would have as my enemy the Magnus and those of his city. They are your allies. I do not know. My neck is before you."

Bar-Lev laughed again. "That has always been so, even if you didn't know it. The Moazians are great plotters. Their allies are their enemies more surely than their foes. But most of all they are their own worst enemies. A bent people. I cannot fault you, who has lived among them, for finding them hateful. This very night two tenths of my hoard are crossing the Ossa. Tomorrow, Moaz shall be without an army and a king. You are fortunate to learn this here and now and not there and then. Fortunate indeed. For fortunate men I always have tasks. And your task shall be to reside with me until I have learned all you know about the Taelien.

So it was that Taxis came to know Bar-Lev and to come under his spell. Strange it would have been any other way.

141

21

MOAZ

The Laso's current wasn't strong, but it rushed the two boats relentlessly onward. All too quickly the torpid air of the fens lightened, the river broadened and the banks fell away.

Getlof was in the boat with Narhad and Golab. With them were one boatman and two soldiers. When the two craft rode closely together, she could hear Doy chattering wit his cousin, apparently content. Renix stared belligerently at the passing scenery. She worried about him. Talo entertained the leader of the guard who was in his boat with two other soldiers. From what she could catch, it sounded like Talo was serving the best of his tales between generous doses of flattery.

In her own boat Narhad sat in the bow. No one had required them to surrender their weapons. He sat with his whetstone on his knee, sharpening his array of knifes. One of the Moazians watched him and after a time asked Narhad about one of his blades, a particularly fine and unusual weapon. Narhad proceeded to do, in his own way, what Talo was doing with the leader in the other boat. Golab stared at the scenery, like Renix; but unlike Renix, he looked frightened. Getlof knew he was thinking the worse and there was nothing she could do to reassure him.

Getlof was at a disadvantage because she had to keep her face covered and, as if she were Olat's daughter, remain silent and as secluded as a woman sharing a crowded river punt with five men would. The situation allowed ample opportunity for reflection. Something was definitely drawing her toward Moaz. Crane, heron, osprey and duck: Moaz they chanted in the beating of their wings. Moaz said the frogs and the sawrucks. She still didn't know the name of the man Talo had left there and that bothered her more than anything else. It made her objective hazy and out of focus.

That night they anchored in the lake. It was cold and damp; Getlof couldn't sleep. She sat bunched up, arms wrapped around legs, chin resting on knees rocking in the gentle motion of the boat. There were no lights on shore, nothing to hear save the slap of the wavelets against the hull. She felt silent and alone.

The night seemed three nights old when she felt a pressure against her shoulder and heard Narhad's whisper softly in her inner ear.

"Getlof," he breathed, "if you will I can take the men in this boat."

Getlof reached out and touched Narhad's arm. Her sense of the inevitable was disturbed by this offer. From far off, the roar of a hunting cat floated over the lake.

"Getlof?"

She walked her hand up his arm, felt for his ear and drew it down to her lips.

"But the other boat, Narhad. They'd be alarmed."

"I know, but don't underestimate Renix and Doy; and even so, you'll be safe and that's the important thing."

For a moment, Narhad's offer was tempting, but then Getlof shook her head.

Narhad sighed. "As you will." He remained beside Getlof and she was grateful for the warmth of his body.

Dawn finally came to attack the night mist with a sky of muted and somber tones of red. The lake surface glittered like a burnished shield. Getlof gratefully felt the sun touch her. The lake fog burned away and through it Moaz appeared like a dream fading away.

Doy's cheerful voice sang out across the water. "Ho, alive or frozen."

"Frozen," one of the Moazians from Getlof's boat replied.

"Aye," Renix said. "Excellency," addressing the leader on his own boat, but in a voice all could hear, "now is no time to be stingy with the wine bags. Bring them out or surely I won't be able to walk when we reach land."

"If I could, I would, but the esteemed Sunol allows no provisions of that kind."

"Ha!" Renix said, "don't strike me down when I say fie on the esteemed Sunol. Stingy man!"

Then Talo's voice. "What say good captain? A brief stop at a dockside tavern will do no harm if it gets our blood to flowing."

The boatmen brought the two craft together. Getlof could hear the indecision in the leader's answer.

"Ah, nothing sounds better, but we mustn't. Sunol said to deliver you to the harbormaster and tell him you are to be taken to the citadel and judged. Let me apologize for his suspicious nature. He's been right once or twice in foreseeing danger and that makes him think he is always right. What can I do?"

Narhad caught Getlof's eye, the inquiry of the night before on his face. Again she shook her head.

They rounded citadel promontory. Caos' fort was a strong looking place, impressive for its towers rising high over the lake. Getlof had seen the Place of Ajum, but she was still impressed. They continued south along the bay to the harbormaster's station on the quays built out from the new city.

When they docked, the harbormaster was nowhere to be found. A subordinate explained that he was up at the citadel and hinted darkly there were rumors of trouble. "Everyone with interests to protect can be found in the citadel these days protecting them."

Well then," the leader said, rubbing his hands, "there's nothing to do but have your drink, Renix. After all, I was ordered to personally hand you over to the harbor master and no one else."

Finding the nearest tavern was a matter of crossing the quay. There the leader showed his true inclinations by throwing himself into his cups with a passion obviously long repressed. Narhad taught them a Gildi drinking game and Renix cheerfully won it three times running. Doy brought out his dice and soon the Moazians were in the midst of a merry time.

Getlof found the interior of the tavern smoky and hot, almost unbearable in contrast to the clear airs over the lake. At last, she truly felt trapped, but she knew she had to let the drinking proceed. Talo was back in command. He would know what to do next.

Talo was huddled with the Moazian officer shaking dice. The officer won the round and gave a shout of triumph. Talo said:

"Congratulations, excellency, you play well. May I say a word before we go another round?"

"Of course, but please, stop calling me excellency." He laughed. "I'm getting to like it."

Talo smiled. "I look to my daughter and see she is not enjoying this sport. (I would be worried if she did.) It would be a kindness, don't you think, to take her someplace where she could rest. I imagine she slept no better than any of us last night."

The leader looked at Getlof with red eyes. "She should let her hood down, get some air."

Talo leaned closer and whispered" "A slight defect under her left eye. She's very shy about it."

The leader nodded knowingly. "Ah, I was wondering why she's been so careful about her face. Well, what place did you have in mind?"

"It's my friend, lord Daken who holds the position of captain of the lower guard in the citadel."

"He's a friend of yours?"

"Indeed. Uncle Daken to my daughter."

"Didn't you explain to Sunol that you had such friends?"

"Of course. I think you've already said all that needs to be said about Sunol's personality. And I hardly need to point out that Sunol is far away and Daken is very close. I'm sure he would regard this as a great courtesy. When I tell him how understanding you've been I imagine he'll want you up to his house tonight. We can drink to Sunol's health; Daken's wines are to the stuff here what they are to swamp water."

"All right. No harm can come from what you ask. How shall we do it?"

"Well, I should go just so he won't get worried like he would if he saw Getlof alone. And the rest of my people too, I suppose. That will be easier, just take my things up in one trip. You should send someone with us and I'll be back before you finish the next game; well, perhaps in two game's time."

"Everyone?"

"Well, I was just thinking that would be best because I don't think Lord Daken will be very pleased when he hears about how I was forced to come here and that will show him that nothing is really wrong."

"Of course. Matta, stand up and go with Master Olat. I'll wait here."

When they were out on the streets Matta sheepishly confessed he didn't know the way. He was a upstream boy and it was his first time in Moaz. Talo said he'd guide. The streets were not as crowded as he remembered. People walked swiftly and no one showed the slightest interest in them. Still, the streets were too crowded for what he had in mind. He turned down the first alley, explaining to Matta it was a short cut. Then he looked back at Renix who nodded. Renix caught up with Matta and swiftly drew him into a doorway. Getlof, not knowing what she had expected, was shocked.

"Keep walking," Talo whispered. "I can find the north gates, but how we're going to find horses I don't know; but its going to have to be fast before the alarm is raised."

Getlof found herself walking between Narhad and Golab. She linked arms with them. Golab looked at her and tried to smile. He was plainly very frightened. The alley ended and they came back on the street. Renix moved in front, stalking aggressively and clearing the way. Talo was behind him, then came Getlof, Golab and Narhad. Doy took the rear.

The street ended suddenly in a square. There was a crowd gathered around a statue of a man with a lifted sword in the center of the square. They kept to the margins because there were armed men around the statue. Then, suddenly, Renix shouted. They looked ahead to see him holding a skinny, teenage boy two inches off the ground. The boy was waving his arms and making strangled noises. A circle of people had opened around them. Talo muttered a malediction and told the others to stay back. He stepped forward and said: "Put him down, Renix."

"I won't. The bastard tried to pick my pocket. I'll kill him."

"Don't be a fool!" Talo hissed, but it was already too late. The soldiers near the statue had noticed the commotion and two of them, dressed in leather armor, dyed yellow, and carrying bows, were pushing their way forward. The spectators gave way, but Renix stood his ground, keeping the boy suspended in the air. Narhad stiffened and Getlof clutched his arm tightly. They backed into the mouth of another street that fed into the square.

An archer confronted Renix while the other held back, an arrow notched. Getlof couldn't hear what he said, but Renix's reply was clear. He held the boy out at arm's length and dropped him at the feet of the archer.

"What do you mean, toad face. This is your criminal. He tried to lift my purse. I don't know what you do with pickpockets here, but where I come from we cut their hands off."

Talo had backed up during this exchange until he was standing in front of Getlof. Without turning he said: "They want to know what he's doing with a sword. Stay away no matter what. I'm going to try to get him out, although why I should escapes me." Then he was striding forward saying: "All right, what's going on."

The archer turned to Talo. "And who are you?"

"Olat of the Xexi, marchlord. Why do you cover my man?"

The archer didn't reply. Talo drew the medallion from a pocket and held it up for him to see. The archer looked at it, then up at Talo then back to the medallion and finally over to Renix. The suspense as he struggled to make up his mind was like the moment when a diver is just about to break the surface to draw the first gasp of air. Finally he made some reply that was inaudible. Whatever it was brought forth a cry of: "Bugger that!" from Renix. He began to pull his sword from its scabbard. The archer's face twisted into a snarl. He backstepped and began drawing his own sword. Suddenly the twang of a released bowstring. Renix fell with an arrow in his throat. The first archer, sword free, turned toward Talo. Talo stood motionless, arms away from his body. Further down the square people were shouting. More archers began running toward them. Then Getlof felt her arm being pulled and Golab was saying: "Come on, you've got to get out of here.

"Easy," Narhad whispered, "don't run." He said this to Golab. Getlof had to be led away, looking until her view of Talo was blocked. Then Doy joined them looking more affected by Renix's death than a hardened guardsman should. Narhad told him to keep a couple dozen paces back and watch their rear. "We don't know what Talo will do."

Getlof looked up angrily to see that Narhad was watching her. He shrugged his shoulders. After that, no one spoke. They hurried through the crisscrossing narrow streets. Then Narhad held out his arm and whispered: "This way," leading them down a different street that opened on their left. Golab asked what was wrong.

"More archers. They'd have looked at us twice after what that idiot fool, Renix, did, may Yetit hold him."

Twice after that they turned to avoid soldiers. The city's labyrinthine geography with its short streets and random intersections made it an easy game to play.

Soon they found themselves in a section pervaded by an air of neglect and decay. The foot traffic had thinned to the point they could walk a block without passing anyone. Getlof even noticed that the people in this area, spotting them, detoured as they detoured around the soldiers. She felt a great weariness and also betrayal that her expectations--as poorly defined as they had been--should turn out thus. They were in a narrow, deserted alley. She sank to the steps of a partially ruined building and said:

"Let's rest."

Narhad squatted beside her. Sensing her distress, his manner softened. "It's hard, I know, but you've been a steady one. Maybe this is our tightest spot yet, but that just means you have to be that much steadier. This city is bewildering, but I've been leading us north. Soon, I hope we'll find the gate Talo spoke of and we'll get out of this yet."

"But what about Talo?"

"Talo is taken. There's nothing we can do for him."

Getlof shook her head. It didn't seem right.

Suddenly Doy, who was watching one end of the alley gave a cry. They all sprang to their feet. He came, roughly pulling a boy with him.

"He's followed us since we left that square. Finally came a little too close.

Getlof stared, wondering why the ragged boy Doy had produced looked familiar. Then she realized he was Renix's pickpocket. Doy pushed him. He sprawled forward, falling at their feet. His eyes were round and white. Narhad grabbed his arm and he shrank back from the dagger that had materialized in Narhad's hand. His expression was so exaggerated, he seemed like a bad actor portraying terror. For some reason this touched Getlof and she felt a vague irritation with Doy and Narhad for being so rough.

"So, what's your name?"

The boy looked around at Getlof in surprise. Narhad and Doy also seemed taken aback by this question. Some people hurried by with heads down.

The boy tilted his head. His Southcoast was accented, but quite good: "Are you playing with me?"

Without thinking what she was doing, Getlof pushed back her hood and held up her hair, letting the cool air find the back of her neck. "Of course not. My name is Getlof, he is Narhad, that's Golab and Doy standing. We won't hurt you."

The boy didn't look convinced, but neither did he look as frightened as just a moment before. "My name is Elp."

Getlof's face reflected her astonishment at this disclosure and seeing that, the boy flinched.

"What's a matter? It's just a regular name."

"I know. I had a friend once with that name." She smiled. "Come to think of it, if he lived here he would probably be out picking pockets like you."

Narhad emitted his characteristic low rumbling noise. "This is getting too friendly. It's not safe to stand around here."

"He's right," Elp said. "If you come with me I can take you someplace safe that's close." He was staring at Getlof, eyes as large as a staring infant's. Then he whispered: "They'll kill you."

Getlof nodded absently. Something in her wanted to accept his offer. She didn't know if it was just a desire to rest or something else. Finally she looked up and said: "All right, take us to your safe place."

"Getlof," Golab objected, "you can't just trust him."

Getlof stood. It couldn't be her desire for rest. She felt fine now; tiredness had disappeared. She looked at Golab and thought that he hadn't been much help since Zoha. "He has help to give and followed us to give it. I will not turn it away."

Golab looked doubtful, but for that matter, so did Elp.

"All right, then," Narhad stood and gave Elp a meaningful look. "Lead, young man. I shall be right behind."

22

BOLT HOLE INN

Elp furtively led them pass unlocked gates, through obscure passageways, and over jumbled ruins. In three minutes Getlof was completely turned around.

Their destination proved to be a derelict building at the end of an alley of tumbled stones and broken planks. Elp knocked once on the door. Narhad stood beside, hand on pommel. Everyone's eyes were on the door and so no one saw Getlof push her hood back again. A peek hole opened and then the door swung revealing a fat woman.

"Well, hello, Elp. Long time no see." She looked at the others not quite so benevolently. "Where'd you find the friends?" Then Getlof stepped out from behind Narhad. The woman gasped.

"Elp, what are you trying to do to me? I can't let her in."

Getlof thought: `Finally, this is what it's to be recognized.' She said: "Please, madam, we need help and a place off the street where we can rest."

The woman snorted. "I imagine."

"Please," Elp said, "I owe them."

The fat woman tilted her head and regarded Getlof as if anew. Then she shook it. "I don't know why I waste my breath saying no. All right, come in all of you, but you," pointing at Getlof, "you keep that hood of yours up"

She led them through an antechamber and into a courtyard tiled with coral flagstones. Past the courtyard she gestured at a door. "Elp knows the way. I'll come down later. You owe me a story for my risk."

Getlof thanked her, but the fat woman just shook her head and lumbered off.

The door opened onto a flight of steps that led down, under the courtyard. The mummer of voices floated up from below. Then they entered a large room set with tables and benches. There were a dozen or so people of both sexes seated about. Several recognized Elp and called out greetings. They looked at the others curiously.

"A thief's hole!" Narhad muttered.

There was a room at the further end of the chamber and Elp led them into this saying: "more private." Inside there was a long table with chairs around it; Narhad pulled one beside the door and sat down, crossing his arms.

"Now," he said, "tell why you were following us."

"Oh," Elp looked back and forth between Narhad and Getlof and finally settled on Getlof as being the easier to speak with. "I saw you at the docks early this morning and thought: foreigners, rare enough to see what they're up to." He shrugged his shoulders. "You looked rich." He seemed to struggle for a second, then produced Golab's wallet. Golab cried and felt his purse. Elp handed the wallet to him and smiled wanly. "No harm, that's how I eat."

"So," Golab said, "you were the death of our companion and not satisfied with that, you followed us to see what else you could get."

"Oh no," Elp shook his head violently. "Not that at all. Didn't you see? Your friend was the death of himself. He should just have let me go. I felt real bad when he was killed, but I was gladder he didn't kill me like he said. Or cut off my hand." Elp shuddered. "I just felt bad. I followed to say I could help because I saw how afraid you were of the yellow chests and you looked like you needed help. And I was curious, but mostly, I felt bad. . . . I don't know why. Mostly, well, I don't know. I felt like I had to."

Getlof nodded. She was sympathetic to Elp's account. All too often, it seemed, she did things not knowing why, except she felt she had to. Then she stood. It was just too hot in the little room to suffer the hooded cloak any longer. She stripped it off and stood, dressed in just the white gown Dedre had given her.

"Elp, remember you said they'd kill me. Why?"

Elp looked at her and swallowed. "I saw one like you a long time ago when I was a little. They killed him out in the great square. Everyone saw."

"I see," Getlof said. "Alright, consider your offer to aid us as accepted. You know what that means, don't you?"

"What?" he asked in a small voice.

"Our danger is now your danger and our fate will be your fate." Narhad interposed.

"That's right. You can begin by telling me what you think they did with Talo. That was the man with the medallion who tried to rescue Renix."

"Oh, that's easy. They took him to the citadel. The yellow chests were surprised to see it. The medallion, I mean. All the lords are supposed to be at the wars with Caos. Lately people have been saying that something funny is happening up there. Disloyalty, or plots, or something. I've heard that. I supposed they figured that if he was a lord then he should have been with Caos and if he wasn't with Caos, he must have been up to something bad."

"I see." Getlof was thinking hard.

"So," Golab said, "the question is whether you can help us escape this city."

"Maybe I can," Elp said. "I know a guard at one of the smaller gates who wouldn't want that much."

"No." Getlof's voice was too loud for the little room. "That can't be our way."

Golab shook his head. "We have to hurry. I know you don't want to hear this, but Talo is capable of buying his freedom by selling ours. In fact, I can't imagine him doing anything else."

"Why does everyone think Talo is so lacking in decency and honor? What he did he did before he knew me. You can't hold that past against him."

"You're being foolish. Even if he is true, there is nothing we can do for him."

"Not so. We can show the loyalty to him that I, at least, expect from him."

"What's that supposed to mean? You want to join him in captivity?"

Getlof closed her eyes. "I mean we can go to where he's been taken and find a way to bring him out."

"Getlof, you're asking us to let you throw everything away and for no reason."

"Golab, why can't you see? What would it be called if I'd been taken and the rest of you, Talo too, had left me? Nothing good, I know."

"But you're not Talo."

"No, she's Getlof," Narhad said.

Golab turned to him. "Look, can't you say something? You know as well as I this can't be done."

Narhad was slow to answer. Getlof watched him wondering what she would do if he gainsaid her as well.

"Well?"

"Who's to say? This is Getlof's road we travel, Golab. We must travel it as she guides for no one knows it better. Maybe there is someway to Talo. Seeking that way is not charging up to the gates and crying vain challenges."

Golab looked at Doy who was standing on Narhad's right. Doy smiled wryly and shook his head.

"Please, Golab. I would do no less for you."

Golab turned and stared at Getlof. Then he sat down and crossed his arms. "Very well. We will seek a way to Talo, as Narhad says. That's all."

Elp had watched this discussion with wonder. Now Getlof turned to him, knowing she needed help and that he was the best she had at the moment.

"Elp?" Then she stopped, unable to think of the question.

Elp waited a respectful moment, then said: "Yes, lady?"

The phrasing of the question gave Getlof her idea.

"Elp, do you know who I am?"

His expression became vague and worried and he looked away. "You told me. You're Getlof."

Getlof folded her hands and didn't reply. Beads of sweat began to glisten on Elp's brow.

"You're one of them. One of the people of the old man of the mountain. But he's dead." Then he blushed and folded his hands in unconscious imitation of Getlof.

"He is dead, Elp, but there's a new one come up from the south. Would you know her?"

Elp looked up again, meeting her eyes like a wounded doe meeting the hunter's gaze Getlof gave no hint of the smile she felt. Elp's gaze fell, vanquished.

As gently as she could, Getlof said: "Elp, why do you fear me?"

Elp shook his head violently. Whatever he was trying to say was lost. Getlof reached out and took his hand. Softly she asked: "Would you know her?"

"Yes," Elp finally managed to say, face bright red. "I mean, yes."

Getlof finally permitted herself a smile. She had never really claimed the title as she was claiming it now; there could be no turning back.

Elp's hand was trembling. Then he said: "There are others who would know you. People who still follow the Old Man." Then, more proudly, "my uncle was one. He told me stories, but he's dead now."

Getlof nodded, as if she had expected to hear nothing else, although Elp's information actually surprised her.

"Can you bring some of them here?"

Elp nodded until Getlof was almost dizzy. "I will, right now." He jumped up, ran to the door and stopped, just as Narhad was about to restrain him.

"Maybe you want someone to come with me. They might not believe me and. . . ." He looked down.

"No," Getlof said, "we trust you, but you're idea is good. Doy, will you go with?"

After Doy and Elp were gone, an uncomfortable silence followed. Then Narhad said he had to step out for a moment. As soon as the door was shut behind him, Golab said:

"Well, you made a conquest of Elp, but why did you deceive him? What happens when he discovers you aren't a woman?"

Getlof regarded Golab, then nodded. It was time to put all that aside. "Golab, I am a woman. I think you must be the only one who hasn't guessed by now."

Golab stared at her, then shook his head.

"What is in you today. Is that supposed to be funny?" His voice trembled.

"You were almost the first to find out, back in Gildesh when you had those men start searching me. Oh, I was frightened then."

Golab leaped out of his chair and began pacing beside the table.

"Is it that shocking. Does it make that much of a difference?"

"Yes! I mean no. There have been female Joshs."

"I wasn't talking about Josh. I was talking about you and me."

"You know," he said slowly, "looking at you sitting there I can believe it. In fact, now I wonder how I was ever fooled." He returned to his seat and put his head into his hands. When he lifted it his face was all seriousness. "Be that as it may," he began, but Getlof giggled. This propelled him to his feet again. Still giggling (astonished that she was doing so) Getlof said:

"Sit down, dear Golab. I'm not laughing at you, just at the way you're acting."

"What's wrong with the way I'm acting. What about the way you're acting?"

Getlof stood, smile still on her lips. "You're making me dizzy." Golab whirled to face her--face working as he tried to form his reply. Then he came up right in front of her, making Getlof look up to see his face. What she saw she

154

didn't particularly like and she thought it was being harder for him to accept then it should have been, when Golab did something very surprising. He drew her to him and embraced her with crushing violence. Getlof returned the embrace softly, but when he bent her head and tried to kiss her she got frightened. She pushed him away and said: "No."

Golab released her immediately.

"Never?"

Getlof's heart was pounding. She wondered what reply she should make, but then the door opened and Narhad reentered. He looked back and forth at them and said: "Still arguing?"

Golab blushed. He said: "Do you know what Getlof just told me? This is no disguise.

Narhad's laugh was clear and loud. "Golab, my friend, where have your eyes been these many days?"

Getlof was grateful to whatever fates had brought her Narhad. He knew when to go, he knew when to come. He saw what he saw. It was all a matter of perception, discipline and concentration.

"Well," as his laughter died down, "I think we're safe enough here, as long as no one gets the idea there's money to be made turning us in. If you're hungry, I'd suggest eating now, while the chance remains."

Getlof realized she was, indeed, very hungry.

They ate and still Doy and Elp didn't return. To pass the time and to put Golab a little more at his ease, Getlof started him talking about the Old Man of the Mountain legend Elp had referred to.

There had been a large community of Pau in Moaz, back in the times before the wasting of Joshin. This was before anyone had conceived the concept of the disembodied emperor. The worship of the old gods was everywhere falling by the side and people were casting about for something to replace it. The old Man of the Mountain was a Moazian name for Josh. There had been much coming and going between Joshin on the mountain and Moaz on the plain; a mixing of people and ideas. Golab told her that the Moazians were the first non-Pauic peoples to embrace the worship of Paulac. That, he said, made it all the sadder that Moaz was now the most dangerous city in Ossa for the Pau.

Getlof listened with half an ear. She had heard most of this story on the Riverrun Road, but Golab had a way of being able to repeat the same tales endlessly and she was glad he could distract himself in that fashion. Getlof herself was curiously ambivalent, as if time and location were suspended. If she closed her eyes she wouldn't know if she were in Gildesh, in the room with the view of all the city, or on the Riverrun with the sun-mottled water rushing beside her, or on the chaparral listening to theology around the fire. It was the threshold's edge and she was poised--about to slide one way or the other. It seemed such a familiar location.

Golab talked on and still Doy and Elp didn't return. Things had reached the point where even Golab was casting nervous glances at the door, as if worry had the power to draw someone through, when there sounded a knock. Narhad glanced at Getlof who nodded and said: "Elp." He opened the door.

Elp came through first. He was smiling broadly. Three strange men followed, blinking from the smoke and dark. Doy was next and the fat lady followed him. She was the first to speak.

"I know its none of my never mind, and doubtlessly, I'd be smarter to never mind, but if plots are to be plotted in my house, I will know what they are." With a nod she settled her bulk into Narhad's chair by the door. The strangers stood awkwardly. Two were old men, the third a youth. All stared at Getlof until she finally smiled and asked them to sit down. With that invitation one of the old men bowed and said:

"Greetings, child. Great joy this encounter gives me. I had though to go to my grave without ever again casting my eyes upon the countenance of the fairest people in all this world."

Getlof nodded briskly. Now that the wait was over she felt herself sliding into the abyss of action adamant. There was no time to waste. She had to know if these people could help or go on to something else.

"I thank you for the kind words. What do your eyes see?"

The old man frowned, the lines deeply indenting his jowls and forehead. "Child, I see you. A Pau in this city that Paulac has forgotten. How you come to be here, I'm not certain and where you will go I don't know, but assuredly, I see you right now. I thought, I'd have seen different. The messenger you sent (although I admit need knows little discretion) is known to me and trusted only with reservation. I am happy my reservation was without basis."

156

Getlof shook her head. "Trust is or it is not; it cannot entertain reservations."

"Ah, you have not known trust betrayed, as have I."

"I doubt not there are many things you have known that I have yet to taste, but now I seek for allies . . ."

The old man interrupted: "And rightfully. This city is a danger to you; you should not have come, but having come will need to leave. Rest your fears. You have found the one aid you can trust without reservation. We can hide you and we will. We can deliver you safely from this danger and we will."

Getlof shook her head emphatically. She had lost the habit of letting people cut her off when she was saying something important. "I asked if you saw me and now I know you didn't"

From across the room Doy's voice: "Be wary, Getlof, this man's a talker. That's why we were so long returning."

Getlof nodded, the secret smile blossoming within. The old man appeared insulted, his two companions unwillingly amused. Getlof felt at the ring beneath her gown and then pulled it out. It was slightly warm to the touch, not burning as it would have been had it truly been sympathetic to her emotions.

"DO YOU SEE ME NOW?"

The old man blinked and took a step forward. The fat lady wheezed with surprise. The old man squinted and came closer still. His eyes began to water and then he fell to one knee. The water became tears.

"Child, forgive me. Truly I see you now." Of the two companions, the elder went also to his knees, but the younger, seeing Getlof's friends still on their feet, did not.

"Get up," Getlof said, "It isn't right for one who has succeeded in reaching your years to be on the floor." He nodded, as if this made sense and slowly got to his feet. Then everyone found seats around the table, except Narhad who remained standing beside the door.

"We know you, but we're still strangers to you, my lady. May I present myself and my companions. I am Iodai the elder," he cleared his throat, "it was my honor, in my youth, to be a neophyte in the service of Josh." And lowered his voice. "Once he noticed me and commended my service. Ah, but if I'd been loyal I wouldn't have fled Joshin when the Moazians were told to go."

"Lady, I am Jerrold," the other old man said. He spoke diffidently, as if unused to speaking for himself in the presence of Iodai. He looked to be of an age with Iodai, venerable in appearance, not yet feeble, but not as indulgently forceful. Getlof turned to the third person and he said:

"I am the younger Iodai." The elder broke in before the younger could elaborate.

"My grandson. Jerrold is my uncle's son. Most of us are related. Caos knows, but he prefers to pretend our conversion is real."

"I see," Getlof said. She noted that the expressions on Golab's and Narhad's faces weren't encouraging and she felt much the same herself; but time was passing. She decided to get to the point at once.

"How many will acknowledge my station and fight to overcome the grievance I have suffered here?"

The elder Iodai blinked rapidly. "That is a difficult question. We cannot gather to meet. . . . I presume you use the word fight figuratively . . ." His voice evaporated under the glare of Getlof's gaze. Then the younger spoke.

"No, grandfather, the Lady means fight. And why not? I know you were speaking of that very thing last week."

"Yes, we were. And what was decided?"

"Surely that is all changed now. How many times have I heard you complain about how you didn't fight last time? Are you going to regret the same non-deed twice?"

Iodai looked down, for the first time without words. The younger continued. "May I answer your question, Lady? My grandfather speaks truly when he says there aren't many of us. Of men not more than three dozens, but what of it? I know that people in this city are tired. They'll fight and not care for what as long as they fight the yellow chests. And when if not now? Caos is in the east. His rule is hardly popular. All fear and most hate him. I have two and twenty years and I can't remember the good old days my grandfather always speaks of, but I know the present times aren't what they could be and I'll fight to make them better."

"Well spoken," Narhad said.

"Indeed," Getlof said. These words sounded right. They were what she wanted to hear. Then Jerrold, who up until that moment had been staring at his hands, looked up:

"Perhaps we may more intelligently commit ourselves if you made your intentions known. Where have you come from, where are you going and why are you here?"

"Fair questions, but you ask in a way which suggests you already know the answers."

Jerrold nodded. "In part. You speak Southcoast. Most people do, these days, but your accent is southern and so are your companions, at least to my eye. That recalls the prophecy, that Josh will come from the south. I presume your people do not yet know you."

"That is true."

"So, the prophecy isn't fulfilled yet. By adventuring here you would put its fulfillment in grave danger. Is that wise?"

Getlof looked down. He was right, but what could she do? She had never worked to make any prophecy true and it seemed rather late to start. "That choice isn't mine. The `adventure' here is laid upon me; I didn't seek it, but I won't run from it."

"So," Jerrold said, "it is your wish that we rise and avenge the death of Josh?"

Getlof shook her head. "Not that."

"No? Elp spoke of a companion of yours who is being held in the citadel. Is it that?"

"More than a companion. He carried the ring in trust."

The fat lady, sitting forgotten in her corner now rose and said: "There was a time when every citizen of this city was entitled to their say. In my house I'm still entitled and will have my say."

"Say on," Getlof said as everyone turned their attention to her.

"Well, I never had dealings with Josh or the Pau and its one to me if they are allowed or disallowed in the city. But I've more than one friend taken by those up on the hill and they'd take me also if I was ever to come to their notice. I know, as you know, that if ever there was a time to be rising, it's now. I've weapons hidden here and know men eager to use them, given a reasonable chance. What I ask is this: is there room here in your plot for more men?"

"There is room." Getlof smiled. She was sliding, but now knew where she was going.

"Good, wait here and I'll bring a few of my friends to this meeting of yours."

23

TALO, RINGWARDEN

Renix lay on the ground, his blood flooding the cracks between the paving stones. Yeti betrayed him in the end, Talo thought sadly. People drained from the square like the blood from Renix's wound. More archers were running toward him. The man guarding Talo stood relaxed, his sword pointed just to the left of Talo's breast.

Talo never looked to see what Getlof and company were doing. The fact that Narhad hadn't waded in, swinging his long sword told him they were long gone. That was the only sane thing to do, but still, Talo felt galled and deserted. After all, he'd only been trying to save Renix from his own foolishness, and only because he thought Getlof would've wanted it. He felt like a sacrifice to her sense of loyalty.

The leader of the archers came striding up and demanded to know what was going on, and who Talo was.

Talo turned, looked him over, and summoning disdain and impatience replied:

"My questions as well."

"He carries the medallion of authority in the superior degree," the first archer offered.

This revelation stripped the officer of his arrogance. There was a dead man on the ground and Talo looked mad. "Sir," he said, "I must ask you your name and the circumstances of your presence here on the streets of the capital, where, excuse me for saying, you have no business to be."

"My business is with the Magnus," Talo said icily. "You, however, will tell me your name and station."

The officer stiffened. "I am Nears, the twenty-third station."

"Very well, Nears, explain to me why my man is laying there and why I am being threatened by the point of this man's sword."

"Sir, we received our orders when the army marched. They have not been countermanded."

"That is insufficient."

"Orders are never insufficient."

"Fool, I didn't ask for philosophy, I asked for your orders."

This convinced Nears a mistake had been made. He wondered if there was a way to extract himself and the men of this station without being saddled with the blame. "My orders were this: All counts and bearers of the Medallions, superior and second degree are forbidden access to the city during the Magnus' absence. There are certain expectations, but you, sir, are not known to be one of them."

Talo saw he had Nears worried and decided next to obligate the man.

"I see, then this is a mistake after all."

"Yes sir, thank you, sir. Obviously you were for the citadel. May I offer an escort. The city is restless and there have been incidents."

Talo, mimicking a man looking for signs of unrest, studied Nears from the edge of his glance; the man was a good officer and not about to forget his orders. The citadel again; but Taxis would be there, perhaps. Talo exhaled. The citadel towers were visible above the low, uneven skyline of the city. Getlof was gone. Of course she was gone.

"Very well. I accept your offer. But first see to my man. I want him to have a military interment. Can you arrange that?"

Nears saluted, balling his left hand into a fist and striking his heart.

Daken, the Captain of the lower guard was surprised to see Talo. Under different circumstances, Talo would have been amused; so anxious to have Talo in his power before, it was clear Daken had no idea what to do with him now.

Talo proclaimed ignorance of the order, pleading he had been far to the south on a special mission for Caos.

The captain nodded. "Searching out Pau. It was no secret. Were you successful? And where is Muk? Was it he they killed in the square?"

"Someone else," Talo said. "As for my success, or lack of it, I must report that only to the Magnus as he wished."

Daken rubbed his nose. His dilemma was that he disliked and mistrusted Talo--had from the very beginning. His instincts said to put Talo away in his deepest, unhealthiest dungeon cell, but clearly that wasn't possible.

"Well, what can I do but pass you on. Lord Raden, whom I'm sure you recall, is sitting in the High Chair as regent. Perhaps you'll condescend to report to him." Pause. "Actually, this comes at a good time for me."

"How's that?" There was something in the Captain's tone that suggested complexities and this recalled to Talo the vague rumors he had heard that morning at the docks.

Daken stared suspiciously for a moment, then shrugged his shoulders. "Of course, you're innocent of all that. It's nothing really. The Magnus leaves and everyone who had the least inclination toward making trouble is free to indulge themselves. Lord Raden is not strong enough to stop it, so we must endure until Caos returns. Then everyone accuses everyone else. It always happens this way. I would sooner not play the game, but what choice am I given. The Upper Captain, Gavin, has even denied my men access to the upper citadel on the excuse they are unreliable--which is pure rubbish. But, I wonder . . ."

"You say it always happens that way, but the situation you describe sounds strange and unusual to me."

Daken clasped his hands behind his back and walked to a window. "I try not to take offense; perhaps I go too far from my way doing so. Actually, there is no telling what is going on up there. It's none of my business and there are always people around to tell me that, but I think I'll round up a couple of men and take you up to Raden myself. This is a good excuse."

Talo shrugged his shoulders. "Whatever. I'm delighted I can finally be of service to you."

The walk up, through the precincts of the citadel was a long one. Memories came unbidden and unwanted to Talo as he passed through courtyards paved with coral tiles and ascended innumerable stairways. He determined that one of the first things he would do was ask Raden about Taxis. It didn't seem impossible that the two of them could get out of Moaz yet; and if Getlof had gotten away, perhaps he would even be able to meet up with her north of Moaz. It was clear the situation he had stumbled into was uncertain; such situations always had their advantages.

They came to the wall that marked the upper citadel, the realm of the Upper Captain's authority, and passed through without problem; a fact which seemed to refute the Lower Captain's fears. From there it was still a long way to the Hall of Light. Talo was struck by the silence in the upper districts. They passed few people. The tramp of their feet echoed in the wide corridors.

At the entrance of the Hall, Daken whispered to an ornately garbed guard stationed there. The guard shrugged his shoulders and, lifting a flap of the curtain that screened the hall from the antechamber, disappeared within. Talo wrinkled his nose at the perfumed scent that lingered. Then, he was back--too quickly it seemed--with word Talo was to be admitted at once. The Lower Captain was to wait outside.

Once more Talo strode down the seemingly roofless hall, filled high with smoke and heavy with odors. The only people to be seen were the guards posted along the walls. Talo walked right up to the dais without ceremony and bowed at its foot. Lord Raden, sitting in a chair to the right of the High Seat, peered down at him and said: "Is that Talo the Taelien?"

"Even so."

"Well, come up. I can hardly see you so far away." He waved a small hand, almost lost in the drapery of his heavy robe. Talo climbed the steps, stopping two short from the top.

"All the way, and get a chair." Talo looked around and saw a small chair to the left of the throne. He picked it up--it was surprisingly heavy--and maneuvered it around the throne. When he was finally seated, Raden said:

"Good, that's better. Now, look about and tell me if there is anyone close enough to hear what we say? My eyes get weaker every day."

Somewhat mystified, Talo did so and replied that they were alone.

"Good. I was glad when you were announced. Finally, someone we can trust. And before it's too late, I hope."

This took Talo by surprise. He hadn't realized anyone in Moaz trusted him particularly. He said: "Did my lord wish to hear a report on my mission?"

"Your mission?" Pause. "Oh, I remember. The Pauic child. No, I don't. We have more immediate danger." He peered around again. "Are you sure no one can hear?"

"Yes, my lord. We may speak in confidence."

"Good. I am never sure these days. Sometimes I think they're all in it. You see," bending closer and grabbing Talo's sleeve, "I have evidence of plotting against the Magnus. Now he is gone they think I'm weak and they can sit in this chair. And there was no one I could trust. This is why it's so lucky you come

163

now. You've been away. You're innocent. I know I can trust you. He said, before he left, to look for your return. He knew there were people who might take advantage of his absence. Oh, this war is risky business."

Talo hoped Raden's hearing was as weak as his eyes so he wouldn't hear Talo's heart beating. "Who do you suspect, lord?"

"Who? . . . I suspect everyone."

"But what evidence do you have. Who is it we must more against?"

"Ah, it's the Captain of the Upper Guard, Gavin."

Talo nodded and leaned back in his seat. The Upper Captain. It could be. "Tell me the evidence so I can more intelligently devise a plan."

"Evidence? I don't need evidence. I have my suspicions and that's enough. But, I'll tell you, I've never liked the man. He's always held too much power. Always goes his own way. Caos always said to let him be; that he's the perfect tool, but sometimes I wonder who is whose tool. The man is positively highhanded. Then, yesterday . . ." he dropped his voice so Talo could hardly hear him, "yesterday I ordered him to come before me. There were certain men I wanted arrested--two of the counts slandering the Magnus' divinity while they hide at home from the wars--and he refused. Not in so many words, you understand. He had an excuse, but the fact remains. He refused and the traitors are still at large."

Talo didn't think this evidence especially convincing; it seemed to him that Raden was enmeshed in a fantasy.

"You are right, my lord. The danger is immediate. Fortunately, I have devised a plan. You must tell me, however, whether the assumptions behind my plan are correct."

Raden nodded, "Good."

The captains of the lower and upper guards hold separate commands, correct?"

"Yes, they are rivals; but the Lower Captain is of little account."

"What of the archers in the city?"

"Elcas has that post. It isn't good to let one man command all the soldiers."

"So, there are three mutually exclusive commands in the city, none of them taking orders from the other. Good, then listen, this is what we must do . . ."

"But wait, there is a fourth command."

This stopped Talo. "There is?"

"Of course, the Magnus' personal guard. A detachment remains for my protection. They, at least, are loyal. And even the Upper Captain hesitates to attack them."

"You mean the troops here in the hall?"

"That is right."

Talo looked out at them. They didn't appear the types of men he would care to trust his life to, especially if there was to be fighting. Still, this was getting better and better.

"Then after I'm gone summon their captain and give strict orders that no one is to be admitted to the hall--particularly the guard of the upper citadel. I'll feel better knowing you are protected. It'll be necessary to create a distraction so that Gavin's attention won't be on me. For that I shall need the highest authority you can give me. If I must answer questions it could be deadly for us both."

Raden nodded and fumbled within his robes for a second, producing, at last, a heavy signet ring.

"It is a duplicate of the one Caos wears. If anyone questions your authority while you possess this, they are not Moazian."

Another ring. Talo gazed at it for a moment, then took it rejoicing in his heart.

"Thank you for your trust. Wait for me here. Before another day is past I hope to return with Gavin. He can explain himself to you then." Talo stood. Then he acted as if he had just remembered something.

"One more thing; like you, I'm uncertain whom to trust. However, there is one person here I trust absolutely and he is a young man named Taxis. He was my companion when first I came and remained here when I set forth on my mission. Can you tell me where he is?"

"Taxis?" Raden mumbled. "Ah, he was a hostage. Yes, I recall him but I can't remember specifically what happened. Some of the hostages were no longer necessary so, of course, they were dispatched. The others went with the army. Yes, no doubt that is where he is."

"I see," Talo said. "Then I must make do. Thank you."

"No, I thank you, fortune sent. Success!"

An attack of nerves hit Talo as he walked down the hall toward the exit, trying not to go too fast. It was certain that Gavin didn't respect Raden's whims; and he would surely consider his handing over of the ring to Talo as a whim.

Talo was almost certain that Gavin, not the lower captain, would be waiting for him. Talo was very glad to discover he was wrong.

"Come on," he said, "let's get out of here. Somehow, I'll feel better when I'm back in your barracks."

Daken looked at Talo strangely and said: "Indeed, this eagerness is new."

"No doubt," Talo said. He gave the captain a quick glimpse of the ring. "I'll explain when we're in your barracks."

The captain nodded, his face suddenly grave.

The trip back was no different than the journey up. Once away from Raden it was hard to believe his suspicions had foundation. If they did, Talo reasoned, would he have escaped from Gavin's lair so easily? This, however, didn't in the least affect what Talo intended to do.

Daken closed the door to his office and said: "alright, I've seen the ring. Now will you tell me what this means?"

"It means, as you suspected, that an emergency exists and I've been given extraordinary power to deal with it."

Daken nodded. Hands clasped behind his back he walked to a window. Then he turned and said, clearly with effort, "what are your orders?"

"Arrest the Upper Captain."

The faint beginnings of a smile. "So, it is that. Of course, you know that is an easy thing to say, but not so easy to do."

"I expect force will be necessary."

"Well, my men are loyal, never doubt that; but in and of themselves, they are insufficient."

"I realize that. A message will have to go to Elcas. By combining his force with yours, we can hope to impose Raden's will on the Upper Citadel."

"What of Raden?"

"He is protected by the Magnus' guard. He seemed to think they'll be enough."

"Not if Gavin gets word of what we're about."

"That's why we must give him something else to think about. I was considering arson in the upper levels."

Daken wrinkled his nose. "That seems a little extreme."

166

"These are extreme times. I can't think of anything that would work as well." Continuing quickly before more objections could be raised: "but first word must go to Elcas. Two hours should be enough for him to assemble the city's forces at the gate."

"It will be dangerous to leave the city unpatrolled."

Talo almost smiled. "No doubt, but the danger here is greater. Now, I'll need about six or seven page boys to guide me and carry messages. Then I'll need a place where I can lay down for awhile. I've been going since yesterday."

Daken nodded and summoned the pages. Talo had the lot of them accompany him to a room within the barracks. There he took the most likely looking ones aside and quickly explained the best ways of making a fire catch and grow. It wasn't difficult. Most young boys are natural arsonists.

24

CONVINCING THE FICKLE

The fat lady was better than her word. First she collected the people in the main basement room. They'd suspected something unusual was happening in their lair, and when they saw Iodai pass, they were certain. She sent messengers out and put people to work moving tables together. Her messengers came back in surprisingly short time with more men. Finally, when everyone was gathered, she invited Getlof in. A hush fell over the room at this final confirmation of strange events in the making. Iodai introduced her with a short speech and the debate began.

Getlof sat at one end of the long table with Narhad and Doy, arms folded, standing behind her. She was unaware of it, but she did look like a leader. The deferential treatment she received from the fat lady, who introduced some important late arrivals to her, reinforced this appearance. However, Getlof was content to watch and listen. The debate quickly revealed two factions. Many had come in response to the call for action; the others -- mostly older people -- had memories of similar attempts that had all failed. But finally, the action party predominated. Even the most reluctant conservative had to admit there would never be a better moment. After several hours it was agreed to distribute what arms there were and to raise the city.

Getlof wanted only to rescue Talo, but her desire had clearly become part of a much greater scheme. The Moazians all agreed their resources would only permit an attempt to control the city. To this end they chose seven captains and divided themselves -- more of less equally -- into seven bands. Each band would attack a barrack at the sixteenth hour, just at dusk. There were more than seven barracks in the city so the seven closest to the northern land gate in the old city were chosen. This was the poorest section of town and there the rising could expect to find almost total support.

After this decision was made, with everyone feeling pleased they had come to a decision at all, Getlof decided she couldn't remain passive any longer. The Moazians, she felt, were ignoring the major obstacle to their success: the Citadel; pretending it didn't exist or would fall of its own accord with the liberation of the city. She stood and waited while all conversation died in the room. Most of the people had been covertly watching her and no one wanted to miss what she would say. The silence, however, was not completely friendly. Getlof could feel the latent hostility and realized that there must be plenty of people in Moaz who shared their Magnus' attitudes toward the Pau. She said:

"People of Moaz, you have decided upon action irreversible, of the most consequential sort. No easy decision it was and I can see it was not made lightly. And yet, what success can you have? In battle, I am told, one must strike at the head and the heart and not be diverted by easier victories to be gained at the extremities. In Moaz, even a stranger such as I can see, that the head and the heart are together in one place: the citadel. Yet, I have heard no plans to deal with this problem. Surely this problem cannot be ignored."

Getlof sat down to see what response her speech would bring. A heavyset, capable looking man, one of the first leaders chosen, stood and asked for the floor.

"My name is Zak. I say that for your benefit, Lady, because most here know me; and they must trust me as well because I've been elected a captain." Here he paused to acknowledge the corroborating nods and grunts from his partisans. Getlof folded her hands and studied him carefully. She felt a challenge coming.

"What I want to know is this: you are a foreigner, that is plain for everyone to see. So are your friends. We were fighting Gildi long before Raos was made Magnus and I expect we'll be fighting them long after we rid ourselves of his son. I don't mean to fight now just to set up another master, Pau or Gildi. Do you understand me?" He sat down amid exclamations of agreement. Iodai and his people (now the several dozen promised) began to contest Zak's words. Getlof had no desire to see the compromise fall apart once again into factionalism. She looked over at Zak and met his eyes. What she saw was not hostility, but rather an open kind of fear; fear based upon lack of understanding of who Getlof was and just what she represented. There was also honesty. It wasn't the look of a man whose mind was closed. She stood once again and again silence fell over the room.

"You have asked several questions, both spoken and unspoken and for this I thank you. Know that I'm in your city by accident. What Pau would come willingly to Moaz?" Some laughter. "My affiliations are my own, my friends are of your city as well as of the south. Some here know my interest in this matter, but I will state it again for all to know. Maybe Caos is my enemy and the enemy of my people, but I have no wish to replace his rule with one of my own." She paused and smiled. "That never occurred to me, I don't think it would be possible, but if it were, I wouldn't like it at all. No, my interest is much simpler. This day a companion of mine was taken. I wish only to secure his release, just as you all seek your own release. If we are blessed with success, I continue my journey north; that is set and I've no choice in the matter. . ." Getlof stopped because she could see she wasn't convincing people as she hoped she would. Perhaps Zak was satisfied, but there was an undercurrent of mutterings she couldn't ignore.

Getlof sat down wondering if it was hopeless after all, and in the very act of facing desperation, received a sudden intuition. The rising needed a head and a heart of its own; otherwise, it would be just a single night of burning and death with no results to guarantee the next morning would be any different. But she didn't know how to say this without appearing to put herself forward; without confirming their worst fears. As if by themselves, her eyes closed. The words of binding, the words to ensure success eluded her.

Her eyes opened. Surprisingly, she noted the room was still quiet; that all eyes remained on her. This brought an empty smile to her face.

"I can only say that my aid is free and it is more potent than you realize. . ." Why had she said that? She was fumbling for words and they were coming from she knew not where. "This is not justification, merely fact. . ." Empty pronouncements, why was she making them? The grumbling was starting again and even Iodai looked worried. . . .

Then the door flew suddenly open. People sprang to their feet, thinking they had been betrayed. The interrupter was indeed one of the lookouts, but his news was far stranger than mere treason.

"The barracks all over the city are being emptied," he shouted. "They are marching to the Citadel. People are saying Raden is dead and the captains are fighting."

In the midst of the cheering Iodai sprang to his feet and, with remarkable agility, leaped up on the table.

"Men of Moaz," his voice cut through the noise like steel through flesh, "let us give thanks." His bearing, his white beard and long cape (which must have been oppressively hot in the close room) were impressive. Getlof suddenly saw him not as a fussy old man, but as a pronouncer of pronouncements and an interpreter of arcane events. "Let us give thanks to the Lady Getlof for it has happened as you heard her speak. Let us feel ashamed we doubted her aid, for indeed, it is more potent than we could have dreamed. Even I who believe had my doubts, I confess." He put an arm across his brow and bowed toward Getlof. "I thank He who is unrevealed and she who is His mouth for not allowing me," his voice rose, "for not allowing us to remain in doubt for long."

It was an effective performance.

"Are there among us any who still doubt?" Iodai thundered, glaring about as if in anger the question had to be asked at all.

Zak stood. "Not I. Excuse me Lady for speaking plain, but when you closed your eyes I thought maybe you were trying to make us believe you could speak to. . . I don't know, but . . ." He shook his head. "I was wrong. The head and the heart, we will do it as you said. Indeed, it is possible now where before it was not."

Then the other captains rose and gave her their support as well. Enthusiasm swept into the room and Getlof felt carried away. It was exactly what she had wanted, but oh, how close it had been.

Iodai spoke again. "Let us all tell of this miracle, for what else could it be, and keep it before us. Who can doubt that with such aid victory will belong to us."

More shouting. Getlof stood and waited until it died away, indicating to Iodai as she did so to get off the table.

"I say this," finally when it was quiet enough to be heard, "let us not forget that we haven't yet begun. Dusk approaches. The plan is the same. We need weapons and the barracks will not be unguarded. Neither must we forget that the walls and gates are garrisoned. I will await at the gates of the citadel. When the city is once again yours, let all gather there who remember me."

The younger Iodai now demonstrated some of the oratorical skill of his grandfather. "I will be there, head and heart, I will be there."

"And I, and I and I" so spoke everyone present.

25

NIGHT OF FLAMES

Getlof was among the last to leave the basement room. The emotion of the meeting had consumed much of her energy; already the day seemed longer than any she had endured, but all that had happened was merely a prelude for all that was yet to come. Cloaked and hooded, she entered the alley with Narhad and Golab on either side. Elp, with Doy beside him, proceeded them and following were a dozen men of the Pauic faction. The younger Iodai was their captain.

The city was quiet. It was dusk, still heavy with the heat of the day, breathless and charged with anticipation.

Getlof glanced at Golab. His face was downcast and shadowed. He seemed older, but Getlof thought her impression was probably an illusion of the uncertain light. She leaned closer so their shoulders were touching. The need for some kind of contact was suddenly overwhelming. This was for Getlof a strange sensation. She whispered so that only he and Narhad could hear: "Tell me what you think, Golab."

He glanced up, banded shadows dancing back across his face. "What do I think? I don't know. I've a prejudice against revolt." A short laugh, more of a bark, followed. "That was the way I was brought up."

"Not that."

"I know. You mean the miracle."

"You know it wasn't. I had no idea."

"Really? Well, you acted liked you knew; like you expected that man to come running in with the news. I found the whole thing convincing and extremely effective."

"It wasn't a miracle."

Golab shrugged his shoulders, breaking his contact with Getlof. "As you wish. Call it a fortunate coincidence."

"If you believe in coincidences," Narhad said, his deep voice rumbling in the stillness. It has to be one or the other. Nothing is coincidence or everything is. Frankly, I choose to believe in something more." Then he smiled. Getlof reached out and lightly touched his arm.

Elp, who was feeling exhilarated, awed and excluded all at the same time, suddenly stopped. When they caught up he pointed. The alley opened into a square.

"We recognize it," Golab said. "The square where this all began."

"No, not that," Elp whispered. "Look past, above the buildings."

"A fire," Getlof said. "That must be the citadel."

"It sure is," Elp said. Iodai came up. They clustered for a moment at the mouth of the alley watching the bright, tiny flames. Iodai said:

"By morning let the whole place be ash."

Getlof turned and looked at him curiously. "Is that what you want?" But before Iodai could answer, a deep throated bell tolled once from somewhere far away.

"The signal," someone said. "It's dusk."

Getlof paused and listened. It seemed she could hear the tiny sounds of men shouting and steel being raised against steel.

"Listen, it's beginning. Hear it?"

Golab looked down and shook his head and Narhad also, but Getlof was certain. It had begun and she was giving no aid, had no part to play, nothing was expected of her except to wait by the gates of the citadel while others risked death. She looked up. People were running into the square. Word of the fire in the citadel was spreading. She had to do something.

"Come, we have six hours and these folk seem curious. Perhaps they wish to help."

"I don't think . . ." cautious Golab began, but Getlof was already gone. She ran to the statue, cloak billowing and people stopped and followed her, wondering who she was. Getlof reached the statue and scrambled up onto the pedestal. There she paused, breathless, overlooking the milling confusion and wondered what next. Narhad was right below, sword drawn. One of Iodai's company had a torch. It was already growing dark. Then Narhad spoke in a voice that boomed and echoed round the square.

"Harken people of Moaz. Great tidings. Harken and hear."

More people. Where were they coming from? Getlof stood dark and uncertain of form, drapery flowing. A sudden stillness. She began to speak in a voice not her own: loud and harsh. Words came without effort. The agitation and excitement from below lent her eloquence and drove her on.

After a time Iodai the younger jumped up and added his voice. The crowd was alive; some new kind of creature metamorphosed from hundreds of separate cells. On the fringes there were knots of agitation; fighting, paying back the old scores as someone (was it Iodai?) had said they should. Then Getlof was swept up and only with difficulty did Narhad and Doy extract her from the eager embrace of the crowd creature. The statue of Caos was tumbled and the head broken off. People spat and defiled it; then some clever person propped the hollow shell on the end of a pole, and lifted it swayingly skyward crying: "The palace, the palace!" Iodai was beside her. "They're ready. To the palace." Getlof nodded, unable to focus exactly on what was happening. Looking round she saw that fires were springing up throughout the city. She wrapped her cloak tightly about herself and set off at the head of the mob.

It was strange to be suddenly plunged so deeply into her interior when so much was happening without. Public words, she realized, were in some fashion different than private words; they took on meaning not conceived by the speaker. It was frightening, as if to succeed she first had to surrender. Getlof didn't like it, but it was too late to stop or be fainthearted.

The edges of the mob waxed and waned as people joined and others splintered away to collect relatives or to discharge business of their own. Caos' head served to preserve some order to the procession. They funneled through the gates and gaps in the wall that separated the old town from the new. From there Getlof could see that only a small part of the very highest section of the citadel was on fire. She wondered anew at the cause and then the simple, inescapable fact hit her. Talo was there. It had to be Talo's doing. She wondered why she hadn't realized it before and whether he even required rescue. She faltered. Narhad reached out to steady her, thinking she had stumbled. Getlof looked back and was appalled by the number of people following. 'What is the point of this?' she asked herself and the answer came like a little pool of stillness; an anomaly in the storm: it was the effort; the fact she was willing.

The citadel was very near. The crowd wound back as far as the eye could follow, along several parallel routes. The old town was lit under a reddish glow that made the citadel fire seem inconsequential. They turned a corner. Marching toward her (still some distance away but not to be avoided) was a file of soldiers. The people running out in front of the mob were pressed back against the buildings. The soldiers ignored them. Getlof told herself to send out more reliable scouts if she ever found herself in a similar situation. Then, catching sight of the solid mass of people with the profane standard at their head, the lead soldier held up his hand and the file--uniformly hitting the same foot, sending out a disconcertingly disciplined sounding thud--came to a halt. Getlof halted also. She heard Golab behind her frantically whispering to someone to go back--for the sake of all the gods--and spread the word to stop before they were pressed into the soldiers by sheer momentum.

The lead soldier took a step forward and in a voice heavy with command and contempt demanded:

"People of Moaz, what treason is this, coming shamefully forward behind the image of our Magnus, may he rule forever."

The bolder ones booed at this. Getlof wondered why he was asking questions and not just coming forward with drawn sword. The shout of "soldiers!" was moving back along the line and in it Getlof could sense the beginnings of panic. She stepped forward so that she and the soldier faced one another at a distance of ten paces.

"No treason here, soldier of Moaz. Caos no longer rules this city. The people have toppled him from his high place." A ragged shout of support followed her words. The soldier's expression didn't change. He said:

"Gentle people of Moaz, one chance I give you. Repent this folly and leave this false leader. Return to your homes before you meet our blades unsheathed."

The fact the soldier talked around and not to her made Getlof suddenly and unreasonably angry. She was not being taken seriously and all she had come through from the day she had left Dell had earned her at least that right. She dropped her cloak and said:

"No false leader I, soldier of Moaz. I am Getlof Josh, Pau of the line of Josh, ancient and mighty. Put down your arms and stand aside."

This revelation finally brought a reaction from the soldier. His face went from amazement to anger to hatred all in a second. In the moment before he threw himself forward, Getlof felt sorrow that someone should hate her for being merely what she was.

The solder threw himself forward, yelling his war cry. He moved so quickly that Getlof froze, unable to even place her hand on the hilt of the short sword she carried. Narhad was there, however. Thrusting toward Getlof, the soldier was unable to check his momentum to meet the whistling down stroke of Narhad's two handed blade, although he saw it coming at the last moment. Narhad detached the soldier's arm from his body and followed with a kick that sent his torso sprawling to the side. Getlof witnessed this all too vividly: still pictures each separated from the one before by a moment of frozen time that etched the scene in her memory indelibly. There was a final image of Narhad, terrible in his size, lifting his sword high over his shoulder and of the next soldier before him, in a half crouch, the fear in his eyes before the blow it was already too late to avoid. With an effort Getlof forced herself to action, bringing her own sword out. At that moment Golab shoved her back into the crowd bunched up behind.

"Stay back," he cried in a voice she didn't recognize, running up to meet a soldier who was about to attack Narhad from his left side. For a moment Getlof was entangled in people, most of who were pushing their way back against those who were pushing forward and those who were just watching. Then Iodai was pulling on her arm.

"Quickly, we must get away."

Getlof shook her arm free and turned from him.

Golab had successfully overcome his man whose attention had been on Narhad anyway. The next one was more ready. He countered Golab's thrust and followed with his own sword into Golab's side. Getlof turned just in time to see this. She screamed, but didn't hear herself. Running forward she buried her own blade in the shoulder of Golab's attacker and lost it when he jerked up in surprise and pain. Doy had been separated from the others. Now he came bounding up past Getlof to join Narhad who was piling bodies around his feet. Getlof looked back at the vacillating mob and screamed again; unarticulated words that were lost in the confusion. But their sense must have been right because people began to come forward at last, Iodai in the lead trying to redeem his moment of panic.

The soldiers broke. The mob flowed past Getlof. She knelt beside Golab, trying to prevent the heedless people from trampling him in their newfound eagerness. His eyes had glassed over with pain, but he was still alive. Then Narhad was there. He looked at Golab, carefully lifted him and bore him out of further danger. Getlof followed mutely. For a moment Narhad didn't say anything, breathing hard, his eyes shut. Then:

"Ah, I can't talk when the rage comes over me. Lady, you and he should have kept back. The first one was the only good one. The others I could've stood off all day."

Getlof lifted her red, swelling face and said: "What of Golab?"

"I don't know. He's badly hurt."

Elp and Doy joined them. Elp's face was flushed and his voice excited. "We got them all, everyone of them. The people are up to the gate. Iodai stopped them there. They're asking for you, Getlof."

Getlof nodded without really hearing him. Doy knelt down and looked at Golab. Golab suddenly moaned and his eyes flew open. There was no expression in them.

"We have to find a leech," Getlof said frantically. "We can't let him die."

Narhad put an arm around her shoulder. "Aye, we'll do that if we can. Elp, can you find someone and bring him here?"

Elp's eyes had gone big and round as they did whenever there was trouble. He nodded.

"Hurry!" Getlof said.

He ran off. Then Narhad: "Come, Lady, you can't stay here. The people you collected are at the gates and they need to see you."

She shook her head. "I can't leave Golab."

"There's nothing you can do. Doy will look after him until Elp finds somebody. Come, he doesn't even know you."

"He's right," Doy said. "Don't worry, I'll see he's all right." Privately both of the guardsmen thought Getlof was making too much of Golab's wound. Wounds, death, the loss of friends were facts to which they were resigned. Getlof, looking into both of their faces one after the other caught some glimmer of their feelings. She sighed and allowed Narhad to lead her away. They didn't speak until they came to the cleared fields hard against the citadel walls.

"Say something," Narhad said. "They want a word."

Getlof shook her head. "I can't."

Narhad looked down and frowned. "What is this? You brought these people here, didn't you? Well, then, do right by them. Give them what they want. You can't call for bloodplay and lose heart when it begins."

Criticism from Narhad was rare and all the more effective for that reason. It wasn't easy, but Getlof forced herself to do what was required. She raised her voice and didn't think of Golab. She told them that now they had to wait, that they must keep back from the gates and walls so those within wouldn't take undue alarm. At midnight, she said, when the others joined them they would go in. They cheered her and cheered hard, such was their enthusiasm. The encounter with the soldiers had been the threshold. Once over it there was no way to go but forward. When she finished, she saw Iodai hovering by her shoulder. She told him to take over and see her suggestions were followed. She had something else to attend to, but would return before the hour was over.

Then, regardless of what was right or wrong and what her responsibilities were, she went back with Narhad to see Golab. They didn't get far before Elp came running up from the other direction. "Getlof," he shouted, seeing her first, "I found a leech."

"Bless you, Elp. Where's Golab?"

"We moved him into a house. Doy's there."

Elp led her to a large house walled off from the narrow street and constructed around a central courtyard. A tall, matronly woman and her daughter, just a year or so younger than Getlof greeted them at the gate. There were several female servants present, but the men were all out and they didn't know where. Despite her worry, however, the woman spoke Getlof politely. She had heard that terrible things were happening and about Getlof. She expected to meet a terrible person. She was surprised to greet someone much like her daughter. Getlof stayed only long enough to still her worse worries. Golab was still comatose, but the leech had sweet herbs burning and their fragrance seemed to promise eventual recovery. However, Getlof still wanted someone who knew Golab to stay with him. She prevailed upon Doy. Doy wanted to be in the fighting, but when the matron and her daughter added their pleas to Getlof's, his resistance crumbled. Rare is the man who can refuse the entreaties of three women.

Then Getlof returned to the citadel. As she approached she saw that people were sitting quietly along the sides of the streets in much better order than when she had left. Then she saw why. Zak, with a group of grim looking men, walked up the street toward her.

"Ah, there you are. Why, you're covered with blood. Are you hurt?"

Getlof looked down. It was true. But Narhad was too and, for that matter, so was Zak. "No, not mine."

"I'm relieved. I can see you've not been idle. Quite a crowd here. Our work went much faster than expected. We took an armory. Only only four men guarded it, if you can believe that. I've been trying to see that everyone has a weapon, but we didn't expect so many."

They walked as they talked and emerged at the edge of the cleared space. Two hundred paces away rose the massive wall and gates of the citadel.

"That looks difficult," Getlof said, nodding toward the walls.

"That it is," Zak answered. "I've set some people to work building a ram, but I think the gates will hold out against it for tonight at least."

"What about the side door there."

"That's what we'll try, but if it's at all guarded, they'll bleed us terribly."

"And the fire? Is it still burning?"

"I have a man in a tower further back in the city. His last report was that it's still spreading, but slowly."

"We can't expect it to do our work for us," Narhad said.

Zak turned to him. "No, lord, we can't. But still, I'd give a lot to know what's happening up there."

"Well," said Getlof, "we'll find a way."

"Lady, I have an idea." It was Iodai. She hadn't seen him approach.

"What is that?" Zak asked. Getlof's heart was thudding. Iodai had startled, even frightened her and she didn't know why.

"Why not try a ruse? We can get uniforms for several dozen men, I should imagine. We must have killed at least that many coming here. . . ."

"That has merit," Narhad said, cutting off Iodai. (Getlof remarked this and wondered why, knowing it wasn't something Narhad would do without a reason.) He turned to Zak.

"There'll be a password. Have you taken any prisoners?"

"I certainly hope so. In fact, I think yes. There was a matter of relatives and I said we'd delay judgment."

Narhad glanced at Getlof and saw she was back inside herself again. He reminded himself she was only a girl and worse, new to all this. "All right then, it's worth a try. Iodai, it was your idea: can you see to the preparations?"

"I can," he said, glancing sideways, hoping Getlof would note his eagerness.

Then came word that another company had arrived. Zak went off to hear their news. Getlof was left with Narhad and Elp. Elp had acquired a sword somewhere. He waved it over his head and said: "See, Lady, I'm going to fight too!"

"Ouch," Narhad said, "that is no toy there, don't wave it around like one. In fact, that's something I can do while we wait: hold an hour or two of drill. Might keep a few of them from cutting their feet off."

Narhad gave a yell. He began with ten, but by the end of the hour had a hundred people amateurishly trying to manipulate their unfamiliar weapons. Getlof stood and watched. Two of Iodai's company stayed by her. Several times she had been warned that not everyone who hated Caos liked the Pau and she could be in some danger, but the only reason she accepted the bodyguard was to keep people from bothering her about it.

Time passed slowly. More people gathered to watch Narhad than to participate in his drill. They were ordinary people who had gone to bed that evening expecting an ordinary night's rest. They had a carnival mood fostered by the massive disruption in their routine and all the oddities the odd night had delivered. Getlof was just one of the oddities. Several times she overheard snatches of conversation that recounted how Narhad had held off twenty, thirty, even forty men singlehandedly. And the stories were growing.

At the end of an hour Iodai and Zak returned with twenty men outfitted in the yellow, leather armor of Moaz. Zak had the password and had confirmed it from several sources. He also said that the fire in the citadel appeared to be under control. The scout guessed it would be out within the hour. On the other hand, much of the northern part of the city had been reduced to smoldering ruin, but the wind was from the south so the destruction was unlikely to spread to the new city. All of the seven companies were present and although it was still short of midnight, all was ready.

Getlof looked at Iodai who was so eager he couldn't stand still. She thought how she would rather be looking at Golab and realized for the first time she was blaming Golab's wound on him. She knew it wasn't fair, but that didn't make her feel any different.

Hidden from eyes in the citadel they marshalled the waiting men, speaking in whispers. Then Iodai led them at a run up to the gate. There was a word of challenge. He answered. The small sally gate opened and they passed within.

A moment of suspense followed, but before it became unbearable, the door opened again. A man came out and gestured frantically. Zak was already moving. Groups began to detach themselves from the mob, but a shout from Narhad brought them back. Then, very slowly, the great gates themselves began to swing open. It happened so quietly and quickly that Getlof had no time to appreciate the accomplishment. Narhad grunted and said:

"They must have been practically unguarded." Then he gave a shout and released the mob. They began streaming through the gate. There were so many it took maybe fifteen minutes for all to pass through.

Getlof was near the middle of the crush. Someone was still carrying Caos' head, but all semblance of order had vanished. There was much wealth in the citadel (or so rumor had it), and no one doubted the quickest would get the best.

Iodai was on the banks of the confusion. He shouted at Getlof when she came by.

"Here," indicating a man sitting against the wall, head in arms. "I saved one if you have any question."

Getlof worked her way over to him. Iodai's face was aglow with a light that made Getlof look down. "Good, Iodai," she said, thinking it was only her senseless ill will that made her nervous. "I do have some questions. Your plan worked well."

"It was sweet. We were more than they and with our surprise, it was easy. Hey, on your feet."

Questioning the prisoner proved a frustrating task. He was in a state of shock and was either exceptionally stupid or deliberately uncooperative. Getlof could extract no sense from his answers. She was looking for some hint of Talo's whereabouts. The man's answers were of the: "it depends" sort. The interrogation degenerated into something of a riddle game and finally he was asking the questions of Getlof. Narhad had left to have a final word with Zak and the other captains who were struggling to preserve some semblance of discipline. He returned to Getlof's side to hear Getlof ask:

"Perhaps you know his name?"

"Oh, I doubt it. I ain't never had nothing to do with outlanders."

"Well, maybe you do. Its Talo the Taelien."

A look of intelligence flickered through the man's eyes. "No, never heard of nobody by that name."

"Excuse me, Lady," Narhad said, "but I think you lack the touch. Now, I'd wager this man just lied to you and. . . ." He turned. A man was running by with a torch. Narhad yelled: "Hey, bring that fire over here." Back to Getlof: "And if I put the question to him again, I think we might just get a different answer."

The captive saw he was about to experience a change in technique and before he could become a witness to Narhad's more effective methods, he began blathering.

"No lies, I know of no outlander by that name."

"Ah," said Narhad, who was using the torch to bring the end of a stick to a red-hot ember. "But you **do** know Talo the Taelien."

He nodded sullenly.

"Good. I think you want to tell me about him."

"Nothing to tell. I'd never heard of the man, least before tonight. But order came this evening and they were for most of the men to march up the hill, quick: even those as was off duty. I remember the filecaptain saying they was strange orders and he thought it funny because they was countersigned by that man, the one you're asking about. But they had the seal on them so he couldn't very well not obey. That's all I know."

Narhad stared at the prisoner, who made no pretense of meeting his eyes. At last he stood. "Sounds unlikely, but if true, it explains one or two things I've been wondering about."

"All true. Now, give me a clean death with the sword. Yours has seen some work, I see."

He was talking to Narhad, but Getlof answered.

"Why should we kill you?"

"You killed my mates."

"But they were fighting us. You no longer are."

"Oh, but if you let me go, I will. I must. It's my sworn duty."

The man had given Getlof good news and she was feeling generous toward him for it. She said: "Stand up."

He complied, expecting his request for a clean death to be honored. Narhad stepped back a pace and watched Getlof. The captive had his eyes on the ground.

"Swear a new oath. To me."

This brought his eyes up. He glanced at Narhad and then at Getlof. "But who are you?"

This puzzled Getlof. She had come to think it was obvious. "I am Getlof the Pau, of the line of Josh."

The prisoner gasped. Then he smiled. "So, I see a Pau. I always thought they was little black folk, you know."

"Well, I suppose I'm darker than most. Will you swear to me?"

He turned to Narhad. "Excuse me for asking, but does she hold your oath?"

"Aye," Narhad rumbled. "I'd answer quickly. Will you or won't you?"

"You're a fighting man and that's no mistake. Yes, if the likes of you follow this child, who am I to refuse such an offer. I swear to the Lady Getlof the Pau to be her man and fight her fights and to die, if she asks, my death."

Iodai could restrain himself no longer. He burst out saying: "I don't believe my ears. This man is our enemy, why do you shirk from doing what you must?"

Getlof turned to him with a frown. "Iodai, you heard him swear. Doesn't that satisfy you?"

He shook his head emphatically. "He swore an oath to Caos as well."

"Yes," the ex-captive said, "and I fought for him and was ready to die for him and would've died."

"But he's my prisoner."

"Iodai, he's a prisoner no longer. If you haven't killed enough I expect there will be more of it to come. Let there be peace among us."

The man's name was Nidot. By the time they were done questioning him, the area around the gate was deserted except for the men of Iodai's company and about fifty of the mob who had lingered to hear the questioning. Getlof told Nidot that she wanted to find Talo and so they set off toward the upper citadel where he thought it most likely Talo would be found.

Their way led through a series of wide halls, each one terminating in a staircase. On the left arched entries gave access to a repeating series of courtyards, all exposed to the sky. These opened to smaller chambers beyond. Nidot explained that court functionaries lived in these. On the right, locked doors faced the arches. Maybe one in ten showed evidence of violence. Similarly, most of the chambers were undisturbed. None-the-less, Getlof insisted that each be checked before they proceeded. She had learned her lesson about caution.

The stillness was remarkable. Finally, when they were in the third hall up from the gates, Getlof whispered:

"With my own eyes I saw thousands of people entering. What happened. Some came this way, but not many by the look of it."

"Most went up the main passage, I imagine," Nidot said. "We are making a detour. Seemed quicker."

"Beware the false guide's detours."

Iodai made this comment. Getlof whirled to face him, her patience snapped. "What is wrong with you? Just leave him alone."

Iodai froze, a snarl captured on his face. Getlof intoned a malediction she had picked up from Renix. Her anger, as quickly as it had jumped from whatever hiding place it resided in, turned back on herself. She was about to apologize for speaking so harshly when shouting from the end of the hall diverted everyone's attention.

At first, there was no accounting for the disturbance; then Elp came bounding down the stairs followed by three other people recognizable as townsfolk.

"Soldiers," Elp yelled. "Next level up, coming down."

'Finally,' Getlof caught herself thinking, surprised at her own reaction. In the next instance she was saying: "Quickly," and with Narhad's considerable aid, was shepherding everyone into one of the courtyards.

Getlof wanted to avoid incident and let the soldiers pass, but it was impossible to hide almost a hundred people so quickly. A few panicked and started running back down the way they had come. The first soldiers coming down the stairs at one end saw the last of the runners exiting from the other end of the hall. A shout:

"There're some." And: "You, you and you, check to see if any are hiding in the courtyards."

The first soldier to stick his head into their courtyard saw Narhad first. And last. His companion cried and fled. This display of fear greatly encouraged the townspeople. When Narhad shouted and leaped into the hall, they followed, echoing his Gildi war cry. Getlof felt what she thought the others must be feeling: a frightful emotion that was full of joy. She shouted also as she was swept into the hall, forgetting she had lost her sword and was unarmed. The main body of soldiers had already passed the courtyard. They turned and turned again and began running. It was as simple as that. Narhad stopped the townsfolk at the end of the hall, but not before several had experienced for the first time the uncertain emotion of striking a man down.

They regrouped, laughing and confident. Even Getlof, normally wary of overconfidence, was elated. But Narhad kept his head.

"Come on, come on," he shouted." Don't expect the next group to be so easily spooked. Those of you as don't have weapons, take one. This will probably be the last chance. Come on, what if they come back."

Getlof saw a soldier laying near her with a short bow clutched in his hand. Her own bow has been long lost, but it was the weapon she preferred, if weapon she had to have. She stopped, retrieved it and tested the draw. Stiff; really too heavy, but much more flexible than the long bows the city archers used. Getlof decided to take it; it would serve at short ranges.

When the scramble for weapons was over, Narhad turned to Getlof and asked: "Shall we proceed, Lady?"

"Yes, and quickly," feeling suddenly nervous about standing so long. Narhad looked at her closely and nodded.

"I know what you mean. This is a chancy game we play. He glanced over the people waiting instruction." All right, Elp, you did a good job. Take the lead again. We need a reliable rearguard now as well."

Getlof nodded. "Iodai, can you take a half dozen people and stay behind us, about a level?"

Iodai's eyes were half-closed. He gazed at Getlof for a moment and finally said: "Lady, give not that task to me. I would rather be in the front. Elp, or anyone can do it."

It was the tone more than the words which were disrespectful. Getlof shook her head, slipping into the confrontational mode so common to her life in Dell.

"No, the rear is the most important now. I want you to take the duty."

Her tone of voice caused Iodai to blink. Then he made a mock bow. "As you say, Lady." Getlof turned away, called for Nidot and the march began once again.

26

CHAOS PAYS A CALL

Talo lay staring at the ceiling. His habit of napping before action always impressed people; but now, with no one to impress, he couldn't sleep. He felt numb and alone and wondered if his condition came from a lack of confidence or resolve. When he heard footsteps outside his chamber, he closed his eyes.

The Lower Captain ripped aside the chamber curtain. His face was flushed, body twitching with imperfectly suppressed anger. Talo opened his eyes, put on a look of irritation and said:

"The city forces are gathered?"

"There is rioting in the city!"

Talo sat up and swung his feet over the edge of the cot. "How bad?"

"Any is bad enough."

"In other words, not that bad."

Daken wove a gesture of frustration in the air and turned away. "I admit I don't know. It appears to be across the city in the old town, but with the city garrison in the citadel, you may be sure it'll grow worse."

"Ah, then the city forces are gathered."

"Listen," the Captain began, turning back, pointing a trembling finger. Talo stood.

"No, you listen. You forget your position, Captain. The city may burn, but we are responsible for the chair of the Magnus himself. I wear the ring. I have the trust and authority of the regent. We will do it as I say it will be done."

Daken struggled for a second, then nodded curtly. Talo crossed his arms and said nothing. Finally: "Yes, the city forces are gathered."

"Good, the day goes on without us. Now, I've been studying a plan of the citadel. There are four gates. We'll have enough men, I hope, to force entry to the Upper Citadel at each of these points. I want you to select the three officers most senior to lead them. I'll explain the plan when its time. The fourth group you'll command and I'll accompany. Our sole task is to rescue Lord Raden and bring the Upper Captain to judgement. I'm sure this task is not totally objectionable to you."

Dalem had to shake his head and admit it was not.

"Good, let us not waste time."

With Daken behind him, Talo strode into the barrack courtyard, passing into a scene of cacophony and commotion. Several hours before he had ordered the Upper Citadel sealed off from the lower precincts. The population of the Lower Palace, the functionaries, courtiers, poets and their slaves and servants had been herded, bewildered and whining into the courtyard. It was fortunate Caos had taken such a large train with him to the wars or there wouldn't have been room for them all.

Talo stopped and inspected the scene.

"Haven't you made any explanation to them?" he asked the Captain.

"No, of course not. You said I shouldn't."

"Did I? Well, the time has come to do so. We'll have less noise and more cooperation that way."

"Do you wish me to make an announcement?"

Talo shook his head, turning so the captain couldn't see how this suggestion amused him. "No, I mistrust your public speaking and I suspect they'd mistrust it even more." Saying that, Talo plunged forward into the throng. He halted before the man who seemed to be complaining the loudest: a gentleman attired in a coral robe stretched tightly against his considerable girth.

"Good evening," Talo said pleasantly. "So you want to know why this is being done?"

"I am Pitas, free count of Moaz. I demand to know why this is being done."

"Free count? Then you have more reason than most to be grateful." Talo suddenly shifted the tone of his voice, making it low and harsh. "There is murder in the Upper Citadel, fool. Gavin is in revolt. Are you so eager then to flee this place of safety?"

This silenced Pitas. He held his stomach with both hands and said: "Murder? Gavin?"

"Be discrete with this news and stand tight," Talo said and abruptly turned away.

187

The Lower Captain caught up with Talo. "Aren't you going to make the announcement?"

"I just did."

"But just one man and even that we don't know to be true."

"Some overheard and I judge Pitas has a mouth large enough to take care of the rest. Besides, I suspect they'll believe a rumor more than any announcement."

For the first time Daken looked at Talo with an expression denoting appreciation.

Just as Talo was about to exit from the courtyard, an old man dressed in a gown of orange and yellow stepped into his path. "Ho, foreigner," he said, "ware of my words."

Talo stopped, memory of a similar encounter in Yebol--it seemed so long-- caused his stomach to flutter, although this man looked normal enough. Still, his words were politer than otherwise would've been the case.

"If they are few, I will. If you have a sermon, give me your name and I'll hear it some other time."

The colorfully garbed man blinked, but recovered his poise before the silence lasted too long. "Ware, stranger. The Red Star is in aspect with Arkspure. There is great burning and unlooked for death. A night of woe. But this will not touch the foreigner. Strange surprise is his lot."

Talo, fearing more, quickly slipped a silver Istel into the old man's hand and continued walking. But the magician's warning was not so easily put out of mind. How could any surprise not be strange? He'd arisen that morning in company with Getlof, Golab, Narhad, Renix and Doy. Renix was dead. Of the others, who could say. That seemed strange. Raden had given him the ring. That was stranger still. He was about to lead most of the remaining forces of Moaz in an attack on Caos' residence in the name of Caos. That had to be strangest of all. Talo's mood was strange. He felt fey and invincible. The prospect of great burning suited him.

Things always took longer than they should. It was shortly before the fifth hour when Talo's group of over a hundred men at arms and city archers reached the side gate of the Upper Citadel closest to the Hall of the Chair. They found the gate ajar with no one guarding it. The Lower Captain was shocked to see this. He whispered:

"Something is amiss, very seriously amiss."

Talo smiled in spite of himself. "Are you only just realizing that, Captain?" Daken looked at Talo, then he dropped his gaze and shook his head.

"Perhaps I am."

They passed under the gate, expecting at any moment to be challenged, but no challenge came. Talo didn't let Daken see, but this worried him also. Where was Gavin? He must have been aware of the preparations they had made--the evacuation of the Lower Citadel and the gathering of the city garrison. The smell of smoke was growing and between the dark shapes of buildings, he could see tiny flames flickering around the edges of the tower far above them. But it wasn't a large fire. Where was Gavin? The Lower Captain was hurrying his men saying: "Quickly, I fear for Lord Raden's life."

They left the region of the gate at a run, no longer trying for stealth. Up long stairways they ran, becoming strung out on the climb. Talo finally slowed the march, fearing they'd be too winded to fight, if fighting there was to be.

Not far below the Hall of the Chair they passed a single soldier who sat, holding his bleeding head in his hands. He looked up and stared dully at the armed men clattering past. They didn't stop for news. His presence and condition were news enough. The body of a lady lay on the next level up. Her back appeared to be broken. Then they were at the entrance to the hall. The doors were smashed and off their hinges. They paused to regroup before going in. Talo noticed that Daken was trembling. He felt momentary pity for him, the loyal servant and then whispered, so all could hear: "This is it, treachery. Our worst fear. Move in slowly, treat the guard of the Upper Citadel as enemies." He nodded and let a file of fighting men proceed him.

The great hall was strangely empty. Men fanned out and slowly walked down its length, footsteps echoing. Even the sound of breathing was loud. Talo was more surprised than anyone. He had been predicting such an occurrence, but hadn't really expected it to happen. Had Lord Raden's suspicions been correct after all? Or had his suspicions themselves brought this about?

As Talo approached the throne of Moaz to ascertain that it was indeed empty, he noticed that the men preceding him had stopped. A few more steps and Talo saw why. The hall was almost totally dark, but there was, unmistakably, someone seated on the chair. Talo walked through the silent group of soldiers.

"Lord Raden?"

In reply, a short laugh, almost a cackle. Talo was uncertain whether this was a yea or a nay. He came closer, to the base of the dias. Peering up he saw that the man was dressed in yellow. He put one foot on the steps.

"Who are you? By what right do you sit in the High Chair?"

Another laugh. "Good soldier with the foreign accent, Talo the Taelien, I'd wager, come back too late, I am Unsari the poet, out of favor, languishing in the Hall while his master wars and does great deed of which this poet will never sing. I sit here because there is no one else to do it."

Another step. "Where is Lord Raden?"

In reply a single note plucked from a stringed instrument, incongruous in the silence. Then a wavering voice, reciting in measured cadence:

> Lord Raden is dead.
>
> He died the ignoble death
>
> Trembling in the High Seat.
>
> His nephew's guard,
>
> No pity had they
>
> Nor care for their trust.
>
> Lord Raden is dead.

Then a cough and silence again.

Talo took two steps forward and saw, indeed, the man was not Lord Raden; until then he had been uncertain. He told himself to give the magician another coin, if he ever saw him again.

"Was it the Upper Captain's men?"

"No, no, that was clear in the poem. Weren't you listening?" He shook his head. "It was the guard. The Magnus' guard, you know. They did it. The Upper Captain was too late, though not as late as you. I told Gavin this would be a bad day. The aspects are in dangerous positions: the Red Star and Arkspure."

"I know," Talo said. "Where is the Upper Captain?" He had climbed to the top and was now face to face with the old man.

"He followed the fighting. The guard, they ran, heh, heh. Raden didn't have the ring. That's what they wanted." He suddenly dropped his voice. "No one knows he gave it to you. It looks good on your hand, but I wouldn't wear it, not yet."

Talo looked at the ring. He had been wearing it as a reminder to the Lower Captain. It was big and heavy and not comfortable; not at all like Getlof's ring. But it wasn't a question of looks; it was a question of power. Getlof's ring was only a sign, but this one actually had the power to command allegiance. A quick vision of himself on the High Chair passed before Talo's inner eye. It was not unpleasing, but he took the ring off and slipped it into his purse.

"Keep your seat, poet who has lost the light of his lord's favor. Keep the seat and give news to those who come seeking, in prose or verse as you choose."

"I will, foreigner. You wear the ring graciously."

Then came indecision and whispered arguments. The other three forces were supposed to meet them at the Hall, but they hadn't arrived, nor was there any news. Scouts were sent to the four quarters of the Upper Citadel. As they waited for some word, the bell tolled another hour.

People emerged from hiding places where they had waited out the bloody events in the Hall. They corroborated and elaborated Unsari's story. Ladies and gentlemen in waiting, refined faces unclean and in shock, told the tale of how the Upper Captain had come with force and demanded entrance--to kidnap Raden all had believed. But the Magnus' guard, after barring the door, had not protected Raden; they turned on him. Raden and all the people of the court they slaughtered with a fury bespeaking hatred immense and long suppressed.

Finally, when Gavin's men forced the door, but too late. The guard retreated fighting, taking the body of Raden with them, as one girl affirmed. She said they thought then they were safe, but Gavin's men entered with the word "traitor" on their lips and their swords in their hands. The massacre went on. The Lower Captain couldn't believe it. He kept saying that soldiers of Moaz would not do such deeds; but the evidence was there, not to be denied. The archers from the city were especially aghast. They muttered in groups and when Talo, tired to waiting, stood and asked if they were agreed that this outrage had to be avenged, their shouts of yes were the loudest. Then one of the scouts returned, breathless, so that it was a minute before he could deliver his tidings.

Two of the columns had run into the fighting and joined it. They were allied with the Magnus' guard against Gavin's men. Of the third column there was no news. He also reported that he had seen extensive fires in the city--especially at the northern end. What that meant, he couldn't say.

"Riots," an archer said. Talo nodded. The spirit of violence had come to Moaz that night. As they exited from the hall, Talo heard his name called. The old poet came running, holding his gown and displaying surprising agility for a man his age.

"You were right, it's a seat too cold for me to warm."

Talo paused. "I never said that."

"No? Well, it is and you have the luck tonight. If you've no objections, I would accompany you with an eye for your deeds and the poems they will doubtlessly make."

Talo laughed. "Especially if you're along. Come then, but don't view my deeds so closely you come to harm." Then the Lower Captain shouted for speed and Talo had no time to pay any further attention to the poet.

The scout led them to an open balcony above a large quadrangle. Talo looked up and saw that the stars were obscured, as if some spirit were holding a black cloak over the city. There were some archers crouched by the railing and with them a few of the Magnus' guard. Talo's force burst in on them and proceeded to cut the guardsmen down. One or two of them took an arrow before the archers realized they were firing on their own. When the balcony was secure, Talo looked cautiously over, into the quadrangle below. He saw many bodies, but few men. Apparently Gavin's men were occupying the margins and buildings on the high end. The archers and guardsmen held the lower end. The gallery dominated the whole scene. With the fifty archers he had, Talo was confident he could keep the courtyard clear; the only problem was how to separate the archers from the guardsmen. Before he had time to consider this, however, shouts reverberated from behind. Gavin's men were attacking the gallery, aware of the position's importance. Suddenly the Lower Captain jumped on the railing.

"Peace, men of Moaz. I am captain of the Lower Citadel." A lull followed and the Captain went on: "There have been acts this night that can never be forgiven. The regent has been murdered! We fight the Magnus' false and ignoble guard that did betray him. Let there be peace between us!"

The attackers wavered. Then one man stepped forward and shouted: "He lies!" And followed this accusation with a thrown dagger--a skill in which Gavin's men were trained. The Lower Captain was hit in the shoulder.

"Sweet god," Talo muttered, addressing no god in particular. The Captain wavered on the railing and then fell inward. They had no choice but to beat the attack off.

Talo ran to the Captain and wrenched the dagger out.

"It's not a killing wound."

The Captain moaned. Then his eyes fluttered open and he struggled to a sitting position. Talo said: "Be careful of the bleeding."

"What are we to do? They have all gone insane. All of them. You must show the ring and command peace."

Talo shook his head. "The only true servant who obeys the ring is you, Captain. I can do nothing but leave them to their insanity. You duty is to protect the Lower Citadel before this spreads to the innocents there."

The Captain coughed and nodded. At that moment, the shouting intensified. The Captain and Talo's eyes met; then Talo looked over to see the cause. Figures were spilling into the square from beyond the positions occupied by the guardsmen and archers. (who were fighting each other now, having heard the Lower Captain's denouncement). These new people weren't in any uniform. While Talo wondered who they could be, Gavin's soldiers gave a shout and launched yet another charge across the quadrangle. Talo bade the archers hold their fire. He was past deciding right or wrong; they could fight and he would wait. Then someone said the new force was townspeople. Around him Talo listened to the men speculate how they had come to be there, who they were following and if news of Raden's death had already reached the city. Talo just watched. He noticed the poet crouched beside him, licking his lips and shaking his head.

The complete randomness of it frightened Talo also. The dealing of death was never a gladsome thing, but it had its forms and observances; its rules and even traditions. Below him was a bestial scene which had nothing to do with form. It was random and meaningless death--the worst of all possible spectacles.

The newcomers to the melee, the townspeople (or the people apparently in the garb of townspeople, Talo was beyond making assumptions based upon appearances) were in the vast majority and although they were extracting a heavy toll, they seemed to be losing more of their own in the process. The Lower Captain had his recall sounded, but most of his men were too involved in the fray to extract themselves. The men on the gallery, once they understood they weren't going to be flung into the fight, began to relax, looking for acquaintances below and even wagering on the outcome of individual duels.

Talo looked away. They were taking such a long time at it. Soon the guardsmen would be squeezed out, either dead or fled. Only Gavin's men would remain. Talo's stomach gave a jump. It wasn't the best of times to be experiencing pains in the belly. He tried to ignore it. Gavin was an enigma. Talo knew he would never acknowledge Talo's possession of the ring. He would have to be dealt with, either now or later. Then there would be no one to dispute his holding of power. His stomach jumped again. Only Caos. It was a rich situation and he didn't want to make any mistakes.

The noise began to abate somewhat. Talo listened and ran over his options again, aware he was delaying, not deciding. The Lower Captain slid down next to him.

"I can walk. Is there any reason to stay and watch this? The sight of townspeople worries me. They must be in the Lower Citadel as well."

Talo still hadn't made a decision. This left him vaguely irritated at himself. "Captain," he snapped, "you may be certain that if there're townspeople here, there're townspeople in the Lower Citadel."

Before the Captain could reply, the pandemonium below intensified again. This time, however, Talo heard the distinctive "Kah la la la," the Gildi war cry. Talo and the Captain looked at one another, astonishment mirrored in their eyes. Then Talo made his decision. He jumped up, heedless of the danger and stood on the railing. More townspeople had appeared taking Gavin's men in the rear. Leading them was a tall man wielding a long sword and harvesting his confounded enemies. Unmistakably Narhad. And behind him a small figure cloaked in black, now kneeling and drawing a bow. Who else but Getlof? Talo stood there a long moment feeling an emotion akin to shame. It was hard to be certain because shame was an emotion he didn't know well. `Getlof,' he thought, `did I remember you so well?' Then, from the corner of his eye, Talo saw an archer raising his bow and taking aim at Narhad.

"No," he shouted, suddenly angry at Narhad for leading her into such danger. "Both are guilty. The city avenges us." The archers and men-at-arms looked at Talo uncertainly. "We join the fight." At the top of his lungs Talo screamed: "Kah la la la!" and ran to the stairway. The soldiers were still uncertain, but then the Lower Captain said:

"Follow the ringwarden. We must trust for the evidence of eye and ear has no worth this night."

Talo was stumbling down the steps and the men began to follow, enthusiastic now that constraint had been lifted and a clear course lay before them.

Into the quadrangle, screaming the cry again and hearing, with gratification, the others taking it up. The guardsmen and even Gavin's men began to drop their weapons and run. Some surrendered, but some continued fighting. Talo had no mind for this. He worked his way through the battle, parrying blows when he couldn't avoid them, but giving out none in return. Then he was suddenly standing in front of Narhad. Narhad saw him, but didn't see him. He was lifting his sword and Talo was in the way. Talo thought of the magician again. Surprise indeed. Then a voice shouted: "Narhad, stop!" Narhad's face was a mask, otherworldly in its aspect. Then he recognized Talo and this look was slowly replaced with another, grimly amused and maybe sarcastic.

"Master Talo, we've been seeking you."

Getlof was there before Talo could reply. She threw herself at him in a most girlish manner. Talo returned her embrace. She was indeed real.

"You're safe. I knew it."

Talo put his hands on her shoulder and held her back.

"It'd be foolish to ask what you're doing here, but why?"

"Talo, I couldn't go on without you!"

Talo gazed at her as if for the first time. Never had he been so surprised in his life.

Then Narhad said: "come." They hurried to a place of relative safety on the margins of the quadrangle.

"I can't believe," Talo said, "after all the bother I went through to cover your escape, you would do something so dangerous and so foolish." As he spoke, the falseness of his words struck him; he ended in a voice smaller than he began. Narhad was looking at him shrewdly and Talo wondered what he was thinking.

"You did all this for me?" Getlof said, apparently noticing nothing. "When I saw the fire in the tower I knew it was you."

Talo was saved from further compromise by a new voice interjecting itself into their conversation.

"Well, foreign soldier, I see there is more to your tale than first I imagined." It was Unsari, the poet, regarding them with tilted head, still running his tongue over dry lips. Getlof and Narhad looked at him with surprise and he bowed to Getlof. She smiled and bowed in return. Then Narhad said:

"There is no longer any point in this. With your permission, Lady, I will recall and attempt to end this fighting."

This reminded Talo of his own responsibilities. He looked around and saw the combat had reached a point where, given the slightest encouragement, it would end of its own accord. The men-at-arms of the Lower Captain were regarding the townsfolk warily. Gavin's men had retreated and the Magnus' guard was mostly dead. Narhad and Talo moved into the quadrangle waving their arms and calling upon the exhausted foes to separate themselves before a new round could begin.

It was strange that the moon choose that moment to lift itself above the horizon of the building behind them. Talo noticed the line of milky light suddenly drawn across the ground. Not until this contrast was made did he realize that all had taken place in the dark, or at best, in the half-light of torches. He looked over toward Getlof and noticed she was shivering. She saw his glance and smiled, making his stomach jump again; although for a different reason than before. There was a group of people drawn up around her he didn't recognize. Strange the changes one day could bring. He looked for Golab and Doy, but didn't see them.

The Lower Captain approached limping, supported by one of his men. Talo thought it an interesting reaction to a shoulder wound. The Captain said: "You seem to know these people; or is this a parley?"

Talo took his other arm and led him to Getlof. Narhad had rejoined her by this time and Talo began with him.

"This, Captain, is Narhad, late of the Gildi guard, my traveling companion from the south. And this is Getlof the Pau, Josh. The others I don't know."

"And this gentleman, Talo? You neglect your introduction."

"He is Captain of the Lower Guard of the Citadel of Moaz, Daken."

"Your prisoner, Lady," he finally said wearily.

Getlof frowned. "Are you not a friend of Talo's?"

The Captain smiled feebly. "A friend of Talo's? No, Lady, Talo commands me by the authority he holds: the ring of the Magnus of Moaz given him in trust by the regent."

"I see," Getlof said, although she didn't really. "Then these were your men we fought."

"No, Lady."

"Its confusing, Getlof," Talo said. "I'll explain, but not right now."

Getlof nodded. Suddenly she felt cold now that she was standing and no longer jumping from one danger to the next.

Zak found them still talking. Three of the elected captains were with him; the others had fallen. Daken was seeking someone to surrender to. Zak was uncertain if he was that man. Finally, Narhad suggested a parley saying no right decision could be made in the night chill on a field of so many deaths. This was agreeable to all.

Gavin's men had been completely routed, but scouts reported he still held the main building of the palace and the fire blackened shell of the Great Tower as well. They decided to vacate the Upper Citadel and to post guards at the four gates. No one had energy for more conflict that night. Denizens of the citadel were emerging; slaves and servants mostly--people with the good sense to survive when most of those they served were dead. Some were put to work removing bodies. Others were sent around to spread the word to any of the Lower Captain's men who remained in the Upper Citadel of the cession of the fighting and the evacuation. The Lower Citadel was still being looted. Zak issued a call for the townspeople to return to their homes, but most choose to ignore it -- the ones who got the message at all -- and there was little that could be done about that.

Finally the survivors were all gathered. The Lower Captain led them to a suitable hall just below the walls of the Upper Citadel. It was the fourth hour of morning: a strange time to begin business. Now that the initial gladness of finding Talo had worn off, Getlof was no longer sure how she felt. Her eyes penetrated clearly through the smoky dark. A chill wind blowing off the lake seemed hot. But her body, the thing that felt and saw, was somewhere lost; couldn't imagine the things it had done, nor any other way they could've been done.

Narhad by her side, Talo just there a moment ago, but now up ahead, whispering something to figures, bright black on black. And whispering motion behind; many people. Still very many people in spite of the rampage of death. Muttered conversations; shouts, a scream. That far away. And again. Or was it constant? Beyond the edge of hearing. Constant. . . .

Getlof looked suddenly up and over. Above the tall, formless buildings that edged up and away from the narrow path they followed. In and Out; the mighty inhalations of . . . what?

There it was; not on top of, but above the domed edifice ahead and to the right. No stars shone behind. Its color superceded black: jet radiance like some obverse sun. A figure beyond menace, but sitting pacifically; crossed legs, back straight and high. Watching Getlof.

She wanted to look over to see if Narhad saw it also, but couldn't see him; just the shape. Both arms raised: black flames flowing down them, curling up from hands. Cupped and held up. Getlof shuddered, or her body did, somewhere far away. It was this and if nothing more than those cupped hands held her: extinction.

A question, like an icy grip squeezing her heart. But in that embrace she felt something warm and familiar and dared to answer yes. Legs continued to carry her body forward in mindless motion.

Yes.

And again:

Yes.

Irony, vast and remorseless, but already the grip was melting. The figure, now perpendicular, stood and as Getlof passed by, vanished.

There was Narhad. His brow was furrowed, head tilted up stabbing at the night with his eyes. Behind, the whispering stilled. No screams. Nothing.

Everything had stopped. Narhad still stared at the sky, but most stood with heads down. Getlof turned slowly in a circle and saw everywhere it was the same. No one seemed to notice her. She said softly, but in a voice that carried: "It has passed."

Then Narhad looked down. He rubbed his eyes. "Getlof, what has passed?"

Other people were stirring now. Before she could answer, Talo was saying: "Why have we stopped?" And: "here is the gate, and the hall we'll use is just beyond."

They filed into the hall and found seats around a wide table within as guards hurried to cover the perimeter. Zak spoke first for the rebelling townspeople. The Lower Captain represented the old authority, although certain of the

Moazian nobility--free counts who had long ceased to be free and who counted for nothing--attempted their best to assist and oversee him. The Captain wanted Talo to speak for Caos because he held the ring; but Talo now insisted that the death of the regent and the events of the past few hours made him nothing more than a transient depository for the ring:

"Just like a padded chest, locked for safekeeping until you all decide who has the key."

Talo noted that Getlof seemed oblivious to all that was passing and he briefly wondered what was wrong, but he could also feel Narhad's eyes. He would be a long time explaining his recent adventures to Narhad's satisfaction.

The room was crowded with townspeople, residents of the citadel and soldiers of several different sorts, all pressing around the table. But all were quiet; listening to the debate as if eager to observe the forms of courtesy; feeling, perhaps, that manners could unspell the recently discovered violence within themselves and lend at least the appearance of self-determination. The Lower Captain begun by standing and formally asking who were the people who attacked the house of their lord; and if their objective was to dispute his rule and question his divinity. He addressed these questions to no one in particular. People looked at Getlof, but as Talo had noted first, she did not seem fully aware. Finally Zak rose and answered.

He spoke of the city's dissatisfaction with Caos' rule and of its injustices and wastes. "From times not so far past, times that many alive remember, the Magnus was merely the first citizen of the city. He was no god nor the ancestor of gods. The blood of Caos today is so rare only because he's murdered most of his family."

One of the Free Counts, actually a third cousin of Caos, interrupted at last and asked the Captain how he could listen to such slander. "Have you forgotten your duty?"

The Captain answered slowly. "I have always remembered my duty, this night no less than any other. But I have transgressed without meaning to transgress and I have erred without meaning to err. I follow the law exactly as it is written, both from old and still today. He who wears the ring of the city is my lord and he commands my sword until the return of the Magnus. And you all must surely realize Caos will return with his army behind him. Still, the man who holds the ring is Talo the Taelien, given to him by the Regent, who is now dead.

Lord Raden is dead." (Many gasped upon hearing this news.) "And the ring was given to the Regent by Caos himself. Thus, the chain of command is still clear."

All eyes were now on Talo. He glanced at Getlof sitting to his left, but her mind was still elsewhere. Then he looked at Zak. If Getlof was giving him the choice, than choice he would make: the Moazian who had, apparently, given her the greatest assistance in winning through to him.

"I can see this man commands the city, the true city of Moaz. If I understand correctly what Magnus means, then he should have the ring. I unlock the chest and deliver the ring of the city of Moaz to Zak."

Zak shook his head, as if trying to shake off the emotion Talo was building for him. "I am nobody. How can I take it?"

His answer was a wave of shouting proclamations from the many citizens of the city packed in the spacious hall.

Getlof was listening to all this, despite contrary appearances, but the words came to her like something said last year. Still, Zak was the proper choice. She stood and waited for the noise to die away.

"Listen to them, Zak. Someone must take the ring and rule this city. It can only be you."

Zak stared at her, then nodded slowly. "You have been right in everything else, Lady. I find it hard to believe you are right in this; I would rather you were wrong, but I will take it. Only from you."

Getlof looked at him, standing across the table. She was about to answer when a sudden wave of dizziness took her. She shook her head to clear it and Zak took this as a negative reply.

"Lady, this is no light matter, for I must oppose Caos when, as the Captain reminds us, he returns with his army behind him. I must be the right choice and only if you give me the ring will I believe that I am. Do it as a sign that this city's abuse of your people has ended."

The dizziness passed and for the first time since her vision in the plaza, her mind was completely clear. "I will, then, Zak," she managed to say. " But realize, I do not choose you; you are obliged to me for nothing. Rather I owe you." To everybody, because she couldn't believe that something as simple as Zak's, or anybody's promise could change the spirit of two generations of genocide: "Realize this is not my place and I cannot stay." Then Talo put the ring in her hand. It was unlike her own: heavy, ornate and she suddenly felt, more than merely a lump of crafted metal and stone. Talo whispered to her:

"Getlof, do you feel all right? This is what you want to do?"

Talo's question was distant; the period of clarity had ended. The ring of Moaz was suddenly repulsive and that because it was suddenly so attractive. She let it rest on her open palm and made her way around the table, feeling small, lost and unbearably cold in her heavy cloak. There was a power in the ring and it frightened her. She was frightened to give such a thing to Zak, but couldn't keep it. Zak's hand was massive. The ring fit perfectly. The shouting started:

"Hail Zak, Magnus of Moaz."

This came to Getlof very faintly; she had delivered the ring, herself briefly Magnus of Moaz, but only felt a giant hand suddenly upon her. She fought it, putting her strength into the effort of standing. Zak came suddenly into focus. He looked discomforted. Getlof could understand, but she couldn't hold it any longer. She crumpled and didn't see the man who had stood. She didn't hear his shout and she didn't know he had thrown a dagger at her. The knife passed through empty air and hit someone on the other side of the table, but she didn't know that either.

27

A GOOD MENTOR IS HARD TO FIND

Summer passed. Taxis was retained close by the side of Bar Lev, mainly, it seemed to entertain the great and powerful lord. Bar-Lev drank with a thirst never ending Taxis' stories of the free companies; particularly the tale of the Prince of Sidoc. Old gossip was all Bar-Lev's had to feed his craving for news of Talo because Talo had apparently disappeared. The rumors from the west were ambiguous and contradictory. Moaz was in turmoil and Bar-Lev was content, for the moment, to let it burn. Reports from the south told of a land girding for war. The fleet, captained and manned by Tarhadians and renegades from the coastal cities, was raiding the Innersea and massing for a descent upon the Gildi coast. The Riverrun was barred and probes against its defense had not fared well.

Bar-Lev lingered in Zoha. His great leap from the Tarhad had given him extensive lands to digest; the next leap required careful preparation. It seemed to Taxis that Bar-Lev's greatest worry was dissatisfaction within the tribes. These he considered his strength and when reports came in that certain small family groupings had fled to the west, to take up again their wandering life, he reacted strongly and with great anger. Each clan was centered on its oldest female member, called the mother. These women he gathered into a closely guarded quarter of Zoha.

Bar-Lev was a fascinating man to know, and dangerous. The force of his presence didn't decrease with familiarity. The pattern of his moods and reactions were less evident with acquaintance. The only certain thing Taxis could see was that Bar-Lev didn't recognize any limits to his abilities or powers. Talo shared this quality, but in him its expression was far subtler. Taxis was flattered by the attention he received, dangerous as it was. Without realizing it, he was slowly becoming mesmerized.

Fall brought definite tidings from Moaz. There appeared to be a new player. Bar-Lev called his advisors to help him consider the matter.

"We finally have news of the Taelien, and strange news it seems. He has overthrown the citadel and fled Moaz; the remaining captains indulge in civil war. More interesting, he operates behind the guise of one called the Josh. A young woman. Thera, remind us of the reports last spring from Gildesh."

"Great Lord, shortly before your capture of Zoha, we received reports from Gildesh concerning the Taelien. They spoke of him entering the city in the company of one called the Josh, a young man. They reportedly found great favor with the boy Emperor, Ducitos and were given an escort comprised of his personal guard. The accuracy of this news was doubted. First, it is well known the Taelin is hateful to the Gildi. Second, it makes no sense to throw a possible resource into the center of a battle. Third, what knowledge we possess of the Josh tells us he was killed a generation before in the northern wars of the Magnus Raos and his line was ended at that time. Fourth, the Josh was the leader of a sparse people known as the Pau. The Pau are found only in the northern mountains and this person reportedly entered Gildesh from the south."

"Yet, we hear of this Josh again and again in connection with the Taelin. Only now, instead of a boy, we have a girl. An interesting riddle, but one not too difficult of solution. Speak to that Xelli."

"Great Lord, there are stories of such a person to be heard from the lips of the mothers of the western tribes. This person, Nivila, is a girl whose coming is foretold in a time of war and uncertainly to protect the tribes and restore them to freedom and to act as their mouth and their ear to the old gods. I have heard similar legends exist along the Shon and the shores of the other lakes."

"Does that not make it plain? The Taelin is a subtle and a dangerous man. He clearly smarts under the shadow of my hand and endeavors to raise the west against me. He knows these stories, or has learned them recently and discards his male Josh for one who is female better to fit the legends he seeks to use against me."

"Great Lord," Rowenna said, "you undoubtedly have penetrated to the truth of his manipulations. Yet, have you not already frustrated this design? What tribe will desert its mother? What power remains in the west? The farmers of Shon? The ghosts of the Pau? The rump of Moaz? South lays our task. Do not let the empty posturings of the Taelien distract your eye."

After this speech, Bar-Lev sat silent and his advisors also. Finally: "The season is passing away. We shall give the Taelin room. The more he draws the west together, the easier will the plucking be. Merck, you will form a column, every man in my hoard who has knowledge of high places, and march south in one week. I want maps of the Xexi Mountains both east and west of the Riverrun. I want forts built on the passes. I want roads built if there are none to serve our purpose. I want you to make the mountains friendly to me and dangerous to the Gildi so that come spring, I may, if I choose, march that road to the fields of Gildesh."

That year winter was especially mild. The wagon roads to the east were clogged with caravans bringing foodstuffs from Tarhad and beyond. Parties ranged throughout the eastern half of Ossa finding victuals for the host. The orchards of Moaz were felled for firewood. There was fighting in the vales of the Long Valley, nasty raids and counterraids. In the Xexi, the Gildi bitterly contested Merck's attempts to win the passes. But it was a very mild winter. The lance heads were honed to a razor's edge.

The first thaw had come, turning the plains into a vast sea of mud. Rills and rivulets tumbled into gullies. Gullies, engorged with rushing brown water, spilled into the rivers. The rivers flooded and eagerly consumed the plains. It was a time when nothing moved and so it was a strange time for the news that Taxis heard. Two couriers had been captured far to the west, heading north. They were slowly being brought to Zoha with an interesting document: a letter from Ducitos XI addressed to The Josh.

This news was confirmed over a week latter when the captives were brought into Zoha. Winter had been a difficult time to be near Bar-Lev; he obviously fretted under the constraints of the weather and so had directed his energies toward testing the loyalty of his subordinates. Taxis had survived and this very fact caused a strange pride and a loyalty to his new master that suggested the loyalty of a suicide toward his noose. The capture of these couriers, however, delighted Bar-Lev. Privately, Prince Rowenna (another survivor) told Taxis that their lord's mood had swung as if he had won a major victory. The relief in Zoha was great; the scouts responsible for the capture were feted like returning heroes.

The couriers were a strange pair. One turned out to be a Gildi guardsman, the other a young and none too intelligent citizen of Moaz. The letter was more interesting still. Taxis learned of its contents directly from Bar-Lev himself. He had been called to examine the couriers, to see if he recognized either of them as known associates of Talo. He did not, but afterwards, Bar-Lev called him to his private tent (even in Zoha, Bar-Lev resided in a tent pitched on the stone paving of a flat roof high in the citadel).

"You have ever given me honest and good counsel; no one among my people knew the Taelin better. I would have you consider the contents of the communication between the Gildi and the Pau and advise me of your impressions. Can you read Southcoast?"

"Great Lord, I can read it after a fashion."

"Better than I, no doubt. Rowenna has gone over it with me so there is little uncertainty about the meaning, but here, try it yourself."

As Bar-Lev handed him a roll of soft and supple leather, Taxis felt washed by pride. The greatest man in Ossa -- evident from the hundreds of thousands he could command -- valued his opinion; and, apparently, his company. Nothing had made these facts more concrete than sharing Bar-Lev's pleasure over the captured letter. Taxis laid out the roll and bent over the difficult cursive script.

"Great lord, it says:

> Greetings to Josh, known as Getlof. Great pleasure was mine when I received your letter and read the tale of your high deeds. Particularly I noted the honor given you initially by your kin did not equal the honor bestowed you in this city. Forgive me for taking pride in the demonstrated acuity of Our instincts. It does not surprise to hear that you felt it necessary to hide your gender during the hard beginnings of your journey. Hearing it I can well believe it because you are so fair in a way that is uncommon to a man. I think you succeeded with your disguise only because your race is rare and no one could say what is normal or not normal in the appearance of a Pau. Still, it excites my heart and I must rebuke you for not telling me.

Ossa

It is unhappy time we now live in, but I can not say I am unhappy. The year since you left has been the best in My life. You have not heard of Angus, probably. He uncovered treachery in Zoha and overcame it. The treachery extended deep among the nobility of my city. Angus held Zoha for many months against the false one who has beguiled the people of the east and still managed to return to me with many of the people he defended, escaping on the lake in a thousand boats. Angus has been my strong staff this winter yet, I have come to see that there are times when I must take my own counsel and act according to my own wishes. Seeing you so fearless has made me ashamed of my own fears. I know we shall meet again and that time I anticipate with expectant pleasure.

Your messengers have been treated with every honor. I am pleased to hear that the few men of my land who have remained with you have played such a large and loyal role in your successes. There are many things for us to discuss, but this will wait for our next encounter, may it be soon.

Signed with His seal. Ducitos XI

Taxis put the letter aside and looked up. Bar-Lev was regarding him intently.

"Great Lord, this seems to tell us many things. Master Talo is not mentioned. More interestingly, it tells us there's only been one person the entire time acting the part of the Josh. Apparently the rumors of the honor given by the Gildi is true and apparently this honor was enough to overcome the hatred they held for Talo. I read this as telling us they are real allies."

"As do I. But I can't believe, either, that it is so simple."

"Simple or complex, I cannot say, Great Lord. I find it curious that he dwells at such length about the girl's being disguised. It sounds to me like a young man who is in love, but knows not what love is."

"Excellent! That's what I wanted to hear. And what girl, regardless of what she knew of love, would spur the attention of Ducitos? Yes, the puppy is sniffing. But perhaps Ducitos does have some idea of what he's about. And maybe his idea isn't so bad. You may leave Taxis. And as you go present this chit to Thera; your advice today has earned you a reward."

The Prince Rowenna, the subtle, soft-spoken surviving remnant of the class that ruled Tarhad in the days before Bar-Lev was the next one called into the presence of his absolute master. And there he learned his new assignment; a journey far, far to the unspeakable west. A rose-petal journey it was to be, remarkably enough, for Bar-Lev had decided to court another wife.

"I don't expect you to return with immediate agreement, though I expect you to exercise the full power of your tongue to get it. So, for that eventuality, I will have you take a sealed gift to be presented upon her refusal. Upon her refusal only." Bar-Lev uttered his deep and oddly attractive laugh. "I'm going to plant a seed, me, the sod-breaker's bane. She must begin to learn whom she presumes to oppose."

26

THE DREAM

This was the dream: Great winds, sky scoured blue and a narrow path spanning a chasm like a stone rope. Peaks surrounded, learning forward, tipped with rocky cairns like rotted teeth.

And Getlof. Getlof standing on the point of this horizon: With two clear ways and still not certain which was forward and which was back; or if her ways were really clear at all.

The wind had a voice, but she couldn't understand. It stroked her roughly, sweeping in from one side, then the other, then from all sides at once. Balance was a precious thing; fear everything else. The real terror was not going the wrong way; it was falling. That would be extinction.

Then came the idea that perhaps she'd already fallen. Maybe she was standing on some species of tongue and was looking out of the mouth of the world. Getlof tried to blink the water from her eyes, afraid to wipe them because that might break her concentration on the path. She went forward, because that was the way she was facing. One step only brought her to the other side--to some high point marked by a single granite stone. The stone might have been a caricature of an old man, standing upright but stooped. She slowly touched it, then jerked her hand back. It was cold, so cold she left skin from her fingertips behind.

The voice in the wind plucked at her comprehension. It seemed she should know its language; that she was being very stupid. Coaxing? Threatening? The voice of extinction or of life?

A man stepped from around the stone. He was not a normal man, his limbs and features were tangled, but his carriage made Getlof wonder whether she was the abnormal one. He smiled an irregular smile and bowed. Getlof stepped back, right to the edge. The wind tugged and pulled.

"The Mountain Sobruins dance today."

Nonsense, but this was her dream. It was The Dream. And every time before she had backed another step; the sensation of falling had always caused her to scream and waken. It was a habit strong and well established.

Getlof bowed back. "The Sobruins?" Her voice small and indefinite.

"You and I, and the mountains. The Mountains of Decay, of Tears, and to you, the Mountains of Terror. Come, dance with me."

Getlof looked up. His name was the proper one. The peaks around her were whirling, whipping the wind to a frenzy. She could barely balance.

He laughed like an avalanche. "Almost ready, but not quite." Then the deformed man started growing. His feet, the left turned forward and the right one back, became as mountain slopes; his head, bent forward and askew, pierced the vaulted sky. And still he grew.

That was when some part of the wind's message suddenly made sense. There were things she was forgetting. Important things. Something she couldn't know about asleep.

"She stirs!"

That had been a normal voice. Just like Golab's. Was it that her eyes were now merely closed, or was some fresh dream sequence attempting to guile her.

"Is she waking?"

"I thought so."

That was the way of dreams: the lost surfaced while the familiar dissolved. What had she been dreaming before? Already Getlof couldn't remember. She opened her eyes, somewhat amazed at how easy it was.

It was Golab. He leaned over and touched her forehead lightly. "Getlof! Thank Paulic you're awake."

She nodded wonderingly. "And you alive." She saw the dressing around his right side. "Where are we?"

Talo's face was suddenly beside Golab's. "Still Moaz. It's the second day after . . ."

He stopped because Getlof was struggling to sit up. Talo had appeared from midst flame and smoke. She had been running up dark, frightening corridors. . . .

"Please," Golab said. "You're weak. Just lay down."

It was hard to struggle with someone who had obviously been badly wounded. Golab's color was wan, his demeanor frail. Getlof lay back. She was returned from her night journey, was merely tired. "All right. Where's Narhad?"

"He's sleeping," Golab said. "Sat with you all night."

"Oh, I thought. . . . Not sure what I thought."

"I think you should sleep a little more, if you can," Talo said. "You'll be fine now. We'll be here when you wake."

Getlof nodded and closed her eyes. It really was easier than keeping them open.

Getlof came awake again that evening, this time instantaneously. Doy and Elp were in the room. She watched them for awhile before they noticed her. Elp sat with his arms clasped round his knees, watching Doy whittle. They were chatting in low voices. Then Elp glanced over and saw Getlof's eyes. He jumped to his feet. Getlof sat up and said:

"Hello, I'm glad to see you two. What's the matter, Elp?"

"You're awake."

"I couldn't sleep forever."

"It seemed you were going to, Lady," Doy said. "We've been worried. Elp, get the others. Iodai has been demanding to see you as soon as you wake. He was mad he missed you the first time."

Iodai. That was a problem she had forgotten. "He's not still mad I took his prisoner, then?"

Doy was confused for a moment. "Oh, you must mean the younger Iodai. I was talking about the elder. Young Iodai is no longer with us."

"Oh." She wasn't exactly sure what that meant, but it could wait. "Do I have any clothes here? I want to get dressed."

"I'm not sure. Maybe you should wait."

Getlof spotted a white dress lying folded on top of a chest. She tossed the covers off and climbed out of bed. A rush of dizziness hit her, but Doy didn't seem to notice.

"If you'll step outside or turn your back, or whatever, I'll put this on." Doy started to protest, but when Getlof began pulling her night shift off, Doy stepped outside.

Getlof was running her fingers through her hair, wishing for a comb, when someone knocked. She walked over and opened the door.

Golab was the first inside. "What are you doing up?"

Narhad, Talo, Iodai the Elder and Zak all followed him in. There were more, but Narhad shut the door on them. Iodai and Zak greeted her formally, but with evident relief. She wondered why everyone was treating her so gingerly.

"Hello. I feel fine. I'm well. What's happened?"

Zak smiled and Iodai turned to Narhad. "She doesn't know?"

"I'll tell her," Talo said.

"Tell me what?"

"What people are saying. You won't remember, Getlof, but in the hall, after you gave the ring to Zak, an attempt was made on your life. You fainted just as the assassin threw his knife. You fell a quarter second before the knife passed through the space where you had been. It was a neat coincidence."

"I don't remember." It was like a story about someone else. "It sounds like I was pretty lucky."

"Personally, I agree. However, it was a well witnessed event, and the stories I've been hearing say something a little more than luck was involved."

"What do you mean?" She still wasn't clear why everyone was acting so strangely.

Talo looked at her oddly. "Can't you guess, Getlof? Let's see:" he held up a hand and began to count off on his fingers. "First, you contrive to make the soldiers leave the city; second you raise the city -- you, a Pau. Third, the revolt succeeds; fourth, you are protected from harm."

"But Talo, you know that's not true. You made the soldiers leave the city; the lady from the inn brought everyone together. I did less than most in the fighting and I only fainted at the end." Actually, she could remember a little. It was as if something, someone, had pressed her down at the moment she needed saving. But she couldn't bring that up--it'd be misunderstood too easily.

Talo shook his head. "I'm not saying this or that; I'm only telling you what people are saying."

"It was a sign, Lady," Iodai said, "that is what you must understand. I greatly regret I wasn't there to see it. The hand of the unmanifest Lord lies upon your brow. He delivers you from harm and breaths success into your undertakings. He smites so you might be uplifted. . . ."

"All right. I fainted just as a knife was thrown at me."

"Aye, you did, Lady, just as it was thrown." Narhad said. "And the whole city knows it. Everyone."

"I see."

"No, perhaps you don't see yet," Zak said. "The city is sorely divided about this. Half of them now remember the power of Paulic and say the destruction and death is a punishment from him. Fine, but the other half says you are a witch and they wait Caos' return. Do you see the problem?"

Getlof nodded slowly. It was as if they were talking about someone else. "But, I gave the ring to you, Zak."

"Yes, for the time being, I have the ring. But not until yesterday did the last group of soldiers in the city lay down their arms; and Gavin still holds the Upper Citadel. And then there is Caos. We have scouts out so he will not come at us unaware, but no one can guess how this will end."

Getlof nodded. She didn't know who Gavin was, but at the moment it didn't seem important. She looked at Iodai, thinking of his grandson.

"What of Iodai the younger? I can't remember seeing him at the parley."

"He wasn't there," Narhad said. "I had people look for a body, but there was none."

"And Nidot?" suddenly suspicious.

"He is dead, Lady. I found his body myself."

Getlof glanced at the elder Iodai. She let the subject drop without following her suspicions further.

"So now, Zak, you wonder what I do next."

"That is correct, Lady."

"Don't be frightened by what they tell you of the city's mood," Iodai said with sudden vehemence. "Emotions are high, but people will settle down and accept what they talk against now."

"You all have heard me say I can't stay in Moaz."

"Yes, but . . ."

"What buts? Iodai, of all people you should be able to appreciate why I can't stay. Nothing has changed for me; I'm still bound to do what I set out from Dell to do."

"Don't be offended, Lady, but it gladdens my heart to hear you speak thus," Zak said. "You have become a symbol of this city's division and I fear it will never be whole as long as you remain."

"No offense," Getlof said, relieved, in fact, that Zak would be her ally in this. "We are in agreement."

"What agreement?" Iodai said. "Let us discuss this thing. You don't know what reception the Pau will give you, even if you can find them. Lady, here you will be held in the highest honor. The lands to the north are wild and unsettled. What good can you do if you come to grief at the hands of a wandering band? Stay in Moaz."

"Iodai," holding back a smile, "you told me I was protected."

"You are, but no one should presume on it."

"Oh, I never have and never will. But I must do what I said I'd do. What's happened here doesn't change that."

Iodai swept around the room, while the others watched him. Finally: "Very well. Your mind is set and I see I can't dissuade you. My mind is just as firmly set, however. I will follow."

The discussion was draining Getlof's still precarious store of energy. To finish with Iodai she said: "Very well, I won't deny you that," and didn't pause to consider the implications. Even the way Narhad and Talo frowned on hearing this decision didn't make her consider.

"The next thing is to decide when. Is there any reason why we can't leave tomorrow?"

"No reason," Talo said. "We've been ready, but are you?"

"Just a moment," Iodai said. "What is this talk? I will have many preparations."

Talo and Iodai commenced arguing, but Getlof shut them out. The decisions were made; others could handle the details.

It happened that Iodai's statement that he would follow Getlof had collective implications. He wanted to bring as many followers as possible. Talo tried to get Getlof to renege on her promise, but she knew no way of doing that. It was clear that Iodai would follow regardless. The season was growing late and the northern winters were long and cold. That factor had to be considered with everything else.

Golab finally suggested an acceptable compromise. Getlof and her immediate circle would depart and travel to the site of Joshin in the Middle Hills. Iodai and his people would follow as soon as they were able. They would winter at Joshin and Getlof would go to Hilev the following spring. It was a delay, but unavoidable in any case.

Her physical condition bothered Getlof more than any prospective delay in her journey. She continued to suffer from spells of lightheadedness and fainting and was continually tired. She tried to hide this from the others, but Golab watched her closely and was hard to fool. She blacked out when the two of them were sitting in her chamber and after that she had to come out with the whole story; everything but the dream which she couldn't remember anyway. She refused, however, to linger in Moaz, so they arranged for her to travel in a cart. The distance to Joshin was not that great--nine days or a little more--and not overly dangerous. In Joshin Getlof would have a whole winter to rest and recover her strength.

It was the same party as before, less Renix and with two additions. Elp begged to be permitted to travel with Getlof and she couldn't refuse him. The second addition was Unsari the poet. A friendship had grown up between him and Talo and they were often seen together. Iodai expected to lead a large group, maybe a hundred or more. They would follow in a few days.

29

UNSARI TELLS A TALE

Getlof departed Moaz on the fifth day after her arrival, eleven days out of Zoha, slightly more than two months into her sixteenth year (as measured by the party in Dell).

She set forth from the citadel at dawn in a covered cart, down the broad avenue that led to NorthGate. Peering through the curtains, she looked on the city for the first time since the uprising. A low wall of rubble--old bricks, broken masonry and burnt beams--ran parallel to the road on her left. She recalled a time in Dell when a canal was under construction. The children had piled up the dirt from the ditch and played war, pretending the ditch was a moat and the dirt a rampart. They had not been playing here.

At the northern end of town entire neighborhoods were burned out. Getlof noticed people sleeping in the streets. At a place where the avenue broadened into a square, she also saw a gallows with six bodies dangling from it. Getlof was glad when the wall (tall and serene) rose into view.

A delegation was waiting there to see her off; Zak and Daken, the Lower Captain, still faithfully serving, and Iodai and other citizens as well. They spoke in low voices, without cheer. Already rumors of Caos' return were sweeping the city. The scouts had given no support to these tales, but none-the-less, everyone seemed to think the tents of the army would be outside the gates any day. Getlof was sorry she had to say goodbye in such an uncertain atmosphere. When Zak asked for a word in private, she could see he felt it too.

"I don't know if this is a proper question, Lady, but can you tell me what you see?"

Getlof leaned back on her cushions. She knew what Zak meant, and although she was tempted to say that she saw no more than he did, she couldn't refuse in that fashion to give what he wanted.

"That's hard to say, but tell me, Zak, have you ever seen a success that brought so little joy and so much fear?"

He shook his head. "No, Lady, you speak the truth there. I almost wish Caos was here so this thing could be finally settled."

"Even so. We make the future. Here there is doubt where there should be joy; silence where there should be celebration and fear where there should be confidence. That's really all I can say." Zak was staring at his clasped hands as Getlof finished. She watched him, wondering if he was satisfied.

"Thank you, Lady. I understand." Nodding solemnly. "A last favor. Will you bless me?"

At that moment, shouting broke out behind the cart. Zak muttered a curse, spared Getlof a quick smile and disappeared running. A female voice, shouting hysterically: "There she is! Right there, the witch. Murderess! Burner!"

Golab came running and awkwardly swung himself into the seat; Doy, right behind, jumped into the rear of the cart. It took Getlof a moment to realize the voice was referring to her. She tried to see who was saying such things.

"Stay down," Doy said. "If they see you it'll get worse."

"Who is it?"

"Just some crazy lady. Don't listen."

Then the shouting turned to screaming. Golab shook the reins and the cart lurched forward, sending Getlof sprawling back into her cushions. Doy crawled to the rear and looked back.

"Move over and let me see."

"A moment, Lady, its not safe. Ah, there, they have them running. By Yetit, what a crowd. Where did they all come from?"

Suddenly it was dark inside the cart and then light again. They had passed the gate and were outside Moaz.

Doy turned and smiled. "A rude sendoff."

Getlof nodded. She was very close to tears.

"Now Getlof, I mean Lady, you can't let that bother you. It was only talk."

Getlof nodded again. Then she did begin to cry. "Lady, please . . ."

From the front Golab said: "What's wrong?"

Getlof tried to stop, but she couldn't. It had been a long time since she had cried. Doy looked at her helplessly, then he climbed to the front and sat next to Golab. Getlof heard Golab whisper: "Better leave her alone; her feelings are hurt." Golab, of all people, should have known feelings were all she had.

Narhad, Talo, Elp and Unsari rode out the gate pell mell after Getlof's cart. Talo was laughing.

"Well, that is that," he shouted. "And good riddance, I say."

Narhad looked back, shook his head, but made no comment. Elp and Unsari looked frightened, both probably wondering what they had gotten themselves into. Talo laughed again. The sun was raising level over the plains. Already it was warm.

Narhad rode up to the cart but the other three lagged behind. After they had put a little distance between themselves and the walls, Talo turned to Unsari and said:

"This is a fine morning; not too hot and not too cold. Do you have a poem to celebrate it? Some little gem from your great store of rhyme that will do it justice?"

"Ah, that I do; many gems any one of which would do justice to this fine morning. And you cannot guess what a pleasure it is to be asked to recite. I needn't tell you how long it's been. But, sad to say, I cannot."

"Fie on you. What good's a poet who can't recite?" Talo asked merrily. A debate was even more to his taste than a recital. "Is there some reason for your disability?"

"There is," with offended dignity.

"And what might that be?"

Unsari looked over his shoulder. Then he drew his horse in closer to Talo's. "The truth of the matter is," whispering, "I have been frightened and badly and that is the worse of omens."

"Frightened by what? The mob at the gate? I took that for a good omen."

"You misunderstand. This harkens back to a similar fright I had once before setting out on a similar journey; and it probably adumbrates yet another fright that will happen on this journey. That is what worries me and stops my tongue. Do you see?"

"I only see why you were out of favor. Tell me about this past journey."

Unsari nodded seriously. Talo couldn't tell if he was acting or not. "There are some things no one understands and what I'm gong to tell is one of those things. But first, you must tell him to ride forward," pointing to Elp who, sensing the story, had closed up. Elp blushed.

"But why? The lad is a full member of our crew and if we're heading into bad luck or danger, surely he has a right to know. Come Elp, beside me. Now,

Unsari, what is this marvelous thing you're going to tell us that no one understands?"

"You won't laugh?"

"Of course not."

"All right. This concerns Joshin."

"Good, seeing that's where we're going."

"Yes, I've been thinking about that. Its haunted, you know."

"The Howling Ghost without a head," Elp whispered.

"Even so, even so, young man. You're more intelligent than I'd supposed. But pray, don't interrupt me again. The Howling Ghost without a head. Some say it's the spirit of Josh, crying out for retribution; others that it's Raos seeking an end to the curse Josh laid upon him. A strong case can be made for either view. You know they both died by decapitation, Josh at the hands of Raos and Raos at the hands of assassins who may or may not have been agents of his son."

"No, I didn't. Interesting."

"Interesting? Well, yes, you might say that. Caos never encouraged speculation about the matter; but I've been to Joshin myself so I know these things first hand."

"I might have guessed."

"Yes," Unsari went on, ignoring Talo. "During the great campaigns when Raos was smiting his enemies both near and far, ever seeking new fields to exercise his army. I was younger and much in favor then. I accompanied him everywhere; even to Joshin, which turned out to be his last campaign."

"Is this going to be a story about Joshin or ghosts? Speaking for myself, I'd prefer one about Joshin."

"Listen and you shall hear both." Unsari cleared his throat and glanced around to make sure he had their attention.

"I traveled in the rear, with the Magnus' baggage. Of course, I had nothing to do with the fighting; stayed as far from it as I could, so I can't tell of the heroic attacks and desperate defenses. Only once did I ever see the battle and that from a distance. Joshin overlooks an east-west canyon, on the north face far above a river. The slopes are steep; when you see it you won't believe anyone could live there, much less build a city; but that didn't stop the Pau. The city was like a giant staircase and so were the farms below. To an honest plainsman like myself, I find it difficult to understand why people would go to so much trouble terracing a mountain when so much flat land here goes begging. But, as I was saying, my first view of the city was from the south ridge. That was the line of Raos' approach. He'd left his main camp back in the foothills. The land's too rough to be dragging around tents, harems and poets; but I wanted to see the famous and much maligned city. It aroused my professional curiosity. I rode out, a day behind the army, with assorted other grandees, to view our lord's progress.

"I remember it was a difficult ride we had, down the mountain and across the river and back up the steps on the other side. Some of the generals had even said it was too difficult and that the city should be left alone. Raos ignored such talk. He was out for glory and dominion and thought to find it in Joshin. Don't think I'm defaming the old man, I wouldn't do that because I was fond of him; but I was there. You're lucky to be hearing the true story. You too, young man.

"We arrived at the south ridge about noon. I remember it was a beautiful day. It had rained all morning, which, no doubt, made the going a bit nasty for the soldiers below, but it made the air clear and fresh for us. Our men had already crossed the river and were slowly working their way up the other side. We had a general to explain the military aspects of the view. He pointed out how the soldiers had to bunch up at the paths leading up to each terrace: how each terrace was being used as a rampart to keep our men back and how poorly the Pau were fighting. Our good general claimed that with one or two thousand men he could've held that city forever. We watched the tiny figures bunching up at the terraces, just like the general said, inevitably moving up, terrace by terrace, until, by late afternoon, they were at the walls themselves . . ." Unsari paused and coughed.

"Pardon me if I'm being wordy, but I want to describe Joshin to you because of all the sights available to my eye, in all my days, the sight of that city was unparalleled.

"I said how clear the air was. One of those days that the far seems to be near. By evidence of my vision, I could've touched the tiny buildings. Colored flags and pennants bravely curled out from the high places. It was a city of bright surfaces. The sunlight delighted in it no less than I. If I wasn't a poet and didn't know better than to use hackneyed expressions, I would have called it a jewel set in the demon's eye -- the demon, of course, being a dual metaphor. I felt distant regret for its inevitable destruction."

He paused again to clear his throat. Talo was engrossed to the point he was no longer interrupting.

"That was the prelude. Joshin fell two days later, but I was back in camp and didn't witness. But Josh, I can't recall if he was twenty-second or third, disdained flight and was captured.

"We were all in attendance the day he was brought before Raos. He'd obviously been ill used, but was still an impressive figure; a lot of past to live up to. Raos intended to keep him alive for the parade back in Moaz, but Josh, when he stood before Raos began to curse him. He spat bitter curses: your fortune will betray you to unknown enemies, he said; your meanest slave shall know more of joy and success; your wife shall cuckold you with your son; your death will be early."

"And the curse was fulfilled?"

"It was. Raos never knew joy after that day. He undertook no more campaigns, convinced they would fail. He started to suspect everyone and he died before his time under suspicious circumstances, as I have related. I know because those were my days of greatest favor. I wrote the epic dirge, "The Curse of Raos." But I'll tell you what you won't find in that poem: I don't think Josh was truly responsible. Raos seemed to believe in Josh more than himself. He tried to prove his superiority by taking Joshin, but in the end only proved he was superstitious."

"How does any of this bring us to the Howling Ghost Without a Head?"

"Know this: Joshin was not completely deserted. Raos tried to settle it with veterans, thinking to hold it if the Pau of the north attempted revenge, which they never did.

"At first everything went well with them, but then men coming back to Moaz began to complain. It was an unwholesome, spooky place. Duty there became unpopular. Raos vacillated. Sometimes he spoke of rebuilding Joshin, and once, toward the end, when he was fully into the curse and not completely sane, he even spoke of moving his residence there. Finally, he decided to raze it, He died shortly after coming to that decision."

"When did the ghost first appear? Before or after his death?"

"Patience, that part is coming. I give just the facts in their proper sequence.

"When Raos died, Caos was seventeen year old. Of course, his first act as Magnus was to proclaim a progress to honor his father and celebrate his greatest victory; a great funeral march from Moaz to Joshin. That was the occasion that brought me a commission to do that poem. Raos' body was placed atop an enormous wain, especially constructed. On top with the coffin were piled various trophies and treasures deemed fitting to go with the old man. Caos put thousands to work constructing a road to accommodate the wain. This road we finally rode along--the army to escort, most of the court, especially the elder intimates of Raos, and people such as myself. The holy widowed mother was left behind to govern in her son's absence."

"Is she still alive? I was wondering about that part of the curse."

Unsari smiled and shook his head. "But don't distract me. That's another tale, longer than this.

"As I said, there were many who suspected Caos of having played an important, say significant role in the death of his father. Naturally, it was an uncertain time for old friends of Raos like myself. I recognized more than a few faces among the members of the conscripted work gangs (they formed the largest part of the audience that witnessed the Progress once it left Moaz) and naturally, my work from those days was fulsome in its adoration of the new Magnus. My foresight proved correct, as usual, but it was luck, not praise that saved me from the massacre. But I'm getting ahead of my story.

"We made the Progress and it was slow going. Caos was his ever youthful, charming self; drinking by night and hunting by day. The object was for all to have a good time and most of us did. Until the hunting accident. One of the free counts, a close personal friend of Raos', I've forgotten his name, shot at a stag and hit Caos' horse. I wasn't there so I don't know the true circumstances. Caos, at the time, choose to regard it as an accident. He teased the unfortunate count about his poor marksmanship, and that just increased the tension. We arrived in Joshin just a few days later. Then strange things began to happen.

"First it was the garrison. Their number had been depleted by desertion; their moral was low and discipline nonexistent. They had been drawn up to welcome the dead Magnus back to Joshin and to acknowledge the new. But the review ended in a riot with the troops demanding relief and a return to the city. The wain that had been two weeks working down the canyon and across the river and back up the other side, was toppled and the body soiled by contact with the ground.

"When order was finally restored, Caos went ahead with the planned ceremonies. It would've been pointless not to, but there was no feeling in them. After such terrible omens that was no surprise.

"There was a hall at the northern, that is, upper, end of the city. I'll be curious to see if it still stands. Workmen had been sent ahead to prepare it for the ceremony of exorcism which Caos preformed. Then he dedicated a plaque for a monument to be constructed on the ridge overlooking the city. Finally, the poets were called in to praise Raos's memory. I was to have given a series of three odes, but in the riot, I had received a nasty cut across my temple -- this is the scar -- and was excused. That was my great luck. After the poets were done, the body was laid out and all Raos' ex-confidants were invited to come up and do final oblation. Caos had decided it would be too much effort to haul the body back to Moaz, so Raos' final resting place was to be beneath the monument. As the old men were passing the body to say farewell, the doors to the hall swung shut and soldiers appeared from behind curtains. Caos presided over the slaughter of all his father's men. The poets, I might add, were included in the massacre, victims of place and chance."

Unsari stopped and stared into space, as if contemplating his accidental escape from death. Talo was looking forward more than ever before to seeing Joshin. For a city with such sacred associations, it seemed to have been the site of an uncommon number of deaths. He looked up at the cart and thought it a pity Getlof wasn't hearing Unsari's tale.

Elp broke the silence. "Aren't you going to tell about the ghost?"

Unsari jumped. Then he looked at Elp with a frown. "What do you think I've been talking about if not ghosts? There are thousands of ghosts there, thousands of them. Haven't I made that clear?"

"Umm, I guess, but I thought you were going to tell us about the Howling Ghost without a head."

Unsari threw back his head and laughed. "That's right. I'd forgotten." He turned to Talo. "I was leading you before, pretending my fear was greater than it is in order to spark your interest. Not that there isn't any reason to be afraid. After all, a lot of people have died in Joshin and that does affect a place. The Howling Ghost without a head appeared shortly after the massacre in the hall. That night, in fact, if my memory serves me correctly, which, these days, it hardly ever does.

"I'd been informed of the turn events had taken and was not about to bring myself to the attention of Caos. Did I say the city was largely in ruins? Well, you might have guessed. Most of the procession preferred to tent it outside the crumbled walls, but I was inside in a repaired house the garrison had fixed as a hospital. I was woken that night by a long, drawn out wail, a horrible sound. My first thought was another victim, but as it went on, I couldn't imagine how anyone could suffer so long and still keep their voice. I wondered if could have been some species of hill animal, a jackal or lion, but at heart, I didn't believe that either. The howling ceased after a time, but few people went back to sleep that night.

"By morning it was all over camp. A ghost, more specifically, a howling ghost without a head." He turned to Elp and smiled. "It seems a sentry saw what he took to be a man prowling the corridor outside Caos' residence in the old palace. When he challenged him, the man turned around and the sentry saw his, ah, deformity. The story has it that he stared in astonishment until the ghost commenced howling and advancing toward him. At that point, the guard fainted. Of course, the howling roused other guards, but they saw only their unconscious comrade. The fact his hair had turned white lent credence to his story. Having heard the howling myself, I had no trouble believing."

"Did the ghost reappear?"

"Yes and no. The next day Caos decided it was time to leave. He took the household troops and left the court to follow. The engineers who were to build the monument were especially unhappy because they were expected to stay. The garrison also felt deserted and they began to slip away in sizeable numbers. I had to stay for two nights more until I was strong enough to travel. I was only a little less old then than I am now. Both nights the howling was heard, although never so close at hand as that first night. When I rode out Joshin was practically deserted. Raos' coffin was buried in the dirt and a most unsuitable monument had been hastily erected. I remember that the chief engineer killed himself, even though it wasn't his fault. Caos had set the example and after that no one was going to stay. I think we can, in all confidence, expect to find Joshin deserted."

"That was a decent tale, Unsari. You are done, aren't you? I can understand several things better now, but what I don't understand is why you are so blithely accompanying us to Joshin if you believe its haunted?"

Unsari chuckled. "That's easy. I wouldn't want to leave the tale I currently appear to be in just for fear of a ghost, especially a ghost that never hurt anyone, as far as we know. After all, we are men and we must be reasonable."

Talo turned to Elp. "How about you? Afraid of ghosts?"

Elp nodded. "I don't like ghosts. I've seen them before, but Getlof is with us and I think the ghost will leave her alone."

"That is an interesting point you raise, young man. The effect of Josh upon the ghost, what will it be? If the ghost is Josh, there is nothing to worry about.

On the other hand, if it is Raos, he will be after her to lift the curse. Either way, we won't know for some days."

Talo looked up at the cart. "Well, I'm not worried and I don't think Getlof will be either. They've been quiet up there. Maybe I'll see how she's doing."

Talo tied his horse behind the cart and squeezed onto the seat next to Golab and Doy.

"She's sleeping," Golab whispered.

"Indeed? Well, I suppose there's not much else to do, but she's been sleeping a lot lately." Talo glanced back into the cart. Getlof was lying with her mouth slightly open. Her face was flushed and red. He looked back to see Golab watching him curiously.

"What were you talking about back there?"

"Were you listening?"

"Not really. I couldn't hear anything beside the voices."

"Unsari told us an interesting story. Are you afraid of ghosts?"

"Well, no. I don't think so. We don't have that sort of thing in Gildesh."

"Of course not. I'll try to get Unsari to tell it again."

Golab nodded. Talo leaned back in the seat. Unsari's story gave him a lot to think about. The horses were stirring clouds of powdery dust that hung languidly in the air. Talo squinted through the haze trying to see the outlines of the Middle Hills. If they were up there, the land was not yet ready to have them revealed. All Talo could see were the plains -- flat lands stretching away in every direction. He wondered what Getlof would think of Unsari's story; if something like that would frighten her. As it happened, he never found out.

30

SNATCHED!

T alo pushed the group onward all morning and into the afternoon, glad to be quit of Moaz and back on the road. Getlof slept this entire time. After a brief break late in the morning, Talo, Unsari and Elp switched positions with the Gildi guardsmen and rode ahead of the cart while Narhad and Doy followed behind. Talo dropped back every half-hour to check Getlof's condition. Narhad rode forward even more frequently to do the same. They were reluctant to wake her for nothing. It had been their fear the journey would tire her and it took time to perceive that danger might come from another direction.

In the mid-afternoon they came to their first obstacle: the road ended abruptly at the bank of a deep gully etched into the plain by a seasonal watercourse. They paused and considered this barrier.

"We've been riding all day," Unsari said. "That's hard on an old man like myself. Perhaps we can make this the occasion for a rest. A hot meal will sit nicely and so will a stretch for my poor body."

Talo nodded. "I know. Don't think I'm so young myself. But I'd like to get the wagon on the other side first. It looks like there used to be an approach, but the banks have been eroded away."

"Two years ago it rained all winter and the Shem flooded," Elp interjected helpfully.

Talo nodded. "We can get the horses down over there," he pointed, "and probably lower the wagon safely if we back it down. Getting it back up the other side is going to be the problem. Getlof will have to walk."

Narhad and Doy had been lagging to avoid the dust. They now came up. Doy saw the gully and emitted a long, low whistle. Narhad shook his head and made no comment.

"Is Getlof awake?" he asked perfunctorily.

225

Golab shook his head. "I'll wake her," and under his breath, "if I can." He disappeared into the interior of the cart. They waited only a moment, then Talo dismounted and joined him. Elp turned to Narhad and in a small voice asked:

"What's wrong with the Lady?"

Narhad shook his head. "I don't know. It doesn't seem like anything should be." Then Talo climbed out. Golab reappeared next, holding the repine form of Getlof. He handed her to Talo and jumped down.

"She's not dead?" Elp whispered.

"No, she breathes and her brow is cool enough, but we can't wake her." The others dismounted.

"An impasse," Unsari said. "Do we go on or turn back?"

Talo shook his head, face grey. "I didn't expect this. She's just like she was before, after that attack."

"And before there was no help to be had in Moaz," Narhad said. "And she came out of it herself. I think it would be foolish to retrace our steps."

Golab: "Perhaps you're right, but I don't think we should move her further today. Not until she shows some sign of life."

Talo: "In any case, we have to get this dray across the gully. We can camp on the other side and see what change the morning brings."

Narhad stood there, stroking his chin. He looked at the cart, then at the gully and finally at Getlof. "All right, we'll do what Talo suggests. You, poet, can watch Getlof while we work."

"A congenial task. This side or the other."

"The other," Talo quickly said.

On the other side of the gully, about a hundred paces back from the lip stood a giant pepper tree. It was the only landmark in sight. Around it were the decayed traces of a burned out homestead. Getlof was carried to the base of the tree, wrapped in a robe and left there with Unsari. The others began the task of lowering the cart down into the gully and coaxing it back up the other side.

The shade was welcome to Unsari. His face was beginning to feel tender from too much sun. He had missed his afternoon nap. The pepper tree emitted a sharp, but not unpleasant fragrance. Hundreds of grasshoppers buzzed aimlessly through the dry grass. Unsari resisted the temptation to emulate Getlof, but it was a struggle. He could hear the others working: shouted instructions, curses and once, a loud crash. He considered getting up to see what happened, but felt so lazy and comfortable he didn't move. Besides, someone, probably Narhad, was sure to get angry if he left Getlof unattended. Unsari was frightened of the big man.

He looked at Getlof. His feelings about her were not so clear. She was so young, nothing more than a child, delicate and small. Her appearance was not the appearance of power, at least as he knew it. But he also knew that appearances could hide rather than reveal. She excited his interest and even his hopes, although what hopes he couldn't say. At any rate, it was good to be participating in events (or a story, as he preferred to think of it) once again.

A grasshopper jumped on Getlof's face. Unsari bent forward to brush it off and almost didn't notice her eyes were open. He paused, heart suddenly beating rapidly. Her gaze wandered, then suddenly focused and she said:

"Where?"

"On the road to Joshin, Lady. I am so glad you're finally awake. We were all worried."

"How long?"

"This is the afternoon of the day of our departure from Moaz."

Getlof nodded, but frowned. They were all dreams, then. It seemed so much longer than only part of a day. "I remember. We have crossed the river."

While Unsari didn't know what to make of this remark, he felt an unexplained excitement welling up from the pit of his stomach. She was awake, but at the same time still asleep. He stroked her brow and said:

"I'll get the others."

"Who are they?"

"Who?" Then Unsari realized she had been looking at something specific the entire time. With sudden fear he looked slowly around and saw four men just a few paces away, watching silently. Nomads, but not from a tribe he recognized. Their blond hair was gathered into a braid, starting exactly on the top of their heads. On their faces two blue scars ran diagonally from their nostrils past their mouths, giving them permanent scowls. They were dressed in brightly colored corsets of leather armor and little else. Unsari rose slowly to his feet. Nomads were unpredictable people.

He greeted them first in Moazian, then Southcoast and finally in the two nomad languages he was falteringly familiar with. Nothing elicited a response. Behind him Getlof struggled to a sitting position and spoke a word he didn't recognize. The foremost nomad's face underwent a flickering change of expression. Then, a brief, incomprehensible speech followed. Helplessly Unsari looked back at Getlof. She caught his look and smiled, which was brave, he thought because there was no way he could've managed a smile himself.

A fifth nomad appeared, as if from the ground, and exchanged words with the others. He pointed back toward the gully. The first nomad gestured to Unsari and Getlof, holding a finger to his lips and then drawing it across his throat. Unsari stepped back, shaking his head. Two nomads stepped forward and grabbed his arms. He managed a surprisingly vigorous shout before he was struck on the head. Getlof made neither sound nor move. Unsari had spoken of the others, but she had no idea where they were. The word she had spoken was one taught her by Golab, long ago, it seemed, while riding up the Riverrun. He had said it meant 'Great Mother' and was used by nomads of different tribes to give one another peace -- all nomads being ruled by old women.

Getlof was picked up and hoisted into a saddle. She saw Unsari lying unconscious across another rider's horse. There was sudden shouting from somewhere behind her, but she couldn't twist around to see what it was. Then they were off, riding north across the plain.

Getlof could see only the hands of the man in the saddle behind her, gripping the reins and urging his horse on. She had to gasp for breath, such was the speed of their passage; but it was invigorating also. Her body, if not her mind, held the memory of the day's journey--the heat of the closed in box, the sweat soaking her dress and covers. All of that was gone. She looked at herself and saw she was hardly attired at all. Her hair, which had been growing for two months, whipped about, flying into eyes and mouth. It was strange, stranger than any of her dreams, but real. Stranger still was Getlof herself. She did not feel like a snatched person; quite the opposite. She felt like the abductor herself. These strange men were flying north at her unexpressed command. The direction was right. The speed was right. The others would find her.

The loud crash Unsari had heard was the wagon slipping from its stays and bouncing back down the gully where it ended on one side, axle broken. This mishap caused tempers to flair and absorbed everyone's attention during the critical moments when Unsari and Getlof were confronted by the nomads. Elp heard Unsari's shout, although it reached him as just a noise, not a cry of distress. He was also the closest, standing on the north lip of the gully, holding the bridle to the team of horses that had just unsuccessfully tried to haul the cart up.

Elp looked back toward the pepper tree. A rise in the ground prevented him from seeing its base. Nothing looked amiss, but he decided he should investigate. Since the night in the citadel when he had drawn praise for keeping the advance watch he fancied himself a scout and a warder. This conceit enabled him to risk Talo's anger for leaving the horses unattended. He ran to the rise and saw a dozen riders and Getlof being lifted up on a horse. It was his shout that Getlof heard. Several riders detached themselves from the group and galloped toward him. He turned and ran for his life, flying down the rise. The pounding hoofs behind grew louder and louder still and he expected at any moment to feel a lance entering his back. Finally, when the sound were all around him, he threw himself to the ground and rolled to his left, bunched into a ball. He missed seeing Narhad and Doy drop the two leading riders with arrows, thereby saving his life. The nomads wheeled their horses and withdrew to the top of the rise. Elp scrambled down to safety as Narhad got a third with a long shot. With a cry of defiance, shaking their lances, the nomads collected the three riderless mounts and disappeared to the north. For a second everyone was silent, then Talo said bitterly:

"A fool. A fool I am after all this to lose her like that."

Narhad was already running to calm the team of horses. All nine had been hitched to the cart and fortunately that kept them from stampeding. Still, two horses suffered broken legs. They were killed. The other seven were quickly saddled, but it was a long fifteen minutes before they were ready to give chase. With Narhad's acid comment of: "that takes care of that problem," they began to follow the trail of the nomads. It was already evening. To Talo nomads meant one thing only and that was Bar-Lev. He explained his fears to the others and they pressed on all the harder. Fortunately the moon that night was early rising and three quarters full.

31

MUK'S ADVENTURES CONTINUE

Muk crouched back from the road as the raiders silently infiltrated the town; when the fighting began he intended to be well out of the way. He watched the sentries fall, one by one; each death lightening the misery of his heart. Then he heard the scream. The attack began and he saw it was premature. He lingered, thinking if anyone deserved a miracle surely it was he and almost lingered too long, being caught in the rout when the Gildi guard swept down toward the inn. Then Muk ran and ran fast enough to escape harm.

He worked his way to the raider's prearranged rendezvous several leagues back up the Riverrun. One failure wasn't enough to make him admit defeat; but, as he waited all night only to gather a half dozen of the raiders, he finally had to concede that most of the survivors considered their duty done and had chosen the hills over loyalty.

Yes, it was clear Talo had planned his treachery well; that he had intended it from the first and that such blackheartedness would not be easily vanquished. But Muk's resolve was steadfast. He would succeed because he had to.

The next day Muk and six men who still followed him slipped past the town and followed Getlof's escort at a safe distance. They followed through the mountain gate and into the plains, never coming so close as to be detected. They saw their prey enter the fort and, the next day, saw them depart afloat with a destination that clearly could only be Zoha.

Muk choose to approach Zoha from the eastern side of the Last Lake, crossing the Ossa below the fort where the river was wide and sluggish. During that night two of his company slipped away. This was bad, but not disastrous. He knew Caos planned to attack Zoha and also that he expected the help of Bar-Lev. If anyone was going to escape north out of that doomed city, they'd have to do it quietly, without many followers. Muk planned to be waiting. If the odds were even slightly in his favor, he wouldn't fail a second time. The idea was inconceivable.

The first day of travel along the Ossa's eastern shore passed without incident. Muk and his party covered more than half the distance to Zoha; an incredible feat of riding made possible by Muk's constant goading and the fact that each man had two horses. That night one of the raiders assigned to guard duty ran away. Muk had never imagined himself a leader of men and after playing that role, he never would. But any task, regardless of its repugnance, he'd attempt to bring about his reunion with Kisti. He was only vaguely aware a darker and stronger one had supplanted this motivation: revenge on Talo.

The group was only hours south of Zoha when they spotted a cloud of dust to the north. Muk had his men dismount and lead their horses into a dell where they were out of sight. He did this not because of the danger that the dust marked Gildi scouting south of Zoha, but because he wanted no distractions. He wanted nothing to happen that might divert him from his chase. He never considered that if he could see them, they could see him; or that maybe they had even seen him first.

The drumming sound of hoofs grew until it seemed the other riders would pass almost next to Muk's hiding place; but just when the noise should have begun to grow fainter, it stopped. Muk looked up and saw riders on the lip of the dell looking down. They were not Gildi; that much was instantly clear, being blond and mostly naked except for leather armor dyed all sorts of improbable colors. Their faces were scored with blue lines and their skulls were bald except for a single braid emerging from the crown. They were nomads and clearly followers of Bar-Lev. Muk relaxed slightly and even had a brief fantasy of what it would be like to lead several hundred men such as these against Talo's party. That would decide things. Then the nomads drew their swords, a horribly brisk sound, and the fantasy vanished.

Muk jumped up and held his arms out saying: "Peace. We are Moazians." He said it in Southcoast, Moazian, in Xumi and in Tumi. Finally, one of them, apparently the leader, showed his teeth and said, in Southcoast:

"Moazians? Frightened Moazians. What do you on this side of the river if the sight of men frightens you?"

Muk didn't care for nomads--most normal people in Ossa didn't--and the manners of this one irritated him. He took a pace forward and said:

"Keep your insults. I am Muk, slave of the Magnus on high commission for my master. Enemies of both our masters, enemies of the highest consequence, travel north to Zoha. We give pursuit."

The nomad laughed. "You lie, slave. We have ridden this shore since before dawn and you are the first we have seen."

Muk shook his head. Strange things had begun to happen to his temper and even stranger things to his self-control. "No, I tell the truth. My commission is this." He showed the medallion of Caos. "My enemies sail on the lake. I follow as best I may."

The nomad looked at the medallion and it was clear he had seen such things before. Then, in a more reflective voice: "Six boats did pass us in the night. We saw and counted them. If these were the enemies you chase, they are in Zoha City now. Yet, news of consequential enemies will interest the great Bar-Lev. Thank your gods, Moazian, you live. Kill the others and bring their horses."

And they did. Muk made no protest. If was enough if he lived.

The Levite camp was situated a half-day's ride due east of Zoha. Muk saw first a smokey pallor in the sky caused by thousands of campfires. When he was led over a small rise and saw the camp itself, he was moved to wonder--as insensitive to that emotion as he normally was. Tents spread over an area seemingly twice as large as Moaz; everywhere people swarmed. Never had he imagined there were so many nomads in all the land of Ossa.

Muk was taken to a wooden hut on the edge of this jostle where he passed the night under guard. He spent the next day in the same circumstances. By the second evening he was certain he'd been forgotten. No revenge; no Kisti; nothing. To think he'd been frustrated by a chance encounter on the road was a thought ever more unbearable. By the second night he was ready to do something about it. The cost didn't matter.

It was apparent the Levites didn't pay much attention to detail. Muk had the same guard and no one had come to relieve him. The man was clearly bored and desperate for some other duty. Muk spent the evening with his head in his hands making piteous sounds (he was unable to force himself to cry); reinforcing the guard's low opinion of his charge. Then he began to snore and after not very long, the guard was snoring as well. From there it was easy. He killed the guard with his own knife and found--to his relief--it was not a hard thing to do. He had no hope of disguising himself as a nomad--his skin was too dark and his hair the wrong color. Moreover, Muk had no desire to look so absurd, even if it might save his life. He spent the rest of the night digging a hole under the wall in the back of the hut. He didn't know the front door was unguarded and that he could have simply walked away.

Muk hadn't been forgotten. News of his capture had reached the all-encompassing ears of Bar-Lev himself sparking his interest. Bar-Lev, however, was a man with many demands upon his time. Perhaps it was for this reason he was accustomed to conduct business at the oddest hours of the day and night. It wasn't strange at all that he should summon Muk an hour before dawn.

Muk heard the door opening. He had time only to turn and hold the dagger before him, expecting to be attacked and killed. Three men crowded into the hut, holding torches. Muk blinked. Silence, then laughter.

"Look, the Moazian lizard-eater killed Cara-Cara." They seemed to think it a fine joke. But then, Muk had never claimed to understand the nomad mind and he had never met anyone who did.

Still chuckling, they disarmed him easily, although Muk attempted to resist. Then he was bound and led through the camp to a yellow tent, little different from all the many tents he had been led pass. Muk had been told he was being taken to see the Great Bar-Lev, but he presumed his captors were playing with him. By the smokey light of torches, it looked a mean sort of place to find a great captain of many men.

People were just waking and engaging in domestic chores. Muk's senses had been dulled considerably by two days of semi-starvation in the dark hut; none-the-less, he found the smokey, greasy, human smells that pressed him quite horrible. He was led pass the cooking fires into the large yellow tent and then into a smaller black tent pitched within. In the light of a smokeless oil lamp three men sat on stools around a low table. They were drinking a steaming beverage with a bitter smell. The men of Muk's escort halted and made low obeisance to these men -- none of whom looked up. Muk repeated their bows, but he did a better job of it, sweeping the floor with his forehead. At this he was noticed. One of the men said, in Southcoast:

"This must be the slave."

The man who said this was on the far side of middle age with a pitted and eroded face and thick, scarred shoulders. Muk thought him crude and majestic looking and deduced he was Bar-Lev. The other two men were younger. The one in the middle was just beginning middle age. His face was clear and his eyes a startling, deep blue. The third man was younger still. Muk paid him no attention.

"I am the slave, Muk, commissioned by Caos, my great Master, sorely delayed by your servants, oh Awesome One."

Muk said this to the older man. However, it was the one in the middle who responded. "Muk, that name seems familiar for some reason. Ala-Medan, leave us. I'll see you next week." The youth stood and withdrew silently. Then: "I am Bar-Lev, slave. He is E-Toyoc."

Muk bowed again, this time even lower. Bar-Lev's voice was even, cold and frightening.

"So, you informed my scouts you followed an enemy--an extraordinary enemy--on special commission for your master. Name this enemy and the commission."

Bar-Lev made no threats; clearly he didn't need to. Muk told first about the Pau whom Caos considered highly dangerous and the advent of Talo in Moaz. He told how he and Talo journeyed to Dell and he didn't leave out the story of Talo's treachery. Then he told of the chase, the failed ambush and finally his capture. Muk left nothing out. He didn't notice when the lamps were put out, nor did he feel the heat of the morning sun when it came streaming through the flap in the tent. He poured forth his tale in a manner he never realized he was capable of. When it was over, Bar-Lev grunted and turned to his councilor.

"Extraordinary. I thought we'd heard the last of our Taelien friend when we burned his ship last fall."

The counselor nodded. "We hoped, but we didn't expect. To hear he's holed up in Zoha is bad news indeed."

"You think of Sidoc, I know. But Zoha is no Sidoc; it's weaker and I'm stronger. But this is indeed extraordinary intelligence. Caos left Gavin behind in Moaz. Do you think he'll let this opportunity pass? Of course not. I know that type. Caos is a fool in love with himself. This has decided my mind."

Bar-Lev looked at Muk who was standing, wondering what his fate would be.

"You, slave, inspire generosity in me. I have no use for fools, but a man who helps himself is a man to my liking. They tell me you killed the guard set over you and were preparing to escape. I conclude the guard was a fool, but you show possibilities. What did you intend when you escaped?"

"One thing only, lord," Muk replied without hesitation. "To carry out my commission and bring retribution to the Taelien."

"Ah, you say commission softly, but retribution, that word has force behind it. But we mustn't forget the Pau. A female, you say. Is she fair?"

"I know not, lord. I never saw her."

"Almost certainly fair. Probably beautiful. They say the Pau are a dark race. I find that appealing. A danger in the hands of my enemies, but an asset to me." He turned back to E-Toyoc and counted off on his fingers: "In Zoha we have the Taelien, certainly a dangerous man. We have the Pau with claims to the title of Josh, under the control of the Taelien and perhaps the Gildi. Dangerous. We have Caos moving his army south expecting us to do the work of taking the city and then to hand it to him." Then back to Muk: "Tell me, slave, what course would you advise?"

Muk had heard enough to get a sense of what Bar-Lev liked and he replied without hesitation: "Lord, without betraying my master I can say he is an uncertain friend. This is no secret. In Zoha your enemies are gathered. Your forces are overwhelmingly strong. You are needed by Caos, but you need him not at all. Gavin contemplates revolt. He needs you likewise and likewise, he is nothing to you. Moaz is the power in the middle lands and the power of Moaz seems likely to fail. These, lord, are merely the facts. If I was your adviser, I would counsel exactly what you intend."

"Would you, slave? I can see you have qualities I can use." Bar-Lev clapped his hands and a girl appeared. "This man is Muk. Find him quarters in my compound and give him something to eat."

When Muk was gone, E-Toyoc said: "But lord, do you intend to trust a man who betrays his lord so readily?"

Bar-Lev laughed. "Trust? I trust no one, E-Toyoc. But I will use him. He hates the Taelien and that hate will hold him to me."

That day the Levite hoard struck camp and began to slowly move east. Muk was given a horse and a companion who, in fact, was a guard: a young nomad, the son of a minor chief, named Pa-Mares. He didn't speak Southcoast and Muk was instructed to teach it to him. Muk, however, with an eye to his own future, used the young nomad to practice his own Tumi.

It took the hoard two days to cover the half-day ride to Zoha. Muk didn't see Bar-Lev during this time. He spoke with Pa-Mares and learned that his duty with Muk was bitter to him. There was to be fighting and he would not have the opportunity to participate owning to his guard and language duties. Muk thought it rather incredible and slightly inhuman a person would prefer a chance at death to safety, but that was the typical nomad way of thinking.

Finally they reached the bluffs of the Ossa overlooking Zoha. It was a city invested. Moazian camps ringed it and a ditch was being dug across the spit of land between the Shem and the Ossa. Muk was able to see these things because he rode in Bar-Lev's party. The Moazian army looked sufficient for the task before it, being a large host, but even Muk could see its numbers were nothing before the Levite hoard. Then ambassadors rode in from the Moazian camp. Bar-Lev had Muk stand in a position where he was able to hear everything. Muk recognized several of the Moazians, prominent among them Count Lejo-Lie a division commander. During the parley that followed, he noted that several times Moazians he knew looked at him speculatively, but no one made a definite sign of recognition.

Bar-Lev bespoke the Moazians graciously at first. They reported to him the progress of the siege. The circle had been closed for two days and already they had launched an assault. Bar-Lev laughed at this and asked if Caos was then waiting to receive him in the halls of Zoha. Count Lejo-Lie sadly said no, the attack had failed. Bar-Lev then said he had certain intelligence that the indomitable captain of mercenaries, Talo the Taelien, was inside Zoha directing the defense. Now it was Lejo-Lie's turn to smile. He said that was impossible-- even going so far as to suggest Bar-Lev was still obsessed with the near thing at Sidoc. However, it was certain that an equally fearsome captain was in Zoha and that man was none other than Angus, captain of the Gildi guard.

All this time the Levite hoard continued to arrive and to spread itself around the Moazian camps as the Moazians were spread out around Zoha. Then Muk saw that a force had forded the Ossa and was on the same side as the city. Lejo-Lie noticed this at approximately the same time. He asked Bar-Lev if it wouldn't be better to keep the two armies separate until a cooperative plan of attack could be formulated.

"Otherwise, there might be cause for misunderstanding and fertile field for incident."

Bar-Lev choose to take the pastoral image as an insult and coldly informed the Count that he and his men were not farmers. The Count blushed and quickly said it was not his intent to offend. Muk noticed most of the nomads appeared to be trying hard not to laugh. The Moazians noticed it as well and began to look about nervously. Then Bar-Lev did laugh, deep and loudly. This must have been a signal because at that moment horns began sounding from all the Levite positions. Hidden archers released a volley into the Moazian party and Bar-Lev's guard rode forward to complete the work. Count Lejo-Lie was one of the few to draw his sword. Muk saw that Pa-Mares had his sword drawn also, but that he was watching Muk, not the fight. Muk stared at him as his heart beat violently; but he made no move and neither did Pa-Mares. Lejo-Lie killed two Levites, but by that time he was the sole surviving Moazian. Nomads came forward one by one to challenge him. He took a third and then a fourth. Then Bar-Lev himself gave a great shout and spurred his horse forward. Lejo-Lie turned to face him, hope suddenly lighting his face, but Bar-Lev quickly proved himself the Moazian's master in swordplay as well as in deception. They fought dismounted in a circle of shouting nomads. Bar-Lev continually forced the Count back then ended it with a thrust into the right armpit that made the Moazian drop his sword. Bar-Lev said:

"You are a brave man for a Moazian and you know how to fight. Join me and I'll give you command of a hundred."

Lejo-Lie shook his head curtly. Bar-Lev shrugged and beheaded him. Then Bar-Lev looked around with a grin, acknowledging the cheers of his men. When he had remounted, Bar-Lev rode over to Muk. He said, in Tumi, to Pa-Mares: "Has the slave behaved himself?"

Pa-Mares replied: "He only watched."

In Southcoast: "A watcher. I knew it. Come, slave, with me and you shall watch the end of a fool. Then we will have to think of a new name to call you by."

Muk followed, riding by Bar-Lev's side, encircled by his guard and captains to the edge of the bluff. At that point they had a clear view of the city and the battle now being fought outside it. Muk understood at once why it had taken the hoard so long to make their movement to Zoha. Bar-Lev had sent divisions in wide circles so that they were now coming at the Moazians from every side, even blocking the retreat back to Moaz on the far shore of the Shem. Then he was able to pick out Caos' campaign pavilion. It was well away from the walls of Zoha. He pointed it out to Bar-Lev. Bar-Lev nodded and spoke to a man who then rode off the bluffs in that direction. Within moments, it seemed, a large force of nomad horse swept into that section. Tiny fires were springing up everywhere and soon the entire view was obscured under a cloud of smoke and dust. Bar-Lev seemed well satisfied. The last thing he said to Muk before riding off to hear his captain's report was:

"So much for Caos. Now the midlands shall know me as the eastlands do. There shall be but one Lord in Ossa, slave no longer. Thank your gods you serve him."

The siege of Zoha dragged on. Bar-Lev ordered an assault on the day following the destruction of the Moazian army, but it was repulsed. The next day was the same and that night same again. Bar-Lev was utterly convinced Talo opposed him and this made him conduct the attacks with a special fury, but also a special respect. More than once the walls were attained, but each time counter attacks threw the Levites off. The nomads began to speak of the defenders with respect--telling tales especially of a corp of giants who could always be found where the fighting was the bitterest. It was a respect they had never accorded the Moazians; a respect facilitated by the certainty of victory. On the second week an assault finally held a portion of the wall. A small gate was captured and Zoha was doomed. Then, as the Levites were pressing in and fires beginning to break out in the city, an amazing thing happened. The water gates opened and a large flotilla of wildly assorted craft made a break down the Ossa. Bar-Lev had few boats available and those weren't in position to hinder the escape. Fire arrows from the shore took their toll, but the majority of the flotilla broke free, traveling down the Ossa under sail and oar. Bar-Lev sent parties to pursue them along both banks of the river, but it was clear the band of escaping boats would outdistance them to the Riverrun. This incident spoiled an otherwise complete victory.

Angus was among those who escaped and with him were the nine remaining members of the guard. He would've been content to die in the city's defense, but he was more concerned about Gildesh. Angus had no illusions about his duty. If young Ducitos was to survive, he was going to need all the help he could get.

32

THE ASPECTS OF DESTINY

Emotions sometimes fail to correspond to the experiences that engender them. Getlof was being swept through the night over the unfamiliar, high, northern plains of Ossa. Her every sense was engorged. Drumming hoofs reverberated against the horizon; wind scoured her body and drenched her in the scent of nomad sweat, oiled skin and cured leather. The stars washed the alien landscape in a dim, exotic light and seemed crowed overhead, as if gathered to watch. Getlof's last, certain memories were of the attack on the citadel. Although she had no knowledge of her kidnappers or their intentions, she had a feeling, strong enough to be labeled knowledge, that she was being guided along the right way. The confidence she felt was unreasonable, but certain.

After several hours they arrived at their destination. Small fires burned randomly on the plain and in the backwash of their light, low, domed structures flickered in and out of sight. The riders walked their horses slowly through the camp, stopping near one of the fires. Getlof suddenly slid off her horse. Someone yelled. A figure emerged from the light, reaching to grab her. Getlof evaded him, hardly sore at all from the ride and walked to the fire. She hadn't been dressed for a night ride and was completely chilled. The man who'd tried to intercept her shrugged his shoulders and sat down close by. There was a thud. Getlof looked back. Unsari had been dropped. She left the fire and ran over. He was semiconscious, laying face down in the dirt, emitting small, piteous groans. When she turned him over, he looked up at her, gave a small smile and moaned.

Getlof tried to lift him, but he was too heavy. Looking up she noticed their abductors were watching. She said: "Will one of you help me?" There was no response. Knowing they probably didn't understand, she got angry anyway. In a slightly higher, and more demanding tone: "I said, help me."

Blank stares. Standing at the edge of the firelight Getlof surveyed them. Then she walked over to the closest one and kicked him in the shins. So her meaning would be clear she pointed at Unsari and then the fire. The man howled and grabbing his afflicted shin, hopped around on one foot. The others laughed. That broke the spell. Unsari was dragged to the fire, and the rest squatted near by, talking among themselves, paying no further heed to their captives. Getlof got on her knees and examined Unsari's cuts and bruises. When she asked for water someone tossed her a waterskin before she had to ask twice.

Unsari had a purple bruise on his temple, but mostly he just seemed frightened. After a few minutes of attention his eyes fluttered open and he whispered:

"It seems like the last thing I can remember is your face. You were laying down and I was stroking your brow. How is it I'm laying down and you're stroking my brow?" Then he noticed the fire and the men around it. "Ouch, never mind. I wasn't keeping my eyes open. We were snatched."

"Don't worry. Everything will be fine."

"Say that when you're on the block. At least you have that to look forward to; I'm too old to sell. I don't understand why they didn't just kill me back at the tree rather than drag me all the way here to do it. It wasn't a pleasant journey."

"You were brave to call out like you did. As for the rest, don't worry. No one will kill you."

"You speak with such confidence, little one. How would it be if I killed him now?"

Getlof looked up. A tall man was standing just beyond the fire. His Southcoast was heavily accented and he spoke with a mumble making him doubly difficult to understand.

"Don't joke like that. It frightens him."

One of the nomads spoke a few words to the newcomer. He laughed. "So, you're a dangerous one. I have to watch my step with you, is that right?"

Getlof saw that while events had placed her in a situation where her cause could be advanced, she couldn't sit back and wait for that to happen. She stood and faced the tall nomad.

"That's right."

He tilted his head and studied her. "You're a funny child, I see that. A northern speaking the tongue of the south. I don't see how you're dangerous, however." He stepped forward and lifted Getlof's chin. She stood for the inspection, meeting and out meeting his eyes, much to his surprise.

"Where did the rider find you? Where are you from, child?" voice becoming hard and suspicious.

"Be careful, Getlof," Unsari said from the ground, propping himself on one elbow.

"The old man is right, child. Foolish conceits will make your stay here a bad memory."

Getlof stepped back and said to Unsari: "Tell him who I am." Her form was silhouetted by the firelight, shift pressed gently against her body by a slight breeze. The conversation around the fire died. People walked over to watch.

Unsari stood slowly, impressive in his feebleness. He glanced around, at the tall nomad, at the people listening and at Getlof. He felt the tension and expectation and realized that whatever he said, it had better be good.

"She is the one . . ." His voice wavered and then grew unnaturally loud. "Her blessing is a blessing and her curse is a curse indeed. She is the one who looks and truly sees; who listens and truly hears; who knows without being told. She is the one who brought the city down; the one whom heroes follow." Unsari suddenly stopped. The echoes of his last statement rolled into the night. In a more confidential voice: "Indeed, tall rider, she is dangerous." Then silence. Unsari looked around once, coughed, then half sat, half collapsed on the ground.

A translation of Unsari's speech ran whispering around the fire. Getlof heard the word: `Abala' being repeated. Suddenly the tall nomad turned on them and furiously spoke words that reduced his fellows to silence. Then he turned to Getlof.

"I told them you are just a foolish child with a foolish old man coached to make foolish claims." Before Getlof could answer, he turned and stalked back into the dark from whence he had come.

Getlof sat down beside Unsari, conscious of being stared at. Unsari took her hand and held it as he lay beside her.

"I'm sorry, Getlof, if I made trouble." A smile behind his eyes betrayed his apology.

She squeezed his hand. "Thank you, Unsari. You did it exactly right. I'm glad I have a poet with me."

Unsari's smile broadened. "Oh, child, I mean Lady, you have your way, don't you."

The remaining nomads still seemed agitated. Getlof looked up and tried to smile at each person individually and to meet their eyes. Two of the nomads smiled back, but the rest wouldn't look at her. She found herself wondering which of them had carried her over the plain. There was no way to tell. To Getlof their clothing was outlandish and their hairstyles even more so. She couldn't readily tell them apart.

With his head pillowed in Getlof's lap, Unsari quickly dozed off. Getlof never had any thought of sleeping. She was completely awake; more awake than she could ever remember being.

The fire had burned down and that the moon had risen. When a woman stepped out of the shadows; the first woman Getlof had seen in the camp. Unlike the men the nomad woman looked almost normal. Her hair was in two braids and her face was unscarred. She was holding a baby, extending it toward Getlof, speaking softly in the nomad dialect. Getlof didn't know what she wanted, but she smiled and after a moments hesitation, took the baby. As she did so, she saw his body was covered with large, open sores. The sight suddenly overwhelmed her with tenderness. She rocked the baby in her arms. Then she remembered Elp's little brother, Earp had been similarly afflicted in the time before he was able to crawl. Elp's mother had made a paste of mud and had succeeded in drying out the sores. The waterskin was still beside her. Getlof splashed some on the ground and mixed it with the dirt. She proceeded to dab little spots of mud on all the suppurations, singing in a low voice to calm the child. The mother watched with wide eyes. When Getlof finished, she returned the infant with a smile, confident she had done the right thing. The mother took her child, looked at Getlof then scurried away into the dark.

Elp shook Talo awake. He turned with a groan, feeling heavy and sluggish. The moon had just risen over the eastern horizon. When he saw it, he remembered what had happened and why it was important to get up. Getlof was in serious danger and already it might be too late. He stood and shook off his sleep like a dog shakes off water. It was hard and, he reflected, getting harder every year. Talo didn't mind middle age except for those times when things that had once been easy were suddenly difficult. He glanced over and saw Narhad standing impatiently by his horse.

It didn't take skill to follow the nomad's trail. They had ridden hard and straight to the north and west. The land was flat and grey in the milky light. It seemed to stretch out forever. Talo, looking up at the constellations thought of the sea. This was not much different.

Dawn was a whispered suggestion in the sky when Elp and then Doy caught the faint and far distant scent of smoke. The nature of the land had gradually changed during their ride. Flatness had imperceptibly given way to low hillocks and shallow dells. To the northeast the line of the Middle Hills hovered on the edge of sight.

"Can you smell it?" Doy asked. Talo shook his head and looked at Narhad, who shook his head as well.

"Well, I can. We're getting close."

"Then we'll have to begin taking care. There'll be scouts and if they know their business, they'll see us long before we see them."

"Do we sit out the day and come by night?" Doy asked.

"Aye, if we knew where their camp was and if we knew they'd stay put all day," Narhad said, unsuccessfully sniffing the air again. "As it is, I don't see how we can take that chance. Too careful and we'll never catch them. Too late and what's the good of that?"

"And what's the good of blundering in? It won't help Getlof if we get ourselves killed."

Talo and Narhad locked gazes, each trying to stare the other down. Elp looked back and forth anxiously between the two.

"What if Getlof escapes. She could, you know."

"She could," Talo said, looking away. He knew he was inciting Narhad, but he wasn't sure why. "We shouldn't underestimate her ability to help herself, but if Unsari is still alive, would she leave him? I doubt it."

"Listen," Golab said, breaking the silence that had engulfed him since the chase began, "we're just wasting time. I'm tired and would welcome the chance to rest, but my heart tells me that would be wrong. I agree with Narhad." Golab still hurt from his wound and his color showed it. Talo shrugged his shoulders. He had only been voicing the problems, not advocating a position. That was something Narhad couldn't seem to grasp.

Getlof watched the waning of the stars and the advent of day. It was a slow and majestic process. She felt she was seeing it for the first time. Unsari slept, head still cradled in her lap. The fire continued to smoulder, although no fuel had been added for hours. Around the ashes, in various recumbent positions, emitting various noises, lay six sleeping nomads. Except for an occasional horseman riding ghostlike through the camp, everything was still. Getlof thought there was little to prevent her from getting up and walking away; nothing except there was nowhere to go. But she was not considering escape. She watched the day slowly define itself and waited.

As it happened, she didn't have long to wait.

The stars were gone and the sun hesitating below the eastern horizon when Getlof noticed a woman approaching. She was dressed in leather breeches with a skirt over them and a long tunic over that. Getlof found this abundance of clothing remarkable considering how little the men wore, even while sleeping in the open. The woman carefully didn't look at Getlof, but Getlof knew. She smiled a secret smile and waited.

Suddenly she was squatting beside Getlof. "You are the one brought in last night." She spoke Southcoast, but like the tall rider, not very well. Getlof nodded and said:

"This is a beautiful morning."

The woman suddenly grinned. "If you're awake to see it."

Getlof lifted Unsari's head off her lap and stood. "I'm ready." The woman gave her a funny look.

"The Mother wishes to see you," she said in an after-the-fact tone of voice. "Follow me."

Unsari stirred when his head was removed from its comfortable resting-place. He watched, still half asleep, as Getlof walked away. Then, in a sudden panic, he got to his feet and followed.

As Getlof walked with the woman, she inspected the camp with interest. It wasn't as large as she'd imagined. The beehive structures revealed themselves to be oddly shaped tents and from them the community was beginning to emerge. Fires were being built up. Naked children ran in the dirt. Horses were being fed.

The woman wound her way silently through all this. Getlof saw she was beginning to draw notice, but the woman ignored it, so Getlof did the same. Then they stopped before a large and ornately decorated tent. Standing in front was the tall nomad. He and Getlof saw each other at the same moment. She smiled and, surprisingly, he smiled in return.

"So, little one, you have come to tire the ears of our Mother with your nonsense. Be careful, she sees the meaning beneath the word and the intent beneath the meaning."

"As you have learned?" Getlof suggested. From behind, muffled laughter. He looked up to see its source, a frown flickering over his face. Then, as quickly as it had come, the frown disappeared.

"Maybe so. . ."

The woman who was guiding Getlof ended this exchange with a sharply spoken word. The tall nomad laughed, and stepped back into the crowd that had formed around the Mother's tent. As the flap was lifted and Getlof passed within, she heard again the word: `Abala' being whispered.

Inside it was dark. Two oil lamps flickered bravely, but without much effect. Getlof paused on the threshold to let her eyes adjust, but before they could, she was addressed by the most singular voice she had ever heard. It was low and musical, modulated to catch one's attention and hold it. Getlof squeezed her eyes shut and opened them, trying to hurry her sight along. The voice's attractiveness was all the greater because Getlof could detect in it evidence of decay. As much as there was, it had just the slightest waver to suggest it had once been more. Getlof was so caught up in its quality, she failed to hear what was said, as if the loss of one sense contributed to the temporary disfunction of another. She was like a person receiving an important message admiring only the paper upon which it was written.

"The Mother has asked you to approach her," an ordinary voice hissed in Getlof's ear. This startled Getlof. She looked around and saw her eyes were doing better. The far side of the tent was visible. In the middle distance an ancient woman sat amid a pile of cushions and rugs. She didn't look like she could have been the source of the enchanted voice, but there was no one else. The old woman wore an expression of amusement.

"That's right, child. You're not afraid of me, are you? No, you aren't. It must have been something else." Her voice was still charming, but this time Getlof had no trouble with her meaning. The greatest power seemed to be on first contact. Her Southcoast was perfect.

Getlof stopped still three paces away, but the Mother held out a wavering hand and said:

"Closer. My eyes can still only see a blur. Come sit beside me." Getlof obeyed, sitting down in the cushion next to the Mother. She still hadn't spoken.

"There, much better." She studied Getlof's face, seeming to derive much amusement from it. Her smile broadened, then she began to chuckle.

"Dear me, now I understand why you confused poor Dadallean so. I heard your little exchange with him at the entryway, of course. My ears, at least, work perfectly well. You are a Pau; a very pretty one and very far from home."

Getlof smiled at this. It was hard not to like the Mother.

"Ah, there's a pretty smile. With a smile like that you must be careful, child. The men will see it and you'll never be rid of them."

Getlof nodded. At the moment her thoughts were not on men. She looked up full into the Mother's clouded eyes and whispered: "Who are you?"

The Mother laughed. "Now that's the very question I was going to ask you." Her eyes left Getlof and quickly passed over the interior of the tent. The other woman was still inside.

"Child, wait outside. We'll talk alone." The woman complied reluctantly. The Mother watched her go with a smile. There seemed to be no end to her amusement.

"That's who I am. She's my daughter. They're all my children; a good many by actual birth, the rest because it's so. I'm the oldest of this people. The custom in your land is different, isn't it? Of course it is. The people come to their Mother to have their disputes settled; to have their babies blessed; to have an important choice made for them. That's who and what I am. Now, child, tell me who you are. Dadallean has already told me a little, but I think maybe you might be someone different than he thinks. You don't strike me as the great fool he halfheartedly claims you to be."

Getlof, who was looking down, nodded. Surprising herself she said: "Mother, you have a beautiful voice."

The Mother laughed. "Thank you child. That is about the only beauty left me. But are you trying to change the subject?"

"No, I just wanted to say that. Its harder to tell you who I am than it was to have someone else tell . . . Dadallean?"

"Dadallean. That's right. A grandchild of mine."

"My name is Getlof. I am a Pau, but I've never seen my people because I was born far to the south, in Dell, which is a village in the land of Istel. I was raised by a foster parent. His name was Geto. I never had a mother, although Mother Riza tried to act like one. I came of age this year and came onto the token left for me." Getlof paused, reached into her gown and pulled out her ring. "This."

The Mother took the ring in the palm of her hand and squinted. "Do you know what this ring is?" as she handed it back. "No, I apologize. I'm far too old to be asking silly questions. Of course you know. You might even be surprised I recognize it. That's because I've seen many things. Now, if you showed it to Dadallean he would think it very pretty and scheme to steal it from you. But I remember the Pau and I remember Josh. I have spoken with their bards and listened to their tales, back in the days when those tales were still being told. Now, here at the end of my days, I get to hear another tale of the Pau. Who would have thought it?"

"Do you want to hear my tale?"

"Please, most anxiously. We have all day. The people are curious about you, but so am I. Their Mother will tell them who you are."

So Getlof told her tale. She told of her birthday and her discovery of the tokens and how Geto had sold them. She told about Talo and the court of the Gildi. She told about her disguise and how Golab almost discovered it. (This part amused the Mother. She touched Getlof's face and said: "So, they thought you were a lad. You couldn't have fooled the people like that.")

Getlof told about the march to Zoha and the incident of the burning inn. Talo's question of loyalty was mentioned in its proper place, although Getlof was careful to say it wasn't his fault. Then she told of Moaz; of the horrible night of fires, Golab's wound and Talo's unnecessary rescue, passing over nothing. She described her vision and her sickness and the departure from Moaz. Finally, she told the mother about her own people; how they had snatched her away and how her companions were, no doubt, tracking her even now. When she finished, much time had passed. The Mother sat silent for several long moments, reserving comment. Finally, she stirred and said:

"Oh, that was a long story; the best I've heard in some while. You must be famished."

Getlof realized this was true. She couldn't remember the last time she had eaten. The Mother smiled and nodded.

"Of course you are. You'll eat here with me. Then I can repay you with a story of my own which I think properly belongs to your own story. No questions, we shall see." The Mother reached down and rang a bell that sat on the cushion beside her. The daughter quickly reentered the tent, concern creasing her face. The Mother said:

"No child, I'm not tired. In fact, I'm most refreshed. And hungry. Will you bring in some food so our friend and I can eat. And see if someone can find Dadallean."

The woman walked up and felt the Mother's cheek. Then she nodded, gave Getlof a curious look and departed. The Mother sighed.

"When I die she shall be the mother. I wonder if she'll prove capable; her sense of humor is lacking, although, I must admit, when I was younger I was more serious also." Then, just as she finished the flap was thrust aside and Dadallean came striding in. He gave Getlof a half mocking smile and said: "I've come, Mother."

"Yes, so I hear. And very quickly. You weren't lurking around outside my tent, were you?" She laughed and in the dim light Getlof thought she could see color rise on Dadallean's face. Still chuckling, the Mother waved a hand as if to dismiss any embarrassment Dadallean might have suffered. She said:

"You might as well know first seeing as how you know already, even if you don't know you know." She continued to chuckle. Dadallean, obviously used to her ways, waited. "This is Getlof the Pau. She is the heir to Josh. Do you know who that is?"

"I have heard the tales," now staring openly at Getlof.

"Yes, I wondered if you remembered my telling them." She shook her head. "I don't know why I'm so fond of you, child. Now listen, Getlof has friends, five of them. They'll be seeking her, but I want you to find them first. I want you to give them peace and bring them to me. Can you do that?"

"Mother, they killed three riders."

"I know and three riders is a loss. Blatta led that party, didn't he. He was careless and I'll speak to him. And now that you've reminded me, did you send out extra riders to watch against the rescue Getlof tells me is coming?"

Dadallean shook his head.

"I didn't think so. You've been lurking around my tent. Well, no harm, I hope. Go and find these people. I shall be very displeased if any of them are harmed."

Dadallean nodded sheepishly. As he turned to leave, Getlof suddenly said:

"The short one is called Talo. The big one is Narhad. Bespeak them by name and they'll listen."

This was almost too much for Dadallean. He paused at the entryway and seemed to struggle against the reply on his lips. Finally, the Mother said:

"What? You're still here? Go child and remember those names: Talo and Narhad."

Getlof watched him go. The Mother noticed this and said: "Remember, I warned you about him."

Now Getlof was embarrassed, until she reminded herself she had no reason to be. She said:

"You're wicked. I was thinking of Unsari. He must be feeling worried and neglected by now."

The Mother laughed. "That's telling me. I think I'd be interesting in seeing your poet briefly. When the first daughter brings in the food I'll send for him."

The food came, finally, and shortly after, Unsari was ushered in. He stood looking, as Getlof predicted, worried and neglected. The Mother shook her head.

"Man of Moaz, don't look like that. I can tell how you look even without seeing you. Come join us in our repast. Afterwards, you and Getlof can await your friends. I shall have some meditating to do."

Unsari looked expectantly at Getlof, but she put her finger to her lips.

33

REUNIONS

The nomad camp proved to be further than the evidence of Doy's nose had indicated. It was midmorning before they sighted it, apparently undetected despite Talo's fears. The horses were left with Elp and Golab in a deep gully. Talo and the two Gildi guardsmen crawled to the top of a rise to spy out the camp.

"I count thirty tents," Doy said.

"Not more than a couple hundred," Talo muttered. It wasn't what he'd expected and feared.

Narhad grunted. "Ten thousand or a hundred, we can't walk up and ask for them back."

"Don't you see?" Talo said, with a touch of asperity, "how strange this is. That's a tribal group, not a war party. What is a tribe of the Xumi doing this far west?"

"You're thinking of Bar-Lev; I'm thinking of Getlof."

"I'm thinking of no one but Getlof. Its just that there must be something in this situation we can take advantage of if we can only find out what it is."

Narhad grunted.

"If we could just take one alive, I'd be able to tell a lot."

"Wait," Doy said, glad there was finally something to distract Talo and Narhad from their debate. "A big group is leaving the camp."

"Several dozen," Doy continued, after a pause, knowing he had the best eyes. "Now they're splitting up into groups of three. One group is coming toward us."

"Well," Narhad said dryly, "you might get your prisoner, but will you have a chance to question him?"

"Just a moment," Doy said, "they carry lances with blue pennants."

"Blue?" Narhad said, "that means they want to talk, but with whom?"

"With us, of course," Talo said, "who else is there? Perhaps Getlof has impressed them with her importance and they seek ransom."

"Whatever, they'll be here soon. We have to make up our minds, and fast. I still think it could be a trap."

"You know little about nomads," Talo said, unwrapping a blue sash from around his waist. "They're honorable people after their own fashion. "I always wear something blue just for situations like this."

"A moment," Narhad said. "I can't recall reaching any decision."

"A moment, a moment, there're no more moments left." With that Talo suddenly stood and waved the sash over his head. Narhad was almost as fast. He grabbed Talo's trousers and pulled him back down, but it was too late.

"They saw us," Doy said. "But they've stopped. One rider is leaving to tell the others. The other two are waving their lances. I think they do want to talk."

"All right, Doy, I can see," Narhad said. "Go down quickly and have Elp and Golab bring the horses up." Talo sat on the ground watching Narhad with an uncertain expression. Then he abruptly stood again.

"Get down," Narhad hissed.

Talo shook his head. "Are you going to force me?" Doy was gone; they were alone. For a moment, Talo thought Narhad just might; he looked like he wanted to. But instead, he stood as well.

"Alright, we'll have it your way. Give me that damn rag, I'm easier to see."

By this time a single nomad was riding toward them. Standing together, tall and short, they watched him come. The others joined them on the rise with the horses. When he was several hundred paces away, the nomad dismounted and climbed the hill on foot. No one spoke until he was only a dozen paces distant, then the nomad said:

"I seek two men named Talo and Narhad and their three companions. I think you are them."

"We are, brave rider," Talo replied, trying to keep his surging emotion from his voice. He had been right and everything would be fine. "How is it you have our names?"

The rider smiled, seemingly in spite of himself. "I am Dadallean. I was told your names and the signs by which I could recognize you. A young woman told me. She has found favor with the Mother. In her behalf the Mother has instructed me to give you peace and honor and to conduct you to her presence."

The others exchanged glances behind Talo's back. Talo said: "Lead and we shall follow, but answer one question first. Do your people serve the will of Bar-Lev?"

"From the corner of his eye Talo could see Narhad scowl. The question also seemed to irritate the nomad. His face, not overly friendly to begin with, clouded and he seemed about to make a curt reply. Then, as quickly as it had come, his ire passed.

"So, you westlanders fear Bar-Lev." He laughed harshly. "Well you might. No is the answer to your question. The people are free and serve only themselves. Now, come if you will. The Mother waits."

They followed Dadallean toward the camp. Elp, for some reason couldn't stop staring at him. He rode close by stealing glances until Dadallean acknowledged him.

"What are you gawking at, little one? Have you never seen a warrior?" Elp, circulation excellent as always, blushed.

"I'm friends with a very great warrior." This he whispered and Narhad, who was several horse lengths back, didn't hear. He did, however, note the calculating look Dadallean gave him. Narhad nodded at Dadallean who suddenly grinned and nodded back.

"Indeed, little one, a great warrior."

When they were near the camp Getlof and Unsari came out to greet them, finally putting Narhad's fears largely to rest. They were all amazed by the change in her: just the afternoon before she had been pale and unhealthy. Now she was glowing and her smile enormous. She had exchanged her white shift for short breeches that left her legs bare to gleam darkly in the sun. Her tunic was of a light material that exposed her arms and more than that, suggested the silhouette of her slim torso beneath. Golab gaped and tried to detect something special for him in the glad greetings they exchanged. It was hard to believe he had held her and even tried to kiss her and not that long ago. When he caught himself thinking things better ignored, he looked away, irritated with himself.

After the reunion, Getlof led them through the camp to the tent of the Mother. The nomads gathered round and watched them. They had been exposed to more wonders in a day than they were used to in a year. First, the strange girl who was doubtlessly Abala (overnight, the baby's sores had begun to heal and the grateful mother was singing Getlof's praises throughout the camp); then the armed outlanders who rode freely through their camp. But they had great love and trust in their Mother. If she chose to provide them with wonders, than that was good; they loved her the more for it.

They gathered in the dim interior of the Mother's tent, the seven who had ridden out of Moaz, with Dadallean and the first daughter as well. First there was silence. This heightened the sense of expectation. Getlof found herself wondering if the Mother's voice would have the same effect on the others as it had upon her. Then, the Mother spoke.

"My eyes think to give up the struggle before my body. I have to humor them, which means you'll have to humor me. So that I can know who I speak to, I ask each of you to come forward so I may see you and touch your faces."

Talo stood at once. "I am Talo the Taelien, good Mother."

"Yes, short and round, but sure of deed. And you," as Talo sat back down, "great and mighty, you are Narhad. What is your city?"

"Gildesh, Mother," submitting himself to her inspection.

"Ah," significantly. "But there are three others whose names I know not. Come forward, children, and tell me your names and cities."

Golab, Doy and Elp, one after the other, obeyed. Golab was vaguely insulted that Getlof had told the Mother about Talo and Narhad, but not about himself.

When the Mother was satisfied, she sat for a moment in silence, then she began to giggle. Her giggle turned into a full laugh; a laugh that seemed absurd coming from such a frail vessel. Those who were seeing her for the first time exchanged glances. Finally her laughter abated sufficiently for her to speak.

"No, I haven't quit from my senses, if that's what you're thinking. That hasn't happened yet. Its just that we have here a Taelien from the far west, three Gildi from the south, two Moazians from the midlands, three Xumi from the east, and from the north, a Pau. When has such a group of people from such far-scattered lands gathered together in Ossa. I couldn't tell you. And we meet, all in one form or another of exile, in a land that belongs to no one." She chuckled again. "I call that amusing. But its not unrelated to the story I want you to hear. Is one group of plainsriders, nomads, that is, the same as another to you all? It shouldn't be, not at least to the Moazians." She paused and Talo took it upon himself to answer.

"You ask if we find it remarkable your people are so far from their pasture? We do, or at least, I do. Your people, the Xumi we call them, are reputed to follow the banner of Bar-Lev. Yet, Dadallean states this isn't the case; that you are a free people."

"We try to be, but lately, that is the last five or ten years, its been a struggle. Our presence here, in the west, is related to that struggle." She looked up and around at the group. "Indeed, I found it necessary to lead my people to new pasture in the west. I had no wish to see my sons remain as soldiers of Bar-Lev, or my daughters become widows and camp followers."

"Yet, the people who follow you are only a small group in the numbers of the Xumi," Talo said. "What did the other Mothers do?"

The Mother smiled at Talo. Things were always so much easier with someone to ask the right questions.

"Perhaps Dadallean should tell it. He's a young man and they sounded the war cry more directly to him than to me."

Dadallean coughed and looked around. "What is there to say? Two years ago the first ambassador from Bar-Lev came to our camp. He spoke of a mighty lord of the riders come from the east who swept through his enemies like a fire through the plain. He spoke of the glory our people could share and to some, who remembered that our pastures were small where once they'd been large, this sounded good; but it wasn't."

"Tell them why, Dadallean. They'll trust the word of a man at arms more than that of an old woman."

Dadallean nodded, warming to his tale. "Well, Bar-Lev crossed the river, the Tarhad, summer before last. The mighty Tarhadian lords were all either dead or become his men. That was good, because in the days of their power, they raided across the river into our pasture for sport and slaves. Then he sent the war call out to our people saying join me or oppose me as we would. We joined because there was no opposing him. His riders turned the plains dark.

"That summer we reduced the islands of the Tarhad delta and returned their farms into pasture. Then we rode south along the coast doing the same. Finally, in the autumn we came to the city of Sidoc. Until then there had been little fighting. At Sidoc it was different. The city fought desperately behind a famous captain. We learned the reason for his fame directly and cursed him; the taking of walled towns is not work for riders. But Bar-Lev wouldn't leave it behind. Ha, I remember they put us in a gang lifting stones to build a causeway out to the island. What sort of work is that for a warrior?"

"Its work a warrior sometimes has to do," Talo said, "but you're right, its no task for riders lacking siege equipment. If the prince hadn't sortied with his fleet, the city would stand yet."

Dadallean nodded. "That is how it was. Where did you hear the tale?"

Talo smiled wanly. The anger was gone, but the sadness of it would be with him always. "I was there."

"Dadallean," Getlof said softly, "Talo is the captain of whom you spoke. He led the defense."

Dadallean starred at Talo, then the Mother laughed. "So, even you see what I mean, Dadallean. This is too remarkable a gathering to be just chance. We're all in need of assistance, or shortly shall be. That assistance we can best find among ourselves. Not so?"

This was exactly how Talo felt. He looked at the Mother with new respect. And having the memory of Sidoc evoked so clearly reignited his smoldering passion for revenge. The notion that this encounter was the beginning of that revenge excited him tremendously.

"I agree with you, Mother, but one thing. How is it, after serving Bar-Lev for a season, you are here, fled from his overlordship?"

"I'll tell you, its no secret. I spoke against following him even for that one season when the Mothers of the people met to consider the question. Some supported my view, others didn't; but like Dadallean said, we had no choice. I had my say then, but knew better than to oppose events further. A sister of mine, however, did. It happened, no one was sure how, that unfriendly riders set upon her family at a time when they were beyond the aid of their kin. The men were slain, as is the way in such happenings; the boys were sent to slave regiments; and the woman suffered what women suffer. Afterwards many of the mothers were frightened. I held my peace that summer while my children swam in blood. They came back, after Sidoc, when the snows began to fall, their taste for blood sated. But the prospect was for more of the same for as long as anyone could see. Riding under a foreign captain is not as sweet as riding free over the plains. But there was more. A greater reason made me gather my people that winter and fly like fugitives from our own pastures." Here the Mother stopped and began to sway slowly on her rugs and cushions. She appeared to sink into herself.

"I had a dream," she finally said in a voice Getlof remembered from their first meeting. "No passing dream it was. A beggar came to me. No common beggar was he; he came not to ask but to give. That was strange in itself, but he was stranger; bent and crippled, but more comely than a king. He knew my distress and whispered softly into my old ear that I was not to worry. When it was time, he would send me a girl-child: no child as I have ever seen. Where, I asked and he said in the west. I asked him how I would know her and he told me I would know. When I awoke that next morning, I had the idea of leading my people to the west. I told them of my dream and they believed its meaning. They gave the child the name of Abala, which is an old name from an old tale. And that is why, master Talo, we no longer serve the will of Bar-Lev, although once we did."

The Mother's final sentence dropped into their midst like a flower in a stream. It was gone before they marked it, save Getlof who knew what was next.

"I am tired and will rest. Daughter, you will tell the people that Abala is among us, if they don't already know. Dadallean, see to the comfort of our new friends. Getlof, are you going to tell the Mother she's wrong?"

Getlof shook her head. She was staring at the carpet design. It was geometric; lines zigzagging together and apart in a pattern replete with hidden meaning. "I had a feeling as well when I was brought here. A feeling of correctness; an absence of worry. No, Mother, I'll not say you're wrong."

"Eh, you're willing to take a lot upon yourself for a child."

"I wasn't always, but, if a thing is meant to be, I must help it be so."

The Mother laughed.

34

THE CAMP AT THE MIDDLE OF THE WORLD

Talo and the Mother quickly discovered they had much in common: both were plotters by nature. It was impossible for the less practiced to keep abreast of the convoluted schemes they devised. Getlof didn't try. She only made sure they knew she was going to Hilev and put that journey first in the various futures they discussed. Beyond that, she was willing to let their greater experience be her guide.

During the three days they remained in the nomad camp, Getlof had more opportunity to be alone with Golab than any time since Gildesh. His wound was healing, but he still rode with pain and walked with care. To speed the healing process, and also hoping to recapture their interrupted intimacy, she insisted he accompany her on walks out of the camp through the bittersweet, late summer chaparral. The Golab whose company she courted was not the Golab she remembered from Gildesh: his behavior seemed more guarded; his opinions more critical. It was clear he didn't share her enthusiasm for the Mother; that she grated his court bred sensibilities in much the same fashion Talo did. While it disappointed her they weren't sharing the old intimacy she'd anticipated so eagerly, Getlof went out of her way to ignore these feelings. It was easy to account for his reticence in terms of the wound and to think that as the body healed, the mind would surely follow. Yet, even his enthusiasm for her pilgrimage to Hilev seemed soured.

"And afterwards, aren't you worried what it'll be like? Regardless of how much Talo and the Mother scheme, don't you realize the Pau will have their say? The only possibilities I see are for conflict."

Getlof laughed and failed to see the scowl that passed quickly over Golab's face like a squall over the water.

"Oh, I hear what you're saying. Talo and the Mother are building plans around me and why don't I stop them or at least speak my piece. The truth is, I don't see how it matters. It seems every plan I can think of, my own included, has been changed. Circumstance and chance will determine what really happens."

The sage was flowering. Golab brushed a plant and sent a cloud of pollen into the air. He didn't think she was deliberately trying to be difficult, but the effect was the same. Getlof had changed so much in those short months since they had walked the corridors in Gildesh; it was hard to adjust to the fact she was no longer his pupil. Even less imaginable was that he would take her in his arms and claim the kiss she had said someday might be his . . .

"Whatever. Doy and Elp will be riding out this afternoon. If we want to say goodbye, we should get back to camp. They'll be hurt if we don't"

The plan of wintering in Joshin had been discarded. It was too unaccessible for the Xumi. The Mother had suggested a more suitable site at the western edge of the Middlehills. A river rose there, which the Xumi called the Anne and the Moazians the Djuna. Just out of the Middlehills, the Anne flowed through a pleasant woodland, the Anneglen. Doy and Elp set out that afternoon with guides from the camp to find Iodai and inform him of the change in plans. Talo was rather sorry he was going to miss Joshin, Getlof didn't care and the others, inspired by Unsari's stories, were secretly glad.

Talo was happier than he could remember being at any time since Sidoc. He finally felt he was doing something positive toward revenging that disaster, the Daughter of Shee and his reputation. His sense of urgency was suddenly overwhelming and delays drove him to the limit of restlessness. In his opinion the journey to Hilev had become unnecessary and even dangerous. Like Golab, he saw conflict as the most likely result of this journey; at the best there'd still be new obligations and new problems at no gain. Getlof belonged to him, not the Pau.

The opportunity for Talo to express these opinions to Getlof came after the nomad camp had been broken and they were slowly making their way north and west over the plain to Anneglen. He mentioned he had a private matter to discuss and led her away from the dust of the march so they couldn't be overheard.

"Getlof, things are changing for us quickly. You started off by yourself and look at you now! You've taken responsibility after responsibility and I admire you for it; but you know, by accepting the Mother's new name you've gotten into a situation that may delay the trip to Hilev. Have you thought about how you'd feel if it was postponed, or put off altogether?"

At first Getlof rode next to Talo silently. This surprised him, having expected some resistance before she agreed. The sky was blue and the day startlingly beautiful. They didn't know it, but it would be one of the last fine days before the weather broke.

When Getlof finally turned to Talo, her face was lined with tears. She shook her head repeatedly before saying: "Talo, how can you say that? With company or by myself I'm going to Hilev. I care about that more than anything and I thought you understood."

Talo had his arguments, but looking into Getlof's face, he thought better of bringing them out.

"I know you expect war with Bar-Lev, but I refuse to go looking for it. If its going to happen, it'll happen and your plans won't change a thing. Don't you see?"

As Getlof stared at him, Talo was going to reply that planning had always served him well in the past, but before he could, she suddenly wheeled her horse and galloped back to the caravan.

Talo watched for a second before he followed Getlof at a walk. He was forever stumbling over old habits; they gave him no more freedom than Getlof's compulsion for Hilev gave her.

The next day, as they were nearing the end of their march, Doy returned with news of Iodai. He had been on the road just outside of Moaz. The trouble everyone had expected had arrived sooner than expected. Only two days after Getlof's departure, Zak, preparing an assault on the Upper Citadel, had fallen victim to an assassin. Being the glue that held everything together, his death resulted in everything falling apart. The Upper Captain had swept out of the citadel, but his force had proven insufficient to control the city. Apparently he had renounced his oath to Caos and was claiming the title of Magnus. The elements that had elected Zak were unable to agree upon his successor. The result was a nasty, three-way civil war. The city was largely in ruins, each faction holding out behind their lines and citizens were fleeing in great numbers. Many of the richer merchants had taken ship up the Laso to the Shemite cities of the Great Lake and Roganspire. Others were going south and still others had chosen to link their fates in with Iodai. Thus, Doy reported, his following was much greater than they had expected. This was the only thing he could report with certainty. Of Caos there was no news whatsoever; events in the south were a mystery.

These tidings saddened Getlof especially; she couldn't help but feel responsible for pushing Zak to accept the Magnus' ring. It caused her to think about responsibility. Talo had praised her for so readily accepting obligations, but she was beginning to see that accepting was the easy part. The hard part was carrying things through. She had failed in large duties--the people in Moaz certainly seemed worse off for her intervention--and she had failed in small duties as well. Getlof remembered, for example, her promise to write to Ducitos. If they sent a scout to Gildesh, as there was talk of doing, she resolved to give him a letter to carry. And that was only the first of many promises she made to herself.

Then, more news arrived which was more amazing still.

Scouts had been sent out to the east and south the day after the company had been united in the nomad camp. Now, the first of these returned. He had ridden all the way to Zoha, seeking news in a land that was ominously empty. At Zoha, the reason for this void became apparent: the neck of land between the conjunction of the Ossa and Shem was covered with tents.

The scout, his name was Xellia, was a daring man. He rode past the pickets and into the tent city itself. He discovered it was the encampment of Bar-Lev himself. Xellia even gathered the current campfire gossip: the hoard would winter in Zoha and the next spring, would advance either up the Shem or down the Ossa, depending upon the successes of the Levite fleet in its battles with the Istelians and Gildi. Caos was dead and his army destroyed. Bar-Lev had attacked him at Zoha even as he was attacking the Gildi, triumphing absolutely over both. Xellia had ridden out of Zoha just ahead of an army Bar-Lev was sending to occupy Moaz. Finally, Xellia reported, news of the events in Moaz had reached the Levite camp and it was brimming with tales of a new power in the west: a Pauic queen, or witch. Informed opinion held that in the spring the hoard would move west, not south.

This intelligence gave Talo a perverse sense of satisfaction. He hadn't talked with Getlof since their ride the morning before, but he was nearby when Xellia finished his report. She caught Talo's eye and to his surprise, smiled. Then she edged her way over and whispered: "This has certainly been a day for news. It seems your plans are being justified."

"You've reconsidered?"

She shook her head. "No, even if Bar-Lev puts himself between me and Hilev, I'll go forward. But I'm not angry anymore. I want you to know that."

Talo nodded. He was glad, at least, for that. Had he known Getlof was now thinking of him as one of her responsibilities, he would have been flabbergasted.

That day the weather turned cold.

The following morning a low fog clung to the ground and made the going uncertain. They knew they were near the Anneglen, but it wasn't until late that afternoon the outriders finally stumbled across the Anne.

Iodai was there already with a portion of his people, huddled apathetically at the southern eves of the forest. Talo wasn't happy about the way they'd just come up on the Moazians without them being aware, but after seeing the condition of the refugees, he refrained from criticizing. Iodai had complaints of his own. His delivery of them reminded Getlof of their first meeting. Iodai hadn't changed. He wanted to know what had happened; where all the strange nomads had come from and why Joshin was longer their destination. Elp was with him and had already explained all this, but Getlof had to explain it again.

Iodai, however, was not to be convinced. Finally, in desperation, Getlof took him in to see the Mother as soon as her tent was set up. The Mother took in the situation with a glance (it didn't matter that she was practically blind). Her first words to Iodai were:

"At last, they bring me a man of age and experience to strengthen our counsel."

Iodai came out of the tent enthusiastically agreeing with everything he'd previously been unable to understand. His change in heart had almost everyone laughing behind their hands. In the days that followed, he found all manner of excuses to visit the Mother. Getlof was pleased he'd found someone to lavish his attention on.

Iodai's story was interesting. He'd been fortunate in having completed preparations for the move when the fighting broke out again. What delayed him and caused his people to become strung out on the march was that so many discovered a hitherto unrealized desire to join him his party. Iodai decided to accept everyone, regardless of their true beliefs about Paulic. Although Getlof agreed that he had no other choice, she privately wondered what they would do with so many people.

Iodai's handling of the flight from Moaz provoked no criticism. He had displayed courage and competence in the fulfillment of a difficult task; in spite of a personal tragedy. Iodai the younger had disappeared in the fighting at the Citadel. Everyone presumed him killed. However, he had turned up again in the Upper Citadel with Gavin, spouting diatribes against his grandfather and Getlof. Getlof was hurt when she heard this, but for some reason, it didn't surprise her.

Throughout the week that followed, people continued to drift into camp until their numbers exceeded a thousand. Work was started on huts and, more importantly, on gathering food. Large hunting parties were organized and sent out daily. Dadallean thought up the idea of a raid to the west to see what the dwellers around Lake Shon could contribute to their upkeep. When Elp told this to Getlof ("right now he's choosing his riders!"), she quickly found Dadallean and put a stop to it.

"Why?" he asked angrily. "These people have come seeking your protection. Would you have them starve?"

"Of course not," more amused than anything by his anger. "Your idea **is** good, it's just the way you want to go about it. Why can't we buy food from them? I'm told it's a rich land and the harvest this year was supposed to be good."

He snorted. "I don't know much about buying and selling, but I was always told it took money."

This confrontation took place in the center of camp where the Xumi had pitched their tents. The riders who'd been selected to participate in Dadallean's escapade sat around listening with a mixture of interest (Dadallean's and Getlof's disagreements were becoming famous and were well attended whenever possible) and fear. To them Getlof was Abala, whatever the others might call her, and they were nervous for their comrade's sake, worried he might go too far and turn her patience into anger, or something worse.

"I concede, you're acute as always, but we must have something worth trading for food."

"We do," triumphantly, "protection!"

Getlof laughed. "Dadallean, we need the good will of the people hereabouts. We won't get it if we rob and threaten them." She paused. "I have an idea, should've thought of it at first. I was among the Moazians today and I've noticed most of them didn't bring much, but what they do have seems to be of value."

Dadallean grinned. "I've noticed as well. The jewelry on the women. But I'd really like to know what's in the chests I've seen some of the men guarding so closely."

"Exactly. We must have plenty of money. We just have to convince those who have it to, ah, donate."

"Good luck. I'll be waiting here when you change your mind." Dadallean stood to his full height and shook his lance. Getlof thought it made his look boyish rather than fierce. She smiled and said:

"Yes, Dadallean, I can see why the Mother is so fond of you." Then she ran off to find Talo, leaving a much perplexed Dadallean still holding his lance over his head, to the laughter of his comrades.

Doy, ever tireless, ended up in charge of the expedition to Lake Shon. The idea of handing over their portable wealth didn't delight the Moazians, but after Getlof called a general meeting and they realized that they didn't have a whole lot of choice, most cooperated. Those who didn't were given the chance to leave, but there was no place to go so very few actually took that option.

Getlof was rather surprised she had enough authority to make the women surrender their earrings and the men open their chests, even though the Mother helped her. The Xumi were not without their resources and she saw that they contributed a generous share. Getlof was coming to realize the importance of not favoring one group over the other. They were still mutually suspicious and only the strictest impartiality would keep acrimony to a minimum.

The two weeks that followed were the busiest in Getlof's life.

"More refugees from Moaz. Where do we put them?"

"Ask the Lady."

"A scout has returned. Where is the Lady?"

A quarrel over food, over housing, an insult, a misunderstanding: "The Lady will decide."

Yes, she soon realized she knew nothing about responsibility. In truth, it was the most demanding master she'd ever encountered.

By no means was Getlof the only busy one. The nights were already dipping below freezing; timber had to be felled and huts constructed. There was no way to get ahead of the food problem and everyone who could be spared was out in the forest hunting and gathering. All the basic problems of staying alive had to be confronted and solved. And, as if these problems were not enough, they had to worry about the situation in the south.

Talo coordinated the activities of the scouts. The arrival and departure of riders was a daily occurrence. He was the generalissimo of their new city (for such it was becoming) and when people could be spared from their other tasks, he labored to give them military skills. Actually, this work was Talo's specialty. In his time he'd won many victories with irregular forces. The Xumi were already superb soldiers, but they suffered from an ignorance of discipline. With Dadallean to help, Talo introduced them to his "new" style of fighting.

Golab's talents and temperament were such that he had little to do in the organization of Anneglen. At first nothing physical was required of him out of consideration of his wound. It was his own choice that kept him out of the decision-making sessions Getlof was always calling. Part of his diffidence was a feeling that he was not qualified compared to people like Narhad and Talo, not to mention the Mother. Then there was that secret wish that Getlof would come to him and throw aside that barrier that had arisen between them after his foolish attempt to kiss her. When Golab saw Getlof bantering with Dadallean, a feeling swept him; one he knew was bad, but one he couldn't fight. He could only turn away and wait for his heart to stop pounding and his vision to clear. Knowing well the dangers he was facing, Golab tried to take himself in hand; but the attempt only taught him how little self-control he really had. Getlof never came to him the way he wanted and only the pride of self-pity kept him from admitting how unhappy he was.

Additional help from a most unlikely source came to the bustling camp at the end of the third week. Late one morning a picket from the southern watch came roaring down the dirt alleys that separated the new huts with news that they'd sighted a large group of mounted men at arms with a larger train of women and children approaching a days ride away.

"Of course, this could mean anything," Talo said to Getlof and the other leaders when they gathered, "but we shouldn't take any chances." He paused and looked at Getlof.

"This is what you do best, Talo. I just don't want any fighting if there's anyway to avoid it."

"No, of course not. Dadallean, collect a hundred lances; better make it the first and second companies. I'll collect the first two companies of Moazians as well. They could use the practice. Narhad, will you stay and see that the other four companies are ready, just in case?"

One of the Moazians, in charge of the hunting detail that day, protested that if every company was set to arms, there'd be no way to check the traps. No one heard him and after a second, he realized he was in the second company and had better get his bow.

When Talo and Dadallean rode out several hours after the first report, they were followed by two hundred fighting men, half the total available in the camp. It was late afternoon before the outriders reported the intruders were at hand. Even at that distance from the Middle Hills, the plain was scored with gullies and gentle ridges. This made it possible to conceal the Anneglen riders while Talo rode out to have a look.

As the scouts reported, the column included women and children and a few wagons as well. The men at arms were dressed in the colors of Moaz, but even from a distance Talo could tell the normally bright uniforms were stained and worn.

"They still don't know they've been watched for almost a day?" Talo asked the scout who accompanied him.

"No, we've been careful."

"Well, its time." They mounted and ascended a knoll in plain view of the column. The reaction was instantaneous. The soldiers drew in and formed a defensive position around the wagons. Then a single rider with a blue pennant detached from the group and came galloping toward them. Talo stroked his chin, a smile slowly forming.

The solitary rider was soon within shouting range. He reined his horse in and said: "Ho, strangers, we seek peaceful passage through this land."

"On what business?" Talo shouted back.

"We travel to find the Lady Getlof, Josh."

"Under what captain?"

"Daken, once captain of the Lower Citadel. We are his men and with us are our families. We have been driven from Moaz and we seek the Lady's city and her sanctuary where we hear so many of our citizens have found peace."

Daken, the Under Captain, and his men didn't arrive in Anneglen until the next morning. Talo was quite glad to have him and so were most of the Moazians. In the last days he had acquired a reputation for moderation and fair dealing, acting first as Zak's right hand and after his death, as the chief resistance to the Upper Captain. The transformation of the Captain's reputation since the uprising began was remarkable. Now people were saying: `Daken was always a good man, it was just his job.'

Getlof's memories of the man were favorable, and she was glad for the addition to her strength (she was beginning to think in those terms) even though her first reaction was `more mouths to feed!' First they took Daken and his filecaptains around the camp deciding on sites for new huts and setting some of the arrivals to work. Then they went to Getlof's hut to hear Daken's story. Always capricious, the weather had turned decent in the last few days enabling them to sit around the hut rather than crowd inside. People gathered from all around to listen. Getlof noticed Daken looking curiously at this and said: "We have no secrets."

"I see. For one accustomed to the councils of Caos, this is strange." Daken sat cross-legged on the ground, hands resting on knees glancing neutrally about.

"You are acquainted with the facts of Caos's death?"

Daken looked up with surprise. "I am, but I hadn't thought you'd be. It was news the telling of I anticipated with pleasure. Caos is dead and I'm free of my oath."

"What's happening in Moaz?" Iodai asked.

Daken laughed bitterly. "Well, the Citadel still stands, but large parts of it are gutted. The city is also in ruins. Few people linger there. But Gavin is Magnus now. There's no one left to dispute him that."

Talo laughed. "Oh yes there is. Haven't you heard? Bar-Lev has taken Zoha. Our scouts say he's dispatched a force to occupy Moaz. By this time I suspect Gavin and all his people have passed into history. That's why we met you with such force."

Daken shook his head. "I didn't know. It seems I bought my people out none to soon. Does Bar-Lev know your presence here?"

"We think he does," Getlof said. "But, the season is late. We hope to be safe until the spring."

"Which reminds me. I have a gift for you."

"A gift?" Getlof said, with the slightest frown.

"In a matter of speaking. Actually, it belongs to you already." He reached into the purse slung over his shoulder and produced a precious and intricately worked casket.

Getlof took it, her frown transformed into the broadest of smiles. "Thank you, Daken. I know what this is, but how did you get it?"

"It was in the palace. After the rising there was much to be had for the taking. I had read the reports on this and knew it belonged to you, so I made a special effort to find it."

The whisper went around the camp that the Lady had recovered her magic casket and now her powers were complete.

When the weather turned cold for good and the first snow was laying lightly on the ground, Doy and the expedition to Shon returned. They had enjoyed success beyond all expectation. The packhorses were loaded with grain, dried fruits and smoked fish; but that wasn't all. A company of sixty Shonians, men and women both, came as well.

"They heard stories," Doy explained. "And I guess we told a few of our own. They wanted to come and see you for themselves. They call you Nivila. It seems they've heard of you before this. You're not mad, are you Getlof?"

The Shonians proved to be valuable friends. They were accustomed to the climate and being foresters, possessed skills both the Xumi and the city dwelling Moazians lacked. They treated Getlof with awe, being shy and deferential when she was present. Her closer friends experienced the Shonian's elaborate respect by way of their association with her. It embarrassed them at first, until it came to be accepted as just a feature of the Shonian collective personality.

One day, not long after the arrival of the Shonians, Getlof and Narhad discussed them as they rode over the plain south of the forest. It was a warm day, melting the light snow and Getlof had proposed the outing to enjoy it. All that was most pressing had been done and restlessness was beginning to afflict her.

"I like them well enough," Narhad said, "and they're wizards in the woods. I thought we were beginning to deplete the game here around, but five of them can find more venison in an hour than fifty of the Moazians can scare away in the day. I just don't like the way they're always bowing and scrapping whenever I walk by."

Getlof laughed. "I thought people like to be bowed and scrapped to."

"Some do, to be sure, but not me." He laughed suddenly. Narhad's laugh was rarely heard, which was a shame because it could be merry and unrestrained. "I don't think of my old life, Lady. I'm not sorry about what I left behind, but if only my old barrack mates could see me now. They'd be rubbing their eyes."

Getlof smiled. "No doubt, and maybe they'd bow to you as well." Just then her horse started a hare. It reared up as the little animal darted out from beneath its hoofs, but Getlof quickly regained control.

"You've become a good rider. I remember back in the first days when we were on the Riverrun watching you ride and thinking you'd never make it."

"I wasn't that bad, but I admit to being better now. In fact, Narhad, I've been thinking its about time to take another ride. The camp is set up and functioning as well as it ever will and Hilev is not so very far away."

At that moment, black clouds blocked the sun. Narhad looked up and said: "Far enough. We'd better turn back before that catches us." He glanced over and saw he hadn't said what Getlof wanted to hear.

"Don't fret, Lady. I'll get you there, and then . . ." He stopped. "And then, what? Do you know?" Getlof didn't answer so Narhad felt bound to continue. "More and more people are gathering around you. The Xumi call you Abala and the Shonians say your name is Nivila. Does that bother you? Do you think they are looking for someone else?"

"I can't help but think those things, but I can't let it bother me. Abala, Nivila or Josh, does it really matter? They all must need someone; why else would they be so ready to come to us? I can't start worrying about it or I'll never stop. I just do what has to be done and that seems to satisfy.

"But you asked me what was next. That was your real question. You know I don't know. That's one reason why I'm so anxious to get to Hilev. It's always been important and now it's more important than ever. I hope that when I'm there I won't be so confused; that I'll be able to see what is right and not worry about doing it. Now, it's so hard with one person saying this and the other that and my feelings a third thing altogether."

"I wonder if what happens will be different than what people expect, especially Talo."

"You still don't trust Talo, do you Narhad?"

"I can't deny it Lady. He's deep and full used to getting his own way. In the Gildi wars he stuck with the forces of all the gods when they won their victories, but when things turned bad, he ran. I've heard tell it was the same in Sidoc."

"There is something about Sidoc that bothers him, I've noticed. As for the other, did you fight at Pendaflex or the battles that followed?"

"No, I was too young."

"Then you just know what people say. Be generous and admit that what people say is not necessarily what happened. I know that Talo's desire to oppose Bar-Lev is so great it keeps him from seeing all there is to see; but neither can I deny this war is growing. If it won't leave us alone, what choice do we have but to walk Talo's path?"

"What choice indeed."

"I know, Narhad, isn't it terrible." She laughed. "We actually have so little choice. See, the storm is closer already. Come, I'll show you how my horsemanship has improved. Keep up with me if you can."

With that she spurred her horse and set off toward the camp.

Winter settled in for good shortly after Getlof's and Narhad's talk. Pleasure rides on the plains became impossible. Indeed, there were stretches of a week and more when it was impossible for all but the Shonians to set foot out of the camp. Getlof thought it was terribly cold, but she was assured that it was, in fact, a mild winter. Narhad caught a chill that developed into fever and he was out of his head for almost a week. Getlof insisted on nursing him herself. She needed something to do and there was so little to be done, except wait.

Talo was an anomaly, enthusiastically busy the whole time. The Shonians, in particular, delighted him. He said they were the best archers he'd ever seen. They considered the bows used by the Moazians to be toys. Compared to the Shonian long bow, they were. He soon had hundreds of bows made on the Shonian pattern curing in the ground and was training a company of the Moazians to use them. Dadallean, whose weapons were the lance and the mace, had a go with the long bow at practice. It frustrated him when he saw the Shonian women out draw and outshoot him. He soon gave it up, having learned nothing except, perhaps, respect for the Shonian women. Others made progress, however, and soon Talo was enthusing that they would have the best force of archers in Ossa. When Narhad recovered, he went out and built his strength back up in the exercise ring, drilling those who would acquire skill with the sword. Doy helped and in his free time taught Elp all there was to know about dice. Golab occupied himself by learning the Xumi language. His tutor was a young woman named

Inna-Se. Getlof was surprised by the feelings she had when first she saw the two of them working together. She was careful to keep these feelings to herself.

Time passed and the blizzards became a little less furious, and the clear periods between them a little longer. One day Narhad was practicing one of his better pupils, a Moazian named Farwe. A crowd had gathered to watch, standing around the margins of the circle of beaten snow that formed the exercise ring. Talo was among them. Narhad and Farwe sent at it with their long swords for a longer time than usual. Then Farwe succeeded in slipping past Narhad's guard, giving him a small cut. Narhad dropped his sword and embraced Farwe.

"That was well done. I haven't been wasting my time with you."

Talo stepped out from among the spectators and said: "Some of them are getting good."

"Some of them are getting very good," Narhad panted, picking up his sword. "By this summer, with a lot of work, you'll have a force that, man for man, will be the equal to any in Ossa."

Talo nodded happily. "That was my thought."

"Its just we're so few."

"Of course," Talo said. "Bar-Lev has a hundred divisions of riders, each of which is equal to the numbers we have here." He raised his voice so everyone could hear. "Of course, their numbers are great and we are few. But who do they follow? A bastard from the east, a robber, a murderer and I hear he's very ugly. Who leads us?"

"The Lady!" several shouted.

"The Lady," Talo said. "Do any doubt all things come to her?"

They cheered and shouted no.

Narhad looked down on Talo sourly. Then he said: "Farwe, you've earned the right to lead the drill. Talo, will you come and have a word with me?"

Narhad's bearing was black as he led Talo out of the camp. Talo had to bob along to keep up with his giant strides. "What is it, Narhad," he finally asked before he was totally out of breath. Narhad stopped and whirled around so suddenly Talo stumbled, falling forward. Narhad caught him and for a second, it looked like they were embracing. The touch embarrassed Narhad, being so incongruous with his mood. He backed away before Talo had fully recovered his footing and caught his own foot against a root in the path. This sent Narhad crashing back against a pine tree. Its burden of snow spilled over his head.

"Oh my," Talo said, knowing better than to laugh. "I've gotten you all wet now."

Narhad shook the snow off like a bear come out of hibernation too early. "My fault," he muttered.

"We'd better go back. You're all overheated from your swordplay and this could make you sick again."

"That can wait. I'll have my word with you first."

Talo nodded. He realized Narhad's word was like to be hard and he had hoped to take advantage of the opportunity his clumsiness had given to advert it. As it was, the snow had chilled Narhad throughout. His speech didn't come out as hot as he'd intended.

"I know what you're doing, Talo and I want you to know I don't like it."

"We go to Hilev this spring. I've done naught against that project. Is that what you mean?"

Narhad shook his head. "It's not that. I mean just now, when I was in the ring and you were putting Bar-Lev together to the people with Getlof; saying he's this and she's that, as if the two of them were in competition. That's not good and I don't like it."

"But they are competing, in a sense."

"I don't see it. She doesn't either."

"Look, Narhad," Talo said, suddenly squatting down in the snow so that Narhad had to squat as well, or strain his neck looking down. "What kind of person do people usually follow? A person not unlike themselves; neither wholly good nor wholly bad. Some are better than others, of course, but I question if that is by intent. Then, suddenly, I see two leaders in Ossa who are completely the opposite. It's as if the terminus that separates night from day were to march visible across the sky with no twilight between. The two opposites must compete. They have no choice. It's the people who have the choice. Never will they have such a clear choice. You and I, Narhad, we've made our choice; it is up to us to see that others get the opportunity to do the same. If it's all Bar-Lev in the westlands as its been in the east, then harm will be done to Ossa that will last unto our children's children's time and beyond."

Talo's body quivered with the force of his words and Narhad had no choice but to accept his sincerity. But he still wasn't convinced.

"I don't see it. There have been wars and conquerors come out of the east before. It has never been our concern and I don't see why it suddenly should be now."

"Come, you know as well as I that his riders are in Moaz. Do you think he'll be content to stop there? He didn't stop at the Tarhad; he didn't stop at the Ossa. Getlof's Dell is threatened, if it isn't gone already. Even Gildesh will not hold, don't hedge you bets by thinking it will. He's different. Like you, Getlof doesn't fully realize it yet, but like you, she must."

Narhad shook his head. He couldn't find words to express his opinion and it was so hard to talk around Talo, especially when he seemed to be making sense.

"Come," Talo said, taking Narhad's arm. "Getlof will be angry with me if I don't make you change. You can think about what I said. Talk it over with Getlof, if you like. And the other thing, about inciting people, I'll try to stop. I don't always know when I'm doing it, but I'll watch myself." He smiled. "At least until after we go to Hilev."

Golab had an uncommon ear for language and a taste for knowledge strong enough to bring him to the attention of the Gildi lore-masters back in the days of his childhood. These qualities had never left him. They had, in fact, almost against his will, drawn him into the life of Anneglen. In his contact with the Xumi, he found himself picking up words and little by little, curiosity overcame hurt pride. He found himself collecting bit of lore and knowledge for no reason other than they were there to be had. There was a master of Xumi lore in Gildesh and Golab fantasied about how he would be able to amaze the old master if ever he returned to that city.

One cold day Golab found himself working a trap line with a tall Xumi woman. She had no Southcoast at all, but did possess clear, handsome features, even white teeth and a ready smile. Golab had no recollection of having seen her before, but she knew him. She knew he stood close to the Lady and she had sensed in him a secret distress. She'd spent days arranging it so she'd be out on the lines with him, alone. Her name was Inna-Se. Like the Mother, she had a taste for foreign men and found the Xumi men of her age boorish.

Walking through the lonely, white world they might have been the only people alive. Golab found Inna-Se a ready teacher, patiently willing to name all the things he pointed out; making him repeat a word until he got the sound of it right. His quickness amazed her. Soon they were laughing, not knowing what they laughed at. After that, they discovered that two bodies together produce more warmth than one alone. The lines farthest away from camp they saved for the next day.

35

THE ROAD TO HILEV

Getlof woke suddenly, amid bright, unfiltered light. For a moment she thought she was dreaming because she was sweating as if running from nightmare, but quickly realized it was only because she was warm. Next she wondered if she was ill, but then a sound: water dripping.

Getlof tossed off her covers. The icicles along the eve of the hut were melting and an astonishingly warm wind was blowing. Becks and rills had claimed the footpaths. The Xumi standing guard looked at her and grinned. "Warm, huh?" he said happily in poor Southcoast. Getlof nodded and looked around wonderingly.

"Do you think this is the beginning of spring?"

He looked confused for a moment, then his face lit up with comprehension. "Yes, spring."

They held a council that day. It was still early, but the Shonians agreed this was the big thaw. It might freeze over again, but the power of winter was broken. "A late, warm winter, an early spring." Iodai said it was a sign and no one disagreed with him, not even Narhad.

The Mother brought up the topic of Hilev.

"Child, there's nothing holding you back. If you want my old woman's advice, you'll select your company today and set out tomorrow. They're right about the thaw. When you've seen as many springs as I, you get a feel for it. No false spring here."

Hilev was not far away, considering how far Getlof had come, but it was far enough; a week to ten days of steady riding if things went well and the rivers weren't too high. Getlof decided to take a mixed escort: twenty-five Moazians and twenty-five Xumi. She would have preferred fewer, but Talo insisted the escort be large enough to deal with any problems they'd be likely to encounter along their way. The tribes of the Sumi occupied the land north of the Middle

Hills and south of the Green Ossa. They were reputed to be primitive and unfriendly.

As the discussion went on, Getlof watched Talo covertly. She had the impression he'd rather remain in Anneglen to contentedly drill his recruits, but he didn't trust her to come back without him there to see that she did. It was also decided this was the time to send someone to Gildesh to learn the situation there and also to carry the letter Getlof had finally written to Ducitos.

The letter was a long missive that described Getlof's life from Gildesh up to the founding of Anneglen. Golab transcribed it from Getlof's dictation. The choice of messenger was both difficult and easy. Easy because it had to be one of the three Gildi; no one else was certain of the way and assured of a hearing in the Gildi court. Difficult because none of the three Gildi was so homesick for his old city he wanted to miss Getlof's excursion to Hilev. Finally, Getlof decided on Doy.

Doy had known from the first he'd be the one and he was able to accept the inevitable with grace. Elp was chosen to accompany him. (A decision which both pleased and dismayed Elp. He and Doy had become close companions, but he did want to go with Getlof.) Two Xumi completed their party. They left that afternoon.

Xellia for the Xumi and Daken for the Moazians were left with the task of seeing Getlof had a place to return to. The Mother and Iodai were left in charge of all other matters.

Three Shonians completed Getlof's party. Their names were Lavrens, Asmid and Korni. Besides Getlof, Korni was the only female. She volunteered herself, wondering why the Lady always had to be in the company of men. This amused Getlof and she said that Korni must then come. Asmid could speak Sumi and was included on the basis of that talent. Lavrens was a leader among the Shonians.

On the morning of the next day the whole camp gathered to see them off. Someone shouted, "don't leave us, Lady!" Others took up the cry and for a moment, Getlof wondered if, at the end, she was to be stopped after all. She held up a hand until the shouting died away.

"What is this? Do some doubt I'll return?"

"Yes, Lady, you will go among your people and forget us."

"Don't you know you are my people? You are. So hear my pledge: I shall return. One full moon, wait and before the next moon has waxed to its full, I shall be back. Await me in good cheer. That is my command."

Before they could begin again, Getlof held her ring high above her head. It caught the light from the sun and sent a dazzling reflection off into the sky. Then they cheered. They cheered the company out of the camp and upon their trail for almost a league before Getlof bade them goodbye.

The first week of the journey passed with few incidents. The greatest trial came on the first day. The Anne was in flood and they had to ride south along its bank for an hour before finding a ford. Then, one of the Xumi drowned. His horse panicked, he lost his head and was swept away into deep water. None of the Xumi could swim; they were all afraid of water. The first evening they camped at the northern end of the Anneglen. The next day they entered the empty land north of the Middle Hills. The thaw had touched this land but lightly. The vegetation, mostly chokeberry and shrub sorrel, was covered with a cold shroud of white and the going was uncertain. The horses were forever stumbling into hidden depressions, but luckily, none of them suffered broken legs. There was no sign of human habitation.

Now that Getlof was on the last stage of her journey, her emotions had become curiously equivocal. The closer she got, the further fulfillment seemed. The trip was going too well. She'd come to expect difficulties and it worried her there were none, beyond the biting wind and treacherous ground. The further north they went, the greater her worry became. Every member of the company who had eyes could see a change in their Lady. Talo, Golab and Narhad had seen it before and so held their peace. The others, particularly the Xumi and Shonians put a different interpretation on her mood. "The Lady," they whispered, "does battle with the devil of the north. He seeks to block our passage, but she holds it open."

When Narhad heard this talk, he accused Talo of having instigated it. Talo denied all. "And what's the harm in it anyway?" he asked. "It does the others good to think Getlof is doing her part."

The first two days on the plains the weather held clear and cold. On the third day it clouded over. A storm raged far off to the north, but its only effect on them was to send the temperature up considerably.

"She holds it at arm's length."

The fourth day was the same. Light snow in the morning and a heavy stillness all afternoon. In the afternoon of the fifth day, which was just like the fourth, an outrider reported he had seen the line of the Green Ossa. The fact there were landmarks after all raised moral. They rode more quickly, eager to see the end of the white, lifeless plain. Dadallean took the lead and called for Getlof to ride beside him. He said it was fitting she should be the first to see the Ossa. After awhile, she noticed the plain, which had been absolutely flat, was beginning to slope away. Then she saw a black line drawn across the horizon. As they rode, this line seemed to come no closer and she was surprised when they suddenly came upon it. The plains ended abruptly. Dadallean and Getlof paused on the brink. The river was far below them. The edge was so sudden and regular, it seemed like a wave frozen at its crest, poised over a trough it would never flood. The others, as they came up, were suitably impressed; but then, something happened which impressed them more. To the north the overcast suddenly broke and some great, unfelt wind sent the clouds scudding aside. The sun came out and in its light the Great Mountains stood forward. A ripple of awe swept the company. Only Getlof seemed unimpressed, as if she had expected the sight. Some of the company noted this and nudged one another. The Devil of the North was standing aside. He could not hold the Lady back when it was in her mind to come forward.

Talo swore an oath to the eyebrows of some deity or the other and said he had never seen mountains so great. Lavrens, the Shonian, laughed at this (he was a carefree and confident man) and said first they had to cross the river and to his eye, there were still ice floes in it.

The river valley was broad and deep. As they descended, the air grew warmer and the mountains dropped from sight. The snow lay only in patches, but, as Lavrens foretold, the river was choked with ice. Willow trees grew both in and out of the water. They rode to the bank, sat on their horses and stared. Finally, Talo selected several of the better riders and sent them east and west to seek a crossing.

The western riders returned just after dark. They had ridden two hours out, but the thickness of the ice kept increasing. Although there were spots where the river narrowed, it was also deep and swift in those places.

"That's probably for the best," Talo said. "Hilev is to the east. Let's hope those who went that way bring better news."

That night, however, there was no news at all. A few people muttered that it had been ill advised to send anyone out so late in the day with unfriendly Sumi possibly about. Lavrens, who had some experience in these lands, made light of such talk. "Its like they were caught by night and will return in the morning. The Sumi are famous cowards and would not attack even an old lady unless they had fifty riders and all are drunk. They'll avoid us, sure and the scouts as well. We're a very great company to be traveling in this country at this time of year.

The next morning the sun shone bright and the air seemed warmer still. "At least we don't have to freeze," Golab said to Narhad, stuffing his cloak into his bag.

"Aye, but it would be better if we did. A solid freeze and we walk across yon river."

The scouts returned before the company was an hour on its way. They had found a small encampment along the river two or more hours to the east.

"Did they see you?" Lavrens asked. He was riding next to Talo. The further north they went, the greater say he seemed to take in their decisions.

"No," the scout replied. "It was coming on dark and they seemed to be all inside. We counted the smoke from seven fires."

"Good! Master Talo, may I have your permission to ride forward with Asmid and several of the Xumi? It may be that we can surprise these folk and get from them some news of a crossing. If there are any fords over this river, they'll know."

Talo glanced at Getlof who gave no sign of having heard. "Getlof," he said, "what do you think of Lavren's idea?"

Getlof jumped. "What? Talo, I'm sorry, I wasn't listening."

Talo frowned. He was beginning to wonder if Getlof was going strange on them as she had done after Moaz. Lavrens repeated his question, a smile playing around the corners of his mouth.

"Oh, did you need my say so? Lavrens, go, but be careful. I'd like the good will of these folk."

"Worry not, Lady. I'm a gentle man and Asmid will be there. The Sumi think it marvelous when a stranger can bespeak them."

Lavrens set out with Asmid and six of the Xumi. At the last moment, Narhad decided to go with them. He didn't trust the Sumi to be as cowardly as Lavrens claimed. If they stumbled into more than they could handle, he suspected his aid might render it manageable.

After two hours the company approached the Sumi camp. Narhad rode out to greet them.

"Lavrens was right. We came on them and immediately they commenced to wail and beg us for our mercy. It's a little tribe, no more than twenty-five people. Come, Asmid is trying to get sense out of their Mother."

The Sumi were in a sorry state. Their dwellings were mean and poorly constructed. They appeared half starved. Getlof asked Narhad about this.

"Oh, I don't know the whole story. Apparently they don't usually winter here. As mild as the winter's been, they're close to starving. Lavrens can tell you more."

Getlof found Lavrens at the dwelling of the Mother. The contrast between this Mother and the Mother of the Xumi was absolute. She looked poor, downtrodden and old before her time. When Getlof entered the dwelling (it was in slovenly order and had a peculiar odor that made her catch her breath) Lavrens came up and kissed her hand. He whispered: "She's over the worst of her fright. Wants to know what such a great company is doing marching east along the Ossa. Asmid has been telling her about you. I think she's ready to help us if you'll give her a push." Getlof nodded and stepped around Lavrens. The Mother rose unsteadily to her feet. Her eyes were large and deeply inset. Getlof took one of her hands. It quivered in her clasp. Her cheeks were pinched. On impulse, Getlof kissed her there, then she turned to Lavrens.

"These people *are* starving. Go to Talo and tell him we'll pause and feast them and tell him I don't care how low the stores are. These people need help and we can give it."

Lavrens bowed. "My thought also, Lady. I'll see to it."

When Lavrens was gone Getlof noticed Asmid and said to him: "Has she told you why they're in this state?"

"Yes Lady. They're not in the habit of wintering so far north. It seems that last summer they were harried from their pastures along the Lower Ossa. Their Mother spoke of great numbers of soldiers. They lost most of their animals then and they've had to slaughter the rest this winter. She doesn't know how they're to last another year."

As Asmid spoke, Getlof watched the Mother. Her eyes were nervously flitting back and forth; but in them was a new quality. Getlof fancied it was hope and it stirred her to see it.

"What did you say to her of me?"

279

"Why, Lady, I told her you are Nivila."

At the sound of this word, the Mother whispered: "Nivila?" and pointed at Getlof. Getlof looked down, making no answer; indeed, showing no sign she had heard. She wasn't sure what answer to give; but, as it happened, no answer was right. The Mother suddenly threw herself on the ground and delivered a loud and piercing wail. She followed it with tears and clutched Getlof's knees. Getlof was going to raise her up, but Asmid said:

"Let her be. She wouldn't think it right. She's thanking her gods they have brought you and saved her people."

"Oh," and Getlof suffered her knees to be clasped.

They fed the Sumi who had difficulty believing such kindness could come unlooked for out of the wilderness and from armed strangers at that. This in itself was proof Getlof was no ordinary person.

After they'd shared their victuals Getlof said: "Now it's time to ask their aid. Asmid, explain to them our desire and ask if they know where we might cross."

As Asmid did this, Golab leaned over and whispered to Narhad: "Note how she is taking the lead now. And before no one could get two words out of her."

They knew a place. It was another day east, down the river. They didn't set out, however, until the next day. The Sumis broke their camp and proclaimed they would follow on foot as best they could. Talo tried to say no, but Getlof told him to let it be.

"We'll go slowly to the crossing place so they can follow. There I'll tell them to wait. I think their situation won't be so hard if they have something to wait for. That was half the problem before, you know; they'd given up." She saw that Talo wasn't convinced and laughed: "Think of the challenge, turning these famous cowards into brave warriors. It was my thought you'd welcome it."

Getlof didn't doubt there would be a crossing place, but she didn't expect it to be as good as the Sumi promised. The river had been ever broadening, forcing them toward the base of the bluffs. Talo, less trusting, bade Asmid to ask about this lake. The only reply he could get was: "We're almost there."

Shortly after they saw it: a bridge stretching bluff to bluff across the whole river valley. As they approached, they noted that it rested on twelve pillars. These looked large, even in the immensity of the setting. Through the twelve arches the river crowded with an ever-swelling voice. Golab's comment was:

"Of course there would be a road from Joshin to Hilev. It doesn't seem to get much use these days."

"More's the pity," one of the Moazians said. "Such a fine bridge and out here in the middle of nowhere."

Getlof said: "Surely we're somewhere."

To Getlof the bridge was more than just a means of crossing. It was the first work of the Pau she'd seen, exclusive of the ring and casket. While the sight gladdened her, there was something ominous about it as well. Rather than being a monument to the power of the Pau, as intended, it was a symbol of the passing of that power.

When at last they arrived at the approaches, Getlof took leave of her negative thoughts and turned to the task of parting with the Sumi. This proved easier than Talo had predicted. They made some hue, but didn't seem eager to cross the Green Ossa into the lands of the Pau. Through Asmid, Getlof received their Mother's promise to wait. Through him she bade goodbye. As they rode out onto the cracked stone roadway, Talo watched Getlof. He was content. Each such promise she made and received was additional insurance that Hilev wouldn't claim her.

36

THE MOUNTAINS

Across the Green Ossa they followed the broken remains of the Joshin road, zigzagging up the bluffs on the northern side. From that point the Great Mountains were again visible; the land swept up to meet them. The intervening distance, being foreshortened, made them seem only a short run away. High overhead, ivory clouds spotted the countryside with shadow.

They made swift progress and people, the Moazians in particular, began to act as if the journey already over. Getlof, however, was filled with a curious dread. She'd tried to rein her expectations and ready herself for disappointment, even denouncement, if it came to that; but she seemed to lack the inner energy even for pessimism. The sharp air and sparkling light was so different from the plains, it made the uplands seem a magic place. Yet, in the unexpected and utter desolation of the countryside, a place of eerie magic. Golab had said the kingdom of Jep, of which Hilev was the main town, began at the Ossa. However, except for bridge and road, they'd come upon nothing to indicate any Pau lived there or ever had.

That afternoon they began to pass tumbled mounds of stones along the roadside, suggestive of dwellings long ruined. These somber signs of decay dampened the happy feeling of spring that was in the air. Despite the gay brook that paralleled the road and the wildflowers that brightened the dells and hollows, the impression of ruin came to dominate. Most began to wonder if their journey would prove meaningless after all.

That night they camped under a low hill crowned by the overthrown remains of what Talo guessed had been a watchtower or some sort of fort. The mood in camp was subdued. Getlof was unable to sleep, fearing that this close to the end her dreams would be unbearable, that they would return like a discarded habit in revengeful fury. She lay awake watching the silent sentries and the wheeling stars. Sleep came upon her unaware.

The next morning the mountains seemed closer than anyone remembered, as if during the night they had edged up on the company. They set out quietly, the more superstitious wondering if Getlof's control over the mountain demons was beginning to wane. They were high into the foothills, a region creased and folded like crumpled paper. Looking back, the peaks of the Middle Hills stood out on the skyline across a vast gulf of empty space. The valley of the Ossa had been swallowed by the nearer horizon

The sun was almost directly overhead when Korni, the Shonian maiden, who was riding near the front, gave a cry. When Getlof rode forward, Lavrens pointed to the source of her distress: a man's silhouette against the crest of the slope they were ascending. The news rippled down along the column. Narhad and Golab hurried to the front. The figure began walking down the road toward them. He was alone. Talo glanced over at Dadallean and saw, to his satisfaction, the nomad had unslung his lance.

The figure stopped at a distance and held up his hand, palm out.

"I want to go on alone," Getlof whispered. She wondered why everything seemed so ordinary. Narhad nodded and halted the column. Getlof dismounted and began walking up the slope.

As Getlof got closer, she saw that the man was indeed a Pau. He was no taller than she was and just as dark and as fine of feature. He was the oddest-looking person she'd ever seen and for the first time Getlof experienced an appreciation for how others saw her. As she got even closer, she saw he was smiling.

The Pau spoke first. Rapid words.

"I'm sorry, I can't understand you. Do you speak Southcoast?"

He bowed. "Yes, I do. That is why I was chosen to come forward and to ask what errand your company has in this land." Getlof thought she detected just the slightest suggestion of disappointment in his reply.

"Do you want to know?"

"No, no daughter," he laughed suddenly. "I see the ring upon your finger. I know what has brought you. Have your companions come forward. The valley of the Jep is over this rise."

In silence Getlof walked beside the Pau. The others followed. When they reached the top of the slope the Pau stopped. The land opened out before them. The silver line of the Jep flashed along the valley bottom. Both the nearer and further slopes were dotted with wooden cabins and stands of pines. On a shelf in the further slope above the Jep stood a little, walled town.

"The old city," the Pau said, noticing the direction of Getlof's gaze. "No one lives there any longer, but in days gone by, it was the largest and fairest city in the northland."

"Then this is Hilev?" Getlof asked, spreading her arms to indicate the whole valley.

"No, not strictly speaking. You can't see the new town from this point. It lays to the north, beyond the next ridge."

"So deserted. I can't see a soul."

The Pau smiled wryly. "Two days ago we received word of your party. We were prepared to oppose you with flight. But they are near. They will hear me."

Talo was in time to hear this last remark.

"What?" he said, "can such a little company ride into the center of the kingdom of Jep and send the inhabitants running?"

The Pau turned and bowed. "These things are decided, good lord, and not by me. I shall call them out."

He craned back his head and put his hands to his mouth, like a trumpet. The results were astonishing. His words were:

"*Ire sie alviso*," repeated over and over.

The rest of the company had gathered at the lip of the rise. The echoes from the Pau's voice rolled off the further hills. There was no visible result.

"Come, they will be approaching to greet you."

Getlof could hear the silence behind her and wondered if the foreignness of the situation that made her companions so quiet. For herself, she discovered she had nothing to say to anyone and so rode, as silent as the rest.

Halfway down the ridge, half way to the river, people began to appear, singly and in groups. At first they merely watched, but their guide shouted to the new arrivals and in his speech, Getlof caught the word: "Josh." By the time they had reached the banks of the Jep, all shyness had vanished, replaced by a shouting, singing crowd. Adults ran beside the members of the company, offering food and flowers. Children rode on their stirrups, laughing when they were pulled off by other children who took their places. The transition from constraint to gaiety was almost too sudden. Getlof wanted to be assured, but she wasn't. Looking back at the pleased faces of the company, she realized her lingering reservations were not shared.

Getlof made no sign of how she felt. She smiled and waved, striving to be happy. They halted at the dike that contained the swift flowing Jep, opposite a bridge into the ruined city. The guide turned and faced the entire band, bunched up together in the center of a crowd of Pau.

"The elders and highborn will be wanting to see you. I imagine by this time the news has been sent ahead, but they never believe without seeing. If you're willing, I'll continue to guide you up to the city of Hilev." There was something in his tone that alerted Getlof. She answered saying;

"I am willing, but tell me, I get the impression from the way you name these people they are, in some fashion, different than you."

He smiled. "Different? Yes, they are; but it is their station that is different, not their appearance. We who live in the valley have our function and they have theirs. We feed them and they guide us."

This last was spoken in a low voice only Getlof could hear.

"But the road is not easy, nor safe. There is no need for your whole company to come. It would displease them to have such a large crowd of outlanders in the high city."

He was speaking very plainly, but leaving out much beside. Getlof struggled to think of the proper question to ask, but could only come up with:

"You've never told me your name."

"Lady, I am honored by your interest. My name is Mahap the scribe."

Yes, she had no doubt; it was a warning. Getlof would have liked to question him further, but too many things were competing for her attention. Paus were pushing forward to get a closer look at her and her ring. Talo and Golab were trying to interject their advice.

"Very well, Mahap, I'll follow you." Like him she tried to put more meaning in her words than their sense suggested.

Getlof decided that Talo, Narhad, Golab, Dadallean and Lavrens should go with her. Talo didn't like the idea of splitting the company, but Mahap said:

"Don't worry, our sense of hospitality is very great. Those who remain behind will count themselves the lucky ones."

The climb to Hilev began in the ruins of the old city. These covered an extensive area. Talo asked Mahap why no one lived there, but the reason lay so far in the past, he didn't know. "No doubt there are books in Hilev which tell the tale."

On the other side of the deserted city they followed a broad and gently inclined trail. As it mounted the shoulder of mountain, however, it gradually shrank, becoming narrow and obscure. Narhad softly wondered what kind of city could be at the end of such a meager trail. Golab, who overheard, agreed. They were both thinking of Gildesh. Getlof was no more heedful of the trail than she had to be to keep her footing. She had in mind something Lavrens said when they crossed the Jep: 'Now we're really in the mountains.' The air seemed different; it was cleaner, cooler and more refreshing, as if a person could draw substance from it alone.

They came to a section where the trail hugged the cliff face. They had to dismount and walk their horses. The view behind them, of the foothills rolling away, was almost terrifying. "I can see," Getlof heard Dadallean say nervously, "why it was best all of us didn't come." Then the trail turned toward a gate in the rocks. As they passed through, Getlof felt something against her cheek and she looked around, thinking she had been touched. What she saw instead, were the mountains with no intervening features to soften the fact of their immensity. In the middle distance, there was the town of Hilev. In its setting of vastness, it looked small, but as they approached, Getlof saw that this was no illusion. It was as if in such a setting no dwelling of man or Pau could aspire to grandeur. The mountains overshadowed all. The people of Hilev seemed to realize this and had built accordingly.

Pau were waiting outside the city to greet Getlof. The manner of this greeting was more in accordance with the tone of Mahap's voice than the enthusiasm of the valley people, being quiet and formal. An old man with a long, wispy, white beard stepped out from the others and raised his hand in greeting. "Paudin," Mahap whispered: "the oldest of the elders. I will give you to his care." In a lower voice only Getlof could hear: "Never will I forget the joy and honor of this day; or that it was given to me to greet and recognize you first among the folk." Then he smiled and turned, walking back down the mountain.

Paudin greeted them graciously, but economically. Then he led them into Hilev. The streets were broad, covered with green, young grass. The town was a collection of residences surrounded by low walls, some of cut stone, others of wood. The impression Getlof formed was of a cluster of separate, miniature estates. There were no indications that the residents of Hilev engaged in any sort of economic activity."

They were led to a manor with especially high walls, over Narhad's head. Servants met them at the gate and at Paudin's bidding, showed them to chambers where they could refresh themselves. He said he would be in the garden when they were ready to talk.

Basins of hot water seemed to crowd Getlof's chamber (after so many days on the trail, any number of such basins greater than one was a crowd). This luxury alone merited the time she spent on her toilet, but the pleasure of washing wasn't the only reason she was the last one into the garden. Something was coming; she could feel it with every sense in her body. Paudin had been polite, even gracious; but also so correct and cool. However, she'd come too far to have a wasted trip. She determined to meet Paudin on his own ground, conceding nothing.

A servant showed her the way to the garden. She paused when she stepped from the dark interior to the brightness outside. At first, it was to let her eyes adjust, but then to admire. Beds of exotic, early blooming flowers framed a quietly bubbling spring. Several paths led away from that spot and she choose one at random. She wandered, admiring the unknown flora and wondering what it must look like in summer if it was so striking in the early spring. Each step seemed to bring a new surprise and a new delight. After several minutes of exploring, she heard voices. She took two wrong turns, before she emerged into the proper clearing. A tree rose out from a grassy knoll. It's bole was seamed and cracked, it's leaves rustled in the light breeze. Paudin was seated in its dappled shade. The others sat on benches around him. All rose when they saw Getlof. The scene suggested warmth and friendship; Getlof wondered if her early impressions had been overly suspicious.

Talo had been relating incidents of their journey and news of the world. Paudin greeted Getlof and bade Talo continue. Getlof sat and didn't participate in the conversation, although everyone except Narhad spoke at one time or the other. Finally Paudin turned to Getlof and said:

"You're so quiet. Have you nothing to bring forward? That cannot be so for I see the ring. Favor me with your tale."

Paudin's tone was mild, but, in it, Getlof detected condescension. In a voice as mild as Paudin's, she told her story with such economy it wasn't long in the telling. A moment of silence followed. Then Paudin said:

"The test is not easy; nor is it meant to be. The office is the highest and there can be no doubt of a person's election." Abruptly, he stood. "The chill is in the air. Perhaps you hardy travelers notice it not, but an old man like myself finds it biting. My child, I shall relate your story to the elders and highborn this very night. Now, I shall no longer keep you from the hospitality of this house." With that he nodded, stepped behind the tree and was gone. Servants appeared in his place to lead them out of the garden. Talo, walking beside Getlof, rubbed his arms and said: "Burr, he's right about the cold. Tonight my only desire is to bathe in heated water."

Getlof looked at him, thinking she already had. Servants took them to a room furnished with a long table. A fire burned at one end and Talo stood before this while other domestics brought in food. Getlof sat down, Narhad, Golab, and Lavrens did the same; but Dadallean began stalking around the table.

"Is this a feast? Where is the host? Where is his company? Why do we eat alone?" The servants didn't understand. Then a woman walked in from a door beside the fire. She sat on a stool and smiled up at Talo, then over at Getlof. She took out a stringed instrument and began to pick out notes.

"Sit down, Dadallean," Lavrens said, "and eat. Every land receives guests differently."

"He's right," Getlof said. "Let's not seek discourtesy," trying to keep the whispering voice within her mind from doing that very thing.

The woman began to sing. It was a strange, familiar song and very beautiful. Soon, even Dadallean was mollified. Getlof, however, found she had no appetite. After enough time had passed so the others wouldn't think anything amiss, she stood and wished them goodnight. She felt she had to be alone, to resolve her feelings without having to struggle to hide them from the others. She wanted to be confident and resolute when again she met Paudin and she didn't feel that way now.

That night Getlof was a long time in getting to sleep, but when she did, she was visited by a great and wonderful dream.

It began in a strangely familiar landscape.

Getlof was walking along a trail of springy turf, following the edge of a cliff. There was a rush of warm air flowing up from the depths beside her. Within her dream she remembered she had walked this path many times before--it was, in fact, the dream from which she always woke screaming. As her dream self remembered this, the fear made its appearance, sitting on her shoulder in the form of a small, black bird. She walked on, feeling the tiny claws digging into her shoulder.

The trail ended suddenly in a chasm. The upwelling air was hot. Peering over, she saw Dell, tiny but perfectly formed. Elp hid in the rushes. Geto sat on the steps of his house, his pipe in his mouth. Little puffs of smoke rose into the air. Behind, the tall mountains, icy and grey. The breeze touched Getlof's face and she almost woke up then, so horrible was its clammy, familiar feel. As if strengthened by her resistance, the breeze became a gale and thrust her back with its force. The bird dug its claws into her shoulders and screamed for her to jump. She trembled and wished she had taken the chance to leave this dream. The wind tugged and threatened to blow her away. Then. . . .

Then a voice of magnificent stillness spoke and she listened, never having heard it before.

"DO YOU DOUBT?"

And she stopped. The stillness echoed. She stepped off the cliff without considering one doesn't do such things. The bird dropped off her shoulder and fell like a stone. A sweet smell. Getlof smiled in her dreams.

While Getlof dreamt, Paudin, styled eldest among the Pau, convened the congress of elders and highborn. This was not so marvelous a thing as the name implied. Together their numbers totaled less than thirty; a group of men ranging in age from adolescence to older than even Paudin. they met in a pavilion on the grounds of Paudin's residence. The sides were open to the night, but the men were cloaked and didn't seem to mind the cold. The met most every day, there being little else to do in Hilev.

Paudin was the acknowledged leader of this congress and had been for seventeen years, ever since its numbers had been greatly reduced by the events of the Joshin war and the voluntary severing of relations with the other Pauic communities along the foothills which followed. Paudin meant: 'Speaker for the Pau.' Although his parents had acted with presumption in giving him such a name in the time of Josh, events had proven them farsighted. This was a source of constant pride to Paudin. He had worked to make it so.

The sudden advent of (what seemed to them) a self-proclaimed Josh affected every member of this close community. They had grown in the habit of not having to consider Josh; such a habit was not to be broken in the course of a single day. This was true for Paudin even more so than the others. Yet, he recognized that if Getlof's claim was valid (and the brief conversation that day had convinced him it was), then it was a habit he would have to conquer. And perhaps, he thought, as he faced his uneasy companions, it wouldn't be such a bad thing.

There was no real legitimacy in Paudin's position of eldest. The histories offered only ambiguous precedents; the rituals were set and he had no power to write his position in. But now he realized something was possible. He had a nephew named Kaytel who was born for advancement, although slow in taking what could be his. Paudin knew he could easily separate the young man from his freedom of choice. And what better way than by wedding him off to the self-proclaimed Josh. (Paudin realized she hadn't really proclaimed herself, but the fact that foreigners were doing so upset him endlessly.) By this arrangement, Paudin could continue to be the speaker in fact as well as in name, while grooming their child, the true Josh, to his (or her) station. Moreover, he gained the added satisfaction of becoming the great uncle of Josh, ending all doubt his family was highest. Thus, by advancing the claim of Getlof, Paudin stood to advance himself. Of course, all this assumed Getlof was amendable to his plans; but she was only a child. Paudin could foresee no problem there.

The congress of highborn and elders was collectively surprised to find in Paudin an advocate of Getlof; but relieved as well. It would have been difficult choosing between the claims of the two for Getlof had law and custom on her side and of all the virtues, the Pau regarded respect for custom the highest.

The congress went as Paudin intended. (They always did.) It was agreed to accept Getlof as the Josh and Paudin's choice of consort was approved. Some might have preferred to see their family acquire that honor, but all shared in a secret agreement that Paudin deserved some compensation.

37

THE AMBASSADOR OF DAWN

The next morning Getlof woke and thought first of all about her dream. This time nothing had slipped away. But more than just a memory remained; she was permeated with confidence and surprised she had ever allowed herself to feel any other way. She realized what had been given; something more than just a ring-- something forever hers. She had vanquished her greatest fear.

Getlof lay in bed for a moment enjoying the exhilarating afterglow. She wanted to tell Talo, Narhad and Golab that everything was all right; it didn't matter what happened in Hilev. Her obligation was discharged. Of course, there were other obligations, but now she was free to go forward and deal with them. And then, after that . . . After that she would be free. She could do anything she wanted to do. Anything.

Finally Getlof opened her eyes. The first thing she saw was a stranger sitting on a stool beside her bed. He was a Pau, some years older than her, dressed in rich clothes that indicated he was no servant. She sat up and they stared at one another. When he didn't speak, Getlof said: "Who are you?" voice edged with irritation. It would have been no surprise to wake to the sight of a friend, but a stranger!

The Pau stood and bowed most graciously. He answered in halting Southcoast: "I am Kaytel. I am given the charge of you."

Getlof got out of bed. "Thank you," trying to remember where she had left her clothes. "However, I'm in charge of myself and don't need any help."

His smile didn't waver; he didn't seem to understand.

"Please," spotting the pile of clothes which had been moved and folded, "I want to get dressed." Getlof repeated herself twice but Kaytel only nodded and smiled. Getlof finally opened the door and led him out by the arm. When she emerged moments later dressed, her confidence was intact, but her elation was gone.

Kaytel followed a pace behind as Getlof set out to discover where her friends were roomed.

Walking rapidly down a corridor (not knowing why she was hurrying, but definitely in the mood for it) Getlof almost ran full tilt into Paudin coming up a side hall.

"You walk so quickly, my child. I am certain there is no need."

Getlof stopped, resisted the impulse to inform him she was no child, and smiled:

"Just now I was seeking my companions. . ."

"Yes," Paudin cut in smoothly, "you place a high value upon companionship. Tell me, do you not find Kaytel a pleasing companion? He is a young man of whom we all think highly."

"I'm sure. He's most ready with his attentions. Will you, reverend eldest, aid me in my search and point the direction where my companions can be found?"

Paudin smiled indulgently. "There will be time and time enough for them. First, it would be best if we had a talk. Yesterday much was left unsaid: things I would trust to your ear, but not to the ears of your companions, being outlanders as they are. Come with me now and let us talk."

Getlof nodded. Something told her it was too early to sacrifice appearances. She matched her pace to the old man's careful stride. Kaytel had disappeared, unnoticed.

Paudin didn't begin to speak until they stepped out into the garden. It was earlier in the morning than Getlof thought. The mountain peaks stabbed into the sunlight over the still benighted valleys. Frost covered the ground. Paudin took Getlof's arm for support as they negotiated the slippery path.

"Such a beautiful spot this is. There are sacred associations here. One day I will tell you the story of how Mahon, an early Josh, came here in a time of very great doubt and was vouchsafed the knowledge which enabled our people to prevail. For myself, I find my thoughts are at their most lucid in this place. I hope you will find the same to be true."

They came to the tree in the center of the garden. Paudin lowered himself on a bench.

"You are still silent. Have you no questions? If not, you would be a very strange child indeed."

"I have questions, yes," Getlof said slowly, wondering at how transparent Paudin seemed. "But you have things to tell me. I will listen, anticipating answers."

"Ah, a child who prefers to listen. I am beginning to see you are no usual child. But that is the point of this conversation: why you are unusual."

The morning air was chill. Getlof didn't show her discomfort, but she wished she had brought a cloak, like Paudin.

"I won't ask if you know who Josh is for it is apparent you do. It is apparent, in fact, and excuse my bluntness, that you have been schooled by your companions; perhaps particularly by the one named Golab who speaks our language. That is well and good because it has brought you to us. But you must realize, it is one thing to know of Josh and quite another indeed to have all the terrible responsibility--and I say terrible because profound responsibility is terrible--of being Josh. That, my child, is the responsibility you will have to learn. We shall begin to teach you at once, of course, but you must not expect even the beginning of knowledge for many years. Indeed, I am an old man so I see these things more clearly than you, so know this will be the work of your lifetime; and still it might happen that the fulfillment of your office will be realized only in the person of your eldest child. To be honest, we must consider the effects of your pervious life. You have been deeply touched by foreign notions, as proved by your attachment to the strangers who accompanied you. At this moment we are conversing in a foreign tongue. There is so much you will have to forget before you can begin to learn. Do I give you a beginning of an idea of the work before you? Have I made myself clear?"

"You have made yourself clear." Getlof replied slowly, not at all surprised by this speech. She was watching the golden line of sunlight descend from the peaks. Inside the garden it was completely quiet. It seemed right that a legendary Josh had come here for inspiration. Her mind was totally clear; certainty and doubts were split like a ripe pomegranate, like the terminus of the mountain dawn.

"But still no questions? Have I answered them all?"

"You are remarkably to the point."

"Do you say so? That is a strange complement to receive from a child." Paudin smiled, the conversation was going far better than he'd hoped to anticipate. "So, I direct your attentions to Kaytel. I denoted in your manner some trace of impatient toward that congenial young man. You realize this is

293

due to the frustration of not being able to fully converse; a frustration which will vanish as you learn our language. He is born of the highest family. The offspring of your union will firmly reestablish the line of Josh after all this time when so many have given up hope of living to see that glad event come to pass."

The rest of Getlof's morning was spent in Paudin's care. (He'd decided Getlof wasn't quite ready for the attentions of Kaytel.) He took her from manor to manor--all the little, walled estates Talo had remarked the day before--and introduced her to the members of the congress of the highborn and the elders. Getlof's ego was clenched like a fist. She contradicted not a one of the amazing notions or prejudices Paudin exhibited; in her silence it was easy for Paudin to miss the fact that she'd consented to nothing.

Getlof found it disorienting to be thrust amid so many people who looked like her; by seeing herself reflected in every age, condition and sex. But this resembelece would have struck most people as ordinary. What was disorienting was that the people reflected her image, but were so foreign in every other respect. It went on and on and on.

On the way to yet another introduction Getlof decided she'd been tolerant enough. She reminded Paudin she wanted to see the members of her party.

Paudin waved his left hand vaguely in the air. He'd felt his work was proceeding with the inevitability of an avalanche. It was irritating to be reminded it'd take more than a few stern, direct words to wean Getlof from her unwholesome attachments. Still, it wouldn't do to be too direct. "They passed the night outside my manor, child, in the city. Later you will have time to see them, but not now."

Paudin's tone and his expression told Getlof her patience had gone completely unnoticed. To diffuse the impact of her slip, she blurted out the secret thing that had been on her mind since she had first learned her real identity, her one true question.

"Do you know who my real parents were?"

Paudin turned and looked into Getlof's eyes, a tiny smile playing at the corner of his mouth. She returned his stare and, perhaps, learned more in the exchange.

"That question I have been expecting. Alas, my child, the pilgrimage to NorthPointing took a heavy toll of the participants. Few returned and the seed scattering was not believed to have been successful. I will show you the accounts of those who went, however. You will memorize those accounts and in that fashion know your parent's name, for everyone of them is your true parent."

Paudin clasped his hands behind his back and fell silent. His mention of the pilgrimage seemed to depress him. Then: "It is good, in many ways, you don't know. This makes us all your family and no partisanship can arise. Someday you will see what a blessing you have in that."

When they finally returned to Paudin's manor (the best one in the city Getlof now saw) Getlof was excused for a period of rest. The Pau set great store on brief periods of solitude scattered throughout their day; a custom which, at the moment, Getlof heartily endorsed. Paudin set a guard on her door, 'to be ready if she had any commands' but her window opened on the garden. Getlof took that exit. She had no specific design, wishing maybe to test the degree of her freedom; or maybe to experience the peace of the garden of Mahon.

The grounds were deserted. Getlof was walking along the path which led to Mahon's tree when a voice hissed her name. For the briefest moment Getlof was confused about where she was. She stepped off the path into the high shrubbery along the wall, expecting, almost, to see Elp. But was the voice belonged to Lavrens. And very glad she was, when her orientation returned, to see him. Getlof hugged him before he could say a word.

"Well, Lady," holding her back, his hands on her shoulders, "I'm surprised to find you like this by yourself. Talo and the others saw you earlier, but there were too many of them around and they couldn't get close enough to say anything."

"I know," soiling her white dress by squatting on the ground. "I climbed out a window to get here. Sounds like you had to do something similar."

Lavrens grinned. "I slipped away last night when it became apparent things weren't going as we hoped. The Pau are excellent hosts, but I talked with Narhad today and everyone's upset, very upset, at being kept apart from you. I take it you're being held against your will also."

Getlof shook her head. "Who knows. It's like you said, but more; they're overly excellent hosts. I'm testing my freedom right now, I guess."

"So, do they agree you're Josh? What's going on?"

"Its like this: I might be acceptable by the time I'm an old lady, but the real money's on my child. They've picked my husband out already."

Lavrens laughed. "Indeed? And you agreed to all this?"

Getlof smiled. "Not hardly; but I haven't made a fuss yet either. It seems we really walked into something."

They talked until Getlof became concerned about the passing time. They agreed to proceed cautiously; the Pau didn't seem to have much talent for either security or violence. There was still time to wait for an opportunity to reunite everyone without causing an open rupture.

"I'll try to talk to the others. Tonight, if you can get away, I'll meet you here."

"All right, if I can," Getlof said, brushing dirt off her dress. Then she thought of something else.

"Lavrens, if no one knows where you are, where did you spend the night? It was freezing."

He smiled. "Cold enough outside, but not in the fine stables just yon the wall of this grand house."

After that Getlof had to hurry. She got back and changed her dress just before she was collected for dinner. She was very careful not to make anyone suspicious. To that end she even allowed Kaytel to feed her delicacies from his plate. No one ever told her it was her betrothal feast.

38

THINGS PROPERLY IN PLACE

Kaytel, as scion of one of the oldest and, more recently, noblest families in Hilev, had boundless respect for his uncle. He also awed, feared and, at the moment, resented the old man. Usually unthinkable, this later feeling had been growing since early that day. He'd sacrificed a morning's sleep to attend to Josh when she awoke He'd tried to be cheerful about it, but she wrecked his attempt, first by talking so fast in her barbaric tongue he couldn't make heads from tails of what she said. Then she expelled him from her chamber as if he had some sort of rude intention or wasn't worthy to see her skinny body. That was bad, but what followed, that evening, was worse. She misled him at the feast, allowing several intimacies. He attributed her change of heart to the talk she'd had with Paudin; but after, when he tried to increase their familiarity, she repulsed him in so final a fashion he couldn't entertain any delusions about her true feelings. This brought his true feelings into focus. He didn't want to marry her any more than she didn't want to marry him.

Such a problem Kaytel had never encountered in all his uncomplicated life. He was too restless to sit at the congress that evening and snuck out as soon as he was able, confident he wouldn't be missed. The grounds of Paudin's manor were extensive and, like Mahon, he wandered them seeking the key to his agitation. He hadn't planned to pass the wing where Getlof was roomed; but he did. Along the pebbled path, beneath the close stars of the northern sky, he saw a form silhouetted along the top of the wall and heard a thud as it jumped down to the shrubbery on his side. Kaytel froze, more astonished than scared. People just didn't drop in on other people like that. Then more noise on his right. Kaytel stepped off the path just in time to avoid Getlof. The sight of her set his heart to pounding. The first figure stepped out of the shadows and addressed her. Kaytel listened and tried hard to understand what they said.

"Getlof, thank goodness you're here. I'm afraid I've trouble to report."

Getlof reached out and took the stranger's hand. Kaytel clenched his teeth.

"And I've some of my own. But what's happened? Has anyone been hurt?"

"No, but it was close. I told them what you said and then Dadallean did a foolish thing. He escaped from his, ah, host and tried to get in here to see you. That was this afternoon. He struck Paudin's gateman when he wouldn't admit him. Fortunately, Talo was following and restrained Dadallean before there was any bloodshed; trouble is, now their freedom has been restricted and they're in custody. It was all very polite, you understand, but they no longer have the run of the town like before. And they're looking for me now as well."

Kaytel watched as Getlof turned from Lavrens and seemed to stare right at him.

"Well, at least I know what to do. Listen, Lavrens, they're trying to marry me off like I said, but its going a lot faster than I thought. Now I'm afraid if I say no, they'll try to force me. We have to get out of this place.

This was too much for Kaytel. He burst out of his hiding place with the vague intent of striking Getlof for adding insult to the burden of his misery. A dagger that materialized in Lavren's hand stopped him.

"Kaytel!" Getlof exclaimed.

Kaytel wasn't sure if he was about to be murdered, but if so, he wanted the last word. "Are you so good? Ha! I no wish to marry, but is. Our feast tonight. It was."

"What?" Getlof said.

Lavrens chuckled and sheathed his dagger. "Fast indeed. I take it this is your young man and he's trying to say you're already betrothed."

"That's impossible," Getlof began, but Kaytel shook his head. She stepped back. Kaytel felt distinctly uncomfortable, being stared at so. Finally, she turned away. "All right, Lavrens, you see. It has to be tonight. They didn't even tell me."

"All right, but what about our friend here. He'll raise an alarm."

Getlof looked at Kaytel. "I wonder, but I suppose we can't risk it. I have everything I want; if you can persuade him to come, we'll leave now."

Lavrens nodded and quickly searched Kaytel who stood and dumbly submitted to this indignity. "Unarmed. That's one of the things I like about Hilev. Here, you'd better have this," handing Getlof a knife. "I always carry several myself."

Kaytel was quiet as they scaled the wall, making no attempt to resist. He wasn't sure exactly what was happening, but in some fashion it seemed likely to solve his problem. It also seemed likely to make Paudin very mad. In his present mood, that prospect attracted Kaytel.

A grassy street ran on the other side of the wall. It glowed faintly from a covering of frost and crinkled under the weight of their passage. Getlof was thinking hard. It seemed there was an easy solution. Then she had it.

"Show me where the others are being held. I'll go with Kaytel and try to get them released. You go down the mountain and bring the rest of the company up just in case. Try finding Mahap, the scribe. He's a friend and I think he tried to warn me. If I'm lucky, we can meet you coming back up and if not, I think fifty armed riders will be enough to convince them here that I'm not the person they want. All right?"

Lavrens shook his head. "In the first place, Kaytel could expose you with a word and you'd never know it."

"I know, but even if that happens, they wouldn't do anything to me. I want to avoid threats or force if possible, but if that's not possible, well. . . . This seems the way." Lavrens didn't like this plan, but from the tone in Getlof's voice he knew she was going to insist on it.

"I think it'd be better if we went down together."

Getlof shook her head. "It's the feeling I get, Lavrens. I have it now. I suddenly know what to do and even if it's wrong, it's right. I used to be afraid to follow that feeling, but now I'm afraid not to."

What could Lavrens do; the Lady was speaking, obviously, as Nivila.

"All right, but give me a chance to get down the mountain before you stir any trouble. I should make it before dawn." Lavrens turned to Kaytel. "I'll remember if you betray her. It's a deadly thing to do. *Shih?*" (Pauic for understand.)

Kaytel nodded. He did understand. The sensation of being threatened was new and while it frightened him, he was also curiously excited. It was as if he were living in some old tale where threats were common and life cheap. He hadn't realized Getlof's companions were so hard, or that she was so hard herself. This also excited him.

"Well, maybe he'll cooperate, but at any rate, here we are. See that house, the one at the end of the street? That where they're being kept."

"Good. I'll wait until an hour or so before dawn, then I'll go in. I feel it will be right but knowing you're bringing the whole column doesn't hurt."

Lavrens nodded and looked at Getlof for a moment. Then he turned and, walking rapidly, set off down the hill.

Getlof and Kaytel retired to the shadows between two buildings to wait out the long hours of the night. She kept the knife at hand, wondering if Kaytel's manner would change now that Lavrens was gone. Kaytel, however, wrapped himself in his cloak and promptly went to sleep. Getlof envied him. She was far too cold, despite her heavy cloak, to do the same.

She tried to think of a story that would free her companions without causing any of their Pauic guards to come to grief, but it was hard to concentrate. Objectively she knew her plan was irrational and it surprised her that Lavrens had given in to her so easily. Still, this knowledge didn't touch her confidence. Not even the lack of a plausible story did that. She knew that something would occur to her when it was time.

Getlof waited two night's spans, it seemed, but finally she could wait no longer. She shook Kaytel awake and said: "Listen carefully and if you don't understand, say so. We'll go in and if anyone is awake, you'll say we have come from Paudin. A rider has come in tonight with news that has to be discussed at once. You don't know what the news is, but, it's something my friends will be able to advise Paudin about. We came, rather than a messenger, so they would believe us and also so I could explain to them. Alright?"

This was a long speech and Kaytel had her go over it several times. Finally, however, he had it. His stomach was jumping with eagerness; life in Hilev had never been so exciting.

Frost tinkled as they shook their cloaks. Getlof thought of showing Kaytel the knife again, but decided it wasn't necessary. Already she was thinking her original judgement of the Pauic youth may have been a little hard.

The door to the building was unlocked. Getlof pushed it open and stepped over the threshold. Contrary to her hopes but true to her expectations, someone was awake. A single Pau sat in a corner wrapped in his cloak. He questioned them in a mild voice. Kaytel launched into the story. Getlof watched, feeling separated from the scene being played before her. Detached and uninvolved. The Pau was suspicious. Two more guards joined him from a back room, rubbing their eyes. This didn't bother her. Kaytel's voice had taken on a pleading tone and he was casting anxious glances at Getlof. Without knowing why, Getlof suddenly looked across the room at a heavy, bared door. And at that moment, someone began pounding and yelling from the other side. She recognized

Dadallean's voice. The Paus glanced nervously at the door, although the beam was too heavy to be broken. One of them exited out another door and then Kaytel did an amazing thing. He leapt at the warden closest to him and pushed him back against his mate. They both fell to the ground, more from surprise than from the force of Kaytel's blow. Before they could recover, Kaytel ran to the door and lifted the beam. The door flew open and Dadallean sprang out with a triumphant cry. Narhad was right behind. He took the situation in with a glance and grabbed Dadallean's arm before he could reenforce the terror his sight inspired with any deeds. Talo and Golab followed.

Talo spoke first. His voice was almost matter of fact. "Getlof, I won't ask what you've come for."

"We have to hurry," she said, the spell of her detachment shattered. "One of them left to get help."

Narhad was wrenching at a cupboard. He gave a cry of satisfaction when the lock broke. Their weapons were inside.

"I'm sorry, Getlof, but never again will I surrender my sword in the name of peace or manners."

"Are there horses outside?" Talo asked, looking curiously at Getlof. When she shook her head he came closer and whispered: "What are you doing? Is this necessary?"

"It is," Getlof said. Then they heard the sound of shouting from somewhere within the town.

They ran from the house and saw from the twinkling of torches around the stables that they would have to fight to get their horses. This was exactly what Dadallean wanted, but Getlof directed them in the other direction, toward the trail down the mountain. No one noticed Kaytel tagging along.

"This is crazy," Dadallean said as they trotted. "They'll ride us down."

Getlof shook her head, swirling her hair with the force of her negative. "No, these are Pau. They won't fight; they'll end up letting us walk down the hill." Then she told them Lavrens was coming with help. Dadallean was doubtful, especially as he figured it would take Lavrens until the middle of the morning to show up. They trotted on and still there was no pursuit.

They were well out of Hilev, almost to the natural gate that gave egress onto Hilev's plateau when the pursuit finally appeared behind them; a bobbing string of lights; horsemen bearing torches. Getlof looked up and saw that night was lightening to grey. Dawn was near. She sent out a silent call to Lavrens.

The horsemen overtook them just before they gained the safety of the gate. Narhad drew his sword and Dadallean shook his lance. Shaking his head, Golab stood with a long knife. Talo had a sword as well. For the first time, Getlof noticed Kaytel trembling beside her. She was surprised he had joined them in their flight. They formed a tiny circle with Getlof in the center. The horsemen rode in a large circle around them blocking the narrow passage on the other side of the gate. No one spoke. It wasn't what Getlof had wanted, not a bit of it. But she was angry rather than disappointed. Hadn't they brought it upon themselves? It was certainly not this her ring had promised, nor the tablet in the golden casket. The ring was on her finger and it was burning hot, as if resonating with her anger.

The impasse lasted for some minutes. Then Paudin appeared sitting painfully atop a horse. All the people of Hilev seemed to be following him. Paudin spoke first.

"This is the return you give us, stranger, for accepting you and doing you honor." His voice was unsteady, plainly laboring under the stress of great emotion. The grey light was growing, constantly bringing new details of the scene into focus. "Kaytel, is that you? Shame!" His voice grew and echoed off the surrounding walls of rock. "No Josh are you, but a great seducer and betrayer. Kill them all," he screamed, voice cracking. "The child as well."

No one moved, plainly uncertain Paudin had really meant to order murder. To encourage their hesitation, Dadallean craned his head back and screamed the yell of the Xumi warriors. The circle about them seemed to widen. The echoes rolled away and then came a reply from further down the trail that was no echo.

"Lavrens!" Getlof exclaimed.

"Already?" Talo said. "He's quick, but maybe not quick enough."

"Did you hear me!" Paudin shouted, his composure completely gone. "Quickly. There are only six of them."

Still no one moved. Then, ahead of time it seemed, the sun penetrated a cleft in the eastern mountain wall. The light fell on Getlof's group. It seemed unnaturally warm. People gasped and pointed to the pillar of rock that formed one half of the gate. Getlof followed their gaze and saw, standing upon the pillar, an elongated figure: something in the form of a man. He had hair of golden black, was shrouded in robes of red shot with fire. He raised both arms and at once silence descended. The sunlight seemed to emanate from him: his aspect was faceted with myriad reflections, painful and bright. He floated down from the pillar just as Lavrens appeared on the other side of the gate. The sun was completely above the eastern wall. Time was passing strangely. He floated down from the pillar and people drew back. Day, full golden and searing. Lavrens halted and came no closer. The figure reached the ground, a benign smile informed his face. Hushed awe.

Getlof couldn't take her eyes from his. She didn't notice the ring burning her hand. He approached, apparently gliding over the ground. People drew back. Getlof was suddenly alone.

He was there, in front of her.

Two hands emerged from the cuffs of his robe. White and translucent. Getlof felt . . . she didn't know what she felt. Fear seemed appropriate, but there was something more; much more. Hands softly encompassed her face and drew it forward. He placed upon her brow a kiss that burned. His smile never varied. Then he stepped back and gazed upon Paudin. Paudin's face was white. Suddenly he gasped and raked his fingers over his chest.. He swayed and then toppled from his horse. The fall of Paudin had drawn everyone's attention. When Getlof looked back, the golden black man was gone, as if he had never been.

Getlof felt the mark upon her brow and wondered if his kiss had left a scar.

39

RETURN TO ANNEGLEN

Lavrens broke the spell. He walked slowly forward and bowed before Getlof. She gazed at him closely, as if for the first time and then at the crowd around her. People pressed tightly on the narrow path and the slopes above. Faces, light and dark were turned toward her like sunflowers to the sun. Lavrens said:

"I see now, Lady, my misgivings were mistaken. Your plan was clearly the best."

Getlof almost smiled at the familiarity of the reminder. He extended his arm in a gesture of invitation. Getlof started down, between the pillars and through the Moazians and Xumi. Behind her she heard a collective sigh as if hundreds of people had just released their held breaths. Without looking she knew there would be few people lingering in Hilev that day.

The noise grew; whispering and muttering, inside and out. Swelling and receding like a tide whelming the shore. Narhad was there, however, holding back the press. When their eyes met, his serious expression was replaced with a gentle smile. Getlof recalled that clearly.

She also recalled the trail, seeing the valley of the Jep straight down and the spiraling column of people flung on the mountainside above. Mahap walked beside her. He told her he had learned of her betrothal from friends and how he'd passed the news to her company. They mustered themselves and set off up the mountain, guided by Mahap, only to meet Lavrens coming down. He said of Paudin: "A good man, but he'd forgotten he was to follow the forms, not invent them." Of the manifestation: "My Lady, it was Rab, Angel of Forbidding Heights. His colors are black and gold and his time is dawn. The histories record other manifestations, but they were long ago. It takes something very great to bring him down so low. People had forgotten of his existence; but they will remember now. For a time."

Getlof tried to recall if Golab had spoken of this spirit. She looked for him, but he was lost in the press. Narhad was near, of course, and Talo too. Dadallean's voice rose clear above the others. But Golab, where was he? She was being set apart. If Golab had been there, she would have encircled his waist with her arm and cried. He, who should have known better than anyone, knew least of all. What could Getlof do? The girl had a clear vision of the Lady walking outside herself, a web of fire etched all around. It kept her from anyone who didn't come first to her. Asha had set her apart, but only in her own mind. The kiss of Rab did the same for all to see.

When they reached the valley they found that somehow the news had preceded them; kegs of spirits were being tapped and people whirled in circles doing spring dances. Mistrials with high, piping voices, chanted the histories (These had gained a new immediacy.) Poets were even putting the events of the dawn into verse, each hoping his version would be the one incorporated into the histories.

Getlof was guided through this scene by Mahap and certain of the elders and highborn who gathered themselves to her. It touched her not at all. Her mind was on signs and symbols. The past was clear as it had never been before, and the future also. Only the present was obscure.

She received expressions of homage and loyalty from the Pau; accepting all because to refuse was forbidden her. The future she saw, coming as a result, was not the future she would have chosen, but that was out of her hands.

Talo recognized the semi-comatose state into which Getlof had withdrawn. It worried him, but with the perspective gained in his long friendship with her, he didn't worry too much. What did concern him was the elder Pau fluttering around Getlof like merchants to a discount. He sensed resentment from some of them even still and so they wouldn't forget the realities of the situation, he formed the Xumi and Moazians into a escort when they reached the valley floor. One of the elders protested that it wasn't necessary and Talo mildly reminded him that, after all, Paudin had ordered her killed.

There was one moment in the late afternoon as the warmth leaked out of the air, when Getlof suddenly turned and looked at Talo with a focused expression, as if he had just called for her attention with something important to say. All Talo could think of was: "Does it hurt?" speaking of the red-brown scar. Getlof touched her brow. She smiled slowly.

"It does hurt, but on the inside."

Talo nodded, wondering what response to make; but as he wondered, he saw no reply was needed. She was out of focus again.

The appearance of Rab had terrified Golab. When Getlof began the descent after being greeted by Lavrens, he hung back. Who was Getlof? Golab had always thought he knew better than anyone; but now he didn't know at all. What good is knowledge if, faced with proof, it shatters, leaving the knower uncertain and afraid? Knowledge was something Golab preferred to keep abstract, separate from the ordinary routine of day to day life. Getlof was Josh, yes; he had seen that before anyone, but Getlof was also a companion and a friend. What Golab couldn't do was merge these two Getlofs together in his emotions.

The tight stream of people, all Pau, carried Golab along with them. He listened to their excited conversations. The Josh! The Josh had returned! She had come back with power. An old era had ended and Golab heard no one say they were sorry to see it go. How could anything be wrong again? (And Golab, hearing this wondered how anything could be right again.)

When Lavrens found Golab that evening, Golab was touched someone, at least, remembered him. He didn't know Getlof had sent Lavrens and Lavrens didn't tell. He brought Golab back to the camp the people from Anneglen had set up. When he arrived, Golab saw Getlof as she saw him. They looked at one another, but neither spoke. Then Golab turned away. What he didn't realize was that Getlof suffered from constraints of her own and those constraints were stronger than his.

Narhad possessed powers of thought far greater than anyone first meeting him would have suspected. His rare quality, however, was that he knew when not to think. He had long since accepted Getlof as someone extraordinary. Proof affected him as little as doubt; neither made a difference. Whoever else she was, Getlof was still Getlof. And Getlof needed protection. All the manifestations in the world wouldn't change that. After Rab disappeared, he was at Getlof's side and never once during the course of the day did he leave it. He asked no questions. His obligations were clear before him and he fulfilled them with an open heart.

The next day Getlof was one of the very few to rise with dawn. After dressing and doing those things that had to be done, she ran into Talo who had risen early as well.

"Another day," he said, putting his hands on his hips. "Do you think this one will be as full of surprise as the last?"

Involuntarily Getlof glanced up at the mountains that loomed close at hand. "No, there is an ordinary quality in this dawn. It comes on slowly as it should."

"You felt that too. I really couldn't imagine what you were feeling. It was very strange."

Getlof looked down and didn't reply. She was thinking once again of Asha and how different that had been.

"You're silent," Talo went on. "It would be easier for me to be the same, but I can't. Whatever happened yesterday, today you can no longer put off your decision. Every person in this valley awaits your word. I must ask what that word will be."

Getlof hadn't expected this question. She looked up and forced herself to concentrate on what was happening now, not on the past.

"Do you think this has gone to my head?" trying not to let him know it had happened several times before. "Talo, we've come a long way and never in all that distance did I knowingly betray my word. Did yesterday make me so different? I know you were against this journey, but it had to be done. It's done. I recall the word I spoke when I rode out of Anneglen. I said wait one month and in the next, look for my return. There is ample time to meet that promise. Indeed, if we leave soon, today or tomorrow, we should get back within the first month. That's my word and I'm surprised you even had to ask."

Relief was apparent on Talo's face. "Forgive me, Getlof. My old habit of doubt is not lightly cast aside."

"Oh, I know. I wasn't angry."

"You're a hard one to figure. I wonder what you want for yourself?"

Looking past Talo, Getlof saw the tall form of Narhad coming toward them through the morning mist. No doubt he'd found her pallet empty and was coming in search. In a low voice, she said quickly, "I'm getting so I'm afraid to want anything for myself."

Getlof gave her word that day. It was received with consternation by certain of the elders who had looked for a return of the old days with Getlof playing the part of Paudin. The reaction of Kaytel was typical of the younger Pau. To leave the confines of Hilev; to participate in high deeds--indeed, the adventure of the age, which would surely be recorded in the histories and read as long as there was a future, accorded perfectly with the new desires Getlof had stirred in him. When Talo saw for himself this enthusiasm, he rubbed his hands and thought of the new companies he could form. It was clear many of the Pau intended to follow Getlof wheresoever she went.

They left for Anneglen on the third day after the manifestation of Rab. They were a great company indeed. Long lines of Pau followed Getlof's Moazians and Xumi. Some came mounted, but most were on foot. They crossed the Ossa Bridge and Getlof was surprised to learn that most of the Pau had never seen it before. She was amused by Kaytel's reaction. He was impressed and then proud that his people had been capable of such great work. He promised her that in the future the Pau would again build such things.

They collected the bedraggled band of Sumi who were still waiting and entered the plains north of the Middle Hills. The weather was perfect as it rarely was in that region at that time of year. Every day the mountains stood out sharp and clear. The northern plain, cold and white on the trip up, abounded with tiny purple and white wildflowers. They went quickly and nothing hindered their progress. Two weeks from Hilev, they met an outrider from Anneglen. It was fully spring and the beginning of the campaigning season.

40

BAR LEV'S AMBASSADOR

Getlof's return to Anneglen was a triumph. She rode through a sea of faces, trying to acknowledge them all; especially the many she didn't recognize.

Anneglen itself was strangely unfamiliar. Surrounded by a new, wooded palisade, it was already spilling beyond into what had been forest when Getlof left. Iodai rode beside Getlof. He proudly watched her marvel at the extent of the new construction:

"We've been busy, but there was no choice. Just last week a party of several hundred Shonians arrived and I think half the population of old Moaz is here. More come all the time and now, with all these Pau, we'll have to give Anneglen a proper name. I was thinking of New Joshin."

Iodai rambled on and Getlof, for a change, was glad to listen. At least he was the same. He'd heard the story of Rab and thought it nothing extraordinary. He only regretted he hadn't been a witness.

After she had seen all Iodai had to show, (and having shown herself to all the people of Anneglen in the process), Getlof turned toward the section where the Xumi had pitched their tents, anxious to see the Mother.

The first daughter greeted Getlof at the door. To her surprise, the daughter embraced her and said: "The Mother will be happy to see you."

Getlof entered the dim interior of the tent and although she couldn't see, she strode confidently to the spot where she knew the Mother lay amid her profusion of cushions.

"Ah, my child, is it you? Yes, they said you'd returned. It must be you."

Getlof sank to the floor and found the Mother's hand. That marvelous voice had faded to a whispery quaver in the short time she'd been gone.

"Yes, its me, Mother."

The Mother feebly returned Getlof's pressure on her hand and chuckled softly. "I hear your worry. Is it so surprising an old woman should approach her time?"

Getlof didn't answer and the Mother went on, almost inaudibly: "I wasn't going to let go before I saw you again. I'm happy you returned before the effort became a struggle too great. You've gathered many new followers in Hilev, they say. I confess, I feared it would be different. It's gladsome to be wrong, sometimes. Are you going to lead these people as they wish to be led?"

"I'll try," Getlof whispered.

"Ah, but you still wonder if you can, your tone says. Good. There is so much for a leader to beware; but beware most the traps from within. They'll push you from behind to think you are more than you are." The Mother nodded and lapsed into silence. Getlof sat, holding her shriveled hand. Finally, Iodai who stood by the door trying to overhear, cleared his throat. The Mother's eyes fluttered open. "I heard that. Iodai is telling us its time for you to go. You have my blessing, child. And all my thoughts. Be strong."

The next day the Mother died. That was also a sign. Getlof was sad, but in a way, she envied the Mother for the peace she had gained. It was another obligation, but Getlof had so many now it hardly mattered.

Talo had ridden ahead and reached Anneglen half a day before Getlof. It had been torture for him to be out of touch for so long. He found Xellia and Daken and proceeded at once to question them about the situation, cutting short their greetings and questions about the trip to Hilev.

"You'll hear about that soon enough."

When Talo's back was turned, Xellia smiled at Daken. From Talo's manner, one would have thought he'd been gone a day, not a month.

Xellia, the head scout, reported that Bar-Lev was still camped at Zoha; but according to rumor he intended to move his seat to Moaz for the season. He had already sent a division to occupy that unhappy city; patrols from Anneglen had occasionally skirmished with his outriders. Talo was puzzled to find there had been no news from Gildesh. He couldn't understand how Bar-Lev could so lightly ignore that power; nor could he believe Gildesh had already been overthrown. Much depended upon the safe and speedy return of Doy and Elp.

As he listened to the reports, Talo considered the odds. There were now several thousand men in Anneglen capable of fighting. It was incredible how their strength had grown, but it was still just a fraction of the numbers Bar-Lev commanded.. One precious month had been wasted by the trip to Hilev. To balance that loss, he had gained a considerable body of new recruits. But they were inexperienced and untrained. Bar-Lev was moving west, not south as he'd hoped. In a pitched battle, Bar-Lev would rout them. It seemed to Talo that their only intelligent recourse would be to retreat to the forest of Shon and the broken country around the Roganspire. If this were to be done, it would have to be quickly. If Bar-Lev caught them on the march, it wouldn't be a rout; it'd be a slaughter

Talo left Xellia and Daken in a grim mood and settled down to wait for Getlof. He observed the celebration her return set off, but the commotion merely deepened his depression. It was a mercy they didn't know what he knew. He wondered if he'd be able to make her see the danger.

On her first day back, everyone wanted to see Getlof. Talo didn't have the opportunity to discuss his worries with her privately. The second day was the same, but on the third day, the matter was brought to her attention and Talo had nothing to do with it.

Outriders brought word of a party coming from Moaz under the blue flag. Getlof was not in camp when this happened and Talo set out at once to find her. This proved more difficult than it should have been. She was in the forest with a mixed company of Shonians and Pau being educated in the tradition of the Sacred Oak that both peoples shared. Talo wasn't popular among the Pau and he got a fulsome share of nasty looks when he interrupted their arcane instruction. It was the most satisfying thing he'd done in days.

"It could mean anything," Talo said as they returned to camp. "And so, we should be prepared for anything."

Getlof looked at Talo, mildly surprised by his curtness. He had changed in their year together, in his way as much as she. For some reason, these changes seemed especially pronounced at the moment. This Talo was older, more than a year's span would warrant. He had less hair on his head and more lines on his face. It seemed he rarely laughed anymore.

Talo felt Getlof's scrutiny and looked up with a wane smile. "Don't worry about me, if that's what you're doing. Worry about this parley. I've a horrible suspicion they're going to bring us news of the fall of Gildesh. If that's the case, we'll have some hard decisions before us."

The rest of day was spent preparing to receive the Levites. The hall Iodai had raised was cleaned and decorated. Seamstresses frantically set to work stitching Getlof a more regal costume than the white dress she habitually wore. Talo put great stock on impressions.

The Levites rode into Anneglen that evening. Talo and Narhad received them with cool courtesy. They were searched extremely well and their weapons taken from them. Narhad was up most of the night making sure the guard he'd placed around them didn't relax its vigilance. The next morning, their leader was granted his audience with Getlof. He was none other than that champion of diplomacy, Prince Rowenna.

Getlof sat in a raised chair at the far end of the hall. Guards dressed in the best armor a search of the camp could find preserved an aisle down the center. Getlof, thinking the Levite mission should be a public event, permitted spectators to jam the remainder of the hall. She sat with her chin in her hand, listening to the stir that greeted the Levites as they entered the hall through an even greater crowd gathered outside. There were many things she should have been thinking, but her mind was curiously empty. She did wonder about their appearance; rumor had the Levites to be so evil, it would be anticlimactic if they proved to be merely ordinary men.

Finally, the announcement. The door flew open and Bar-Lev's ambassador came sweeping in. He was a youngish man: his clothing and gear rich, but not ostentacious. His manner confident, but not arrogant.' He was definitely not a barbarian chieftain as Getlof had expected. He strode up the aisle looking neither left nor right until he stood before Getlof. Then he bowed low and held it until Getlof remembered herself and said:

"Ambassador."

"Greetings, Lady, Ear of the Unspoken Voice. His Ominous Majesty of the Uncounted Herds, Grandoverlord of the inner and outer lands, Bar-Lev greets the Lady Josh, known as Getlof, through his humble and inadequate mouthpiece, the Prince Rowenna." He capped this greeting with a brilliant smile.

"Prince," Getlof said, inclining her head slightly to the left toward a chair. She was vaguely surprised and even disconcerted, but knew better than to show her feelings. The same could not be said for the crowd in the hall. There was a buzz of whispering as the Prince sat down. He smiled in acknowledgement and perched on the edge of his seat, as if to be that much closer to Getlof. She held up her hand, and when silence was restored, said:

"What word has the Lord of the Uncounted Herds given you to say onto me, Prince. Speak it out and do not delay." Unconsciously Getlof mimicked Rowenna's polite mode of speech.

"Ah, reverent Lady, you are succinct, a quality I admire. Know that my lord has looked upon your rise with amaze and delight. In your advancement, he see parallels to his own elevation and abundant signs that an age of peace and order is at hand. To mark and to ensure these joyous times my lord did bide me fly to your presence and present to you his proposal for confirming the order of this new age." Like a storyteller trying to create suspense, the Prince paused and inclined his head toward Getlof, never ceasing to smile. Getlof couldn't help but smile back, even as she asked:

"What proposal is this?"

"Plainly will I tell you, Lady. It is this: My Lord sends me to you for one reason only; to inform you of his desire for peace and to confirm this peace in the strongest possible fashion. His desire is to wed with you and thus unite the authority of this whole land in one house. Only in this fashion can lasting peace prevail."

For a moment Getlof thought she'd misunderstood. Suddenly everyone wanted to marry her, even the terrible Bar-Lev. The notion was too ludicrous to even upset her. She leaned back in her chair and began laughing softly. The Prince's smile faltered. The hall was suddenly quiet.

"Lady, what am I to understand by your reaction?" Rowenna slowly stood. "Am I to tell my lord that I presented his offer and you laughed? It would displease him greatly."

Getlof contained herself and looked at the Prince. His threat reminded her that she was answering not only for herself, but also for everyone in the hall.

"Prince, stand or sit as you choose, but don't threaten me in my own hall. You must forgive my laughter and realize, if you will, the surprise such a proposal evokes in one who knows Bar-Lev only by reputation."

Rowenna sat, again on the edge of his chair. A brief smile returned to his lips. "Lady, it is no pleasure for me to say that if you know my lord by reputation, you know what he is capable of. Answer now with considered words. Say you yes or no?"

"Prince, it is no gracious suitor who presses a girl he has never met for an immediate answer, but if one you will have then it must be no. I will not marry your lord."

The Prince stood and bowed low. It seemed for a moment he saw the situation much the same as Getlof. He was a likable man. "I hear your words, Lady. I warn you once again that my lord has his own way and you are right, it is not typically gracious, but now I will say no more." Getlof nodded, assuming the audience was over, but Rowenna went on. "I had presents from my lord which the caution of your attendants did not permit me to bring within this hall. I have a present also to be given in case of your refusal. You have refused; may I present them to you?"

Getlof glanced to her right where Talo and Narhad stood. "Narhad, will you see this present is brought in." She was truly curious.

Rowenna sat back beside Getlof in a more relaxed manner. Glancing at Talo, Getlof could see he was worried this present might be some trap or trick. Then a man entered the hall accompanied by Narhad. He carried a small chest. All whispering stopped as they walked between the pressed people. The chest was set on the floor at Getlof's feet.

"Lady, it is sealed with a lead plate," Narhad said.

"Yes, the Prince said, standing again. "And on it you will notice the seal of Bar-Lev. Straight from our lord has this come; untampered, unviolated. You may break it with a sharp blow."

Narhad looked up at the Prince and grunted. Then taking a small, single bladed axe from his belt, he struck the plate with the blunt end. The lead cracked and the lid flew open. Narhad looked in. Then he reached in with both hand and pulled out two head, dried and shrunken, but still recognizably Doy and Elp.

Getlof gazed down sadly in the silent second before pandemonium erupted. She didn't feel fear, she didn't feel surprise. She was angry. Anger, she knew was the emotion of people losing control; it was an emotion she had once known well. Then the hall was rocked by shouting and screaming, shaken fists and stamping feet. Dust motes careened wildly in the entering shafts of sunlight. This allowed Getlof to restore a measure of self-control. She stood and held out her hands and after a time a semblance of quiet returned. Getlof said:

"Prince, did your master know these people were dear and trusted friends of mine?"

Rowenna looked at her; his face was white. Clearly the gift had been as much a surprise to him as anyone.

"No, Lady, I don't see how he could have; but if news of that fact ever reaches him, I do not doubt he will be pleased."

This statement destroyed the audience's uneasy calm. Getlof was some time before she was able to give her reply.

"He will get news of it as quickly as you take it to him. You will thank him for returning these friends to me so I can do their memory the honor it deserves. You will tell him also that the age of peace and order that he envisions is no certain thing."

The Prince began to bow, then suddenly dropped to his knees. "Lady, I will deliver your message faithfully, even if it is the death of me. Your understanding outstrips by far your years. This also I will tell my lord. Finally, if you will accept a true warning from me, a warning I would give." He paused and looked up, continuing only when Getlof nodded. "Bar-Lev will take this as a challenge and his strength is very great."

"Thank you, Prince Rowenna. I have heard your warning. Narhad, will you escort the Prince and see he and his men are allowed to proceed safely."

Getlof's eyes were starting to mist. The trouble with controlling anger was that it let sadness leak in.

41

HOW THE WARNING WAS HEEDED

That year the omens of nature contradicted the omens of man. No one could recall a milder, more favored spring. The worst storms were nothing more than afternoon showers that meandered down from the Middle Hills. Everywhere the bare earth sprouted. Trailing creepers and berry vines worked hard to engulf the huts and fields of Anneglen. Purple wildflowers with tiny white hearts hid the scars of construction. Even tree stumps cloaked themselves with beards of new growth. The muddy, raw looking camp became a new, more pleasant place. It was Getlof's first spring in the northland. Dell had been a favored spot in a dry land, but here, the favors of nature were so profuse it seemed miraculous--almost unnatural. It puzzled her how the northerners took this explosion of growth for granted; even, at times, as a nuisance. To wander alone in the verdure would have been a delight, but the days contained no time for such pleasures.

Unsari wasn't in demand like Getlof. He spent his mornings sitting in the sun, contemplating the wonderful material for poems that surrounded him and doing nothing about it. He wrote only his epigram, the passing of the Mother being a direct reminder of his own mortality.

> Stand here, friend, and look upon Unsari;
>
> A poet once famous in the west.
>
> Cherished and forgotten and cherished again,
>
> He chose his words well; but, alas,
>
> The lute he never mastered.

It was a spring for lovers. Golab, after returning from Hilev went completely over to Inna-Se, adopting her language and mode of dress. Anyone who saw him would never have guessed that only a year before he had been a functionary in the imperial court of Gildesh. He seldom went to Getlof's counsels, although she was now taking special care to make him welcome, and offered no advice when he did. He avoided her at all other times.

Kaytel had no time for love. Getlof allowed him a place not far from her side and this made him a leader among the younger Pau. He filled them with his enthusiasm, an attitude Talo and Mahap, but not Lavrens, were surprised to see him maintain. He spent his days drilling and polishing armor and listening avidly when Narhad or Talo spoke of military subjects.

"He likes to listen," Talo admitted, "and he's not nearly as stupid as he seems."

For leisure Kaytel organized war games in the forest. Xumi youths reported that the Pau showed promise; they were not afraid to do themselves harm.

It was a spring that demanded confidence. The signs, like the days, seemed bright and clear. People said, after the mission of Prince Rowenna: 'The Lady sent him running,' and: 'Did he not kneel to her?' and even: 'She laughed at Bar-Lev.'

Only a few, Talo and people like Dadallean who had served with Bar-Lev, knew better. Talo saw that the mood in Anneglen wouldn't tolerate a confession of weakness like a retreat to the Roganspire. He forced himself to abandon that idea.

Getlof encouraged the mood of confidence; but in truth, didn't know what else to do. The signs people marked didn't speak to her. She recognized the withdrawal that was beginning to creep over her and fought it, struggling to hold to the resolution she had felt when she saw the heads of Doy and Elp. She thought she'd be alright once they were in danger, but that was an uncertain comfort in the absence of danger.

The days grew longer and hotter as spring passed into summer. Bar-Lev had long since received Getlof's reply to his suit, but from the east there was still no sign. Some people interpreted this favorably, others found it disconcerting. Talo was mystified. Hadn't Bar-Lev founded his power on action swift and terrible? He had made a threat and that couldn't be withdrawn or ignored.

And then, one night, Getlof had another dream. This took place in the period of balance, on a hot night shortly before Longest Day.

She dreamed of two riders hurrying across a darkened landscape. Pale silver light dripped from the stars. She didn't need eyes to know these people: Doy and Elp. Within her sleeping breast the sense of loss seemed more real than it ever had awake. Back glancing continuously, but nothing to see; no sign of pursuit. Doy and Elp. Faces suddenly very clear. Frightened. By what?

A breeze mocked her cheek. A tiled courtyard--green and blue, an aquatic scene--and the gentle sound of falling water. A fountain? Asha? But before she could begin to hope, a large, soft man with powered cheeks and fuzzy eyes approached. Bowed. The tinkle of the fountain. `Your lord awaits, Lady.' Oily smooth words. Sudden fright. Those had been happier days. Oh yes! How had the past intruded into this present? Tinkling water. Oh, Asha, Asha, how had this happened?

Getlof wrenched herself awake. Far worse than any nightmare. Pale silver light streamed in through her window. She had to rise and look out before she was sure it was really Anneglen. But then she heard from an unimaginable distance hoofbeats. Two riders were hurrying across a moonlit landscape. She shook her head to clear the web of nightmare. The red scar on her brow throbbed and she touched it. As she did, her orientation returned; past and future separated fell away. Certainty replaced them. She knew, briefly, the present. Quickly Getlof dressed and stepped out into the night. The guard at her door looked up in surprise.

"Lady, where are you going?"

"A messenger is coming. To hear the news."

He looked confused. "I heard nothing. . ." The guard was a Xumi, but Getlof couldn't recall his name. "No one has brought word . . ."

Getlof nodded. "I bring word." Doy and Elp were dead. Why had she dreamt such a dream? "Go to the bell and awaken the camp. I'll be with Talo and Narhad."

"You have spoken, Lady," face suddenly frightened. Did he feel it himself or did the emotion communicate itself through her?

Suddenly Narhad appeared from the true shadows, hand resting on hilt. "I heard voices. Is aught amiss?"

Getlof smiled. "You sleep lightly, Narhad. Come with me, a messenger will soon be here. We'll get Talo up and hear the news." As they reached Talo's hut the alarm bell began suddenly to toll. Narhad looked quizzically at Getlof. She said:

"The time of waiting is past. The time of action now begins. I wanted a clear demarcation."

They woke Talo, something the bell couldn't do and went to find the messenger. All around people were spilling from their huts and forming into companies. When he saw this Talo grumbled: "You're ordering this and we still don't know if there's really a messenger?"

But it happened that Getlof was right. The messenger was a Xumi stationed with the outriders watching Moaz. His news was that yesterday, at dawn, a large body of fighting men had ridden from the northern land gate of Moaz and were headed in their direction. He had ridden all day and night to deliver the tidings.

By dawn the companies were ready to march. Getlof acted with an energy rare even for her most energetic phases. She held nothing back, was everywhere, spoke a word to everyone. Somehow she had awakened from her dream knowing what to do, how to do it and filled with a consuming need to get it done. Questions, hesitations, doubts? She had no time for any of that.

Getlof gave a speech to the companies before they marched. " . . . I refused once and so now he sends an escort to deliver me to my wedding feast. And you, my people, he will send to the end that awaits all who oppose him. Ha! . . ."

Her words surprised and gratified Talo. It pleased him especially that there was no way Narhad could accuse him of having coached her. Talo didn't know what instinct prompted her, but her speech met the situation perfectly.

More information arrived as the day went on. Bar-Lev was still in Zoha; a lessor chief was apparently, directing his first move. Getlof didn't need Talo to tell her it was foolish to underestimate an enemy; it made her both angry and glad the herd lord was taking her so lightly even as she wondered how Bar-Lev could make such a basic mistake. She was filled with confidence stronger than knowledge that it'd be a mistake he'd regret.

Their companies marched quickly while the scouts reported that the Levites were moving slowly. The eastern nomads had yet to suffer a defeat in the westlands and they seemed supremely confident. The scar on Getlof's cheek throbbed constantly; not with pain but with a rhythm by which she focused her concentration. She could close her eyes at any time and hear the sound of tinkling water. It was coming.

On the second day out of Anneglen they set an ambush in the rolling, folded land. The Levites were lured into a valley and, quite simply, flanked. Talo directed the fight while Getlof observed. Her people fought with a conviction clearly absent on the other side. Talo was mildly amazed at how well he had done his work. (He always was.) He was pleased also by the brittleness of the

Levite divisions. The Moazians, the Shonians, the Xumi and the Pau overcame the Levites when they fought and slaughtered them when they broke. They chased them over the plain all the way to Moaz without respite.

On the fourth day out of Anneglen, Getlof, once again, passed through the gates of Moaz. It was a piece of theatre Talo had suggested. She rode a white horse dressed in a white gown. Her army, stepping high with success, marched behind. (Of course, Narhad and a company of Xumi preceded her to guarantee security.) It was theatre indeed. The highway that cut through the city was trimmed on either side with ragged lines of people; more people than Getlof had expected. They cheered as she rode past. Getlof waved (it was something a person had to do in that kind of situation) and recalled the manner of her exit from Moaz the autumn before. Cursed and pelted with rocks; time had been passing very swiftly indeed.

Yet, as Getlof rode down the broad boulevard through the city that had been devastated, repaired and devastated again, she was aware of an edge in the cheering; an edge of nervousness, almost hysteria. This served to remind her that her true journey had really only just begun.

But still they cheered. And even more, they swelled the ranks of the Josh's Army. News of the Levite defeat raced through the westlands faster, it seemed, than a horseman could ride. It was like winter in Anneglen all over again, except it was early summer now and people were more inclined to travel and, perhaps, seek adventure.

Getlof remained in Moaz for two weeks and that was thirteen days longer than she would've liked. Originally her plan was to wait only for the foot elements to catch up with her and then to set out once again, this time for the east. She had confided her plan to no one as yet, not wishing to deal with the objections that Talo, among others was sure to raise. The need for action was driving her and every day without motion was torture.

Daken's infantry came in on the evening of the second day with Iodai, ever increasing in energy himself, striding proudly at their head and setting the pace. When people started volunteering that caused another delay. Many Moazians, seeing how well their compatriots had done with Getlof, were eager to do as well for themselves. More surprisingly, Levites began to trickle into Moaz during the following days to join Getlof too. Most of them were Xumi and their complaints against Bar-Lev were much the same as the Mother's had been. Moreover, the fame of the Lady had reached even their camps. Getlof's victory swelled her already glowing reputation. Talo was more cynical about the motivation of the Levite defectors. He guessed they were afraid to return to Bar-Lev after their defeat and, fearing treachery, he forbade Getlof to visit their camps. In this she indulged him knowing she would shortly require a greater concession from him.

Talo was not completely in touch with the direction of Getlof's thoughts. He saw no reason for haste, especially before he could fully acquaint the new volunteers with his system. He even set people to work repairing the citadel thinking it would be the best place to stand when Bar-Lev moved to restore what his captains had lost. When Getlof heard this she rushed to countermand Talo's orders. This resulted in the worst fight Getlof and Talo had ever had. He told her she had no conception of Bar-Lev's strength and when he heard she intended to march not only to Zoha, but all the way to Gildesh and perhaps Dell after that, he told her flatly she was insane.

Getlof paused after Talo delivered this harsh assessment, then conceded that maybe he was right; none-the-less, she had no choice. Although she didn't understand why, she felt her plan was the best course, but there was no way she could explain it rationally to Talo. After all he'd been through with her, Talo still wasn't able to accept Getlof's intuitions on faith. None-the-less, Narhad was behind her whether her plans were rational or not. Grudgingly Talo finally gave in, burying his frustration by furiously working on forming new companies from the Moazian and Xumi volunteers.

The energy Getlof felt was something she couldn't explain. During the days of delay she spent every second she could find among the companies, infecting the men with her impatience. Narhad always accompanied her. Gathered around their fires a person would suddenly spot Narhad, a head taller than anyone, and shout: "The Lady comes!" Getlof would gravely enter their circle (she reserved her smiles for special occasions now), her skin and hair made darker by the white gowns she wore. They would press around her and listen intently as she talked. And then, when she smiled -- always at the end -- they would cheer.

As Talo suspected there were those among the former Levites specifically instructed to join Getlof's force. Chief among them was Muk. Never for a moment did Bar-Lev believe that a teenage girl was directing the resistance against him. He remained certain his true enemy was Talo the Taelien, foremost mercenary captain in the varied lands and shores of Ossa. Muk's mission was to assassinate Talo. This was a mission that coincided perfectly with Muk's desires;

all hope of regaining Kisti had vanished long ago. All he could anticipate was revenge. Afterwards, Muk didn't care what happened.

Muk saw Getlof during one of her tours and it rather surprised him that Talo wasn't with her directing speech and action. Then he thought of how far he had chased her. All that way and this was his first sight of his long sought goal. But for Talo's treachery all might have been so different.

Talo threw himself into the task of organizing the irregulars. In part, his activity was meant to repress the ideas that had floated to the top of mind following his big argument with Getlof. Briefly he considered calling a general meeting and having it out with her for all the world to hear. And then, when she refused to consider his most rational objections, as he knew she would, being stubborn and naive, he would declare his intention to strike out on his own with all who cared to follow. What really prevented him from doing this was the thought of the satisfaction it would give Narhad. He also realized such action would be strongly reminiscent of his deeds during the Troubled Time in Gildesh and the siege of Sidoc when it appeared he had left his followers to a fate he didn't care to share.

Midway through the second week Getlof called a conference. This was held by the outer walls in what once had been a watch room. Very seriously she outlined her plan. Even at this point she held back from declaring Bar-Lev her enemy. Of course, if he undertook to oppose her march, she would fight. Her plan was faulty, she admitted, in that they would be dependent upon Bar-Lev to react, but at least, they would have the open land behind them, if worse came to worse, while Bar-Lev would be between the Shem and Ossa, neither easy to cross at any time of year. Still, the bad taste of her argument with Talo lingered so she proceeded to state to the company of leaders every object Talo had raised. She ended by saying that while these objections had merit and deserved consideration, she was under a strong compulsion to do what what she had proposed to do.

Lavrens stood then and told the company that he had some experience with Getlof's compulsions. At first view they seemed unsound, but they succeeded beyond expectation. He went on to say he was confident this case would be the same; his days of doubting Getlof's judgement were over.

Dadallean stood. He said he didn't understand what all the discussion was about. The Lady had acquainted them with her plan. What more did they need?

She certainly wasn't proposing they put it to a vote. Dadallean sat down amid general expressions of approval.

Something in this frightened Getlof. Once she could never have believed so many men could so readily follow her intuition in such a dangerous undertaking. Especially when one with such greater experience was so against it. It was her feeling; she had to follow it; but what if she was wrong?

As Dadallean sat down Getlof felt the weight of the company's eyes come down on her.

Never any time to pause and wonder. Never any time when it was needed. Getlof waited, but no one else rose to speak. She looked at Talo who sat on her right. His chin was resting in his hand and he seemed to be staring at a point in the wall on the other side of the room.

"Talo," she said, trying to postpone the moment, "I do a poor job of advocacy, it seems. Will you explain you reservations to the company more fully?"

This request caught Talo by surprise. He had supposed Getlof's advocacy of his views had just been her way of trying to put their argument behind them. Moreover, he was in a surprisingly good mood. The best mood he could remember for a long time; and it had come when he surrendered his own opinion and resigned himself to the future. Why the turnabout? If Getlof thought he had a grudge, there was no sense in letting her continue to think so.

"No, Getlof, you presented my reservations plain. Tomorrow we march and here's to success."

Instantly the room was on its feet. Getlof turned to Narhad who was on her other side. He made a slight gesture with his head as if to say: 'I know, but it's done.'

42

PRELUDE TO BATTLE

When the scattered, defeated remains of the Moaz garrison came trickling into Zoha, Bar-Lev acted angry and surprised, but he wasn't really. Several commanders foolish enough to return with their troops were crucified along the public ways, but only because his people expected such shows. The attack had been a probe and had served its purpose. Bar-Lev had his opposition gauged. The Taelien who had frustrated him for so long in front of Sidoc -- curse the luck that had permitted him to escape -- had returned; but Bar-Lev didn't intend to be frustrated again. He acknowledged the Taelien's talent and wished it was working for him; he admired the way Talo was manipulating the situation, finding and then using the Pauic girl as a symbol to rally people against him. But he was moving too swiftly, making mistakes all of a sudden. His true worry, that he'd have to chase the Taelien over the Roganspire and down the Tain was, thankfully, nothing more than a worry.

One thing had kept Bar-Lev from marching north and west with his hoard to finish Talo off: this was the ongoing threat of the Gildi Empire. His navy had suffered a serious check the autumn before trying to force the island barrier of Istel. Every rebuff required a swift and overpowering response. Bar-Lev was balanced between these two obligations. The Gildi were the more powerful, but the Taelien was the proven foe. Already word had come to his ear that stories of the Pau were being told around campfires in Zoha. This was no bad thing in itself; Bar-Lev's plans definitely contained a place for her. What concerned him was that the Taelien's army included a sizeable number of Xumi, said to be renegades from his hoard. That was something he had to punish as quickly as possible. Thus, when Bar-Lev received the news that the army of the Taelien had quit Moaz and was marching toward Zoha, he couldn't believe his luck. He could remain in position, let the Taelien come to him and still have time to turn south afterwards. Bar-Lev had every reason to be well satisfied.

Ossa

He had paid close attention to Prince Rowenna's report. Although the Prince had tried to conceal it, Bar-Lev could tell he had been highly impressed with the Pauic girl. Listening to the story, Bar-Lev shared this impression. He especially liked her reply after receiving his 'present.' He was full tired of having people cower whenever he raised his little finger. It would be nice to have someone with a little spirit at his side. He let it be known that he would be highly displeased if any harm came to the girl in the upcoming battle. He promised the regency of Tarhad to whoever delivered her safely to him. Already, he thought with satisfaction, the rumors were running wild in the harem. It would do them good to worry.

Muk was assigned to the irregular division. He worried about how he would get close enough to Talo when the time came. He'd received his instructions from Bar-Lev himself. It couldn't be done too early, not before the armies were actually in contact. Muk kept his place in the long line of sweating men and tried to imagine what satisfaction must be like.

"You're worried about Talo, aren't you," Narhad said to Getlof as they rode side by side near the head of the columns.

"I'm worried about everybody. And I'd think you'd understand why. You've never expressed an opinion about all this, Narhad. Do you think I'm being foolish?"

Narhad smiled and shook his head. "You're asking the wrong man. Besides, what is foolishness anyway? At this point I can't say. What I can say is that you're in a position I wouldn't occupy for the world, Lady. I know you're following your heart as best you may; what more can you do?"

Getlof smiled the private smile of a young woman amused with herself. "I suppose you must be tired of hearing me talk like this; but you're the only one I can speak my doubts to these days."

Narhad nodded. "We've come a long way thought many doubts. I find it amazing you haven't grown overconfident. As for the other thing, I can see you miss Golab. If you'd let me speak with him I can straighten his foolishness out."

Getlof laughed. "And you just told me you didn't know what foolishness is anymore. No, leave Golab alone. I think he'll come around in his own time."

Lavrens rode at the head of a company of Shonians and Pau. Kaytel rode at his side, chattering away in his execrable Southcoast. Lavrens was thoughtful despite his proclaimed confidence in Getlof. Kaytel was exuberant. The death of several friends in the first engagement had only fed his battle lust. He considered them lucky; they were assured a place in the epic. If he were to die, Kaytel was ready. He just prayed death came in a worthwhile and public manner so his name would appear in the records.

Dadallean headed the Xumi division. His men sang a warrior's song as they rode in the hot sun. He knew the Mother would be satisfied if she could see them, despite the uncertainty of their future. He could picture her saying: `A person can take any path, Dadallean (are you paying attention?) just so long as they accept the consequences.' Dadallean hoped for victory, but he didn't fear defeat.

Talo rode up and down the line of march making sure no elements lagged and solving problems as they arose. Mahap the scribe and Unsari the poet were often seen in his company. Mahap had shown a talent for organization which complemented Talo's. Talo found him a valuable aid. Unsari had no such skills, but his conversation was diverting.

Daken headed the first company of Moazians. Iodai marched with him. He saw a multitude of signs along their way that promised victory. He pointed these out to his people and their moral was very high.

The season of high summer had settled over the land. Even as they marched, Getlof imagined she could see the hills and plains wither, becoming brown and parched. Dust rose in great clouds coating skin and clothing; mixing with food and water. Every day the heat seemed more intense.

The region along the north shore of the Long Lake had once been prosperous and densely settled. Now, however, the road was lined with untended orchards, fields gone fallow, burned out villages. More than once foragers turned up mounds of human bones, grim evidence of where the population of the North Shore had gone.

On the morning of the fourth day from Moaz they came to the town of Ria which once had marked the frontier between Gildesh and Moaz. This town, like the land behind it, was wasted. At Ria they encountered their first Levite horsemen since the battle west of Moaz. Disdaining surprise, the Levites launched themselves at the advance guard and a freewheeling melee developed until the arrival of the rest of the army put them to flight.

Having claimed the battlefield with little loss, the army moved in and, with spade and shovel, began the tedious task of preparing a secure camp. Talo sent scouts across the neck of land between the Shem and Ossa--less than two leagues wide at that point--to warn of any flanking moves.

It was evening and the camp was almost completed when scouts came galloping into Ria with news that yet another delegation under the blue flag approached from Zoha.

It was the Prince Rowenna again. This time he had only two attendants and no presents. Getlof met him in what had once been Ria's square, her captains around her. The Prince stopped at a respectful distance and bowed low. He spoke as if they were old and dear friends.

"Lady, it gives me the greatest pleasure to be able to greet you like this once again, before this strife ends all possibility of friendly intercourse."

Getlof shook her head and tried not to smile. There was something so incongruous about diplomacy.

"Prince, the pleasure is mine. I am especially glad to see that your concerns regarding the news I left you to deliver to your master didn't cause you harm. But tell me, do you come with more presents from your lord, he of the uncounted herds, or is it just words this time. Or have you decided to walk the path of your desire choice and add yourself to our strength?"

The Prince looked long and carefully at Getlof before he replied. "It is the second of the three possibilities you named, Lady. I have words for you from my master."

"And they are?" Getlof said, noting that the third choice had surprised and tempted him.

"They are these: With abounding patience and understanding, my master informs you that even now time remains to reconsider his earlier proposal.

However, because of the lateness of your acceptance, he is bound to make one condition and it is this: The captain known as Talo the Taelien must be handed over. Be advised, my master cautions, that this man is corrupt and troublesome and is responsible for this needless conflict." As he spoke these words, the Prince scanned the captains around Getlof and wondered which of them was the infamous Taelien. His eyes settled upon Narhad, even if he did look like a Gildi, not a Taelien.

Getlof paused before she replied. She thought it remarkably strange Bar-Lev was going to such lengths to parley with her. According to Talo he took what he wanted, when he wanted and made excuses to none. For the briefest of moments she wondered if the picture Talo and the Mother had presented to her was accurate in all respects. This gave her an idea and she decided to test it.

"Prince Rowenna, my friend," (She didn't know why she added this, but was glad she did because by his expression which tried to hide everything and instead told everything, she saw it flattered him.) "Return to your master and tell him this: No follower of mine, be he captain or camp follower will I surrender. I will not marry him either. However, I have every desire for peace. Before this can be, however, he must vacate these lands he has taken in his most recent campaign for I say they belong to me. He must withdraw across the Ossa, at least, north of those mountains called the Xexi in these lands. Then it might be possible for us to meet in some neutral location to discuss our differences."

The Prince shook his head. "Lady, you make an ambassadors' life difficult. I will swiftly return to my master and tell him your proposition." He started to turn away, then stopped and added: "I hope it will be possible we will meet again under such happy circumstances."

One week before this meeting, shortly after the Levite garrison of Moaz was routed, the will of His Imperial Majesty, Ducitos VIII, finally prevailed. In the year since his encounter with Getlof, Ducitos had so changed it seemed a different person bore his name. To the frustration of Lord Xem and others like him, the boy emperor had begun to take an interest in everything. He began to ask questions and demand explanations. No longer was his name bandied about court as a synonym for dullard. He was on the threshold of adulthood; he had entered into his estate.

With separation, his memories of Getlof had become idealized. She came to represent all that was good. Their interview was the dividing line between what he had been and what he hoped to become.

After Angus escaped from Zoha bringing a tale of treachery and defeat, people said the Josh was lost to the Gildi because she had been foolishly permitted to leave. Ducitos was the true target of this criticism. He never believed it. Then, when word came that winter from Moaz, Ducitos was vindicated. He didn't let his counselors forget it.

The letter came at the beginning of spring. The tale it contained was better than Ducitos expected; it solidified the change and confirmed Getlof as his example. He honored Doy and Elp as if they were lords. It was then his resolution to become an active force in the northern conflict solidified.

It took the considerable support of Angus, captain of the guard for Ducitos to get his way. His plan was this: to personally lead an army north. The recapture of the Gildi city of Zoha was the expressed objective of this plan, but actually Ducitos hoped it would lead to a meeting with Getlof. The army, especially the guard, had been chaffing with inaction, doing nothing while the forces of Bar-Lev used one a Gildi city as capital. Ducitos' triumph ensured his popularity with the military. The preparations have long since been made. The route chosen was over the Xexi on little known paths. It was hoped they could surprise the forces at Zoha and with superior quality, make up for their disadvantage in numbers. Ducitos wondered what it would be like to hear his name spoken with genuine respect.

The scouts brought back news of a very strong position about a league south of Ria; a hill surrounded on three sides by a deep ravine. After scouting it out for himself, Talo decided they would be better able to withstand an attack there. The ravines would prevent Bar-Lev from effectively using cavalry, his main strength. The move was made secretly at night. By dawn the army had occupied its new position. From the south there was silence. Except for the skirmish at Ria, Bar-Lev appeared to take no interest in their movements.

Golab volunteered for the work crew that was formed to dig a ditch on the exposed side of the hill. He had been feeling especially useless ever since they'd departed Anneglen. Golab had marched down with the company of irregulars and not with Dadallean's Xumi as he'd wished. Always in Anneglen he had never belonged to any company at all; his close association with Getlof relieved him of that responsibility. However, in the days after the first mission of Prince Rowenna, when it seemed certain there would be fighting, Inna-Se nagged him about this. She asked him why he hadn't joined a company if he chose not to advise the Lady. She got angry and refused to speak to him for two long days when he said he didn't plan to join a company at all.

They were reconciled, but not before Golab promised to do as she wished. ("But only because you want it, not for any other reason." "How can you, who were with her from almost the beginning, feel that way; especially now when this might be near the end?")

Dadallean turned Golab down when he asked to join the Xumi.

"Friend, this is nothing personal, but we are fighters! Warriors! Of this craft you know little and even now, at this late point, I've noticed you make little effort to learn. You belong at the Lady's side where you have always been. Don't come to me."

Golab swore he would never return to the Lady's side. Instead he joined the irregulars where his lack of killing talents was not so apparent. There was one time in the march up country when Getlof made a surprise visit to their campfire. He stood off to the side while the others greeted her. When he felt her eyes seek him out, he didn't respond. Afterwards he noticed his comrades were less friendly to him than they had been.

Finally, on the day they came into Ria, Golab prevailed upon Dadallean and was given permission to ride with his Xumi which formed the advance guard. He didn't know that the news of his desire had come to Getlof's ear and it was her intervention, not his badgering, which changed Dadallean's mind. That was the day of the skirmish. Golab lost control of his horse the moment the Levites yelled their warcry and charged. This threw the counter charge off so that the Levites broke through their first line. The second line held and Golab was unharmed, but both the men on his left and right were killed. Afterwards he went to Dadallean and said that he saw now why he was unsuitable. Dadallean said yes, but now he was with them he would learn. But Golab's pride didn't permit failure. He went back to the irregulars. That was why he had volunteered to help dig the ditch.

Getlof's first reply to his ambassador had impressed Bar-Lev. Her second reply amused him. It was amusing to think he would surrender land he had rightfully taken by conquest. The two men who accompanied Prince Rowenna gave their reports before Bar-Lev saw the Prince. His version of events had deleted Getlof's invitation to join her. This amused Bar-Lev as well. He had the Prince arrested but he decided to delay punishment until the Pauic girl was by his side. It would be interesting to watch her reaction to justice.

As the Prince Rowenna was being taken out one door, Bar-Lev summoned his captains in through another. His mind was made up. The hoard would ride and he would lead it.

43

ENDINGS: HAPPY AND OTHERWISE

It began as an uncommon day. Giant, gray thunderheads peered above the northern horizon; an unseasonable, gusty wind harried the ground, lifting whirlwinds of dust.

"This feels like the autumn wind we call Marya," Narhad said, squinting his eyes as he, Talo and Getlof walked the lines.

"They called it The Puka where I was a lad," Talo said, "but it feels the same. Early spring, early autumn; the seasons are ahead of themselves this year."

Getlof had her cloak wrapped tightly around her body. She was silent. They had only completed their inspection of the first of the four sides when a lookout up the hill sang out that a rider approached. On the fourth side, where the ditch had been dug, a wooded bridge provided the only easy entry into the encampment. They hurried to this bridge and stood atop the rampart of dirt that had been raised behind.

"One of our people," Getlof said, shading her eyes, "but look beyond. See the dust in the air? Many men are moving. I fear today will be the day."

"I can't see, but I've no doubt you're right," Talo said. "At least we're ready."

At last the rider clattered across the plank bridge, drew up his horse and rather clumsily dismounted. He had a scarf wrapped around his face to protect it from the wind. When he unwound it, Getlof was amazed to see Kaytel.

"Lady," he panted, "they're coming. Great numbers. From one river to the other they fill the land."

Getlof nodded. Talo was already sending runners out to alert the captains. "Thank you, Kaytel, but what are you doing with Dadallean's company? You're supposed to be with Lavrens."

Kaytel grinned and blushed. "He seeks dangerous duty," Narhad said. "He's eager for great deeds."

Getlof shook her head. "There will be plenty of opportunity for every sort of deed today, I imagine. But what of Dadallean?"

"He fights with their advance riders, Lady. He sent me to you. He says keep the bridge down because, when he comes, he comes fast."

"I can believe that," Talo said. "Kaytel, go to Lavrens and have him move his, your, company up to the bridge. We'll need the best archers if Dadallean is too closely pressed. I'll see Xellia is prepared to sortie."

Getlof nodded. Kaytel was already gone. Talo paused and added: "Lady, where will you be?"

Getlof looked at Talo curiously. It was the first time he'd ever addressed her directly as `Lady.' "Here by the bridge."

"Alright." Talo looked up and squinted. "At least the wind is blowing in their faces. A little advantage but such things tell."

Lavrens' archers deployed two deep along the rampart; Xellia's Xumi poised behind. Dust clouded the air, making things close at hand seem far away. The land to the south was under a yellow pale not even Getlof's eyes could penetrate. The tension was so heavy Getlof caught herself gritting her teeth. Looking to the north she could see that the thunderheads were taller, closer. She wondered if it was this that made the air feel so strange. Or was it the fact so many people were walking so close to death?

The sound of shouting began faintly to intrude. The dust cloud was closer, about to engulf them. Then riders began emerging from the obscurity. In groups of two and three they crossed the bridge. "Dadallean is coming," they gasped, "he is coming. They press him on every side." Getlof strained her eyes, trying to make some sense of what she could only dimly see. Then it became clear. The battle was suddenly raging up against the ditch. There were Levites intermingled with Dadallean's Xumi and it seemed impossible they could make the bridge. Then she heard a shout and a hundred voices repeated it. It was the Xumi warcry and they were shouting her name. Xellia swept across the bridge, leading his company to his kinsman's aid. The battle migrated away again. The clamor grew and then all was suddenly silent. Getlof watched as surprisingly orderly lines of horsemen emerged from the cloud and crossed the bridge. Then she finally saw Dadallean, looking left and right, an enormous grin on his face. He saw her at the same time. His grin became broader still and he raised his lance in greeting.

"They have come to know us, Lady. They will know us better still."

Getlof waved in reply. Her intuition suddenly told her that Dadallean expected to die; was pleased to be still alive. A gust blew a string of hair across her eyes. When she brushed it away, Dadallean had already ridden past. Then she looked up and saw that the wind was blowing the dust to the south. For the first time she beheld the hoard of Bar-lev. Black it seemed and the motion of so many men gave the vista the aspect of a seascape, except the color was wrong. Her heart began pounding and the thought crossed her mind: `What have I done? Where have I led these people?' And then: `Dadallean is right. He knows and he is right.' Along their entire line silence had fallen; a hush inspired by awe. Then Dadallean's clear voice rose above the wind.

"Look, do you see them? Many warriors brave and strong. My lance has drunken deeply of their blood and it wants more!"

Another voice: "All hail the Lady. To the center of great deeds she has led us. All hail!" Getlof realized it was Kaytel. His cheer was picked up and repeated, louder and louder by every voice in their beleaguered island. Getlof found this amazing.

Golab cheered because it would have been unseemly not to, but his thoughts closely paralleled Getlof's. `What has she done? Where has she led us?' Then, as if by its own volition, his mind leapt back in time. He was laying wounded in a house in Moaz. A cool hand touched his brow. He reached out and clasped it, thinking it was Getlof and thinking: `She is a woman. I can love her without shame.' But it was the daughter of the house. She told him to lay still and rest. The Pau had been in earlier and she had cried. She would be back. He slumped in despair, thinking she wouldn't be back. She had undertaken the impossible and would never be back.

Golab shook his head and endeavoured to return to the present. He realized his left hand was at his side groping for a wound that was no longer there. He was sweating. All around people were cheering even though it was their death they faced. He realized he was still cheering as well.

`Who is she? What is she? Why are we cheering?' He looked up and saw her, a spot of white in a field of darkness. It suddenly seemed to Golab she was looking for him. Golab threw down his short sword.

"Hey, where are you going?" The man on his left said.

"To the Lady. She's calling me."

The man shrugged his shoulders and let Golab go. He knew who he was, had heard those stories and could never understand why he avoided her. If their positions were reversed he would show the Lady what true loyalty was. Of course, he still could, but she'd never know.

They were cheering still as Golab pushed his way through the crowd, seeing only that spot of white. Then he was beside her without knowing how he covered the final fifty paces. He heard her say: "Golab!" and felt his hand being taken by hers.

"Getlof, Lady, I'm back. I'm sorry; I don't know why."

"Don't try to tell me," she said. "I'm happy without knowing."

He squeezed her hand and she returned the pressure. Then an amazing fact hit her. She was happy. She had led these people into a situation they couldn't escape and they were cheering her. When her hopes were at their nadir, Golab had returned. It all seemed backwards. 'This is it,' she told herself. 'It seems wrong, but it must be right.' Suddenly she lifted her arms into the air and the cheering died away. They'd been calling for a word and now she had a word to give them.

"I am happy," she shouted. "You have made me happy. I am strong. You have made me strong. We see the consequences of what others will call our rashness and we are not afraid. They shall know us and they shall know us well!"

The wind brought their cheering down into the ranks of the Levites. Bar-lev heard it and thought it astonishingly out of place. His men heard it and were confused. It had been a long time since they had faced a confident enemy. Imperceptibly the advance faltered and then stopped.

"Why aren't they moving?" Bar-lev shouted. "Does noise frighten them?"

That was the dawn when Ducitos, Angus and the Gildi army came on Zoha after a long night march. During the darkness the advance riders had found the ferries opposite the town hardly guarded and seized them intact without alerting the opposite shore. They took prisoners and learned that Bar-lev had marched only the day before. They learned that Getlof was not far away. This information led to a hurried conference among the twelve Gildi captains as dawn broke over the sky.

"This is it, isn't it?" Ducitos said, still awkward at reconciling his inexperience with his responsibilities. "The Josh is at hand and in dire need of our assistance, it seems. If we hurry across we can catch the Levite from behind."

A twisted smile from Angus. "Lord, a secure base would be an important advantage. I strongly recommend a surprise attack upon the city before we rush north. Anticipating your orders, I have already begun the preparations." Ducitos consented, but he didn't feel good about the delay.

A small force of rider disguised as Levites crossed the Shem. They found Zoha's main gate open to permit the exit of a convoy of wains filled with foodstuffs. They rushed the gate, took it and held while Angus hurriedly ferried reinforcements to them. Ineffectual surprise was a kind way to describe the Levite response. Angus committed only one company of a thousand men, but this was more than sufficient to win the gate. The garrison swarmed out through the lesser exits and dispersed upon the plain. Angus had set up a picket line to intercept these people, but it was too thin to contain them all. Before noon the Gildi army of two guard companies and nine regular divisions, less the one left to garrison Zoha, was ready to march north. The ease of their victory elated the Imperial army and erased the weariness of their long march and lack of sleep. They gorged themselves on the captured food and eagerly anticipated their orders for more bloodplay to the north.

The first assault came against the ditch. The Levites massed at about three hundred paces, just beyond bowshot. There was a moment of stillness; then, along the lines, drums began to beat a measured cadence. They came forward walking the first two hundred paces, suffering two volleys in silence. At a hundred paces a single voice shouted the Levite warcry. Thousands, repeated, the sound crashing against the sky. Their pace picked up to a trot. Getlof positioned herself on a small rise behind the rampart near the bridge. Talo stood by her and calmly issued orders. The Shonian and Pauic archers released two volleys more, extracting a terrible toll. The Levites flooded into the ditch and began struggling up the side. As the first of them neared the rampart, the archers retired behind a line of Moazian men at arms. The assault smashed against this barrier. For a half-hour they struggled to throw the Moazians off the high ground. When Talo ordered a counterattack, the Levites fell back in disorder. Even Getlof could see Bar-lev was withholding his best troops.

Twice more the ditch was assailed while the rest of the hoard spread out and encircled their hill. Twice more the attack was repulsed, but with a margin ever narrower and losses ever greater.

Getlof had lost all concept of time. She screamed and shouted encouragements until her voice began to crack. Narhad and Golab stayed beside her except once when a group of Levites finally managed to gain the top of the dirt rampart. They were slowly expanding their toehold and no reserves were present to check them. Narhad said to Golab: "See she doesn't follow." He sprang down with a terrible shout to join the fight. The attackers fell under the sweep of his sword. The defenders took heart and slaughtered the intruders.

The Levites threw themselves at the other three sides of Getlof's position as well. The army of the Josh was like a drowning man in a stormy sea. Yet, it kept its head above water. The ravines were more difficult of access than the ditch and the attackers fared no better there, even though Talo kept most of the regular companies at the ditch. Finally, the attackers receded at all points and a lull followed.

Getlof had lost track of Talo. Now he suddenly appeared at her side from out of nowhere.

"Well, Getlof, so far we've held our own." Getlof looked over (Talo was shorter than he used to be, or had she grown?) and saw he was smiling. In fact, his whole manner was changed, as if the Talo of a year ago had reappeared. "Only thing is, the archers are beginning to run low on arrows. I've sent some parties down into the ditch to see what they can salvage." Before Getlof could reply, the clash of battle came to them from the other side of the hill.

"What's that?" Talo said looking up. "I was just there and it was quiet." They listened and Talo began to frown. Then a Pau came running up out of breath.

"They're on the north side and already at the top of the ravine," he shouted. Getlof could detect the beginning of panic in his tone. Talo muttered a curse.

"That's where I put the irregulars. How in the names of all the gods did that happen?"

The boy shook his head. "They were hidden in the ravine and surprised us. Kaytel sent me. He's trying to find people to push them back."

Talo looked and saw a new attack forming to their front. "Alright, I'm coming. But we can't spare any people here." Getlof was suddenly struck with the feeling her presence would be needed as well.

"Coming?" Talo said when he saw her, Narhad and Golab following. "Well, hurry." He laughed. "If Kaytel has found anybody, he won't wait long. Your kinsman is an eager one, Getlof."

They found Kaytel at the top of the hill, haranguing a collection of Pau and Shonians. He saw them and came running down.

"At last! They push us back. I have these cowards, but they ignore me. You they will obey."

Talo stood on the sharply sloping hillside and looked down. Getlof wondered why he paused. She felt Kaytel's urgency and the situation certainly looked grave enough to warrant immediate action. A tight knot of Levites had formed on the inner side of the ravine. Very slowly they were bulging the line of defenders.

Talo shook his head. "Not so bad, Kaytel. We're giving up ground slowly. Frankly, I'm surprised they're holding so well. But you're right, its about time to give them a little encouragement." At that point, Talo's face suddenly changed. He saw a man throw down his weapon and turn to run; several others saw this also and did the same. Kaytel looked at Talo, then Getlof, then he shouted something in Pauic and ran down the hill. The little group he had collected hesitated, then followed.

Talo hurried after Kaytel to confront the deserters. Narhad held Getlof back from following. "No, Lady, if you fall no one will stop them from breaking."

Muk was in the line when people around him began to run. He cursed them. The day had not gone according to his expectations. First, there had been no sight of Talo and no way to slip out and seek him. Muk had hoped the confusion of battle would give him his chance, but when the attack came, a strange thing happened: Muk forgot himself. His blood began to course and adrenalin swept him away. He fought and thought of nothing but the fighting. All the fury and anger he had ever harbored came roiling to the surface and with each blow he struck, a tiny bit of it was discharged. For the first time he understood why men sought danger. But now people were running and he had to give ground or be cut down. Then Kaytel's Pau were hurrying up and around him. He stopped and turned back to face the battle. A strangely familiar voice said: "Good man!" and he understood it was directed at him. Muk looked over his shoulder and saw the Lady standing on the hill. The giant was beside her. Such an oddly matched pair. Muk lifted his sword and prepared to rejoin the fray, but instead he paused.

Muk paused in the midst of the bloody confusion because something was bothering him and he didn't know what. He looked to his right and then he realized. Talo was standing not two paces away, bullying the waverers. It was he who had called him a good man. At that point Muk stopped thinking. He walked over. Talo's back was to him. He set and then pushed his sword into the resisting flesh as far as he could. A long piercing wail, but not from Talo. Talo made no noise other than a slight gasp. And somehow he retained the strength to stay on his feet. Muk stood there, making no effort to run. Slowly Talo turned. He looked at Muk. His face was full of confusion. Then it cleared.

"So . . . Muk . . . you finally found me." Then Talo fell.

Muk looked up at the sky and saw that it was dark. He was being jostled. Then cool metal entered his belly. Somehow he wasn't sorry. He slid to the ground beside Talo, hoping it had been as easy for Kisti when she died.

Getlof shouted for them to bring Muk to her, but her words were lost in the wind. The Pau who killed him thought she was calling for vengeance. Narhad shook his head, then jumped down and recovered Talo's body. The Levites didn't notice Talo's fall. Kaytel was a dark fury. His attack caught them just as they thought they might prevail. He rolled them back and drove them into the ravine and the irregulars rallied around him and his men.

The thunderheads had been creeping south all day, but their approach, impressive as it was, went unheeded until the first bolt of lighting flashed overhead, followed in less than an eye blink by a long deafing roll of thunder. Then the warriors of both sides faltered and looked overhead. An exciting and hopeful rumor encircled the defending lines: "The Lady has summoned aid from the north. The Cold Mountain god and even He who is unmanifest have strode on long legs to succor her." They fought with renewed energy until relief did come. The clouds opened up and a torrent of rain came smashing to earth. On every side the attack broke down and the Levites pulled back to regroup.

Getlof stood, face to the sky, letting the rain substitute for tears. She didn't move until Golab wrapped his cloak around her and said: "Getlof, you'll get sick dressed in that gown." The captains, Lavrens, Daken, Dadallean and the others began gathering for instructions and to report their losses. The rain quickly spent its violence. Getlof stood and saw Kaytel. Unsari was there as well. He had found Talo's body and was sitting on the ground, little rivulets streaming off him and around him, staring at Talo's face. Xellia was dead, she was told. So was Mahap the scribe. Old Iodai had died attempting deeds beyond his strength. The list went on.

Getlof walked over and stood by Unsari. He looked up and nodded mutely. "Talo was the only one who knew me before I became this." Getlof covered her face with her hands, at first thinking he was speaking as if he were her. 'It's true,' she thought, 'Now I am what I am and there is no return. Who would believe what I was?' She tried to recall Geto's face and found she couldn't do it. She herself was unable to believe what she had been.

"Lady," Lavrens said, "the storm is passing quickly. They'll come again. Will you take command now that Talo is lost?"

She shook her head. "I lack the knowledge. Let Narhad set the dispositions and command the reserve. I'll remain by his side with Golab." She was weary and glad to have two such supports. Many such supports. She looked around at their faces, loving every one of them. The sun broke through then, pouring sudden warmth on them. Narhad nodded. "Let us tour the lines. The men will want to see that you're safe."

The storm rapidly passed over the heads of the Gildi. The eleven companies emerged into sunlight at a point not far from the Levite outer line. Angus rode beside Ducitos. "There she'll be, majesty," Angus said. "On that hill they have the Josh besieged." Ducitos was seeing the Levite hoard for the first time. The sight left him slightly stunned.

"They are so many. How can we win through to her?"

"We are bound to try anyway we can," Angus said gravely. "Our luck has been extraordinary getting as far as we have without challenge. Now we must move swiftly before that advantage is lost."

"Very well, give the orders." Ducitos castigated himself for his fears. He was doing what he had always wanted, after all.

Bar-Lev felt cheated. Success had lay within his hand when the storm broke up the attack. "That is the type of luck they'll be calling a miracle, no doubt," he said to E-Toyoc who rode by his side. He issued orders for another assault and thought they'd have no such luck this time. He would lead personally.

Just after Bar-Lev had positioned himself with the forward companies, a rider galloped up with news that there was a large enemy force to their rear. This seemed so impossible to Bar-Lev he committed a very rare error; he ascribed the report to rumor and went on with the assault.

Getlof stood on the hill and listened to the Levite drums. "See that standard?" Narhad said, "that's Bar-Lev's own. This attack he leads himself." Getlof saw it. Purple and black; it stood out even among the dust and confusing bright colors of the Levite warriors. Her eyes roamed past and beyond. Suddenly she grabbed Narhad's arm. She saw another large body of men coming from the south. Unlike the Levites, they were somberly clad in colors that blended with the earth.

"What is it Lady? What do you see?"

"Narhad," whispering so he had to bend far to hear her, "I'm afraid to trust my eyes. Look past the Levites and tell me what you see."

Narhad shaded his eyes and looked. "I don't know, Lady. It's hard to say."

Golab jumped. "Its more men. Another army. They're attacking the Levites. Grey and green. Can't you see. Green and grey. Gildesh!"

Narhad stared, leery of false hope. The attack began. The Levites came straight at the ditch, threw in debris and withdrew for more. The volume of arrow fire from the hill was causing a nuisance now, not an execution. Briefly Getlof wondered why they hadn't done that before. The other three sides of their position were, for the moment, impassible, filled with swiftly running water from the storm.

The Levites filled the ditch and attacked the rampart behind. Bar-Lev's standard was near the front. Getlof wondered how they could make so much progress so fast. Or was it that time was acting strangely once again.

"We're needed down there," Narhad said.

"No, wait," Getlof said. She had been watching the other battle more than the one before her. "See, the Gildi are nearer. They're cutting through the

Levites. Bar-Lev's banner is dropping back. He's realized his danger." Then confidence came coursing in that familiar fashion. Everything was clear. Bar-Lev was the head of the army; only he held it together. If he was free to turn against the Gildi he would beat them back and they'd be no better off than before. She saw what to do, but there was no time to explain it. She said: "Follow me," and set off running down the hill.

The men in the line had no idea why the attack was being called off. They cheered when they saw Getlof among them, but she had no time to acknowledge. Then Dadallean saw her and hastened up to ask her what was the matter.

"Dadallean," she panted, out of breath more from excitement than exertion, "can you take a horse across the ditch now?"

"I could have before. Now that it's filled anyone could. Why?"

"Because we're getting help from the south. Take every rider who's fit and all the wounded who'll go and attack the standard black and purple under which you'll find Bar-Lev. Do it now. We can't permit him to disengage and meet that attack."

Dadallean's eyes suddenly glowed. "Ride out to attack Bar-Lev in the midst of his hoard. Yes, Lady, I will do that." He turned and began to issue orders. The horses were brought down from the hillside. It took time and Getlof was frantic long before they were ready.

Measured in numbers, it was not a large charge, but its impact was great indeed. Because of the Shonian archers using the last of their hoarded reserve of arrows, Dadallean was able to lead his warriors across the ditch unmolested and form them up on the solid ground beyond. The Levite cavalry was off to the south so Dadallean was able to smash without interference into the mass of disorganized infantry facing him. Getlof raced back up the hill to watch. There she saw that Dadallean was like a stone cast into water. The ripples were spreading, moving out into rout. Then she knew it would be all right and couldn't watch anymore. Getlof wrapped herself in Golab's cloak and sank to the ground and into her thoughts. She was beginning to realize that in many ways victory was more terrible than defeat.

When Dadallean returned with Bar-Lev's head on his lance she was surprised he could be back so quickly. Then she saw it was already evening.

"A present," Dadallean said, exultation in his voice. Getlof forced herself to look at it. The sight surprised her. Bar-Lev died young. His features were regular, strong and handsome. There was even the suggestion of the heroic about him, although this was only a suggestion and not furthered by the state of his remains. Then she was told that the Emperor of the Gildi, Ducitos himself, was due to arrive shortly to pay his respects.

"Ducitos here?" she said with surprise. "Not Angus?"

When they met under the light of torches, Getlof saw that Ducitos was no longer a boy. He greeted her formally. He said that Angus had been most anxious to see her, but had fallen in the attack. The changes Ducitos had undergone became transparent to her vision. She saw he would be a good emperor and a strong one and that he would want to marry her. Her eyes were open and the fullness of sight was upon them. She was looking at the Ducitos of twenty years hence, not the boy-man before her. And herself as well. It was done, but she couldn't seek a quiet or normal sort of life.

" . . .and your friend and captain, Talo the Taelien as well. I am sorry, Lady. Your losses were great."

"It has happened. His face was to the foe, but the sword was in his back. I still don't understand why." Then she had another vision and hoped it would be the last one for a time, at least.

"We'll raise a cairn upon this hill and bury Talo there and beside him we will put Bar-Lev. I have seen they were the same person and it is fitting that their memories thus be mingled."

Ducitos didn't understand, but he let it pass. "And you, Lady? Will you let me give you hospitality before you return to your seat in the far distant north?"

Getlof looked down. That is what she had been doing, but it was Asha she really wanted to see. Narhad and Golab stood on either side of her. She looked up.

"Yes. But then I travel south to pay respects to one called Asha who befriended me first of all. I have taken two of your best servants; Narhad on my left and Golab on my right. Will you confirm my act of thievery?

"Gladly, Lady. With all my heart."

Getlof looked at Golab and smiled. "Will Inna-Se mind?"

Golab's face was bright. "She'll understand.

Yes, this was different. It would be better.

44

THE PRINCE AND THE MATE

The Prince Rowenna sat against the roughly hewn, plank wall of the crowded hut. Around him, the sour scent of fear emanating from the apprehensive hostages and prisoners was as dense as tule fog.

Taxis had been watching the Prince's shadowed face for several hours, aware he'd been high in Bar-Lev's esteem and surprised such a personage was sharing his durance. Taxis was a little stunned himself by his current straits. He knew well what was happening; Talo had resurfaced, apparently at the head of an army -- an army sprung from the empty westlands in the course of but a season -- and Bar-Lev was, at that very moment, destroying him. Taxis couldn't help but feel pride in his old master; he couldn't help but feel angry at his new master's lack of trust and he couldn't help but wonder about himself. Maybe Bar-Lev's mistrust was justified.

Finally, Taxis' reticence succumbed to those adamant enticements, curiosity and boredom. He walked over and squatted beside the Prince.

"I recognize you, Prince Rowenna; it grieves me to see you here. May I ask?"

The Prince looked up with an expression that caught Taxis quite off guard. His countenance was distant, but not fearful or embittered. He seemed enraptured.

"You interrupt my thoughts which I prefer to conversation," the Prince began. Than he stopped at gazed more closely at Taxis. "Ah, excuse my discourtesy, I see I recognize you as well. Is it not Taxis of Istel, the former mate of our horse herd keeper's most hated enemy, the Taelien?"

"I am flattered, Prince, that you should remember me."

Rowenna laughed softly. "A man who utters public words for others must have a good memory for people."

"You have no rivals, Prince; but, `horse herd keeper?' Is that a well chosen description?"

"Well chosen? If you mean careless, perhaps. If you mean intentional, yes, certainly. He does right to lock me away. I am no longer his man for I have found something I can believe in and it was from thoughts of that person you disturbed me."

"And I blush at my presumption, Prince. I'll leave you in peace."

"No, no. Unless, you don't care to associate with a self-proclaimed traitor."

"I may be one myself. If you'll talk, I'll talk gladly."

"A fellow traitor, maybe. I suppose Bar-Lev's jail is where one would expect to find them. Has he caught you out in a secret longing for your former master?"

"I think my confinement was ordered only on the general principle of mistrust. To tell you the truth, I was mad at first. But being here and not having anything to do other than think, I wonder if he doesn't see me more clearly than I see myself."

"Don't doubt that, friend Taxis. Our nomad whirlwind is the finest reader of men you'll ever meet."

"He is. Yes, he is. I think of what Talo has accomplished and I can't help but feel pride. Just a year and a season ago he was completely burned out; his crew was dead, down to two others and me. Look at him now, challenging the mighty Bar-Lev not a day's ride from his capital with a force that could only have been produced by magic. Yes, I compare him to Bar-Lev and I feel, right now that for all his faults and for all the apparent hopelessness of his cause, it's Talo the Taelien I'd rather be following."

"As if by magic. I wonder." Rowenna paused, the abstracted expression returning to his face. "Ah, excuse me." He took a deep breath. A muffled humming suddenly pervaded the confined room, as if from a distant earthquake. The Prince seemed as one about to impart life's most important secret. The noise went on, but Taxis pushed it from his mind.

"But I am forced to disagree with you, Taxis. I think, no, I know, you give your former master too much of the credit. Twice I have parleyed with the leaders of that army. Master Talo, I don't doubt, has played his role, but it's the Lady who has worked the magic, she has gathered that brave force and brought them here to tweak our gaoler's nose. Yes, I know. I've met the world's great men--seen them elevated and humbled--but never did I imagine it was possible for someone so selfless, so sure of the right to be born in this earth."

Taxis blinked rapidly. "But Bar-Lev is so sure. . . ."

"Ha, he is sure of everything but he knows nothing of the Lady; he thinks to have her dragged before him to add her like another jewel to his crown of conquests. He knows nothing. Believe me, my island friend, I will tell you now: I have come to believe in the Lady. She offered me a place by her side and I walked away. Walked away! I thought nothing could resist the force, the horror, the swarming numbers of that eastern barbarian. I walked away though my heart shouted 'stay, stay you fool.' But I will tell you, today is his last day alive under the sun and stars. If the Lady chooses to come here and challenge him, then she shall prevail. She knows the right. Bar-Lev the mighty has met his doom and he doesn't even know her name."

"Prince, I can't believe that. It's just impossible. I'd like to, but I can't."

"You are like I was. But, if you want to believe, don't you think there must be a reason for that desire? Just believe. Once you really try you'll see it isn't hard."

Taxis leaned back. The Prince was crazy. He had a rather attractive kind of insanity, but none-the-less. Suddenly Taxis' attention was wrenched away from his contemplation of the Prince's condition. The humming noise was louder, resolving into sounds recognizable as shouts, screams, the cacophony of battle. But it was impossible for the battle to have reached Bar-Lev's camp. Taxis looked back at the Prince, back at a smile serene and knowing.

EPILOGUE

A nd he came striding, stepping over the dismembered fallen. He, the original poet; a strange sort of man, normally visible only from the corner of the eye.

Up to the cairn wherein lay the bodies of his great creations for that age--the trickster Talo the Taelin and Bar-Lev the mighty. Who cannot shed a tear that they are gone.

> Tis but a rumor I hear
>
> This time you choose to stay near
>
> A struggle that fate
>
> Had set you sooner or late
>
> So this land could briefly forget fear.

And he cast his eyes north and thought on his daughter, the dark skinned one. She would pick her consort and for a generation the many peoples of this land of Ossa would truly forget fear.

Ossa

Books by Vincent P. O'Hara

German Fleet at War (2004)
The U.S. Navy against the Axis (2007)
Struggle for the Middle Sea (2009)
Dark Navy (2009) with Enrico Cernuschi
On Seas Contested (2010) editor with David Dickson and Richard Worth
In Passage Perilous (2012)
The Royal Navy's Revenge (2012)
To Crown the Waves (2013) editor with David Dickson and Richard Worth
Black Phoenix (2014) with Enrico Cernuschi

Mr. O'Hara is a native of Southern California and a noted naval historian. *Ossa* is his first published work of fiction. It was completed in Oakland, California in 1978 and revised in San Diego in 1993.

www.ingramcontent.com/pod-product-compliance
Lightning Source LLC
Chambersburg PA
CBHW050542260626
47157CB00002B/395